"Tobi." A whisper from behind her.

She spun around. She was alone in the office.

"Tobi."

It was coming from the corner over by the desk.

"Tobi. I want you."

From the air vent.

"Tobi. I want you. I'm coming for you. Let me in."

She backed away from the vent. She didn't like this. She didn't like this at all.

"Let me in, Tobi. I'm coming."

She grabbed her radio off the desk and depressed the call button. It was dead.

"Let me in, Tobi. I'm right outside the door."

She leapt for the corner of the room behind the door where she couldn't be seen from its window.

"Tobi, let me in. I've come for you. I want you. I've got something for you."

"Who are you?" she asked, trembling.

"Open the door and find out. I'm right outside. I'm waiting."

The doorknob turned, rattled.

The voice from the air vent whispered: *"Let me in now!"*

Tobi tried her radio again; banged it on the floor. Remaining seated on the floor, her back against the wall, Tobi slid along the wall to the door and peeked under it.

Someone is definitely out there, she thought.

"Or something," came the voice from the vent . . .

<u>BOOK YOUR PLACE ON OUR WEBSITE</u> AND MAKE THE READING CONNECTION!

We've created a customized website just for our very special readers, where you can get the inside scoop on everything that's going on with Zebra, Pinnacle and Kensington books.

When you come online, you'll have the exciting opportunity to:

- View covers of upcoming books
- Read sample chapters
- Learn about our future publishing schedule (listed by publication month *and author*)
- Find out when your favorite authors will be visiting a city near you
- Search for and order backlist books from our online catalog
- Check out author bios and background information
- Send e-mail to your favorite authors
- Meet the Kensington staff online
- Join us in weekly chats with authors, readers and other guests
- Get writing guidelines
- AND MUCH MORE!

**Visit our website at
http://www.kensingtonbooks.com**

THE
PRISON

R. PATRICK
GATES

PINNACLE BOOKS
Kensington Publishing Corp.
http://www.kensingtonbooks.com

*For Tehagan, whom I've always admired much more than
I've ever let on.
Thanks to Millie Arpano for proofing the final draft
of this book.*

PART ONE

1

Corrections Officer Tobi Dowry sat at her desk in the guard's office on the first floor of the Segregated Inmates Unit (SIU), more commonly known as the "Can," and cursed herself in a loud whisper. She couldn't believe she had forgotten it. Hopelessly, she searched through her workbag but it wasn't there. She had already dumped it out twice and ransacked through it fruitlessly. She had been hoping that she'd left it in her car and could get it on break, but then she remembered she had put it down on the washing machine when the phone rang just as she was leaving for work. She had left it sitting there, along with her lunch.

She never would have thought that she would ever need a *book* so badly, especially considering her history.

She had been working at the New Rome Correctional Institute for nine years now, the last three on eleven-to-seven shift in the Can. She hated the hours and the Can at night was a gloomy, depressing, even frightening place. It was always cold in the SIU, even on the hottest nights of the year. She'd heard all the ghost stories about the prison when she'd first started working there—how it used to be an insane asylum and was now haunted by the ghosts of all the lunatics who had died there. She'd also heard that the reason the Can was always so cold was because it used to be the asylum's morgue and was, thus, the most haunted place in the prison.

Tobi didn't buy any of it. She'd figured out that the reason SIU was cool all the time was because the entire building was built of stone—granite blocks, to be exact, and it was under the shadow of the hill's highest ridge all day. It had a deep basement, also built of granite. As far as the rest of the ghost stories went, she had never believed them. Only once in her nine years had she seen anything strange—a light on in the abandoned cupola, now gone, destroyed in a blizzard last winter, on the top of Digbee Hall next door. Others had seen the light over the years, and the story was that the cupola was haunted by the ghost of Myrtle, a former patient who had committed suicide by hanging herself up there. But even that Tobi had been able to find an explanation for; it was obvious the light was a reflection from the tower spotlights, and when the lights moved around the cupola, as they sometimes had, it was a reflection of the lights of small airplanes passing overhead on their way to New Rome Airport.

Tobi was a practical girl and it had never been ghosts that had scared her about working graveyard shift in the Can—keeping watch over a dozen convicted murderers, now *that* was scary, but ghosts? Never. And with all the inmates in the Can locked up at night in individual cells—she never had contact with them; almost never saw them—it wasn't even that scary. Depressing, yes. Boring, *God* yes! It was so crushingly boring that at times she'd thought she'd go crazy.

Never having been much of a reader, over the years she had tried to find other ways to occupy her time. She'd started by stashing a deck of cards for solitaire in the desk, along with a hand-held electronic blackjack and poker game. She tried knitting for a while but had not been able to get the hang of it. When all those diversions had run their routes eating up her first six years on the job, she was as bored as ever, and decided to try reading again after all.

The last book Tobi Dowry had read had been *The Good Earth,* by Pearl Buck, in high school, and it had been such a traumatic experience that she had stopped reading altogether. She didn't get the book at all. It bored her to tears. Literally. She cried daily over the torments of reading the book; in order to pass senior year language arts and graduate, she had to ace the test and report on that damned incomprehensible book. And no matter how hard she'd tried, she never got it.

Thank God for Cliffs Notes and the Internet. She downloaded a book report off the Internet site of some brainiac out in Colorado. All she had to do was send him a picture of herself. Cramming with the Cliffs Notes, she managed to get a sixty on the final, which, with her semester average of thirty-two, should have put her in summer school and bye-bye to graduation, but her teacher, Mrs. Queen, had been so impressed with Tobi's book report that she gave her an A plus plus and told her not to worry about the D minus. Anyone who could understand a book as well as she understood *Good Earth* didn't need summer school, Old Queen had told her.

The last time she'd cried over that book, it was from laughing too hard. It was also the last time she'd read *anything* she didn't have to.

But she found nothing had changed. She tried a book, *Patriot Games,* by Tom Clancy, that her shift commander had recommended to her but, as she'd expected, she didn't get it. It made those long, boring nights even longer and more boring. She had started thinking about bidding for the day shift and/or a different position the next time positions came up, but she liked the extra money of eleven-to-seven and hazardous-duty pay working the Can—fifteen dollars an hour compared to thirteen on day shift, and eleven if she switched to another building.

One night over beers with her friends at O'Brien's Pub she had sparked a lengthy debate about books when she asked a couple of friends what they would recommend. Jane

Mazek, who worked switchboard on eleven-to-seven, suggested Nora Roberts, Danielle Steel, Dean Koontz, and *The
Bridges of Madison County.* Judy Bennett, who worked in I
dorm on day shift and was Jane's live-in girlfriend, told her
to read Stephen King and Anne Rice, then mocked Jane's
picks, except for Dean Koontz. The argument had ensued, to
be periodically interrupted by the barmaid, Regina ("Rhymes
with *vagina,*" she liked to tell people), who was also the
pub's owner. According to her, the only author worth reading
was Anaïs Nin.

Lost in this discussion, Tobi had wandered off to the juke-
box. The next day, though, she'd gone to Barnes and Noble
to check out the authors her friends had bandied about.
When she saw the cost of the books, even the paperbacks,
she thought maybe she should renew her library card. She
was fairly certain none of the authors her friends had mentioned were going to appeal to her, or she wouldn't be able to
understand them, so why waste the money?

At the library she had asked for Dean Koontz and had
been directed to the fiction-horror section. She had considered Koontz no further, for the same reason she wouldn't be
reading Judy's pick, Stephen King. She hated horror. And
though she didn't scare easily, she hated *being* scared. She
had seen a movie about a mad dog that was based on one of
King's books, and had been terrified by it. Of course, it
helped that she was deeply afraid of dogs.

Learning from the librarian that Anne Rice could be
found in the same section as King and Koontz, and that
Anaïs Nin was considered erotica ("Pornography!" whispered the librarian), Tobi had opted for a Nora Roberts novel
and *The Bridges of Madison County.* Armed with those
books, she had gone to work that night with hopes of a quick
shift, but neither book held her. She had been about to give
up and buy a portable TV small enough that she could smuggle it into the prison—even though it was strictly against
regulations and could get her fired—when, one day, she saw
her fifteen-year-old neighbor sitting on her front steps, read-

ing a book. Tobi wandered over and discovered she was reading one of the Babysitter's Club series. The girl said they were her favorite books and the *best* books ever written. Willing to try anything, Tobi had gone back to the library to find a *Babysitters Club* novel and was mortified to be directed to the juvenile fiction section. Fighting feelings of embarrassment, she'd checked one out anyway.

And it had *worked*! The first night she brought it to work, the first half of the shift, three and a half hours, went by seemingly instantly. She *finished* the *entire* novel by *lunch*! She read it again after lunch, then went home and read it one more time. Luckily, the day after that was her day off and she was able to get to the library and take out three more.

From then on she was set and her previously unendurable shift began to fly by each night. She got so engrossed in the books she had to force herself not to read them when she wasn't at work. Even so, she quickly went through the series and reread them several times, devouring and redevouring new ones as soon as they came out. Before long she discovered other, similar series, like *Sweet Valley High* and *Girls, Inc.,* and she was never bored again.

Unless she did something stupid, like leave her book at home.

She pulled the deck of cards out of the desk and dealt a hand of solitaire, resigning herself to a long, dull night.

"Tobi."

She looked up, expecting to see Dave Stirling, the second-floor guard, popping his head in to see if she wanted anything on his way to the break room, but he wasn't there. The door was closed. She got up and looked through the small rectangular observation window reinforced with chicken wire that was set into the door to her office. The corridor, called tier two, between the two rows of cells was empty, and all the cells were dark. The door at the other end of the corridor, which led to the outside and the stairs to the second floor and the basement, was closed.

"Tobi." A whisper from behind her.

She spun around. She was alone in the office.

"Tobi."

It was coming from the corner over by the desk.

"Tobi. I want you."

From the air vent.

"Tobi. I want you. I'm coming for you. Let me in."

She backed away from the vent. She didn't like this. She didn't like this at all.

"Let me in, Tobi. I'm coming."

She grabbed her radio off the desk and depressed the call button. It was dead.

"Let me in, Tobi. I'm right outside the door."

She leapt for the corner of the room behind the door, where she couldn't be seen from its window.

"Tobi, let me in. I've come for you. I want you. I've got something for you."

"Who are you?" she asked, trembling.

"Open the door and find out. I'm right outside. I'm waiting."

The doorknob turned, rattled.

The voice from the air vent whispered: *"Let me in, now!"*

Tobi tried her radio again; banged it on the floor. Nothing.

Laughter came from the vent. *"You don't want to call anyone. Let's just keep this between us. Open the door. Join us."*

Remaining seated on the floor, her back against the wall, Tobi slid along the wall to the door and peeked under it. The space was narrow but she could see the very bottom of a pair of shoes. She peeked up at the window. A shadow moved in the glass. She ducked back.

Someone is definitely out there, she thought.

"Or something," came the voice from the vent.

"If this is a joke, I don't think it's fuckin' funny!" she said loudly, trying for bravado, but the tremolo in her voice gave her away.

"There's nothing funny about fucking." The sound of many people laughing came through the vent.

"This has got to be a joke," Tobi told herself in a whisper.

"It's only a joke if you're laughing. I don't want you to laugh," the voice said gently.

"What *do* you want?" Tobi whispered fervently. Leaning toward the vent.

"WE WANT TO HEAR YOU SCREAM!" came a crowd of voices in answer. *"NOW LET US IN!"* Bellowing voices.

There was a tremendous blow to the door, rattling it on its hinges, shaking the entire room. Tobi shrieked and tried to make herself as small as possible in the corner. The door shook again, a crack running up the middle of it as it bowed inward under the force of the blow.

"No," Tobi whimpered. "No, no, no!"

"Yes!" Boom! *"Yes! Yes! Yes!"* Boom! Boom! Boom!

The blows to the door went on relentlessly, the sound like thunder in the room, making every object inside and every fiber of her being pulse in time with them.

Boom! Boom! Boom! Boom!

"No, *please!* Leave me alone!" Tobi cried; pleaded.

"Let!" Boom! *"Us!"* Boom! *"IN!"* BOOM!

"Nooooo!" Tobi screamed. "Leave me alone! Please, please, please, leave me *alone!"*

Sudden silence.

Her breath caught in her throat and she held it, waiting.

Nothing. No sound but for the ticking of the clock on the wall. She leaned forward and looked at the door, then up at the observation window. She could see nothing.

Softly, from where the door had been split and now bulged inward, came the sound of breathing. Slowly, the split in the door moved inward—*inhale*—and then out—*exhale*. A wisp of curling white vapor seeped through the crack in the door and was suddenly pulled back—*inhale*. The doorknob jiggled slightly. She looked up at the observation window again. Someone (*something?*) was there this time—a shadowy face peering in at her. The crack in the door bulged—*exhale*.

The doorknob turned.

"Now!" came the whispering voices from the air vent.
"Now!"
"Now!"
"Now!"

The doorknob clicked. The edges of the bulging crack curled inward, opening like some alien plant. Cold white fog poured through the opening.

"No!" Tobi whispered.

"Yes."

The door opened.

"No! No! No!" Tobi shrieked hysterically, over and over again.

The fog became a white cloud enveloping her. It was cold, so cold it froze her fingers together; it froze her eyelids open instantly.

"Nooooo!"

Something stepped through the door. It was huge and to Tobi, trapped in the swirling fog of icy vapor, formless and sinister. She tried to crawl away, but she was frozen to the floor.

The thing was reaching for her.

Tobi lost all control. Her screaming pleas of "No! No! No!" became unintelligible shrieks of pure terror. Her bladder and bowels let go simultaneously, the liquids freezing immediately to her skin and clothing.

The thing was reaching for her—its hooked claws inches from her face, its milky white eyes enveloping her, becoming the fog. Her shrieks caught in her throat and she began to choke. The white vapor turned dark, blinding her.

"Tobi? Tobi, what's wrong?"

It was like waking from a nightmare, only she knew she hadn't been sleeping. Suddenly her vision cleared. Dave Stirling, the guard from upstairs, was standing over her, a frightened look on his face. The fog was gone. Behind him, the door was whole, undamaged. Tobi tried to speak but could only make gagging noises and struggle for breath. Dave Stirling grabbed her under her arms and pulled her to her feet, grimacing at the stench emanating from her and frowning at the dark, wet stains around the crotch of her pants, front and back. Once she was standing, he pulled her arms high over her head and held them there.

"Deep breaths. Take slow, deep breaths," he told her.

She complied and within minutes was breathing regularly again.

"What the hell happened, Tobi?"

She flung herself on him, wrapping her arms around him, burying her face in his chest, sobbing uncontrollably.

2

May 6–7

He is standing on a hillside beneath a milky white night sky—a storm sky. The nighttime landscape around him is strangely illuminated, as if from a full moon, though there is none. He turns and sees a long, dark, brick building with a domed roof, on top of which sits a cupola, below him. The windows sparkle with light, as if reflecting the rising sun, but he knows, somehow, that dawn is still hours away and this is not sunlight. There is a deep, bone-reverberating thud, and a sinister black crack opens in the roof of the building; the aged black roof suddenly melts away. Flames leap briefly into the sky. There is a rushing sound, like a gale wind blowing through a thicket of trees, and a great dark cloud emerges from the hole, swirling and spiraling above the building, then descending, diving straight at him.

Bats, he thinks and doesn't know why. Thousands of them. Flapping and squeaking. Though he never actually sees them, the thought of them, their leathery wings beating against his face, their tiny mouths open, tiny teeth piercing his skin—

—brings him awake, drenched with sweat, whimpering like a child in the darkness.

* * *

Several restless hours later, thirty-one-year-old Tim Saget rolled out of bed, rubbed his eyes, and looked at the radio-clock on his night table. The glowing dial read 6:35. The radio, tuned to Oldies 105, was playing Blue Öyster Cult's "Don't Fear the Reaper." Tim cursed and headed for the bathroom. He was going to be late for work again if he didn't haul ass. If that damned dream hadn't kept him awake half the night, he wouldn't have overslept.

Behind him in the bed, Millie—his steady girlfriend for the past ten months—said something he couldn't quite hear. Or maybe he could, but he chose to ignore her. The truth was she had been getting on his nerves lately, and he had been thinking of a way to gently tell her it was over.

In the bathroom, looking at her toothbrush in the holder, her assorted lotions and creams on the toilet tank, and her various shampoos and conditioners in the shower, he realized he had better do it soon. For the past two months she had spent nearly every night at his place. In that time she had begun slowly moving in—a personal item here and there, leaving a change of clothing in the closet, claiming half of one of his dresser drawers for spare undies and nylons. And she had been dropping hints about their living together. And recently, she had begun using the "L" word with a yearning tone in her voice that pleaded for him to return the sentiment.

He got in the shower and turned on the water, feeling it with his toes as it ran out of the tub faucet. When it was hot enough he flipped the lever to turn on the shower and let the steamy water wash over him. The sound of the water brought back the dream and the sound of the bats as they had filled the night sky. He'd always been a very vivid dreamer, but this dream had been over the top in its realism; in its feeling of being a memory rather than something brought on by too much Chinese food. The memory of the dream brought back the memory of how glad he had been, when he woke in a cold sweat, as frightened as a child sleeping for the first time without a night-light, that Millie was there. She had sensed his panic, his fear, and snuggled up close to him, wrapping her arms around him and pressing her warm flesh into his back, murmuring, "It's okay, baby. I'm here." Though he'd never openly admit it, she had comforted him, made him feel safe.

In fact, she did that a lot, and not just when he had a nightmare. If he let himself be honest, he had to admit that she made him feel better in nearly every aspect of his life; more confident, more secure, more of a *man,* and she didn't nag. But then, Tim Saget was not one to be honest with himself for very long, especially when it came to women. It was the reason he was thirty-one and had never been truly emotionally involved with any woman.

Out of the shower, he returned to the bedroom to dress and found Millie sitting against the headboard, hugging a pillow to her stomach. She looked in pain.

"You having cramps?" Tim asked, hopefully. Millie had missed her period two weeks ago. Though she kept reassuring him that she was very irregular and everything was okay, he was nervous.

Millie just shook her head, slid out of bed, and headed for the bathroom. A few minutes later, he heard the shower come on, followed by the radio he kept on the shelf for when he took a long hot bath. Heading downstairs, he thought he heard her say something, but when he called to her, he got no answer. He stood in front of the full-length mirror that was on the back of the apartment's front door and checked out his uniform. At five foot eleven and two hundred fifteen pounds, with his jet black hair, large wide eyes, long straight nose, and straight white teeth to add to the way he filled out his security guard's uniform, he cut quite an impressive figure. *He* would never think so—he thought he was too short and his nose was too big, and he was generally unaware of the attention he attracted from women on a day-to-day basis. He heard the beep of his ride outside and had just enough time to grab a granola bar from the cabinet and a bottle of

spring water from the fridge, his hat and badge from the hall
table, his coat from the stairpost, and head out the door.

As soon as he arrived at the security office on the main
floor of Mountain View Hospital, Tim knew something was
up. All three shifts of hospital security guards—seven men
and two women—were there with less-than-joyful expres-
sions on their faces.

"What's going on?" Tim asked, looking from face to face.
Before anyone could answer, the inner office door, that of
the head of security, Mr. Bowland, opened and the director
came out. He nodded curtly at all present and cleared his
throat.

"There's no sense in beating around the bush; you know
I'm not that kind of guy. So I'll give it to you straight. You all
know the hospital has been having financial problems for
nearly a year, and this economic slump isn't helping. The
president of the hospital gave the word this morning—major
lay-offs of nonmedical personnel. For us, that means we'll
be cutting down to just two security guards on days, and only
one on three-to-eleven and the graveyard shift. Harrison and
Gardino are being cut from eleven to seven, Simpson and
Espana from three to eleven, and Tim Saget from seven to
three. I'm sorry people, but you're through as of today. Turn
in your hats, badges, radios, and hospital IDs. Your last pay-
check will be mailed to you."

A whisper in the darkness.
A hollow sound.
Like sighing, only wetter.
Corrections Officer Darlene Hampton sat up, startled.
She had been dozing. The sound came again and she real-
ized it was her radio.

It sounded like breathing.

The light on the phone on her desk—called a "landline"

and used by prison staff for confidential conversations—lit up. She immediately snatched the receiver up. "Whatchoo doin, fool! You *can't* do that over the radio. *You* should know that. You think people don't know that's you?"

"Take it easy. I'm in Inner Control, relieving Henderson. I called you on the landline so no one could hear me."

"Oh yeah, like they couldn't hear you panting like some horny dog over the radio." Darlene relaxed. "You are such a fool, sometimes," she said, smiling, her voice teasing.

"I don't know about no heavy breathing over your radio—you got another boyfriend around? But I'll agree with one thing: I *am* a fool for you. You got a break comin' up in five, why don't you meet me in *our* place?"

Darlene looked around at the vast hall filled with foldable cots. On each cot slept a prisoner. Forty convicted criminals slept in the room, mostly sexual offenders. It was a reflection of the prison population as a whole; 85 percent of the inmates in the medium security section of the prison were either pedophiles or rapists (what the guards referred to as "diddlers and skinners").

All was quiet. Darlene looked at her watch. It was 2:24 in the morning. Only three and a half hours to go until the end of her shift. "All right," she replied into the phone. "Meet you there." A moment later, her relief, Jack Roy, showed up a few minutes early, sending her on break with instruction to take her time, it was a quiet night.

Darlene headed through the rows of sleeping inmates to a massive steel door at the far wall past the rows of sleeping cons, marked KITCHEN TUNNEL. Using a key from the extensive collection on her belt, she unlocked the metal security door. A quick look back at Roy, who was busy looking at Darlene's *Cosmo* magazine, and she returned the key ring to her belt and went through, heading down a metal staircase.

Darlene had been working at the New Rome, Massachusetts, Correctional Institute, known as the "Hill" to inmates and guards alike, for five years and had been having an affair with the new night shift captain, John Thompson, since the day after he'd transferred from the Cedar Junction facility in Walpole back in March. They had found a place under the prison complex, among the network of tunnels that connected the various buildings and which only guards were allowed to use. It was a side tunnel, a dead end that was used for storage. Hidden behind boxes of computer paper, she and the married white captain had been able to steal some passionate moments on a fairly regular basis.

At the bottom of the stairs leading down from A dorm, Darlene paused. A cold breeze blew over her, tightening her nipples, which were already hardening in anticipation of John's touch. She thought she'd heard a noise, but when she was silent, listening, there was nothing. It was very possible to run into another officer in the tunnels—they all used them to get around, especially in the winter or in bad weather—but Darlene wanted to avoid that. She was pretty sure no one at the prison knew about her and the captain and they both wanted to keep it that way.

She started down the tunnel, one of the few that had recently been redone so that it now resembled a hospital corridor more than a tunnel. The majority of them were typical dank, spooky, dark, and low-ceilinged passageways hewn out of rock that were more akin to mine shafts than anything else.

Another icy breeze tickled her breasts, raising goose pimples and keeping her nipples firm. The tunnels were generally cooler than the buildings above ground, but she had never felt *this* cold down there. It felt as if someone had turned the air conditioning to *freeze,* but that was impossible, for there was no air conditioning in any of the tunnels. As far as Darlene knew, the only fresh air the tunnels got was through the louvered air vents she saw every twenty feet or so.

She turned a corner, making sure to check the concave mirror, hung in the corner of the ceiling, for traffic coming the other way, and reached the first of several locked fire/

security doors. She used a key to unlock a lockbox by the door, used another key inside the box to unlock the door, and pushed it open. She stopped. The lights were out in the tunnel beyond, and the stream of icy air was steady here. It was one of the older tunnels and had been hewn through solid granite. It ran slightly downhill, as if the diggers of the tunnel had been looking for a way under the solid bedrock. The floor was cracked concrete, with a small drain every thirty feet. The walls tended to sweat year round; the tunnel was a nasty, damp place in winter and a creepy, clammy place in summer.

Darlene removed her flashlight from its holder on her belt and sent a beam into the darkness. It was clear for as far as she could see in the light. According to the prison's setup and operation, it was supposed to be impossible for inmates to gain access to the tunnels without an escort, but she heard it had happened, and just recently. In the other kitchen tunnel, running out to the dormitory in A building, supposed evidence had been found that prisoners were using the tunnels at night on a regular basis. What they were using them for, no one seemed to know or wanted to talk about, when Darlene had asked her fellow guards. Since the majority of corrections officers were men, and macho men at that who looked the other way and rarely acknowledged the homosexual liaisons of their charges, she figured the prisoners had been doing just that—engaging in some sort of gay orgy. Also, two prisoners had disappeared during a storm last winter, the same one that destroyed the cupola on top of Digbee Hall, and the consensus was that they had escaped through the tunnels somehow. They were still at large. There'd been talk recently about filling all the tunnels in—they were the prison's weak spot.

Holding the door open with her right foot, she reached around the corner with her free hand and felt for the light switch. She found it, clicked it, clicked it again, and nothing happened. She thought about calling Inner Control and letting them know the lights were out in the tunnel, but decided to wait until after hooking up with John. She didn't want anyone venturing down there until they were done with their business.

Halfway down the darkened tunnel, the lights came on with a buzzing, crackling sound and a whiff of ozone. It startled her and she whirled about quickly, as if expecting someone behind her. After a hundred yards or so the tunnel leveled off and reached an intersection. To the right, the tunnel led to the kitchen, to the left the corridor made a sharp right turn and ended thirty feet on in another locked door that led to the power station, which was beyond prison walls. Darlene and John's little love nook was just before the door. It was a secluded spot; the door was no longer used since civilians ran the power station. Like most side tunnels—and any other available space in the prison—it was stacked with boxes, mostly of outdated inmate files.

Darlene reached the corner and paused, looking back the way she'd come. It was clear. She ducked inside the side tunnel and let out a low whistle. She was surprised when she heard John whistle in return; she usually beat him there.

"Well, ain't we Mr. Speedy tonight?" she said softly, and chuckled. A little louder, she added: "Whatsamatta, Hon, you need to get some tonight?"

He stepped out from behind a stack of boxes, his hat a dark round silhouette, his face and chest hidden in shadow. He pulled her to him, wrapping his strong arms around her and crushing her ample breasts against his wide chest. Darlene loved the way his arms felt around her, the way he squeezed her so tight it took her breath away. His lips found hers and smothered them. His tongue sought out hers and pulled it into his mouth, where he sucked on it. A moment later his lips were sliding down her chin, her neck, seeking out the well of her cleavage. His tongue, snakelike, slithered between the crack of her breasts and roamed to the left, under her uniform shirt and the thin lace bra she wore under it, not stopping 'til it found her rock-hard nipple. She shivered with the sensation and felt her panties getting damp.

Within seconds she was naked, yet didn't remember taking her clothes off. One moment he had her shirt open, her bra pushed up to her throat, sucking, licking, and biting her nipples, switching from one to the other, then squeezing them both together so that he could suck both hard knobs as one, and the next moment she was naked, up against a stack of cardboard boxes, her legs spread, aching for him to enter her.

She never saw him undress, either; one moment he was clothed, the next naked. He stood between her legs, his hands massaging her breasts, fingers pinching her nipples. His penis brushed her inner thigh and it was oddly cold but then it was inside her and she was squealing with delight as he filled her. Not the reason she had originally been attracted to him—he was extremely handsome in a Harrison Ford kind of way—but certainly a big reason why she had let the affair continue was John's more than adequate penis size. Darlene had been cursed with a large womb, and John had been the first man to make her feel full when he was in her. But tonight, it felt like he'd been *working out* down there, if that was possible. Tonight, she felt like she might burst at the seams he was so big. And *hot!* Where his penis had been cold against her thigh, it now felt like the proverbial red-hot poker inside her.

And it kept getting *hotter.*

She had an orgasm at the moment of first penetration, then a series of three more as he worked at her. When she felt his penis begin to burn, she had another powerful orgasm that left her breathless, but he kept pumping, and getting hotter. She came again but it was beginning to become uncomfortable. It started to burn and she felt as though her insides were being rubbed raw. She tried to speak, to tell him to stop, but he clamped his hand over her mouth and furiously plunged into her. A voice in the back of her mind warned her that something was wrong. John had never treated her roughly, but she couldn't hold onto the thought; the pain was getting serious now. He was fucking her faster and faster. She could tell he was building to a climax—the most powerful he'd ever had, to judge by the frenzy of his fucking—so she tried to hold on and bear it until he was finished.

There was a sound from outside their love nest.

Footsteps.

Someone was coming!

Darlene tried to pull John's hand away and tell him someone was coming, but his hand clamped down on her like a vise, cutting off her breath and any sound she might make. His other hand grabbed hold of her left tit, his fingers digging in, and held her as though she were as instantly crushable as paper.

The footsteps came closer.

John fucked her harder.

She caught a snatch of a song, softly sung. Her entire left side went numb beneath his hand squeezing her breast. The voice singing was familiar through the pain.

She finally managed to yank her face free of his smothering hand. "Someone's coming!" she whispered frantically.

"Yeah, me!" he grunted, his voice strange. He was climaxing, his back arching, his head thrown back. He let go of Darlene and grabbed her hips, plunging deep inside her. At first she spread her legs wide, squirming her butt around to help him come quickly before whoever was approaching caught them, but then he started to ejaculate.

As hot as his penis had been, feeling as if it were searing her, his come was just the opposite, scalding her with coldness, sending stabbing icicles of frigid pain through her body. And he wouldn't stop. He kept thrusting and thrusting and coming and coming, and she kept getting colder and colder. . . .

"Dar?"

The voice reached her through the mist of ice particles swirling around her. John was still pumping at her but she could no longer feel her legs. They were numb from his frozen semen. Her breasts, her face, her *mind,* were all succumbing to the frigid invasion. With the vague apprehension of someone on the edge of sleep, she wondered who was calling her. But then John ejaculated another numbing glacier into her and the voice faded. . . .

"Darlene? Are you here, baby?"

But it was back again, and louder. It broke through the film of ice forming across her consciousness and pulled her, shivering, back to reality. John lunged one last deep thrust into her and let out a long, slow gasp.

"Darlene, it's me, Johnny-boy. Are you here?"

It's John, she realized with relief. Now she didn't have to worry about getting caught with . . . him?

She screamed and struck out at the man she had thought was John, but her blow found only air. John was beside her the next moment, his arms around her, staring in shock at the frightened, slightly insane look on her face.

"Darlene! What happened? Baby, what happened?"

"Where is he?" she screamed, looking frantically about. "Where is he?"

"Who, baby? Who?" John asked, looking around. "There's nobody here but us."

She looked up into his face and he had to draw back from her stare.

"You didn't see *anyone* run out of here just now?"

He noticed her lips and fingertips were blue, as if she'd been somewhere cold. But it was May and the weather outside was balmy. "No, babe. I didn't see anyone. Was there someone here?"

She looked at him as if he'd just asked the most outrageous question in the world.

"Was someone here? Was *someone* here? I was just *raped* by *someone!*"

Incredulous, John looked at her. "What are you talking about? How were you raped? You're fully dressed."

Darlene looked down at herself and gasped. She *was* dressed, but just seconds ago she had been completely naked, with freezing come sticking her thighs together.

"Here! Look! Look!" she cried, frantically plunging her hand into her pants to show John the cold, sticky fluid she could still feel clinging to her and dripping out of her. Her fingers came out dry.

"Here! Here!" she screamed at him, pulling her shirt open and pushing her bra up to reveal her left breast. She nearly cried with relief when John's eyes widened at the sight of the bruises there. "I *was* raped. I was! I was *raped* . . . raped . . ." She broke down, sobbing the word over and over again, collapsing against John's chest, staining the front of his uniform with her tears.

Thirty-four miles away, in the small town of Ashton, Tim Saget didn't notice the lights were still on in the apartment when he staggered in at 2:53 A.M.—the same time Darlene Hampton was having a liaison with a man she thought was her lover. Tim was too drunk to notice the lights. Or Millie sitting, curled up with her feet tucked under her, on the living-room couch. He was so drunk it was a wonder he had been able to drive home at all—he couldn't remember doing so—without killing himself or some innocent.

"Where have you been?" Millie asked. Her face was blotchy red and her cheeks streaked with dried tears.

"Wassamatta?" Tim asked, slurring the sentence into one long word, punctuated by a burp.

"Oh, *nothing*," Millie answered, her voice rising an octave on the last word. "Why should anything be the matter?" she continued, her voice wavering between high and normal. "You left the house yesterday morning to go to work and now it's *this* morning and you haven't been home or called or . . ." Her voice trailed off, threatening to become a burble of tears, but she regained control. "Would *you* think anything was the matter if *I* left for work and didn't come home at the end of the day, or that night, until well *after* midnight?" She sat up and, not wearing her glasses, squinted at the digital clock on the VCR under the TV. "What time *is* it anyway?"

"Half pass'a cat's ass an' a quarter to his balls!" Tim blurted out and giggled.

Millie didn't join him. "Funny," she replied, dryly. "I'm glad you think this is funny. I'm *glad* you think it's funny that I've been calling everyone and every place I could think of, trying to find you." Her voice, which had been rising steadily, reached a shout. "I'm *glad* you think it's *funny* that I called every hospital emergency room between here and Worcester, *praying* with every call that you weren't there all smashed up in a car accident, or worse, *dead!* I'm *glad* you think it's funny that your *father* was over here with me until just a half hour ago, worried even *more* than I was—*if* that's possible."

"The Sarge was here?" Tim asked, his speech suddenly clear. He sat in the rocking chair near the door. *"He* was worried?"

"Oh! Now you're concerned! You couldn't care *less* if I was going out of my *mind* with worry, but mention *Daddy* and suddenly you don't think this is funny any more. *You* are *unbelievable!* What the hell is wrong with you?"

"I got laid off," Tim answered, his voice sober and barely a whisper. Millie didn't hear him.

"What?" Before he could repeat himself, the phone rang. Millie looked at the caller ID. "It's your dad," she said and got up from the couch, going upstairs to their bedroom.

Tim straightened and stood, took a deep breath, and picked up the phone. "Hello?"

"You're home," his father's voice came through the receiver, hard and disapproving as usual. "I *thought* I passed you on Pine Street as I was leaving your apartment. So . . . where were you?"

It was more an accusation than a question. Tim wished he could think of something other than the truth to tell his father—like he had been working a second job, or volunteering with homeless people—*anything* other than what he *had* been doing. Just once he'd like to be able to surprise the Sarge and not live up to his worst expectations, but, as usual, this was not one of those times. And forget about lying to the old man; he'd never been able to do that.

"I went out with a couple of the guys from work," Tim answered meekly.

There was a long pause. "You went out *drinking* at three o'clock in the afternoon on a Monday? And you're just getting home now at, what? Three in the morning? When are you going to grow up, Tim? You're thirty-one years old!" He could hear the anger, exasperation, and, above all, *disappointment*, growing in his father's voice. "It's bad enough you wasted your twenties in a drunken stupor, playing the party animal. Are you going to do the same with your thirties? Your forties? Aren't you ever going to *do* something with your life? Aren't you—"

"I lost my job," Tim interrupted the building tirade. "I got laid off."

"What? Why?"

"The economy, what else? The hospital is cutting back on nonmedical personnel."

"Oh." Uncharacteristically, his father was at a loss for words, and for a way to blame Tim for this misfortune, but it wouldn't last long. "Well, ain't that a kick in the head. I swear, you have the *worst* luck. I was hoping things might turn around for you—you might grow up—now that there's a baby on the way and you're going to be a father."

"What?"

It took John Thompson twenty minutes to get Darlene Hampton calm. Once she stopped repeating the word *rape,* she went limp and just lay there against the boxes, eyes glazed. John thought he was going to have to call for help, but then she started to come around and he helped her straighten herself out. While she rebuttoned her shirt, he radioed her relief and told him she was sick and would be late returning from break.

"I think it was one of the prisoners," she said quietly after he'd signed off the radio.

"What?"

"One of the prisoners. *One of the prisoners!*" she said, her voice growing louder and the words coming faster the second time.

"But I didn't see anyone, Hon," John explained, weakly stroking her arms.

"I don't care!" she hissed at him. *"Someone* fucked me in there and if it wasn't you, who was it? If it wasn't you it had to be someone on duty, or one of the prisoners. And since nearly half of them are skinners, I'd say it was a fair bet it was one of them."

"But how would they get down here?" John asked, even though he knew it could have been either a prisoner or a guard. Although prisoners were not supposed to be in the tunnels without an escort, John Thompson knew they had been. Besides the two prisoners who had found some way to escape through the tunnels, pentagrams had been found painted on the walls, and just last month, a dismembered squirrel had been found. Inner Perimeter Security was trying to find out who was using the tunnels for seemingly occult activities but so far had been unsuccessful. Superintendent Capello hadn't thought it was a big deal and therefore neither had John, but he didn't like the looks of this. Even so, Darlene had made comments recently that made him doubt her veracity now.

"John, I'm not lying," Darlene said as if reading his mind. "Someone was in here, waiting, like you would. They must have known we meet here. I thought it was you; it looked like you in the shadows; it smelled like you; it *felt* like you. But he wasn't gentle like you." She began to sob. "He hurt me! I tried to stop him, but he put his hand over my mouth and I couldn't cry out." She broke down again and he held her, shushing her with soft sounds.

"If someone was down here, waiting for you, it's more likely it was one of the guys, not one of the inmates," he said, considering if what she'd said was true.

She jumped on it with a vengeance. "*If* someone was down here? You don't believe me? You think I'm lying?" She pulled away from him. Anger and fear, inflamed by shock, burned in her eyes. "I was *raped*. And either one of the prisoners or one of *your* guards was responsible. And *whoever* it is, I want their *balls* in a *sling* or this place is gonna have one big mother-fuckin' lawsuit on its hands."

This was what John had been afraid of; now she was going to cry *lawsuit*. She'd said something like this just yesterday, threatening a sexual harassment suit because one of the guards had tried to hit on her. Now this incident and all his vague insecurities and doubts about her became hard fact and reality. He had wondered all along why such a good looking young *black* woman had found him, a fifty-something *white* guy, attractive. He knew he was good-looking—he'd never had trouble with the ladies when he was younger, and he kept in shape and all, but still. . . . And *she* had been the one to initiate the affair, letting him know through flirting and body language that he could have her anytime he wanted. And he had gone for it, with relish, but always with the nagging question of *why*? Did she have an ulterior motive? Now it seemed, maybe, she did.

He started to apologize but she pulled away from him and walked off. He thought about going after her, walking her back to her station to make sure she got there safely, but then said, "Fuck it." She hadn't been raped, he was sure of it; there hadn't been enough time for a rape to happen and her to get dressed before he got there. *And* he had seen no one coming through the tunnels.

If she was raped, he thought with a smile, *then it was by one of the ghosts the inmates are always scaring the new blood with.*

Darlene Hampton returned to her station oblivious to the questioning look her relief gave her. He said something she didn't catch or care about and then walked away as if mad when she didn't answer. She didn't give a fuck. She felt like shit. No, she felt worse than shit. She felt like *frozen* shit.

She sat at her desk and tried to pour herself a cup of coffee from her Thermos, but her hands were shaking so badly she couldn't do it without spilling it all over. The combination of shock and the deadly cold that seemed to have permeated every fiber of her being kept her trembling, sometimes violently. She cupped her hands around the steaming Thermos mug and lifted it slowly to her lips. A violent tremor of her muscles and nerves, and the coffee was all over her hands. And though she knew it was piping hot—could tell from the steam rising from its surface—it felt barely warm on her frozen skin.

She put the cup down and looked closely at her fingertips. There was a rim of blue around the fingernails that she had seen before when she had gone hiking on the Webster Cliff Trail in the White Mountains on a November day. She had got caught in an early snowstorm and by the time she and her companions had made it down the mountain, they were suffering from hypothermia; their fingertips, lips, and ears were blue. Struggling against the shakes, she opened the middle desk drawer and pulled out a small compact mirror she kept there. She looked at her eyes, ears, nose, and lips. They were all blue-tinged.

What the fuck is happening to me? She put her head down on the desk and sobbed. An inmate, lying near the desk, grumbled loudly in his sleep and rolled over. Darlene put her hand over her mouth. *Get a hold of yourself, girl! There is an explanation for this. You just gotta* calm *down!*

She took a deep breath. Raising her head, she put her hands under her chin, clasping her jaw and cheeks in the bow of her fingers. *What exactly did happen down there?* She took a quick look around the sleeping room and closed her eyes. She pictured herself walking down the tunnel. She focused on the moment just before she had gone down the side, storage tunnel, when she had looked back, checking the concave mirror at the corner. Had there been anyone following her? Had someone been hiding there, maybe flat against the wall very near the mirror, and she, in her passion, had overlooked him?

She bowed her head and concentrated, thinking, willing herself to see *someone* hiding there in her memory, but it was no use. She saw no one now because she had *seen no one then!* She knew herself. She knew how cautious she was; she knew how methodical she was about making sure her trysts with John were safe. Just as she was sure there had been no one in the tunnel with her when she had gone down the side tunnel.

Just as you were sure you were naked?

Steeling herself with another deep breath, she shook the thought off and imagined herself going into the storage tunnel, whistling for John.

He answered me! He whistled back! She remembered thinking it odd that he had beat her down there. She remembered something else—his silhouette. It had been *John's* silhouette that had come out of the shadows, she was sure of it. In fact, his touch, his embrace, his kisses—everything had been John's. And yet, it wasn't him.

Then who the hell was I fucking? And how did I end up naked one second and dressed the next?

The shivers increased and she bowed her head to the coffee cup, slurping the hot liquid like a pet at a water dish. She'd heard the ghost stories the skinners and diddlers liked to tell the new meat; they were the same stories the screws liked to tell rookies. The prison had been an insane asylum when such places were more bastions of torture and inhumane treatment than medical facilities. Lobotomies, crude shock treatments, water treatments, beatings, and who knew what else had supposedly gone on there.

Darlene had always doubted it. The state hospital had been converted to a prison only in 1987, though she was unsure when the hospital had closed. Darlene doubted that the asylum had been anything but a proper medical institution at least from the 1960s on, *if* it had been anything *but* before that. Besides, she had never been one to believe in the super-natural. The *stupid*-natural, she had always called it.

But now she wasn't so sure. Like her trembling muscles, her beliefs had been shaken by the incident in the tunnel.

She had been so sure *that it had been* John *waiting for her. So sure it had been* him *making love to her.*

"What are you gonna do, bitch?" she asked herself quietly.

"Good question," came an answer, squawking with static over the radio.

Darlene bolted back in the chair, her hands gripping the metal arms of the chrome office-style swivel seat.

"Why don't you meet me back in the tunnel and I'll give you the answer, on your knees!"

Darlene snatched up the radio and hit the *Talk* button. "Who is this? Who are you, motherfucker?"

A low laugh emanated from the radio. *"I don't think you're ready for that, just yet."* Followed by another, more sinister baritone chuckle.

"Who *are* you? I am gonna *fuck* you up, you *bastard!"* Darlene loudly sobbed out the last few words, clutching the radio in both hands.

"What the fuck's all the racket about?" a sleepy voice near her desk cried out. Another inmate awoke and punched the first who'd spoken.

"Shut the fuck up, asshole. I'm tryin' to sleep." More inmates woke and began to yell. In the far corner, a fight broke out. Seeing bodies crashing over the cots caught Darlene's attention and she forgot her rage at the voice on the radio. She pressed the call button and shouted into the radio: "Ten thirty-three," the code for *officer in need of assistance.*

The radio was dead.

"Hello? Hello? Ten thirty-three! Ten thirty-three! Officer in need of assistance in A dorm. Come back. Anyone?"

Nothing. Darlene pressed the call button and banged the radio on the desktop. The battery compartment door popped open and she saw why no one was answering. The batteries

were fried, leaking a white foaming substance she had to assume was acid.

"Damn!" she swore. The fight was spreading, now involv-
ing several inmates, and was in danger of becoming a full-
scale riot. She pushed her body alarm button on her belt.

"Now you're fucked, *aren't you?"*

Darlene froze. The voice was followed by a familiar low,
menacing laugh. She looked at the radio, at its foaming batteries lying disconnected from it on the desktop. Still, the
voice came from it.

"Now you are really *fucked, bitch,"* the laughing voice
added.

Darlene Hampton began to scream.

Tim Saget stood in the bedroom doorway watching Millie
throwing clothes into a large canvas suitcase. She was crying, sniffling, snot collecting on her upper lip. She was randomly pulling articles of clothing from her drawer, balling
them up, and stuffing them into the bag.

"How long have you known you're pregnant?" Tim asked.
Millie said nothing; continued packing. "When were you
planning on telling me?"

Millie replied with a short, barking laugh and a shake of
her head.

"Why didn't you tell me? Don't you think I have a right to
know?" Tim demanded.

"I don't know, do you?" Millie shot back.

"What the hell is that supposed to mean?"

"What do you *think* it means?

"I don't know, Mill. I don't know anything anymore."

"You still know how to party, though, don't you? Well,
after I'm gone you won't have to worry about coming home,
or calling anyone, or caring about anyone, or anyone caring
about you, or loving you!" On the last she burst into renewed
tears, wiped the snot from her nose with the back of her
hand, then wiped her hand on the clothes in the suitcase.

"If you had told me, I wouldn't have gone out. . . ." Tim started to explain.

"Really? I'm sorry, Tim, but I find that hard to believe. It ain't like this is the first time this has happened. It's turned into a weekly thing lately." She sniffed and went on before Tim could speak. "And the reason I didn't tell you is I didn't *know* until this afternoon. I mean, I guessed. . . . I was hoping I wasn't. I was hoping . . . I don't know what I was hoping."

Tim stood there, suddenly mute, not knowing what to say. Millie looked at him hopefully, then sighed and continued shoving balled-up wads of clothing into her suitcase.

"What do you want me to say?" Tim finally mumbled. "What do you want me to do?"

"Nothing, Tim. I don't want you to *say* or *do* anything," Millie replied, angrily. "I just want you to go on with your life, the carefree party animal you've always been. You're never going to grow up, and I need a *grown-up* to help me raise this child."

"So . . . you're going to keep it, then?"

Millie gave him a surprised look. "Of course I'm going to keep it. Did you think I would do anything else? Did you think I'd have an abortion?"

Tim shrugged. "I don't know, maybe; maybe put it up for adoption."

"God! You really don't know me at all, do you? We've been together now—how long? Nine, ten months and you don't know that I would never, *could* never have an abortion or give up a child of mine?"

"Yeah, well, things change," Tim said, lamely.

"Something's maybe, but not this. This is a *life* we're talking about."

"Look, would you just stop packing and talk to me?"

Millie blinked at him. "I'm sorry. I thought that's what we were doing. Besides, what else is there to talk about? I thought everything was pretty clear—I'm going to have this baby, on my own, without you, and you . . . you, you're just going to go on your merry way getting drunk and partying with your friends and never growing up. Just like you did today and will keep on doing."

"I went out today because I lost my job!" Tim said angrily. "I got laid off; a bunch of us did, so we went out for a drink or two. I didn't plan on staying out so long—it just happened. I thought this job was it, was going to be my *last* job, you know? I thought I had a chance at . . . a steady, long-term thing there, a promotion, some security—a future, you know? Despite *what* you think of me I *do* worry about the future and what I'm going to do with my life. I mean, jeez, I'm thirty-one and I've got nothing going for me.

Millie's face softened. "You had *me* going for you, Tim. You still do . . . if you want me."

Tim's eyes teared up in spite of himself. "Yeah, I want you, Millie. Don't go. Don't leave me. I want you—and I want this kid—*our* kid!"

Millie cried and ran into Tim's arms. They kissed and held each other tight, tears streaming down both their faces.

John Thompson was about to open the door to the Outer Control room when it flew open and his second-in-command, Lieutenant Jim Henderson, clad in protective helmet and carrying a long stun gun, which was nothing more than a modified cattle prod, came running out.

"Captain! There's a brawl in A dorm. I called the tact team to assemble."

John swore under his breath. *That was Darlene's station.* To Jim Henderson he replied, "Did you call the dogs in?" The lieutenant nodded. "Okay, let's go!" John pushed Henderson ahead of him and followed, running down two flights of stairs to the armory in the basement of the building. The inside door was already open, as was the one inside the room leading out to the yard. Several officers were grabbing their protective gear: Plexiglas shields, heavy rubber gloves, and riot helmets equipped with gas masks. An officer near the door handed out the stun guns and gas grenades as the clad guards ran past him, up the stairs, and into the yard, where they assembled.

John grabbed his equipment and ran out to the men forming up in the yard. "All right!" he barked. "We got action in A dorm." Out of the corner of his eye he saw the two night-shift K-9 officers come running around the corner with their huge German shepherds straining at their leashes. "Standard Procedure A!" John yelled, motioning to the dog officers. "Canines go in first, we follow. I've got the gas"—he held up the tear gas gun in his hands—"if we need it, then we go to Standard Procedure B! Got that?"

The men nodded and John could see that several of them were practically dancing from foot to foot, pumped up with adrenalin. And that was the way he wanted—needed—them to be.

"All right! Let's do it! Double time—A dorm—second floor!"

Darlene Hampton stopped screaming when a hand clamped over her mouth. It was one of the inmates who had snuck up behind her when the fighting broke out. Darlene could smell him, a mix of onions and too much Aqua Velva, and immediately knew who it was: Billy Dee Washington, a huge black skinner in for raping two teenage girls while their tied-up mother was forced to watch. He'd already been reprimanded for calling Darlene an uppity black bitch and threatening that if he ever got his hands on her he'd teach her about being black—black and blue! At least two feet taller than she, he was able to easily reach over with his huge hand and cover her mouth, nose, cheeks, and chin. His other hand plunged over her shoulder and into her blouse where it shoved her bra aside and grabbed the flesh of her breast as though he would tear it from her body.

No! she screamed in her head. *This can't be happening again! I will not be raped twice in the same night!* Training and reflexes came to her rescue. She lifted her right foot and brought the heel down hard on Billy Dee's bare foot, grinding her boot into his bare instep. At the same time she twisted, pulling free of his hold, and gave him a right uppercut. Being so much shorter, she landed a direct hit squarely to his balls. Washington dropped to his knees with a thud, his mouth open in a silent scream of pain. Darlene stepped back, saw his eyes widen with anger, and added a lunge kick directly to his throat, sending him flying backwards to the floor, where he lay motionless.

She whirled, bringing her baton to her hand in one smooth motion. The dorm room was in chaos—men fighting, leaping upon one anothers' backs, pillows flying through the air, all accompanied by the sounds of fists hitting flesh, grunts and groans and cries of pain, and a whole lot of swearing. An inmate, staggering backward from a another inmate's punch to the chin, stumbled into her, and she leveled him with a swiping blow to the back of his head. He crumpled at her feet. The other inmate stared at her chest and grinned. She looked down and saw that her blouse had been torn open by Billy Dee Washington and her left breast exposed. Walking like Frankenstein's monster, hands held in front of him at arms length, the inmate took a step toward her. She crouched and lunged, sweeping her left leg into his ankles and knocking him off his feet. She spun around, jumped on his chest, and incapacitated him with several furious blows to the face and head with her baton. The sound of dogs barking stopped her assault, and probably saved the inmate's life.

She looked up toward the sound of the dogs approaching from the main stairwell, and noticed someone standing near the dormitory entrance, staring at her. Though prisoners fought all around him, the man stood amid them as if enclosed in a force field that none of the rioting inmates could penetrate. And there was something else about him; he wasn't dressed like the other inmates, who generally wore their prison-issue green boxer shorts and T-shirts as sleepwear. He was dressed in white, like a doctor or an orderly in a hospital. At first she thought that's who he was—one of the infirmary workers who had come to help out with the riot. But that didn't make sense; infirmary help wasn't supposed to respond to riot situations unless called; unless needed to treat seriously injured inmates who could not be transported to the prison hospital. Besides, on eleven-to-seven, the only person on duty in the Health Services Unit was her best friend, Sheila Donner, the night nurse. But Sheila was on vacation, so he might be her replacement, except that Darlene didn't recognize him, and she knew all of the HSU workers. She supposed he could be a new hire . . . but there was something else, something *weird*. He looked *washed-out,* if that was possible, like a pale image seen through a thick glass, or like how a person looks in the movies when they superimpose the image of a dead actor into a new film.

His identity did not remain a puzzle for long. In the next instant, Darlene knew *exactly* who he was as he slowly grabbed his crotch, massaged it, and gyrated his hips while never taking his eyes from Darlene's.

It's him!
Him!
The bastard who raped me!

It didn't take long to quell the disturbance and John Thompson was glad of it. It was always that way with random, spur-of-the-moment frays—what he worried about and dreaded was a *planned* riot and attempted takeover. That . . . and what Darlene Hampton was going to do next.

John sat in his car in the officers' parking lot, glove compartment open, pint bottle of 100 proof Southern Comfort that he always kept there in his hand, and cursed himself for being such an idiot. His shift had just ended, but he couldn't bring himself to go home. He sat there, imagining what inmates and officers alike were saying about him right at that moment inside the prison. As he had been doing, over and over for the past hour since he'd got off work, he reran the whole mess in his mind once again.

It hadn't taken the tact team more than fifteen minutes to bring the dormitory under control—something that John would have been extremely proud of under other circumstances. They were the best response team he had ever seen. It should have been a routine mop-up after that—getting the inmates back to their cots, taking the injured to the infirmary—except for Darlene Hampton. Her shrill voice rang in his head still.

"Stop that man! Stop that man!" she had screamed, running across the dormitory, shoving inmates and tact team officers alike out of her way. Everyone looked around, trying to see whom she meant. Several of the inmates backed away from her, shaking their heads as if to say, "Not me! I didn't do anything!" With her torn shirt, exposed tit, and rabid expression of fury on her face, no one wanted to get near her, and no one could take their eyes off her.

"Where'd he go? Where'd he go?" she asked frantically when she reached the entrance. She had grabbed John then by the front of his shirt and jerked him close until her face was right up against his chest. "He was here!" she hissed, her voice high and squeaky like steam escaping from one of the old radiators lining the walls of the room. "He was *here*, John. I saw him! He works in the infirmary!"

John realized *now* that he had reacted in the wrong way. He had known whom she was talking about, but he was caught so off guard, in front of his men and the inmates, that he blurted out, "Who? Who was here?" The words had been like a lit match to a fuse for Darlene.

"Who the fuck do you *think* I mean? The fucking skinner who *raped* me, that's who!"

Several of the inmates sniggered at that and were joined by some of the guards. John could only shrug—unable to think of how to react—and say, "I don't know who you mean." It was like trying to put out a fire with gasoline.

"You don't know who I mean?" Darlene shrieked. *"You*

don't know who I mean? I *mean* the guy who passed himself off as *you* and *fucked* me sore in the tunnel not more than fifteen minutes ago, you son of a bitch! Of course you know who I mean! What kind of man are you? Some fucking skinner rapes your woman and you act like you don't know what's going on? You fucking *pussy!*"

John looked around and, judging by the knowing looks on the faces of many of his colleagues, knew that his and Darlene's secret sex trysts had not been so secret. Even a few of the inmates were laughing behind their hands at him and exchanging winks.

John took another long pull from the bottle of Southern Comfort. His face flushed hot with embarrassment again as he remembered the awkward silence when Darlene had stormed away from the dormitory. Flustered, he had barked orders at his men to get the injured inmates to the infirmary, and they had snapped to it, yelling at the prisoners in turn.

John had gone after Darlene—his temper sufficiently raised by her actions—but she was gone. She had made a rampaging tour of the infirmary looking for her supposed rapist, then had stormed out of the prison, leaving her shift early. He could have her reprimanded for that; even bring her before a review board and have her suspended without pay, or fired, but he knew he wouldn't do that. She had the goods on him now, not the other way around. If the reaction of his men and the inmates was any indication, he was going to be the laughingstock of the entire facility. And worse, he might just find himself at the shit end of a lawsuit.

Tim Saget parked his car in his father's driveway and shut off the engine. The old man had been calling him every half hour since six A.M. Tim had let the machine get the first seven calls while he and Millie snuggled and tried to ignore the stern tone in his father's voice as he asked—more like *commanded*—Tim to come over ASAP because he had something important to discuss with him. Finally Tim had given up trying to ignore the calls and picked it up.

"Get over here on the double. I've got something important to tell you," his father had growled and hung up. Now Tim sat staring at the house where he had grown up, wishing he didn't have to go in, knowing that he had no choice. It was funny how he'd always felt that way, for as far back as he could remember—as far back as the day his mother died.

He'd been only five when she died of ovarian cancer after wasting away for nine months, but he still remembered her. She had been loving, warm, caring—everything his father, the Sergeant, was not. Tim remembered the day she'd died; it was the first time he had dreaded returning to that house where only the Sarge waited for him. He had stayed with his Aunt Sadie, one of his father's sisters, during the final days of his mother's life. He could still remember that terrible tight feeling in his chest, the mounting anxiety knowing he had to face *him* without the loving buffer of his mother between them. He could still remember it so clearly, for he *still* felt it; had felt it every day of his life while growing up.

In elementary school, he used to hang around the classrooms after school, risking being ridiculed as a teacher's pet, so that he wouldn't have to go right home. The Sarge worked seven-to-three and was usually home before Tim, who got out of school at 3:30. He would clean desks, the chalkboard, clap the chalk out of the erasers—anything to avoid the inevitable. He would walk home as slowly as possible, and if any of his friends invited him to their houses to play, he would gratefully accept and stay as long as he could—until the kid's parents told him to go home, it was time for supper, or the Sergeant called or showed up. Those were the worst times, fearing his heavy-handed wrath and seeing the look of disappointment, even dislike, in his father's face.

His earliest memories of his father were those looks of disappointment; the feeling that he didn't measure up to his father's definition of *son* and never would. It had led him to avoid his father and home as much as possible. Thank God he'd had his aunts, Sadie and Rosie, around. They had taken care of him whenever his father was working overtime— which, after his wife's death, he had done as much as possible. Retired now, he had been a sergeant with the Ashton Police Department for forty years. When Tim was in high school, and after, that fact had kept him from being arrested several times. The Ashton cops turned a blind eye to trouble when Tim was involved, or delivered him into the hands of the Sergeant—a fate worse than any punishment a judge could mete out. And after high school, when Tim had really started partying, being the Sergeant's only son had saved him from more than a few DUIs. All the while, with every new infraction, that look of disappointment, disgust—even *dislike*—had grown. Tim thought nothing he could ever do would change that.

He had tried. He had wanted to be a son that his father could be proud of, but the problem was that Tim had no idea what that was. In junior high he had tried sports, football, basketball, and baseball. The Sergeant never came to a single game. Early on in high school, Tim had tried studying hard, getting good grades and being a model student, but anything less that an A wasn't good enough for the Sergeant, and Tim had struggled to get Bs and B minuses in most subjects, and he never achieved more than Cs in the major subjects of math and English. Behaving and being the model student made no difference either; his father never went to parents' night to hear how wonderfully behaved his only son was. Tim finally gave up and resigned himself to the fact that he would never be good enough for the old man. That was when he'd started down the road to trouble and partying that he still seemed to be trapped on.

Tim took a deep breath and got slowly out of the car. He tried to mentally brace himself for what was sure to be a major ass-chewing from his dad—maybe even as bad as the one he'd got when he'd flunked out of the law enforcement program at Mount Wachusett Community College. That had been his last-ditch attempt to straighten out and please his father, make him proud by following in his footsteps, but he had blown it with too much partying. His second semester his GPA was a dismal 0.09 and he flunked out.

Now he'd lost the hospital security job—a laughable position, he was sure, as far as his father was concerned, but it had been something Tim had *liked*. For the first time in his adult life, he had found a job he actually enjoyed and was good at. Even though the Sergeant thought it was "playing cop," as he'd often said, Tim knew the old man would still be upset; would see it as just one more fuck-up in a long line of fuck-ups by the world's biggest fuck-up—his son. And this particular fuck-up was compounded by the fact that he'd got Millie pregnant. He could just imagine what the Sergeant would have to say about *that*.

Darlene Hampton didn't know how she made it home without having an accident. From the moment she had exploded at John Thompson she had wept profusely—all the way through the infirmary where she had failed to find the creep who raped her, out to her car, and during the drive home. Now she couldn't remember even seeing the road or her street. She had cried; she had driven; and miraculously, she had ended up at home.

She entered her tiny apartment on the second floor of a four-unit building on the west side of New Rome and locked the door behind her. She looked at the doorknob lock and realized how flimsy it was. It had never worried her before, but now she felt a growing panic, knowing that the pathetic button lock would not keep out anyone determined to get in.

The face of her attacker, as he had looked at her in the dormitory, clutching his balls and sneering, flashed before her eyes. That look had spoken volumes: *I'm not done with you, yet bitch! I'm going to get you, cunt!* She grabbed one of her wooden kitchen chairs and propped it at an angle under the doorknob. Her next stop was the metal strongbox she kept under her bed. In it was her .38-caliber Smith and Wesson revolver, well oiled and wrapped in gun cloth. She opened the chamber, made sure it was loaded, and carried it with her as she walked around the apartment, first checking every place someone could possibly hide, then just pacing back and forth, reliving the terrible events of the past evening.

She developed a throbbing headache before too long and went into the bathroom to run hot water in the sink so that she could breathe the steam. She wet a face cloth and put it over her face, breathing deeply of its heat. A sound from the other room made her catch her breath. She lowered the face cloth and stared at her frightened reflection in the mirror, silently telling herself that she had *not* heard the doorknob rattle.

But there it was again. Distinct. Clear. No doubt about it. *Someone was out there. Trying to get in.*

The *skinner!*

Darlene put the face cloth in the sink and retrieved her gun from the top of the toilet tank. Moving cautiously, soundlessly, she slipped out of the bathroom and down the short hall to the kitchen. She stood at the end of the hallway, her back against the wall, and looked across the small kitchen to the front door of her apartment. There was no sound now. Could she have imagined it? She was sure she had heard the doorknob turn and rattle as if someone were testing to see if it was locked.

What was that? A dull *thud* outside the door, or was it somewhere else in the building, and she was just imagining it was outside her door? The apartment walls were flimsy and she was constantly hearing noises from the other units in the building. Half the time she couldn't tell which apartment—below or beside hers—they were coming from.

Get a hold of yourself, girl! Stop imagining things! That skinner don't know where you live!

But was that true? He could have followed her from the prison—she wouldn't have known; she couldn't even remember driving. If he worked in the infirmary, as she thought from his white uniform, he could have looked her address up in the personnel directory issued to all correctional staff.

Sweat dripped down her nose, tickling her, yet she remained still, listening and thinking, but she heard nothing except the panic growing in her thoughts. She had to stop this. She had to regain control. She had to—

—*listen*! The doorknob was *turning,* ever so *slowly,* ever so *quietly!*

Stifling the urge to scream, Darlene took a deep breath and pushed away from the wall. Slowly, moving as though underwater, she stepped into the kitchen, crossed it in a few steps, and was at the door.

The knob stopped turning. Whoever was on the other side was *listening.*

Being careful not to touch the door or make a sound, Darlene leaned forward and put her eye to the peephole. The fisheye view showed an empty corridor—the image of the concave mirrors in the prison tunnels flashed before her eyes—but just to the right of the door . . . was that a sleeve and the edge of a white-trousered leg, of someone pressed up against the wall to avoid detection?

The way he must have done down in the tunnels at work!

A swell of anger rose through Darlene. *The bastard terrorizes me at work and now he thinks he can come to* my *home and* fuck *with me in* my *house? Not fucking likely!*

Moving with a speed developed through years of karate and Tae Bo classes, Darlene grabbed the doorknob, kicked the chair out from under it, twisted and pulled the door open, and leaped into the hallway, gun up and pointing at the spot directly to the right of the door.

"Now! Motherfu—!"

There was no one there.

John Thompson sat in the officers' parking lot drinking until 8:45, then drove home. He slipped quietly into his house, careful not to wake Bella, who was sleeping on the living-room couch again. She hated sleeping alone in their bed when John was working. Which made little sense to John since she never wanted to *do* anything in bed with him other than sleep. At 60—five years older than John— menopause had left her a changed woman, in the bedroom and everywhere else. It was what had driven him into Darlene Hampton's arms when she'd made herself available. Ten, twenty years ago, he never would have considered cheating on Bella, but he was, after all, a man whose sex drive had not diminished along with hers. When she was younger, she had been as horny as he, oftentimes more so. Now most of the time he felt like he was living with a stranger.

He went into the kitchen and took a beer from the fridge. The Southern Comfort had left him with more of a headache and upset stomach than the calming buzz he'd been looking for. He hoped that complementing the whiskey with a few beers would relax him enough so that he could get some sleep. He popped the top on a can and drained half of it, grabbed the rest of the six-pack, and took it upstairs to his office.

The room had been his daughter Kathy's, until she had left for UCLA. She had dropped out after a year, pregnant, and married her boyfriend, a Los Angeles fireman. Bella had wanted to keep the room a bedroom for when they came to visit, but now it didn't look like they were going to. They were supposed to visit right after the baby was born, in May, but she miscarried in February, her seventh month. Instead of them coming here, Bella had gone out there for a few months. His transfer to New Rome and subsequent affair with Darlene had coincided with her absence. Emboldened by it, John had turned the room into his office, something he'd wanted since they'd bought the house. Bella had her sewing and crafts room downstairs; he thought it only fair that he should have a sanctuary of his own. The garage had a workbench, but he'd never been much of a carpenter, mechanic, or general tinkerer. He *had* always dreamed of writing a book—a mystery, or maybe a spy novel. Upon her return, Bella didn't put up much of a fight, so he treated himself to a brand new Gateway computer with Windows 2000 software, complete with Microsoft Word, and had settled down to write. That had been the plan anyway. The reality was that he played solitaire and Minesweeper and surfed the Net more than anything else.

He closed the office door behind him, put the extra beers on the desk next to the metal computer table, and sat in the plush black leather swivel chair. The screen saver showed a mass of pipes growing from one tiny piece and flowering into a complex maze that filled the screen, only to blank out and start over again. He grabbed the mouse and the picture was immediately replaced with the desktop showing the computer's programs. He directed the arrow to the Microsoft Word icon, hesitated, then continued on to the deck of cards peeking out of a box that symbolized the solitaire program.

Numerous games, several beers, and two hours later he was still wired. Bella had woken and popped her head in around 10:30 to ask if he wanted some breakfast, to which he had grunted a curt, "No, thanks." Shortly after, he had smelled bacon cooking. She had returned twenty minutes later to ask again, and he had snapped at her, telling her to leave him be.

The phone rang, but John ignored it. He was about to give up on the beer and solitaire—generally a surefire combination for making him drowsy—in favor of one of Bella's sleeping pills when Bella called up to him.

"John! It's for you. It's Bill Capello."

John felt a leaden weight of dread drop into his stomach. Bill Capello was John's oldest friend; he was also the prison's superintendent and he *rarely* called John at home, and *never* called at a time when John would normally be sleeping. There could be only one plausible reason for his calling, and it was confirmed for John as soon as he picked up the extension in his office.

"John, Bill here. Hope I didn't wake you but, frankly, it's too damn bad if I did. I don't like what I'm hearing around the Hill today. I want to know what the hell went on here last night, and it had better be good!"

Though it was midmorning, the house was dark and quiet when Tim entered. As usual, all the shades—the heavy dark blue kind that shut out nearly all light—were drawn against the brightness of the day. The air in the house was heavy, musty, still carrying the stuffiness of winter. As far as Tim knew, his father never opened a window in the house, relying instead upon central air that he'd had installed several years ago. It was obvious he had not yet turned it on. For a fleeting moment, Tim entertained the hope that the Sergeant had got tired of waiting for him and had gone out.

"Don't just stand there like an idiot! Come on in."

The hope died.

His father was sitting in the living room in the deep recessed shadows of his recliner, parked in the darkest corner. It unnerved Tim to realize his father had been sitting there, invisible, watching him, sizing him up; *judging* him. Tim shuffled into the room and made for the end of the sofa, as far as possible from the Sergeant, but he should have known better.

"Don't sit there!" his father growled. "Sit over here where I can see you."

Several retorts—such as "Ever hear of opening the shades?"—popped into Tim's head, as they always did when he spoke to his father but, as always, he kept quiet. He moved to the rocking chair next to the recliner and sat stiffly in it, not letting his shoulders rest against the chair back. He sat with his hands folded, clenching each other white in his lap, head down, looking at the Sergeant out of the corner of his eye.

His father hadn't changed much over the years. He was still as formidable and military looking as he had been when he was the Ashton Police Department's desk sergeant. His hair—one of the few things to have changed, going from black to steel gray—was cropped as short as ever, just under crew-cut length. The stern lines in his square face, around his eyes and mouth, had always been there but of late had grown deeper, more pronounced. His physique was still imposing—six feet two, wide shoulders, forearms as thick as most men's legs and hands as large as any pro basketball player's. His gray-blue eyes were closed, as they often were when he was speaking to Tim, as if he couldn't stand to look at his disappointing offspring.

"So . . . you've gotten yourself into another fine mess, I see," the Sergeant said slowly.

Yes, Ollie, Tim was tempted to say but didn't.

"You know, it's bad enough you've lost *another* job, but now you've gone and knocked up that little guinea you've been living with. Tell me something, have you *ever* heard of rubbers? Has she ever heard of the pill? Are the two of you so stupid that you thought you could fuck like rabbits and not pay the price?"

Tim said nothing. The Sergeant shifted in his chair.

"She gonna get an abortion?"

Tim shook his head.

"No, I didn't think so. She's a Catholic, right?"

Tim nodded.

"So . . . what *is* she going to do? For that matter, what're you gonna do?"

Tim took a deep breath and let it out, speaking softly. "She's going to have it. We're going to get married." He waited for the mocking, sarcastic laugh he was sure would follow that statement, but it didn't come. The Sarge looked at him directly for the first time since Tim had entered the room and seemed to be regarding him with something other than his usual disappointment. He steepled his fingers together in front of him and cleared his throat.

"How do you expect to be able to support a wife and kid now that you're unemployed—again?"

Tim shrugged. "She can keep working right up to the ninth month, and I can collect unemployment until I find another job."

"You need more than unemployment, kiddo, and now you'll need more than *just* another job."

Tim didn't reply. He'd collected before and it had been enough—enough to keep him in beer; enough to let him go out with his buddies drinking every weekend, but would it be enough to get married with? Enough to have a kid? Maybe the old man was right.

"Tell me something, Tim. Does your girlfriend have health insurance where she works?"

Tim's stomach did a little panic twist. He hadn't thought of that and he didn't know. Millie worked as a receptionist/secretary for a small waste disposal company. She'd been there for five years, so she had to have benefits, hadn't she?

"I think so," Tim lied and was immediately answered by a grunt of disgust from his father.

"You *think* so? You don't know?"

Tim shook his head meekly.

"I suggest you find out before you sign up for unemployment. If she doesn't, you'd better sign up for COBRA coverage at the unemployment office. *You,* at least, had health insurance on your job, didn't you?"

Tim nodded.

"Then COBRA will extend your benefits for as long as you collect, or until you get another job and qualify for coverage there. They take it out of your unemployment benefits and it ain't cheap, but in this case, it'll be worth it."

There was an awkward silence. Tim wondered if that was it. He longed to get up and leave, but on the phone the Sarge had said he had something important to tell Tim.

As if reading his mind, the Sergeant said, "There's something important I want to discuss with you. I wanted to know what you were going to do about your girlfriend and all be-

fore I brought it up. Now that I see you're going to be a man
[he didn't say "for a change," but Tim could hear it implied
in his voice] and do the right thing, I can tell you. Honestly,
Tim, I think getting that girl pregnant may be the best thing
that could happen to you right now. I think it's just what you
need. There's nothing like becoming a father—no matter
how it happens—to make a man grow up and accept responsibility."

Tim waited, expecting a prolonged lecture on the duties
and demands of parenthood, but the Sarge again surprised
him.

"I think I can get you into the state corrections officers
training academy. An old friend of mine, Bill Capello, is the
superintendent of the medium-security prison up in New
Rome. I saw him the other day and he mentioned he's got
some openings. I asked about getting you in. Though they
generally like to get younger guys, he agreed to give you a
shot as long as you can pass the seven weeks' training at the
academy. It's good pay, excellent benefits, and you can retire
with 75 percent of your pension after only twenty-five years.
Not bad, huh?"

Tim nodded but didn't know what to say.

Prison guard? Him?

Darlene Hampton thought she heard someone outside her
door three more times, and three more times she leaped into
the hallway, gun ready, only to find it empty. The fourth time
she heard the doorknob rattle, she forced herself to ignore it.
She went into the bathroom, locked the door, and took a
long, hot shower, soaping and massaging her aching breasts
and genitals. She went straight to bed from the shower, but
could not get warm under a pile of covers. She was filled
with an inner chill that originated in her womb and spread
throughout her body like the bone-chilling cold of a fever.

When she finally did fall asleep, around three, her phone
rang. It was Superintendent Capello's secretary, asking her

to come in for a meeting with the superintendent at 4:00 P.M. Though the secretary "asked," Darlene knew she did not have the option of refusing, not if she wanted to keep her job. And after walking off her shift last night, she knew she was already in hot water—no matter what the reason for her leaving.

She dragged herself from bed and took another scalding shower, trying to get warm. In the light of day and the steam of the shower, last night seemed so unreal. If it wasn't for the soreness between her legs and the bruises on her breasts, she could have written it off as a bizarre dream.

I was raped. It was no dream.

She began to tremble, then cry. The emotion swept over her uncontrollably, driving her to her knees. Her sobs became so powerful they convulsed her stomach and soon she was retching and tasting bile in her throat. She lay in the tub, water spraying over her naked body, and reflexively curled into a fetal position.

By the time her crying jag had run its course, she was late. She had to hurry into a pair of slacks and sweater and didn't have time to put on any make-up or do anything with her short, bushy Afro other than brush it straight back and put her prison cap on over it. She ran out to her car and drove dangerously fast through the streets of west New Rome to Route 140 where she sped at sixty—twenty miles an hour over the speed limit—to the prison on the opposite side of town. Luckily, there were no local cops policing the road, as they were wont to do on a regular basis.

Darlene arrived at Capello's office at 4:20 and was welcomed with a dour look from his secretary, a fish-faced, steely-eyed, gray-haired, buxom old broad by the name of Mrs. Hadley. Capello's office was on the third floor of D building, which housed the prison school and chapel, as well as the administrative offices, and Darlene was able to get to his office with a minimum of contact with her fellow screws. She didn't notice the smirks she got from the two guys working the front gate in C building as they buzzed her through.

"Go right in; he's been waiting for you," Mrs. Hadley said before hitting a button on her desk intercom and announcing: "Officer Hampton has *finally* arrived, Superintendent, and is on her way in." Darlene bit her tongue and pushed through the heavy oak door of Capello's office.

She was not surprised to see John Thompson—looking uncomfortable out of uniform—sitting in front of Capello's desk. She was a little taken aback by the presence of Joe Peters, the corrections officers' union rep, and another stern-looking business-suited man she did not know. Superintendent Capello stood as she entered.

"Officer Hampton," he said by way of a greeting, adding a curt nod. "You know Captain Thompson"—he managed to say it without any inflection or hint of what he was thinking—"and Officer Peters, your union representative. I've also asked Dave Costello, assistant district attorney for Worcester County, to be here. Please have a seat." He motioned to the only empty chair between Joe Peters and John Thompson, and sat down himself. He glanced at a sheaf of papers on his desk, smoothed them, then clasped his hands in front of him and looked and Darlene.

"I'm sorry if this is interrupting your sleep—I know from many years of working the graveyard shift how hard it can be to get the sleep you need—but I think you know why it was imperative that I have this meeting as soon as possible." He paused, cleared his throat, and seemed unsure of how to go on. "There were some rather, um, *indiscreet* shall we say, goings-on here last night and I—"

"You call my getting raped an 'indiscreet going-on'?" Darlene blurted out.

Not one to be put on the defensive, nor have a subordinate be disrespectful, Superintendent Capello shot her a stern look. "No, I don't. But I *do* call trysts in the tunnels indiscreet, inappropriate, *and* unprofessional—not to mention *unlawful*—and downright dangerous," he answered, his voice loud and intimidating.

On the other hand, Darlene Hampton was not one to be

easily intimidated by authority. "So what are you saying? Because I was having an affair with John I *deserved* to be raped?" she countered.

Next to her, John Thompson groaned quietly.

"Don't be putting words in my mouth, Officer Hampton. You know exactly what I mean. And as far as your being raped, we only have your word to go on for that. I've looked at your record, and you used to work for the rape crisis unit with the Brockton Police before coming here so you *know* the procedure for rape, and it is *not* to let the victim leave the scene without a thorough medical examination."

Darlene was fuming and barely heard the last part of what he'd said. "Oh, I get it now! It's not that you think I *deserved* to be raped, you think I'm *making it up!*" She turned to John Thompson. "You spineless *prick*! What the fuck have you been telling them?"

Superintendent Capello interjected harshly and immediately. "That's enough! There's no need for profanity or accusations here, Officer Hampton. I just want to find out what happened last night and why you left your shift early."

"Why do you *think* I left? I was raped, goddammit! I was raped and your *boy* John here was treating me like I was a lunatic, or worse, a *liar.* I couldn't stand to stay in the same place as him, much less stay knowing the skinner was walking around, maybe waiting to get a hold of me again and shut me up for good."

"When you went to the Health Services Unit why didn't you get examined, then you could have left according to on-duty-illness procedure."

"I just told you why—and I wasn't ill, I was *raped!*"

Capello gave her a piercing, narrow-eyed stare and asked quietly, "Did you shower when you got home?"

The question caught Darlene off guard. She nodded sheepishly.

"Did you, um"—the superintendent paused uncomfortably before continuing—"Did you douche?"

Darlene had to laugh at that, a great guffawing, nervous laugh, and shook her head no.

"I'm glad you find this amusing," Capello said sternly, his face beet red with embarrassment. "But I assure you, this is *not* an amusing situation. There were some serious breaches of conduct last night by both you and your watch commander, Captain Thompson. But the worst was your leaving your post without permission."

Darlene started to interrupt but the superintendent held up his hand, stopping her.

"Let me finish! I believe you had a traumatic experience last night, but the fact that you left the facility *and* showered is going to make it very hard to corroborate your story."

"It's *not* a *story*," Darlene said sullenly.

"I did not use that word to imply it was a work of fiction, Officer Hampton, and quite frankly, your attitude is starting to *piss me off!*" Capello's voice went up a few decibels on the last few words. "You are in serious trouble here; the fact of your being raped doesn't change that. If you and John here weren't two of my finest officers, with over fifty years experience between you, I'd quite honestly have your guts for garters. But you *are* two of my best officers and I *don't* want to lose either of you. And, just as importantly, I don't want this to balloon into something that's going to affect the reputation of this institution."

Darlene sat forward, mouth open, face angry, but Capello cut her off.

"Neither do I want to diminish what appears to be a serious crime against you. Whatever you may *think*, Officer Hampton, I believe you and I *do* want to find the person responsible. An attack on an officer of this facility is a serious offense and must be punished. We will find the perp, whether he be an inmate or a fellow officer, and prosecute him. I just want to do it with some discretion and out of the public eye if possible. That's why I've asked Mr. Costello from the attorney general's office to be here." Capello nod-

ded at the man in the suit and Costello smiled reassuringly at
Darlene.

"Now," the superintendent continued, "why don't you tell
exactly what happened here last night."

3

Tim Saget got into the Massachusetts Corrections Officers Academy with an appointment from his father's friend, prison superintendent Bill Capello, who did it as a favor for his long-time army buddy Joe Saget, a.k.a. the Sarge. For seven weeks, starting three days after getting laid off at the hospital, he traveled to Brighton five days a week where he spent eight hours a day learning the ropes of being a Massachusetts corrections officer.

The first week was the toughest. He had to get up at five and leave by 5:45 to get there at seven. Aerobics, running, weight training, endurance exercising, and self-defense filled each morning. Tim liked the self-defense classes the best. There he learned how to use an M-13 baton, along with jiujitsu, aikido, and an in-depth training in the proper physical restraint holds. Three times a week they went on the firing line and practiced with .38-caliber Smith and Wesson revolvers, the standard firearm for Massachusetts corrections officers. After lunch it was actual classroom time, learning the state-mandated rules, regulations, procedures, and codes that are used in all Massachusetts prisons. There was also a heavy dose of criminal and civil law as it pertained to the corrections system and those incarcerated in it.

It was tough; the toughest thing Tim had ever done. Several times he felt like quitting. Everyone else in the academy was at least ten years younger than he—a lot of them stronger and in much better shape than he and most of them smarter. If it wasn't for Millie and the baby growing inside her, he might have just quit. But then there was the Sergeant to contend with.

Since Tim had entered the academy, he had noticed a change in his father. The condescending tone disappeared from his voice and Tim could almost sense . . . pride, albeit a *cautious* pride. Even so, there were times in the middle of the night when he lay awake thinking about the choices he'd made in life and those that had been thrust upon him; when he couldn't shake the feeling that he was falling into a trap, a prison that he would never escape from. It was more than just being tied down with a wife and career; it was a sense of impending doom. Like a killer on death row, he felt he was waiting for the inevitable execution.

His dreams didn't help. Night after night he returned in somnolence to that strange building where smoke poured from the roof and turned into deformed bats, swooping down on him. On several nights he woke to find himself standing in a different part of the house, staring at a spot off in space somewhere, seized with panic and terror. It was one of those dreams he often had that felt like it was more than just a chance dream, more than just a random firing of the synapses in his brain. All too often these dreams had proven to be prophetic. There'd been at least three.

As a kid, a few times he had dreamt of things that would happen, but they had been small, unimportant family events, like the time he dreamt that he won fifty dollars playing keno with his Aunt Sadie at the St. Anthony's fair and then it happened. The first such *important* dream Tim could remember having had been shortly after seeing the movie *The Matrix*. He dreamt that he was with the characters Trinity and Neo, in the scene where they go to rescue Morpheus, but with a few deviations from the script. He was dressed in black—sunglasses, T-shirt, jeans, long leather trenchcoat and jackboots, all in black. Beneath the coat he could feel enough weapons to outfit a small army.

Curiously, he noticed a Nazi armband on the sleeves of his coat and those of Neo and Trinity. That was the first deviation from the film scene. The second was when they marched through the double doors into the building and opened fire. Instead of armed policemen, security guards, and soldiers, they were shooting and killing—*kids!* Teenagers! They ran screaming from the hail of bullets, some escaping, too many being cut down in eruptions of blood. In the dream, Tim realized this was wrong and grabbed at Neo's arm, but it was not Keanu Reeves who turned to face him, but an acne-ridden teenager who grinned maliciously and said, "This is cool, huh? Just like the movie. Now we'll make them pay!"

Exactly three weeks later, the Columbine High School mass murder took place. When Tim saw the pictures of one of the teenaged gunmen, he realized it was the kid he had thought was Neo in his dream.

The second important prophetic dream he had was in August of 2001. For a week straight, every night he dreamt it. In the dream he and the Sergeant were in an underground garage filled with paper debris—sheets of it flying about as if caught in a windstorm. The Sergeant was in a uniform, but not a policeman's uniform. Instead he was dressed in firefighting gear. A line from the Beatles song "Helter Skelter"—*she's comin' down fast!*—kept playing over and over loudly in the background like a CD with a glitch in it. Suddenly, a thick fog, which seemed to come from everywhere at once, filled the garage, making it hard to see and breathe. He lost sight of his father and searched frantically for him in the growing fog. Each night, just before he woke, his father's face would emerge from the cloud, his helmet's plastic faceguard mask cracked, his nose and cheeks bloody within. "Run!" he'd yell, and Tim would awaken.

He forgot about the dream until nearly a year later when he was watching a documentary on the clean-up of the September 11th World Trade Center disaster. The news showed a video of a small part of the underground garage beneath Tower One that had survived the collapse. Tim sat stunned, staring at the place from his dream, where papers were flying everywhere, and dust swirled around the camera as thickly as fog. The camera focused on a fireman's helmet on the ground; the face mask was cracked and bloody.

The most recent prophetic dream had been several months before the actual disaster happened, and the dream occurred only once, but because of the two previous dreams, he had immediately felt that it was a prophecy. In the middle of winter, he dreamed it was autumn. He was in his father's yard, raking leaves and listening to the radio. He heard a sonic boom and looked up to see the contrail of a jet high overhead begin to break up into several smoky streams. Tim could see the jet's wings rip off and the jet itself then disintegrate into many pieces. Months later, when he woke to the news of the shuttle disaster on a Saturday morning and saw the pictures on TV of the destroyed spacecraft streaking across the Texas sky, he knew the meaning of the dream.

But there was one major difference between those dreams and the one he was having now: This dream was one he'd had at least three times since he was a kid, and he had yet to see that building, much less watch it burn and see the smoke turn into a swarm of bats. If it was a prophetic dream, he wondered why he had it so young and kept on having it. When was this dream going to come true?

Maybe it wasn't a prophetic dream, after all.

Darlene Hampton sat in Outer Control at the monitor board. Before her, a bank of closed-circuit TV screens flickered in black and white, showing various parts of the prison covered by the outdoor security camera system. Until an investigation of her rape could be completed, she had been as-

signed to this station on eleven-to-seven to keep her away
from the prison population and to isolate her from the rest of
the corrections officers.

She didn't like it; it felt too much like punishment. Neither
did she like the way she had been treated since the meeting
in Superintendent Capello's office. After telling her side of
the story to the suit from the DA's office, she'd had to endure
nearly an hour of his questions, all with a tone that hinted he
thought she was lying. And the way he kept repeating his
questions, rewording them, the way investigators will when
questioning a perp to try and trip him up and catch him in a
lie, had really pissed her off. But she bit her tongue, gritted
her teeth, and answered every damned question. She knew
from the tone of Capello's voice and the look in his eye that
she was walking on thin ice and she wasn't going to give him
any reason to let her fall through.

After the questioning she'd had to endure a medical examination from Doctor Waskewitz, the Health Services
Unit's head physician. That had been embarrassing; she
knew Walt Waskewitz well and had often joked and flirted
with him, especially when she had been on the day shift a
few years ago. She was given the option of going to a doctor
at the local hospital to be examined, but she just wanted to
get it over. But to have Walt examine her, asking the personal
questions about her sex life that he had to ask in a medical
rape investigation, had been more embarrassment heaped
upon her. After, she wished she had gone to a doctor she didn't
know.

For the past few weeks she'd had to endure looks and
comments—the nasty laughter after she walked by—behind
her back, and right to her face, from her fellow officers. It
was getting so bad that, for the first time since becoming a
corrections officer, Darlene was thinking about quitting,
leaving it all behind. Unfortunately, she had made the mistake of burning bridges when she'd left the Brockton Police,
and her job before that with a security agency in Boston, and
wasn't sure if any police force or security firm would take

her. Glowing references weren't something she had a lot of. Besides, this was *supposed* to be the last job she'd ever have; ever *need*. The benefits were great and she'd be able to retire young and still healthy enough to enjoy retirement.

A movement in one of the top row cameras caught her eye and she glanced up, sitting forward. The monitor showed the front entrance to A dorm, where she was normally stationed. Jack Roy had taken her spot at the second-floor station, and it was he stepping outside and lighting a cigarette that had caught her attention. Darlene shook her head; that was a double *no-no*. Dorm guards were not supposed to leave their posts at night unless relieved, and there was supposed to be no smoking anywhere on state property, which in this case covered the entire hill. Everyone did it, of course, though *she* could say, with a feeling of smug superiority, that she never had.

She flicked a switch, turning on the monitor to the cameras covering the sleeping area of A dorm's second floor. Normally, these monitors were not on in Outer Control, whose surveillance was supposed to be of the cameras set in various outside locations in the prison. Inner Control covered the inside cameras, but those could also be accessed by Outer Control at any time. By regulation, though, such access was to be reserved for emergencies. Darlene knew the regulation, but it didn't stop her. Lately, she didn't much give a shit about prison regulations. Using a toggle switch, she panned first one, then the other of the two cameras set at opposite ends of the large room. Everything was quiet; all the inmates were sleeping.

She started to sit back when something at the edge of the monitor caught her eye—a glimpse of white. She tweaked the toggle switch controlling the camera's movements, but the spot was just outside its range. She switched to the other camera, at the opposite end of the room. Each camera inevitably had its blind spots, but the other camera covered those. She panned the second camera to the spot and gasped.

It was *him*! The *skinner*! He was standing in the corner by the heavy window curtains, dressed in the same white doctor's-type uniform she had seen him in the night of her rape. In front of him, two inmates writhed naked on the floor as he watched over them, moving his arms as if instructing them. Darlene hit the zoom button on the control panel and the monitor blurred, and then refocused automatically showing a close-up of the man in white. Darlene's breath caught in her throat and she began to tremble as he looked up directly into the camera, smiled, and gave her the finger.

Captain John Thompson was having coffee in Inner Control on the first floor of Digbee Hall, which also housed the Health Services Unit on the second floor, and the Awaiting Action Unit and solitary confinement also known as the Segregated Inmates Unit, commonly called the can, at the north end of the hall. The third and fourth floors were un-used, though the fourth was in the process of being reno-vated. At the opposite end of the building, between 7:00 A.M. and 8:00 P.M. it also housed the prisoners' day room where they could watch movies, play Ping-Pong, chess, and a host of other games, or check out a book from the small library, which consisted of one wall of shelves lined with beat-up paperbacks. Thompson had made his rounds, but avoided Outer Control, with Darlene Hampton there. He had stayed on at Inner Control long after the evening bed count had been completed, tallied, and logged. He had thought it best to avoid Darlene as much as possible. But he knew that was not going to last once he heard her voice over his radio.

"Captain Thompson? Adam 21."

It was the code for "Call me on the landline," the private line for when officers wanted to communicate with each other and not have it broadcast over the prison's radio sys-tem. He ignored the smirk on the face of Pete Seneca, the of-ficer on duty in Inner Control, and picked up the landline on his desk.

"What is it?" he asked curtly.

"It's him. The skinner," Darlene answered, her voice quavering.

"Where?"

"In A dorm. I've got him on the surveillance camera." Her voice was a near whisper.

John Thompson turned and looked at the bank of monitors. "What do you mean? Where's Jack Roy?"

"I don't know!" Darlene hissed. "Gone for a walk, I guess. I noticed him going outside, so I turned on the second-floor cameras to cover for him and *he* was there!"

John walked over and looked at the second-floor A dorm monitor. He saw nothing unusual, and there was nothing unusual in Jack Roy stepping outside for some air—every guard on night dorm duty did it; the other guard in the building covered both floors. With all inmates sleeping it wasn't a big deal; certainly no reason for Darlene to break regulations in Outer Control.

"Where's Lieutenant Henderson?" John asked Darlene. Henderson was his second in command and his station was Outer Control.

"Jerkin' off in the bathroom—who knows? Why? Don't you believe me? Ain't you got eyes?"

John looked again, along with Pete Seneca, panning the camera around the room, but neither saw a thing. Seneca looked at him and shrugged. John decided to play it safe and not risk riling Darlene again. Who knew what she'd do?

"All right. I'm on my way over there to check it out," he told her. John hung up the phone and turned to Officer Seneca. "Radio Jack Roy and have him get back to his post immediately. Radio Lieutenant Henderson, too, and tell him to grab the other yard officer and meet me on the second floor of A dorm immediately, if not sooner. Then I want a head recount from every dorm except A. Let me know immediately if there's any discrepancy," he told Seneca before leaving Digbee Hall and heading across the yard.

* * *

"I've got you now!" Darlene Hampton whispered to herself as she turned away from the switchboard and returned to the monitor station. The night switchboard operator—Jane Mazek, a redheaded, brawny fellow officer who was openly gay and whom Darlene didn't like—looked at her questioningly, but Darlene didn't notice. She sat at the row of monitors and swore softly.

"Damn!" The monitor for A dorm, upon which she had been watching the skinner, was now dark. She clicked the button to turn it on and nothing happened; the screen remained dark.

Pete Seneca's voice crackled over the radio: "Two-two-one, you need to report back to your station ASAP. Over."

Darlene rolled her wheeled chair over to the radio console. "You have an intruder in your area, Two-two-one, over!" she practically shouted into the microphone.

There was a pause, then came the reply, "Uh, negative. I'm back on the floor and all prisoners are accounted for. Over."

"I *didn't* say you had anyone missing! You've got an *intruder* on your floor; in the *same* room with you, goddammit! Over!" Darlene shouted into the microphone, causing Jane Mazek to nearly jump from her seat.

"Sorry, Control, I don't understand. Everything's normal as far as I can see. Who's here?"

Just then, John Thompson's voice cut in. "This is One-zero-zero. Control, maintain radio silence. Two-two-one, I am on my way. Over."

Darlene slammed the radio microphone down on the console and stood, knocking her chair over with a loud bang.

"Jesus Christ, Hampton! What the hell is wrong?" Jane Mazek declared, whirling in her chair, nearly causing her headphones to be ripped from her ears.

"He's not going to get away with this!" Darlene said fiercely.

"Who?" Jane asked. "What are you talking about?"

"Mind your own fucking business, dyke!" Darlene shouted at Jane and stormed out of the room.

"Well fuck you, too, bitch!" Jane Mazek returned with a sneer.

John Thompson ran across the east yard as fast as he could. At the south gate, he fumbled with his keys. He hadn't liked the sound of Darlene's voice on the radio. She was losing it, and there was no telling what she might do. As commander of the watch, John was ultimately responsible, and even more so now considering the trouble he was already in with Superintendent Capello. He got the gate unlocked, rushed through, and bolted for A dorm as the gate automatically swung shut and locked behind him. He couldn't see the yard officer and figured he was already inside. That was good. Outer Control was a lot closer to A dorm than Inner Control. John hoped Darlene wouldn't be stupid enough to leave her post *again,* but on the outside chance she had, he wanted more than just Jack Roy there to head her off before he could get there.

As he ran up the stairs to the second floor of A dorm, John Thompson knew deep down that Darlene wouldn't be able to let him and the other officers handle the situation, but he was not prepared for what greeted him at the top of the stairs. Jack Roy, Lieutenant Jim Henderson, and Mike Lecuyer, the west yard officer, stood in a semicircle, their hands raised, facing Darlene Hampton who was brandishing a gun.

"I want to know *where* the fuck he is!" she shouted. The three officers looked at each other, puzzled and frightened. "I *saw* him on the monitor! He was *in* here, dammit! Now you guys are going to stop covering for him or I'm going to shoot your balls off, *one by one*!"

"Darlene, put the gun down."

John Thompson spoke softly, hand outstretched, his eyes never wavering from the pistol in Darlene Hampton's hand. He felt as though he had suddenly been thrust into a video running on slow motion. Next to him, he could hear the scared, labored breathing of Jack Roy, Mike Lecuyer, and Jim Henderson. Within his peripheral vision he could see the sweat running down the side of Jack Roy's face. He could hear his own heartbeat, strangely slow and unexcited, completely out of sync with the panic he felt in his chest. Behind Darlene, inmates moved as if underwater, slowly and languorously, backing away from the trouble. It looked as if all of A dorm was awake and aware of the drama being played out at the top of the stairs.

"He's *here*! I saw him on the monitor!" Darlene said through clenched teeth, her grip on the gun unrelenting. "You're hiding him! I know it!"

"We're not hiding anyone, Darlene," Jack replied as soothingly as he could. "We want to get this guy as much as you do. He's a threat to *all* of us. We're a team, remember? We're a *family*. Remember your training? Remember the first thing they taught you at the academy? We're a *brotherhood*! We watch out for each other. If someone, especially a prisoner, does something to *one* of us, they do it to *all* of us."

Darlene smirked at John. "You can take that bullshit and shove it back up where it belongs. I ain't no part of no *brotherhood;* in case you hadn't noticed, I *ain't* no *brother*!"

"You know what I mean," John said, cajolingly. He took a cautious step toward Darlene. She swung the gun, training it on him, and opened her mouth to tell him to stop, but the words never came out. Her mouth opened and her eyes widened, but were trained on a spot behind John, further down the stairs. Suddenly she pointed the gun at the spot, a ferocious look in her eyes, and fired. John ducked, but the shot was far to his right. He dropped to one knee, his arms up in a futile gesture to protect his head. The other three guards jumped back, cringing nearly as badly as their captain.

"There he goes!" Darlene screamed. She ran to the top of the stairs, made as if to fire again, then swore. "Come on! He's getting away!" she shouted to the others and ran down the stairs, taking them two at a time, her gun up and ready to fire. Within seconds she was gone, and only her retreating footsteps could be heard, then the slamming of the outside door.

John Thompson got unsteadily to his feet and pulled his radio from its holster. His hands were shaking so badly, he could barely depress the transmission button. "All stations, we have a ten thirty-three. I repeat, we have a ten thirty-three. All emergency response team personnel meet me at the south gate."

"I've got you now, you bastard!" Darlene hissed as she shoved through the heavy door to the prison yard from A dorm. To her left, about twenty yards away, she caught a glimpse of white going around the corner between A and B dorms. She sprinted down the steps and across the yard as fast as she could, into the alley between the dorms, and to the rear corner of B dorm. She stopped at the corner, gun up, and peered around it just in time to catch a glimpse of a door closing. It was the old basement door to B dorm, which, as far as she knew, hadn't been used since the place had become a prison. In fact, she was certain it had been locked, sealed, and barred on the outside and from the inside, with the doorknob and lock plate removed; yet here it was, knob and keyhole intact, the edge of the door slightly ajar.

Slowly, gun ready to fire, she reached for the knob, grabbed it, and pulled the door open. A cool, damp, musty puff of air washed over her from the blackness within. She shifted the gun to her left hand and unsnapped the flashlight from her belt. She flicked it on, but its beam barely penetrated the darkness beyond the door. All she could make out were a few stone steps . . . leading downward.

"She's fucking nuts!" Jack Roy shouted. A cheer went up from the inmates of A dorm behind him.

"I'll take care of her," John Thompson told him. "You get

these guys back in their beds and take another head count."
To Mike Lecuyer and Jim Henderson he said, "You two
come with me." Still trembling, teeth chattering, Thompson
led the way downstairs. He stopped at the door leading outside and held up his right hand, motioning for the officers to
wait. Cautiously, he opened the door and peered through the
crack. Seeing no sign of Darlene, he opened the door further
and stuck his head through. She was nowhere in sight. John
opened the door completely and waved for Henderson and
Lecuyer to follow him. They started across the yard at a fast
walk that soon became a run as they made their way to the
south gate, near the front of the prison grounds.

    Darlene Hampton fought the urge to rush headlong down
the stairs after the skinner in white. She went halfway down
and shined the flashlight ahead, and was surprised to see the
stairs led down, not to a basement, as she'd thought, but to
one of the old tunnels that were no longer used by the prison.
She smiled in the faint back glow from her flashlight; if she
remembered correctly, tunnels like this had been blocked off
from the maze of other tunnels under the prison grounds and
buildings. She had the skinner trapped now; there was only
one way out—the way she'd just come in. She was glad she
had smuggled in her pistol strapped to her leg and two
speedloaders in her pockets. Though it was against regulations to have firearms in the prison, except for in C building,
at the rear gate, and in case of a prisoner riot or takeover
when they were distributed from the armory in C building, it
was easy for a corrections officer to sneak one in; they un-
derwent no searches upon entering the prison and did not
have to go through the metal detectors all other visitors to
the prison had to go through.
    In the fervor to get the perv who'd raped her, it didn't
cross her mind to dwell on how the door she'd just come
through had suddenly manifested a doorknob and lock and
had become unsealed and unbarred when, for as long as

she'd been at the prison, it had been unused. In the back of her mind she figured the skinner had something to do with it—was using the old tunnel for some illegal purpose. If it was an inmate, it could be anything from a drug stash to a place for illicit sex with other inmates. If it was a guard or a member of the hospital staff (which was much more likely), it could be a place for a quick nap while on duty—or a place to hide things smuggled in to sell to the inmates. There was a thriving black market in the prison, everything from food to drugs and pornography. Though no one talked about it, guards on the take brought in a majority of the contraband.

A noise from the darkness at the bottom of the stairs—a rustling of footsteps? a whispered chuckle?—made her pause. She shoved the flashlight ahead of her as far as she could, but it still could not penetrate the gloom for more than a foot or so in front of her. Just beyond the perimeter of the light, the darkness swirled momentarily. Was it movement?

"Hey!" Darlene shouted immediately. "If you surrender yourself *now* and come out of there, I won't shoot your ass!" She waited several moments, but there was no answer. "Okay, motherfucker, if that's the way you want it, get ready for a world of hurt."

A distinct giggle rose from the darkness below, followed by the patter of retreating footsteps. A chill trickled down Darlene's spine, but she shook it off and descended.

The eleven-to-seven shift's Emergency Response Team was the smallest of all three shifts; only three officers stood at the south gate waiting for John Thompson. Including Lecuyer, Henderson, and himself, that gave him six men to find Darlene Hampton before she hurt someone, or worse. John Thompson quickly filled in the other officers about the situation.

"Shouldn't we call in the tact team, Cap?" Henderson asked. The others mumbled their agreement.

"No!" Thompson answered quickly, and a little too

harshly. If he called in the tact team, he'd have to notify the duty officer, who'd call the super. "That would take too long," he explained. "We need to find Officer Hampton and diffuse this as soon as possible. She's not . . . acting coherently."

"She's gone fucking *nuts,* if you ask me," Jim Henderson commented.

"Yeah, she threatened to shoot our balls off, then took a shot at the Cap," Lecuyer added. The other officers started to laugh but a sharp look from Thompson silenced them.

"All right," he said, "we're going to have to split up—each man on his own. Maintain radio contact at all times. Officer Hampton is armed and considered dangerous, though I don't think she'll fire on any of us—I *don't* think she was shooting at me before," he added in answer to their doubtful looks. "Do *not* approach her. Just locate her and radio me immediately. I'll have you guys covered from the towers. If it looks like she's going to fire on you, they'll take her out. Otherwise, I think if we can just talk to her, we can get this under control without anyone getting hurt. I'm going to the infirmary to get her friend, Nurse Donner. Maybe she can help us talk Hampton in. As a last resort, I'll call in the tact team. Got that?"

The group of officers nodded in unison.

Thompson gave each of them their assignments, dividing up the prison grounds between them and advising each to contain their search to the grounds until they were sure she wasn't outside. If she did enter a building, the officer on duty in that building would notify him.

"I'm heading for the infirmary and I'll contact the K-9 unit to patrol the perimeter. Remember what I said: Don't try to take her yourself. We want to talk her into surrendering without anyone—officers or inmates—getting hurt. All set?"

They all nodded.

"All right. Let's do it."

* * *

The air in the tunnel was cold and damp. It seemed to cling to her skin and tug at her clothing like slimy, invisible fingers. Darlene Hampton walked slowly, gun held ready in her right hand, the flashlight held in her left. Not that the flashlight was doing much good; it cast a small, donut-shaped circle of light immediately in front of her but did not penetrate beyond a couple of feet. It showed her walls and a stone floor that appeared to have been hewn out of solid rock, evidence that this was one of the oldest tunnels under the prison. She had noticed there were no pipes running along the ceiling, either—further proof that this was a very old tunnel.

She moved cautiously through the tunnel, head cocked, listening for any movement ahead of her. But there was nothing, until she heard a low laugh from *behind* her. She whirled, flashing the light into the darkness she'd just come through.

How did he get behind me? she thought. It was impossible. There was nowhere he could have hidden until she passed.

The acoustics of this place must be playing tricks on me, she figured.

But a few moments later, she heard another sound, a rustle of clothing, from behind her. She swung around, squeezing off a shot in the direction of the noise. The bright flash of the pistol illuminated the length of the tunnel behind her, all the way back to the stairs, for just a second, but it was long enough for her to see the tunnel was empty. No one was there.

Laughter came from the other end of the tunnel, but as she whirled round to face it, it sounded from behind her again. And when she turned back, it came from the opposite end.

"Where are you?" she screamed and fired two shots into the tunnel behind her and another two into the tunnel in front of her. By the muzzle flash of each shot she saw no one and nothing but bleak, rough rock walls, ceiling, and floor—behind her, the stairs, and ahead, empty tunnel for ten feet or more until, it appeared, the passageway veered to the left. The sound of the bullets ricocheting briefly echoed around her and she instinctively ducked.

More laughter came out of the darkness ahead of her and she could swear that it was more than one person now.

That can't be, she told herself.

"Why not?" came a voice from the darkness. Darlene recognized it immediately as the voice she'd heard over her radio in A dorm the night she was raped, just before the fight broke out.

"We all want a piece of you, Darlene."

"Shut up!" she screamed at the voice and fired into the darkness, but the pistol clicked empty. She held the gun up, opened the cylinder and let the spent cartridges clatter to the tunnel floor. From her shirt pocket she removed a speed loader, snapped it into the cylinder and flicked it closed.

"You want a piece of me?" she muttered. "I got *six* pieces here for you, sucka!"

John Thompson swore loudly at his bad luck. Sheila Donner, head night nurse, was not on duty in Health Services. She was on vacation; had been for three weeks. She wasn't due back until next Monday. To make matters worse, there was no psychiatrist on call either. The prison shrink, one Doctor Young, had left for a job in Maine. The nurse at the infirmary desk informed Thompson that the prison human services department had not yet found a replacement. All inmates—and guards for that matter—in need of psychiatric services were to be referred to the Hayman Memorial Hospital in New Rome.

His radio crackled to life and he heard Mike Lecuyer calling him: "One hundred, this is one-five-four. I don't think she's out here, Cap. We've just swept the grounds from A dorm to Digbee Hall and there's no sign of her, over."

Captain Thompson held his radio to his lips. "One hundred to all towers. Do any of you have visual contact? Over."

One by one, the tower personnel, who were armed with AR-15 rifles covering the unarmed guards searching the grounds, reported in—negative.

"One hundred to K-9 detachment. How many units do you have on the perimeter? Over."

"One-seven-three here, Cap. We have all available units on the perimeter. We've got nothing, too. All clear as far as we can see. Over."

John Thompson frowned. On eleven-to-seven shift he knew there were only two dog officers on duty. Their perspective of things being "all clear" was, thus, very limited. Thompson called every man searching the yard, and none of them had seen any sign of Darlene Hampton. Using the landline at the reception desk in Health Services, he checked each of the dorms and Inner and Outer Control. No one had seen anything; all was quiet.

Could she have left the grounds? he wondered. Jane Mazek hadn't seen her go through the front gate. She might have slipped out through the vehicle trap/shipping and receiving gate at the rear of the prison. On eleven-to-seven it was locked down and under surveillance by closed circuit camera only. Darlene, like every officer on duty, had keys for that building. John decided it was time to check the parking lot and see if Darlene's car was still there.

Officer Ron "Boomer" Bromley paused at the corner of B dorm and fished a pack of Juicy Fruit gum from his pocket, unwrapped a stick and folded it into his mouth. He looked around and shook his head in disgust. *That crazy bitch isn't out here,* he thought. *This is a waste of fucking time. I'm missing my midshift nap.* Bromley's station was on the first floor of I dorm watching over sixty sleeping inmates. Normally, he and the second-floor officer took turns napping on a spare cot while the other covered both floors. Bromley had spent the better part of his most recent time off getting drunk and had got only a few hours' sleep, thinking he could make up for it on the job.

"Murphy's Law," he muttered, continuing his walk around B dorm. "Goddamned Murphy's Law. With my luck I should know better."

He passed by what everyone called the "old basement door" to B dorm and gave it a perfunctory glance. There was no way Darlene Hampton could have gone through that door, he knew. It was sealed and barred, always had been. It had no doorknob—there was no way to open it without a crowbar and a blowtorch.

A muffled, distant popping sound made Boomer Bromley pause and look around. It was hard to tell what it was or where it had come from. After standing still and quiet for nearly a minute, waiting to hear it again, he decided it must have been a car backfiring down on nearby Route 140, which ran past the base of the hill. He continued his search, walking away from B dorm and wishing Captain Thompson would call off the search soon so he could get some much-needed sleep.

Darlene reached the bend in the tunnel and paused, her back against the wall. She flashed the light back the way she'd come and, though she was sure it was no more than six or seven yards to the stairs leading up to the outside, she could see nothing but the tunnel disappearing into the gloom as if it went on forever.

A random thought: *There's no way out!* slipped into her mind and was immediately echoed.

"There *is* no way out!" said a voice nearby, just around the corner ahead.

Darlene charged down the tunnel and around the bend and there he was, running sideways down the tunnel as he turned to laugh and wave at her. She fired at him once, twice—was certain she'd hit him, but he didn't fall, just continued on laughing and waving tauntingly as he ran from her in a way that was more of a twisting, teasing dance than a sincere attempt to flee.

Darlene ran after him, but he disappeared around another corner. Within seconds she was out of breath. She found it hard to move quickly; her feet felt leaden and her arms felt as if she'd been carrying heavy weights for hours.

It must be the air down here; not enough oxygen, she thought. Another, unbidden, thought pushed its way into her mind—*suffocation!*—accompanied by a chest-constricting wave of panic.

She stopped and leaned against the tunnel wall, breathing heavily. Her flashlight, now limp in her hand, pointed down at the floor, illuminating a dark wet spot on the stone. She bent, touched it, and examined it more closely in the light.

Blood! I knew I got the bastard!

Energy renewed, she once again started down the tunnel, taking it slow, checking the floor for more signs of blood. Several feet further on there was another, larger stain. Less than a foot from that, more splatter—a whole clump of blood spots.

I winged him good, she thought. *Let Thompson and Superintendent Capello make light of her story when she dragged the skinner out to them.*

She stopped and considered just *how* she was going to get the perp back down the tunnel, up the stairs, and outside if he was seriously wounded, perhaps even mortally so. Judging from the spots and streaks of spilled blood she could now see every few inches within the reaches of her light, the skinner might be already dead. She grinned with vengeful satisfaction at the thought, but another part of her cautioned, reminding her it was better to have the skinner *alive.* She realized if she dragged a dead skinner out of the tunnel, all she had was a *dead skinner*—no proof; nothing but maybe a murder rap on her hands.

Thinking clearly for the first time since she'd seen the skinner on the monitor in Outer Control, Darlene unbuckled her radio and called: "Ten thirty-three! Ten thirty-three! Officer in need of assistance. Over."

She got nothing but static for an answer.

She called again. "Inner Control, this is one-six-nine, come in, please. Over."

Nothing. She tried Outer Control. The same.

"Hello-o-o! Captain Thompson? John? Can anyone hear me?"

"You're on your own, bitch!" came the skinner's voice, seemingly from everywhere at once.

Darlene swung the light around, flashing it back and forth, but there was nothing.

Damn this place, she thought.

"Too late!" came the whisper of not one, but many voices from out of the blackness around her. Laughter echoed.

Darlene broke into a cold sweat. *What the hell is going on here?* Not only had she heard many voices that time, she could have sworn several of them had been *women's* voices.

"But that's impossible," she mouthed, soundlessly.

"Nothing's impossible down here . . . in *hell!*" came the single voice of the skinner again.

Darlene let out a little shriek in spite of herself and heard the skinner chuckle gleefully. That was it; at the sound of that mocking laughter the trembling, panicky, *scared* feeling which had started possessing her suddenly dissipated into anger. She'd had *enough!* No one was going to fuck with her head—especially not some low-life, perverted skinner cracker.

"That's it, motherfucker! Playtime is *over!* This is your last chance to come out and bring anyone else in there with you!"

"Come in . . . come in . . . and—and—and—get—get— US!" came a whispered multitude of voices in echoing answer.

Darlene took a deep breath and, grunting, pushed off the wall and charged down the tunnel, light and gun held up in front of her. Her footsteps echoed, bouncing off the surrounding stone, multiplying into the trundling of a crowd.

Just ahead was the last corner she'd seen the skinner go around. Without pause, she lunged around the corner and came face to face with . . . a stone wall. The tunnel's end, bricked up from floor to ceiling.

What the hell? Where is he? she wondered. She had examined every part of the tunnel on her way in and *knew* there was no other exit, no place where he could have hidden while she passed by.

This is crazy.

She turned around and retraced her steps warily. Something wasn't right. After ten feet or so she realized that the corner she had just come around was *no longer there!* She was in a straight length of tunnel.

That's impossible!

There were whispers in the darkness around her; nothing she could understand. She turned and went back, searching for the corner—she had to have passed it. Several feet back, she came up against the stone wall again.

No! This can't be happening! She *knew* she had walked further than this. A chilling fear filled her. There was something terribly, terribly wrong. She decided it was time to get the hell out of there and get some help.

She backed away from the wall, keeping an eye on it, half expecting it to move and follow her. She stumbled, fell back, but was prevented from hitting the floor by *another wall!* She sprang away from it, flashing the light over its surface. A flurry of laughter—the mirth of many voices—swirled around her. She turned to run and came face to face with another wall.

"No!" she shrieked and spun around, bumping into the wall behind her. Frantically, she looked from wall to wall—she was trapped in a space no more than three feet by three feet square.

"Fuck!" she gasped, disbelievingly.

"Yes, let's!" came the skinner's voice, directly behind her.

She spun around and there he was, tall, pale, eyes glaring madly at her, a sneer of lust upon his thin lips. She fired twice. The first shot just missed the skinner, finding a chink in the wall on his left and burying itself there. The second shot went straight into the center of the skinner's chest—and passed through as if he wasn't there. It struck a protruding stone in the wall behind him and ricocheted up to strike the ceiling, where it ricocheted again, heading straight down and into the top of Darlene Hampton's forehead, obliterating her frontal lobes and killing her instantly.

At 9:15 A.M. John Thompson sat in the waiting area outside Superintendent Capello's office. He was exhausted; it had been a long night, the longest of his twenty-five-year career as a corrections officer. It had also been the worst of his career, and as far as he knew, it might also have been the last. Everything that could have gone wrong, had.

Despite his hope to contain the situation to the eleven-to-seven officers and himself, he'd been unable to. A search of the prison grounds had turned up no sign of Darlene Hampton. By standard operating procedures, he should have called in the tact team then, but he still thought he and his men could handle it.

After finding Darlene's car still parked in the officer's lot, he had paired his available men and set them to searching every building within the prison's walls. It had taken over two and a half hours and turned up nothing. At 6:30 A.M., facing the arrival of the day shift, John had finally put a call into the duty officer who mobilized the tact team and called Capello. Now, as he sat waiting to see the superintendent, the prison remained in full lockdown with inmates confined to their cells and dorms while the tact team re-searched every building and the maze of tunnels underneath the prison. Sitting there, John had monitored their progress on his radio, but there was still no sign of Darlene.

Where could she be? John was stumped. If her car was still in the lot, then she had to still be somewhere on the prison grounds or the Hill in general. But where? Beside the prison proper, there were a dozen or so falling-down structures that had been living quarters for the more socially interactive patients of the state mental hospital, but they had all fallen into ruin and were now only used sometimes as training areas for the K-9 unit. But, just to be sure, he'd sent the K-9 patrol to check each of them out before he'd called the duty officer, and they had turned up nothing. Then there was the small farm of the former hospital caretaker, Joe Jones. He was in his eighties or nineties and had a farm on the hill. The farm had been bequeathed to him by the state in perpetuity for services rendered for over fifty years. When the abandoned hospital had been converted to a prison after lying empty for sixteen years, the state had offered to relocate Mr. Jones's farm, but he had refused. Considering his advanced age, the Massachusetts Department of Corrections commissioner had decided to forgo eminent domain, figuring the old guy didn't have much time left as it was. That was thirteen years ago, and old Joe Jones was still going strong, growing tomatoes, corn, squash, beets, watermelon, and pumpkins on his tiny farm and selling them at a roadside stand down on Route 140 in the summer and fall. John had sent one of the K-9 officers to check on the old guy and warn him. The officer found him at his roadside stand down on Route 140, just outside the prison turnoff, getting ready for the heavy morning rush hour along the road; he had seen nothing and no one.

The superintendent's door opened suddenly.

"Thompson! Get in here!"

Startled, John Thompson scrambled to his feet. He hadn't known the super was already in—he'd thought he was en route. Exhaling a long, slow breath of trepidation, he went inside.

Tim Saget woke in a cold sweat from a new nightmare. It was a chase dream where he was running down an endless flight of stairs, a fire-breathing dragon at his back. The strange thing was that upon wakening, though it was such an unrealistic dream with a *dragon* and all, he *knew* that the dream had taken place in the dark burning building of the other dream. He didn't know how he knew that, but he was certain of it. It was the only thing concerning the dream he *was* certain of—confusion prevailed in all other regards.

He got out of bed quietly and padded his way to the bathroom. Relieving himself, he tried to push the dream, and the sense of foreboding and terror that accompanied it, out of his mind. Instead, he thought about tomorrow, graduation day from the academy. It had been a rough seven weeks, but now that it was over he felt pretty good about himself. As training had gone on he'd felt himself getting stronger, back in the kind of shape he had been in ten years ago. He had passed his physical training and self-defense exams with near perfect scores. He had tied for first in marksmanship. On the written exams, his lowest score, in criminal law, had been a seventy-five. He was ranked ninth in the class of twenty-two, which, for him, was pretty damn good.

But the best thing was the look on the Sergeant's face when Tim showed him the scores and told him he was graduating in the top ten. The man had actually *smiled.* A few hours later the Sarge had called to tell Tim he was throwing a party for him after graduation and had invited all of his relatives. He magnanimously told Millie to invite her entire family, too, and then dropped the big bomb: *He wanted to pay for their wedding!*

Tim flushed the toilet and looked at himself in the medicine cabinet mirror.

Married.

The Sarge wanted to have the wedding in two weeks. He told them he had talked to the Reverend Jones at the Unitarian Church and the man had agreed to marry them.

Married?

Millie, being Catholic, hadn't been too keen on the idea of getting married in a Protestant church until she called her own parish church and found out that they couldn't get married there for a year, and they would be required to attend classes once a week on how to have a successful Catholic marriage. Figuring she was pushing her luck if she asked Tim, who had never attended any church as far as she knew, to submit to that, she agreed to be married at the Unitarian Church.

"Married . . ." Tim said the word out loud slowly, trying it on for size. *Me. Married.* When he was young he had always figured that some day he would get married, but *when* that would be had remained vague in his mind—a time when he was grown up and adult; a time when he became more like the Sergeant.

"I guess that time is now," he said softly to his reflection. Only he didn't *feel* like an adult. In fact, he didn't feel thirty-one. He still felt like a teenager, no older than eighteen at the very most. And he certainly didn't feel he had become like the Sergeant.

But haven't I? His inner voice argued. *I've finally accomplished something that he's proud of. Isn't that the first step to becoming him? I'm going to be in* law enforcement *just like him; I'm going to be a* father *just like him.*

At least I don't look like him, he thought with a smile.

Tim went back to bed and slid between the sheets. It was a warm night, and no breeze came through the open windows to cool the air. He looked over at Millie lying on her stomach, wearing one of his tank-top T-shirts, which had ridden up to her back, revealing her naked butt. Tim became aroused and thought about rolling over and slipping his hand between her legs, or maybe even going down on her while she slept, to bring her into a waking state of arousal, but then reconsidered. A couple of months ago, he wouldn't have hesitated. But now . . . well, now, she was *pregnant.* His *child* was growing inside her.

So what? He tried to tell himself. *You can't have sex with her because she's pregnant?*

He rolled over, tried to ignore the idea, but it was true. Part of it was due to the way she'd been acting lately whenever he'd made advances. The last time they had made love Millie had been very uncomfortable, complaining that it hurt. With his baby growing inside her, the last thing he wanted to do was cause her any pain, thus, he was now wary of sex.

Does this mean I'm growing up? Maturing? Thinking about someone else for a change rather than just my own needs? he wondered, rolling onto his other side, away from Millie, putting his back to her alluring nakedness.

Father . . . me?

Dad!

He tried to imagine the kid calling him "Dad" but just couldn't envision it. Now that he thought of it, he didn't think he had ever called the Sarge "Father" or "Dad" out loud; it had always been "Sir." "*Yes, Sir,*" and "*No, Sir.*"

Dad . . . me, a dad.

A wave of despair seeped through him.

Married. . . . father . . . prison guard?

I don't want to become the Sergeant.

He felt trapped, as if he'd stepped into quicksand that now had a firm grip on his ankles and was slowly, inexorably, sucking the rest of him in.

Darlene Hampton was not found. Her apartment was checked. The prison grounds, inside and outside the walls, were searched and searched again. Every building inside and outside the prison was searched, as were the tunnels connecting them. Surveillance tapes of the front and rear gates were reviewed, revealing nothing. Every square foot of the hill and the woods was combed. The state police brought their K-9 tracking unit to the hill and turned up nothing. The newspapers and TV news were all over the Hill for days and ran Hampton's picture daily for a week with no results. Her car remained abandoned in the officers' parking lot. Since she had no relatives living in the area—the closest was a sister living in Biloxi, Mississippi—there seemed to be no

leads, no clues as to where she had gone on the night she'd
pulled a gun on John Thompson and the other guards.

As for Captain Thompson, he received a major ass-reaming
from Superintendent Capello. It was unheard of for a CO to
discharge a firearm—much less against fellow COs—inside
the prison unless under orders to do so. Capello knew security on COs coming and going from the facility was lax, but
he blamed John Thompson anyway for allowing Darlene
Hampton to smuggle her pistol in on his shift. He was suspended with pay for five days while an investigating com-
mittee determined what had happened. The inquest found
that he was guilty, but only of not following standard operating procedure. No mention was made of his affair with
Darlene. As far as Thompson could tell, there was only one
person he had to thank for that—Bill Capello. The official
verdict on Darlene was that she had left the facility and the
Hill on foot—present whereabouts unkown. The media kept
the story alive for less than a week before moving on to
other, higher-ratings-grabbing tragedies.

Capello *did* take it out on him, though, verbally, emotionally, and financially. He was demoted to lieutenant and put
back on eleven-to-seven shift. His pay dropped with the demotion, and he had to share command with a guy he couldn't
stand, his second in command, Lieutenant Jim Henderson.
Henderson was a stick-up-his-ass kind of guy. Everything
had to be by the book. Several times in the past four months
since John had transferred to New Rome and taken command
of the eleven-to-seven shift, Henderson had questioned him,
his shift captain, on decisions John had made or how he
commanded. It was obvious Henderson resented John's
transferring into a command position, probably one he had
been eyeing himself. Since Superintendent Capello's information about John's actions had been so detailed, he figured
Jim Henderson had been filing detailed reports. It was the
sort of thing he'd do; he was a *prick*.

So Capello got John good. He knew John couldn't stand
Henderson, which was exactly why he'd promoted him to

co–shift commander. John Thompson sat in his chair in Inner Control and contemplated his situation. All in all, he rationalized, he had been lucky. He was still senior officer in terms of service on the eleven-to-seven shift, though now he shared command duties with Henderson, who had been second in command. Despite his intense dislike for Henderson's prissy propriety, he tried to tell himself this was not that bad. All that had really changed, now that he had to *share* command with dickhead Jim Henderson, was that neither could make a decision affecting more than one component of the prison without the other's agreement. He swore loudly at the thought. To have to consult that asshole really bugged him, no matter what he told himself. It bugged him so bad he'd started thinking of retiring. He'd get 85 percent of his pension if he retired now. This wasn't the first time he'd considered it. If Bill Capello, whom he had known all his life and served in Nam with, hadn't asked him to transfer to New Rome and take command of the night shift, he'd be retired right now—he never would have met Darlene Hampton and none of this would have happened. And now, ever since the "Darlene Fiasco," as he'd come to label it, he had been contemplating retirement even more. Having to put up with Henderson in co-command came very close to being the camel's last straw. He had always said that when the job started to get to him, as it had in Walpole, he would retire— and if now wasn't that time, what would have to happen for it to get to him? He thought about it; thought about selling the house. He thought about how he and Bella could move to Florida, or maybe even Southern California to be closer to their daughter, Kathy. Bella would love that. If he did that, he thought, Bella might just forgive him for his affair with Darlene Hampton.

John Thompson had never been exactly sure of what was truly "ironic"; in school he had never been able get around the concept. Usually when he thought something was ironic, it was just bad luck. But now, he was pretty sure he got it, for it seemed terribly ironic to him that ever since the Darlene

Fiasco he had started to appreciate his wife more than he
ever had before, tentatively renewing the spark of their ro-
mance *because* of the Darlene Fiasco, but now it looked like
he was also going to *lose* her because of the Darlene Fiasco.
The long stream of shit that he'd been awash in at work had
overflowed into his personal life when Bella heard about his
affair with Darlene through another officer's big-mouthed
wife. She had become completely unglued.

Life with Bella became a deep freeze of hate and resentment after that phone call. Now, when he got home from
work at 7:30, 8 A.M. in the morning, their bedroom door was
locked. She slept in, some days until noon, and had lost all
concern for his well-being, not caring whether or not he'd
eaten. He was left to cook for himself. He was left to do his
own wash. He was left to clean up after himself. She stopped
doing it all.

The day she found out about Darlene had been a bad one.
They had the worst fight John could remember in their
thirty-year marriage. She wept and screamed and wept some
more—refused to listen to anything he had to say until he,
too, became angry and started shouting, thrusting the blame
for the affair onto her for her refusal to have sex with him.

That's when she started breaking things, smashing dishes
and glasses in the kitchen, moving on to the living room to
throw their wedding pictures and his framed commendation
plaque from the DOC for twenty-five years' service against
the wall. In the bedroom she threw his bowling trophy, won
ten years before and collecting dust on top of the mahogany
wardrobe closet, through the dresser mirror. When she'd
headed for John's office, that's when he'd stopped her, telling
her enough was enough.

She had slapped him then, hard, and kept on slapping
him, both arms flailing, both hands raining fleshy slaps
down upon him. In a moment of anger, he had raised his
hand to strike her back and she had cringed away from him.
Since then they had not spoken. He was struggling to main-

tain his normal routine, acting as if he was in complete control and nothing was wrong, while his wife, his marriage, his family, and his job all seemed to be slipping away from him.

Since the Darlene Fiasco, Superintendent Capello had also authorized some changes: more personnel to be added to the hiring list that would bring Tim Saget to the prison and requiring all COs to pass through the pedestrian trap's metal detector when entering the prison. Eleven-to-seven shift was going to get three more officers—one to replace Darlene and one each in Inner Control and Outer Control to watch monitors. All closed circuit cameras in the prison, even those in shipping and receiving, were to be on and monitored, twenty-four/seven. More cameras and monitors for the tunnels had also been ordered.

John swiveled his chair to look at the Inner Control monitors. His eye caught movement on the screen covering the second floor of A dorm—a man in a white medical uniform, standing near the windows. He got up from his chair and went over for a closer look, but when he got there the screen showed nothing and no one except for inmates sleeping on their cots.

"Did you see that?" he asked Seneca

"What, Captain?"

"That guy near the window in A dorm. He looked like someone from Health Services."

Pete Seneca looked at the screen and shook his head. "Uh, no, sir, I didn't. Sorry. I was looking at the kitchen monitor; it seems we have some cat activity in there again."

John Thompson looked at the kitchen monitor and saw what he meant. Several cats had tipped over a garbage barrel and were feasting on its contents. The prison had a severe feral cat problem. They got into all parts of the prison— mostly where food was available—and no one had yet figured out how they were doing it. They'd even got into the maximum-security unit and into locked cells. Several maximum-security prisoners had been found keeping them as pets. When questioned, they had refused to say where they'd found the cats and how they'd got them undetected into the cells. They had been stripped of privileges for a month and their cells torn apart and searched.

"Yeah, well, we'll let the kitchen staff worry about that in the morning. Keep an eye on A dorm, second floor." He went over to the landline phone, which could connect him to any phone in the prison. He punched in the extension for the second floor of A dorm and waited for Jack Roy to answer. He got Jim Henderson instead.

"A-two. Lieutenant Henderson here."

"Jim, it's John Thompson. How long have you been there?"

When Henderson answered, his voice was bristling. "I no longer have to report my whereabouts to you, *Lieutenant* Thompson! I am carrying out my regular *command* duties."

"I'm not questioning that, I just want to know how long you've been in that room because I saw someone on the monitor, over near the window, who looked like one of the Health Services staff."

There was a pause, then, in a flat voice, Henderson answered, "No. No one's here. I relieved CO Roy fifteen minutes ago."

"Are you sure?" Thompson persisted.

"Positive," Henderson replied and hung up.

"Radio me if you see anything," he told Seneca. "I'm going over there."

Billy Dee Washington lay on his cot, making soft snoring sounds in his throat, dreaming about having sex with the crazy bitch CO who'd pulled a gun on the other screws a month ago. Because of her, Billy Dee had spent twenty-eight days in the Can, solitary confinement. But it had been okay! It was while in the Can that he'd started getting dream visits from that snotty black bitch screw. He'd been dreaming of her every night since, each night the sex getting a little rougher and a little more real. Twice he'd woken, slimy with semen. He was well on his way to doing so again tonight when someone whispered in his ear, "If you *really* want her, follow me."

Billy Dee woke to see a white guy, dressed all in white like a doctor, standing over him. The man smiled, winked, and beckoned with his hand for Billy to follow him. Billy Dee got up to do so, but stopped midway and looked around in amazement. The forty cots filled with sleeping inmates around him were transparent and overlaid with another scene entirely, like a double-exposed photograph. Old-fashioned hospital beds, the kind with the arched, iron-barred head- and footboards, were lined against the walls on both sides of the room. At the base of each bed sat a large wooden foot-locker like the kind used in army barracks, much different than the shallow flat ones he and his fellow inmates had to keep under their beds, some of them decorated with pho-tographs that he couldn't quite make out.

At the far end of the dorm, next to the bathroom door, was a room where there had never been a room before. It had large sliding glass windows lining it, behind which sat a burly male nurse. This room, too, was transparent, filtered over the ranks of sleeping inmates. The two scenes kept shifting, one gaining dominance and appearing to be solid for a moment, then fading as the other grew stronger in its place. It was like looking at a hologram that shifted images depending on your viewing angle and the light.

But the strangest thing was when he looked down at his own cot and saw, interchanging every few seconds, the image of himself sleeping, then one of the old hospital beds, empty. He heard a soft cry and turned. Chained to the wall was the crazy woman guard, naked, splayed out, wrists and ankles manacled to the wall. The man in white stood by her, his hand out in offering to Billy Dee.

"Washington! What are you doing?"

Billy Dee Washington shook his head and held up his

hands against the light blinding his eyes. He looked around. Everything was back to normal and he was standing near the window in his underwear. The dorm CO was shining his flashlight in Billy's eyes. Next to him another, taller screw watched. They both had their batons out and the shorter one looked nervous.

"Get that damn light outta my eyes," Washington muttered. He was aware of movement in the dark around him as some of the prisoners were disturbed from their sleep.

The dorm CO lowered the light a little. "What are you doing over here?"

"Uh, I gotta use the head, *okay*?" he said with attitude.

"The bathroom's this way," the taller CO told him.

"I *know* where it is," Washington replied gruffly. Sullenly, he made his way through the maze of cots, followed by the two COs.

It was just another dream, he told himself, but deep inside he knew that wasn't true.

John Thompson hurried up the stairs to the second floor of A dorm just as Jack Roy and Jim Henderson were escorting Billy Dee Washington to the bathroom. He ignored Henderson and spoke directly to Roy.

"Were any of the HSU interns over here?" he asked, an unwanted tone of urgency coloring his voice. Jack Roy heard the tone and immediately became nervous. Ever since the night Darlene Hampton had gone screwy and disappeared, the slightest things—like an inmate getting up to pee in the middle of the night, or his captain asking weird, urgent questions—could set him off. He didn't like having to take Hampton's station. Normally he was the west yard officer and made the rounds as relief officer for dorm guards to take their breaks. He hoped they hired someone soon to take over Hampton's spot so he could go back to his old position.

"I told you on the landline that no one's been here," Henderson interrupted.

"I wasn't talking to you. I'm asking if *he* saw anything *before* you got here." He looked at Roy expectantly.

"Uh, no, Cap," Roy said quickly. "Nobody's been here."

"Are you sure? Standing right over there." Thompson pointed. "By the windows. I saw him on the monitor."

"You must have seen the prisoner who just got up to go to the bathroom," Henderson said dismissively. "He was standing over there just a few minutes ago. Just standing there. I think he was sleepwalking."

"Is he a white guy dressed like a doctor?" he asked Henderson, sarcastically.

"You know who he is, Cap," Officer Roy offered. "Washington, the biggest black guy on this floor. He just got out of the Can for grabbing Darlene Hampton that night, during the fight."

"Yeah, I know that guy," John told him, then to Henderson, "and that's not the guy I saw on the monitor."

"Maybe you're overtired, seeing things," Henderson said, the slightest smirk playing at the corners of his mouth.

Roy laughed nervously. "You're not catching 'Darlene Disease' are you, Cap?" he asked, jokingly. The look that John Thompson shot him told Roy that he had just picked the wrong thing to kid his former captain about.

"Just keep your eyes peeled!" Thompson growled. He turned and walked away with Jim Henderson following close behind, wondering where John was off to next. Behind Jack Roy, who stood muttering to himself as his commanding officers left, Billy Dee Washington waited just inside the bathroom, the door open just enough to hear the entire conversation between the three screws.

"I knew I wasn't dreamin'," he said under his breath.

John Thompson left A dorm hurriedly, ignoring Henderson's hurled question, "Where are you going now?" He ran down the walkway to the south gate, through it, and around D building to Digbee Hall. Pete Seneca, the officer at the front desk of Inner Control looked up questioningly, but John shook his head at the man and continued up the stairs to the second floor, where the Health Services Unit was housed. Behind him, he heard Henderson enter the building and, out of breath, ask Seneca where John had gone. A moment later he heard Henderson charging up the stairs after him.

Sheila Donner, head nurse in the Health Services Unit on the eleven-to-seven shift, and Darlene Hampton's best friend, was sitting at the reception desk. She and an intern from the Hayman Memorial Hospital in New Rome were the only staff on duty. The intern was a green kid just out of UMASS med school and in only the second week of his internship at Hayman Memorial. His name was Louis Feldman and he was a puny man, only five feet, four inches tall and one hundred pounds if he was lucky. Considering his Coke-bottle-lens glasses and his timid demeanor, Sheila wondered if he'd be able to handle working with cons. The prison employed a full-time medical doctor for the day shift, plus a psychologist/drug counselor and a part-time medical doctor on second shift who worked from 3 P.M. to 7 P.M. A few years before, after several prisoners had needed emergency, lifesaving treatment in the middle of the night, the prison had hired a part-time doctor for the graveyard shift, also; usually an intern from Haymont Memorial that they didn't have to pay much. Generally it was easy duty and the interns got to sleep the shift away and get paid for it, but once in a while they actually had to work.

Sheila heard John Thompson thundering up the stairs and jumped up from the desk where she'd been reading the latest issue of *Cosmo*. From the speed of the approaching footsteps she assumed she had an emergency situation on her hands and wondered why she hadn't been radioed about it. When she saw it was John Thompson charging up the stairs, she clucked in disgust and stood waiting for him, hands on hips, full of attitude.

She had *never* liked John Thompson and had told Darlene

so when her friend had confided their affair to her. Sheila had told her she was making a big mistake. Not only was he married, but there was something just a little too *cracker* about him; a little too redneck for Sheila's liking. "You can't depend on a guy like that," she had told Darlene. "He'll leave you high and dry just when you need him most." And she had been right. He'd done Darlene just as Sheila had warned he would.

But Darlene had laughed at her. "He ain't just no regular cracker, honey," she said. "He's a premium Saltine; he's a Ritz! He's a fuckin' *Triscuit!* The guy's in his fifties and he's got better looks and a better body—and a bigger Johnson— than any twenty- or thirty-year-olds I've ever known."

Now Darlene was missing and Sheila Donner had the feeling that John Thompson, the Triscuit, knew more about it—had *more* to do with it—than he was letting on.

"Sheila! How many staff you got working tonight?" Thompson asked, nearly breathless as he topped the last stair.

Sheila folded her arms across her chest and fixed him with a steely look. "I would prefer that you follow protocol and call me *Nurse* Donner, *Lieutenant* Thompson."

Behind John, Henderson had just reached the top of the stairs and was now breathing heavily and sniggering happily. Thompson ignored him and looked uncomprehendingly at Sheila for a moment. "What the—?" Thompson started to swear, but finished with, "*Fine!* *Nurse* Donner, how many on duty tonight?"

"You know the answer to that yourself, Lieutenant. Same as *every other* night, just me and the intern *du jour.*"

"Where is he? How long has he been working here?" Thompson fired the questions at her.

Sheila raised an eyebrow and let out a long sigh. "You want to tell me what this is all about?"

Thompson gave her an exasperated look. "Not now! Just answer my questions!"

Sheila's return look told him he might as well "talk-to-the-hand" for all it was going to get him.

"Never mind," he said, dismissing Sheila with a wave of his hand. He headed for the staff lounge where the night interns regularly napped when things were quiet.

"Where do you think you're going?" Sheila demanded of him, trying to block his way. Thompson stepped around her and continued.

"Hey! You can't just barge in here like that!" she said to his back.

"Actually," Lieutenant Henderson said quietly behind her, "he can, Nurse Donner."

"Who the hell asked you?" she said crossly, turning on him.

He backed up, raising his hands in surrender. "Just telling you what you already know. On night shift, watch commanders have access *on demand* to any part of the facility."

Sheila gave Henderson a dirty look and went after John Thompson. He had reached the staff lounge. As she came up behind him, he opened the door. Light from the hallway pierced the room and exposed a small, frail-looking man lying on the ratty leather couch within. He was balding, with wisps of fine blond hair clinging to the sides of his head. He was not the man John Thompson had seen in A dorm.

"It's not him," he said, more to himself than to Sheila or Henderson who had joined them.

"It's not who?" Sheila asked.

"You're sure there is no one else here tonight?"

"*No one,*" she answered. "Now what's this about? What's got your panties all in a bunch?"

Thompson mentally debated whether or not to tell her and quickly decided against it in front of Henderson. The last thing he wanted was for it to get around that he was seeing the guy whom Darlene hallucinated had raped her. It was bad enough the guards on the shift already had a name—"Darlene Disease"—for it.

"Do you have a guy on staff with long black hair—you

know, cut in like a Beatle style? He's kind of tall, six feet or so, and has a gaucho mustache? On any shift?" he asked Sheila.

She shook her head. "Doesn't sound like anyone I know, but I don't know *everyone* on the other shifts. It could be someone new on one of them. Why? Tell me, what's this about? Does this have something to do with the guy that raped Darlene? Is it the same guy?"

John shook his head. "I don't know," he said and walked away. At the top of the stairs he stopped. A picture on the wall had caught his eye. It was a group photo of doctors and nurses. There, at the end of the second row was the man John had seen in A dorm.

"Hey! That's him!" he declared.

Henderson had been halfway down the stairs but stopped and came back. Sheila Donner came over also.

"This is the guy, here, in this picture of the Health Services staff. Who is he?" John leaned forward, squinting to read the names printed at the bottom of the photo. Next to him, Sheila Donner gave him a strange look.

"That *can't* be the guy you saw," she said.

"Why not?"

"Because that's *not* a picture of the HSU staff; that's a picture of the state hospital staff from when this place was an asylum for the insane. See?" She pointed at the caption just above the list of names at the bottom. It read: *The Doctors and Nurses of New Rome State Mental Hospital— 1972.*

John Thompson looked at the name for the guy in the second row—*Dr. Jason Stone.* "You sure he didn't stay on when they converted this place to a prison?" he asked Sheila. Behind him, Henderson spoke up.

"From what I know the place was empty for fifteen or so years before the state converted it to a prison."

John Thompson looked again at the year—1972—then at Stone's picture. It had been taken over thirty years ago, yet when Thompson had seen him on the monitor, he had looked the same as he did in the picture; as if he had just stepped out of the frame and decided to take a stroll through A dorm.

"Are you sure that's who you saw?" Sheila asked him.

"No," John said gruffly, turning away. "I guess that's not the guy," he added, but he was lying.

4

"Congratulations, Tim! We're so proud of you!" Aunt Sadie hugged him and kissed his cheek. Behind her stood Aunt Rosie, beaming, and he braced himself for another hug and kiss. Neither of his father's sisters were petite; both were built like the Sarge—as if they'd been poured from the same mold—and outweighed him each by at least seventy-five pounds.

The Sergeant's house was full of people, mostly family—cousins who were all younger than Tim but who were already married with children and ensconced in upstanding careers. Sadie's three kids were there; two of them teachers, the third an EMT with the Fitchminster Fire Department. Rosie's only child, Melissa, owned the Swashbuckler Restaurant with her husband, Isaac, in nearby Leominburg. The Sarge had hired them to cater the graduation party and they were running between the dining room and the kitchen directing their three helpers on which food went where on the buffet table.

Tim stood in the front hall, still wearing his uniform from graduation, greeting people as they came in—a job given to him by the Sarge. A large contingent of Millie's family, some of whom he'd met only recently, when they'd broken the news of her pregnancy and their impending marriage, had just arrived. Millie's father, who openly disliked Tim and made no attempt to hide it, brushed past without so much as a nod, ignoring Tim's outstretched hand, and went directly to the dining room sideboard where the bar was set up. He poured himself half a tumbler full of Sambuca and stood there sipping it and scowling at everyone. Millie's mother, on the other hand, was one of the sweetest women Tim had ever met. After some initial distress at the news that her only child, her *baby*, was going to have a baby, she had embraced them both with the promise that she would do whatever she could to help them. This would be her first grandchild and she was overjoyed at the prospect.

Mrs. Arpano—"Call me Toni" she kept insisting to anyone who was too formal with her—was only five feet, two inches tall, and she was nearly as wide as she was high. But instead of being one of those obese, unhealthy-looking people who can barely get around and who look like every movement is a chore and torture, Toni Arpano was a dynamo. Her cheeks were always rosy red, her eyes sparkling, and she never seemed to sit still for a minute. Tim had wondered how she stayed so fat until Millie told him it was a glandular condition.

Of course, the first time Tim had met Millie's mom the old adage: "If you want to know what your wife will look like in twenty to thirty years, just take a look at her mother," had come to mind. He had been relieved (and felt guilty about the relief) when Millie had told him it was glandular and that it was not hereditary. Mrs. Arpano's sister, Millie's Aunt Connie, on the other hand, was an attractive, still shapely woman of sixty-seven. Tim hoped Millie had more of a chance of turning out like her than her mother.

All of Millie's relatives brought food even though Tim had told her to tell them it was a catered affair. Millie had laughed. "That doesn't matter. We're Italian! We *never* go to a party without bringing something." They had not proven her a liar. Her mother brought an immense casserole dish of lasagna. Her Aunt Connie, a crockpot full of meatballs. Three more aunts and two uncles brought loaves of Italian bread, pasta salad, hot peppers and sausages, a fifth of anisette, and a case of beer, respectively. Millie led them all to the buffet table while Tim made his way through their large assortment of offspring.

After Millie's family came several retired Ashton cops his father had served with and who were now his weekly golfing buddies. They solemnly greeted Tim, clapping him on the back and telling him what a wise choice he was making by joining the corrections department. One of them even went so far as to tell Tim that he had made the Sarge (what they always called Tim's father, too) very proud. He knew that should make him feel good, but strangely, it left him with a feeling of trepidation. He had *never* made the Sergeant proud or lived up to his expectations; to have done so now meant that he could *never* screw up again. If he had finally climbed to the pinnacle of pride in his father's eyes, how much steeper and harsher would the fall be if he fucked up again?

Finally, it seemed that all the guests had arrived and Tim was able to have a beer and relax a little. He grabbed a plate and worked his way around the buffet table, helping himself to generous amounts of chicken wings glazed with Southern Comfort, lasagna, Swedish and Italian meatballs, potato salad, and a hot-pepper-and-sausage sandwich on two thick slices of Italian bread. He made his way through people milling about in the kitchen and found an empty chair on the back porch where he ate and watched his cousins' kids playing dodgeball in the backyard.

Halfway through his meal, his can of beer was empty, and he was just about to get up and get another when Millie's father came onto the porch and handed him one. Taken aback by this show of friendliness, Tim expressed thanks several times while Mr. Arpano sat on the railing and took a long sip of his Sambuca.

"You know, Tim," he said quietly, slowly, "a lot of people believe the old stereotype about us Italians." He continued when Tim looked perplexed. "You know the one—every Italian is in the Mafia or has mob connections."

Tim shrugged by way of agreement.

"Well, in my case, Tim, it's *true*. And I just want you to know that if you *ever* hurt my daughter, or do anything to cause her grief, I will have some very large goombahs pay you a visit. And they will cut off your *balls* and feed them to you, diced with a nice marinara sauce made from your *blood!* Capeesh?" Mr. Arpano smiled broadly. "Do we understand each other?"

"Uh, y-yes, s-sir," Tim stammered. At that moment Millie's mother came onto the porch.

"There you are, Frank," she said to her husband then passed a quick look between him and Tim. "What've you been up to?" she asked her husband.

"Nothing, nothing," Mr. Arpano said. Tim could detect more than a touch of nervousness in his voice. "Just having a chat with my future son-in-law." Tim noticed he couldn't say the latter without grimacing slightly.

Millie's mother turned to Tim. "Has he been threatening you? Has he been trying to scare you? Let me guess, he told you he has connections with the Mafia."

Tim cast a guilty glance toward Mr. Arpano who gave him a narrow-eyed glare. Tim shook his head. Mrs. Arpano wasn't buying it.

"Oh Frank! You can be such a *citrole* sometimes. Tim, don't believe any of it. The closest thing he has to mob connections is his deluxe DVD edition of the second season of *The Sopranos*." She laughed heartily then looked crossly at her husband. "What did I tell you this morning, huh? Leave the kid alone. If Millie says he's good enough for her then he's good enough for *me*. He's good enough for *us*. Now, come on. Your sister Annamarie has to leave; she has to go to work. Come say goodbye; she hasn't seen you in ages."

Not waiting for a verbal response, she grabbed her husband by the arm and led him inside. Mr. Arpano looked angry, but he avoided glancing at Tim. When they were gone, Tim let out a loud sigh and drained half his beer in a few gulps. Not for the first time, or the last, he wondered what he was getting himself into.

Millie came out looking for him just as he was finishing eating. "Tim, Mary and Brittany from work are here. I want you to meet them." She took his hand and led him into the kitchen where her friends were eating standing up, their plates of food on the counter top. Millie introduced him to Brittany, who did the payroll for the small waste disposal company, and Mary, who, surprisingly, for her petite frame, drove one of the trucks. They congratulated Tim on his graduation and asked polite questions, to which he gave equally polite answers—Was the academy hard? ("Yes and no.") Was he nervous about working in a prison? ("Yes and no.") And when did he start? ("In two weeks.")—before turning to talk about where they worked. Tim stood next to Millie, leaning against the sink, arm around her waist, and half listened to the three women complaining about their boss, the owner of the company. From where he stood he could see clearly into the dining room where people still helped themselves to the copious amounts of food. His aunts, Sadie and Rosie, were making their fourth trip around the buffet table, and as they passed by the kitchen doorway, halfway between the cold-cut platter and Millie's mom's lasagna, Tim heard Sadie say to her sister: "It gives me chills to tell you the truth. Who would have ever thought he'd end up there? After all that happened, you know?"

"Oh, I know what you mean," Rosie chimed in. "It's very ironic, don't you think?"

"Ironic? A little *too* ironic—if you ask me it's downright spooky. We never did find out what really happened. By the way, when was the last time *you* went to visit?"

Tim didn't hear Rosie's reply as his father came over to introduce him to John Thompson, an old army buddy of his who worked at the prison also. Tim smiled politely, shook hands, and nodded at everything his father and Mr. Thompson said, but he kept wondering who the heck his aunts had been talking about. At first, he'd had the funny feeling it had something to do with him, but what they had said didn't make sense.

Twelve hours later, John Thompson went up the stairs to Digbee Hall and inside to the Inner Control desk. Lieutenant Jim Henderson was reading the newspaper, while behind him Corrections Officer Pete Seneca, sat at the monitor board. Larger than the one in Outer Control, it controlled all the indoor cameras in the prison.

"What's up, John?" Henderson asked. "You look tired. You okay?"

Thompson nodded. "You wanna go on break?" he asked his co-commander. Even before John had been ordered to share his command with Jim Henderson, it had been routine for him to relieve Henderson for coffee and lunch breaks.

Henderson looked at his watch. "Uh, nah. I think I'll wait a bit." He paused and looked John in the eye. "You know, you don't have to come and relieve me anymore. Remember we're *co*-commanders, and if I need someone to relieve me I can order it myself."

"Look, I didn't mean anything by it," John said gruffly. "It's just that's the way we've always done breaks—if it ain't broke, why fix it?"

"But now that I'm *co*-commander, I'm not always here at Inner Control. I go out and do rounds, checking the entire facility, just as you do. So, actually, it really *won't* work anymore." Henderson gave him a condescending smile and went back to his paper, as if dismissing John.

What a dick! John thought and walked away. He was fuming. It was bad enough to have to suffer the embarrassment of being demoted; he also had to put up with Henderson flexing his command muscles. He wouldn't mind if Henderson wasn't being such a *prick* about it, rubbing it in John's face at every opportunity.

He went down the hall and through the fire door that led to the Segregated Inmates Unit. He went into the officers' break room and got a can of Coke from the machine. He looked over the selections on the candy and snack machine but saw nothing to tempt him. Besides, he was too angry to eat.

He sat at the table, popped the top on the Coke, and entertained a host of comebacks he should have made to Henderson, but that just made him feel worse knowing that he hadn't been able to think of any of them before, when it would have counted.

The landline phone on the wall buzzed. Thompson reached over and grabbed it. "One hundred here."

There was dead air.

"Hello? One hundred here."

Again, no answer. But then, from far away—from far *within* the phone line, John Thompson heard a voice, very faint at first, but slowly growing in volume."

"John!"

"Help me!"

"Help me, John!"

It was—

"Darlene! Where are you?"

"Help me, please, John!"

"Tell me where you are!"

The voice faded, echoing away, and dead air returned.

"Darlene! Darlene! Where are you?"

No answer. Nothing but the faint hiss of electricity in the line.

"You okay, John?"

Thompson spun around. It was Henderson, standing in the doorway, a look of concern on his face, but John could also detect a trace of a smirk on his face.

"She's still here!" he said, excited.

"Excuse me?"

"She's still here!" John repeated. "Darlene—uh, Officer Hampton. That was her just now on the landline."

Henderson looked doubtfully from John to the phone receiver that he still held in his hand. "Where is she?"

"She didn't say; she couldn't say, I don't think. She didn't have time. She was in pain. She cried for help and kept asking me to help her." John realized he was nearly raving but couldn't help it.

"Calm down, John," Henderson said soothingly. "Are you *sure* it was her?"

"*Positive!*" John snapped, irritated by Henderson's condescending tone.

"Why didn't she tell you where she is?"

"I don't know. I told you, she was in pain; she's hurt somewhere but managed to get to a landline. Maybe she's being held against her will."

Henderson's doubtful look deepened. "Oh, come on. Who could hold *her* against her will—especially in here? Are you sure she was calling from inside?"

"Yes!" Thompson declared. "Did you hear Control radio me that I had an outside call?"

Henderson shook his head, but his doubting expression never changed. He knew as well as John that all outside calls had to go through the Outer Control switchboard, then the operator would radio whomever the call was for and they would go to the nearest landline to take it. "So, if she *was* calling you from inside, there are only so many places she could be."

John nodded curtly, as if to say "*Now* you get it."

"But how did she know where you were? How did she know you were here, in the break room on this floor, this building, at this exact moment?"

John hadn't considered that. The answer came to him almost immediately. "She must have seen me come in here. She's in *this* building, or Digbee Hall," he said, standing. He hung up the phone. "We got, what, six landlines in SIU and Digbee Hall, combined?"

"Yeah, one at Inner Control, one at each watch station, up and down here in the Can, one for HSU, one above the prisoner day room at the other end of Digbee, and one here."

"We know she wasn't using the phone at Inner Control or in here, so that leaves four to check. You check the two watch stations here, I'll go across to Digbee and check upstairs in Health Services and then the day room."

Henderson hesitated a moment, started to say something, but he was too late. Thompson pushed past him hastily and was gone—a man on a mission. Henderson clucked his tongue in exasperation. *This is ridiculous.* Darlene Hampton couldn't have been on any of the landlines in the Can or Digbee Hall without being noticed by someone, except maybe for the one in the observation room over the prisoners' day room. That wasn't used at night and the closed circuit camera in there was on the blink; a repairman was coming during the day shift to fix it. But how had she got in there? The tunnel door to Digbee Hall was locked, and only he and John had the key for it. An open tunnel was too much of a risk in a building that housed the maximum security wing.

"Screw him, I'm going to the day room," Henderson muttered. "I don't take orders from *Lieutenant* John Thompson anymore."

It didn't take long for Thompson to come to the same conclusion as Jim Henderson. Halfway up the stairs to Health Services he changed his mind and headed for the observation room on the second floor, over the prisoners' day room. He took the rest of the stairs two at a time and ran the length of the second-floor hall, past the startled Sheila Donner sitting at the main desk of HSU. He nearly skidded to a stop at the end of the hall and had to brace himself against the wall with his arms outstretched to absorb the impact. He quickly unlocked the door to the observation room and flung the door open.

It was dark inside. The observation room was circular,

nearly encasing the first-floor prisoners' day room below. All John could make out was the wall of glass to his right, curving away from him in both directions. The room's main station, where the landline was kept, was straight ahead, twenty feet or so, on the only desk in the room. In the dark, John couldn't see the desk. He reached out and flicked the row of light switches next to the doorway. Nothing happened. He flicked them up and down repeatedly, all at once, a couple at a time, and individually. The room remained dark.

"Darlene?" he called into the darkness. "Darlene, are you in here?"

There was no answer. He pulled out his flashlight and shined it in the direction of the desk. There was no one there. He pulled out his radio. "Outer Control, this is One hundred. Do you show a power outage in the south wing of Digbee Hall? Over," he asked, referring to the name for the observation room as it was labeled on the electric power grid panel in Outer Control.

"Negative, One hundred. Over," came Jane Mazek's voice, answering.

"You sure, Control? Over."

"I'm looking at the grid right now, Captain, and it reads that there is power in the south wing, just like everywhere else. Over," she replied.

There had to be something wrong with the grid, he thought. He'd deal with that later. "Control, ring the landline over here in the observation room in Digbee. Over."

"You got it, Cap. Over."

John walked over to the desk. Though he was waiting for it, the phone ringing startled him. He let it ring twice before picking it up.

"Okay, Mazek," John stated to say, but the voice on the line cut him off.

"Help me, John! Come find me, please!"

Darlene! But how could that be?

"John, I need you to find me! Find me, John, before *he* comes back!"

"Who, Darlene? Who's got you?"

"Save me from him, John. Save me from the doctor."

The doctor?

"Darlene!" he shouted into the phone. "Where are you?"

"Help me."

Far in the background, tiny and tinny, John could hear Jane Mazek's voice: "Say what, Captain? Hello? Can you hear me?"

"Help me, John. He's coming back. The doctor . . ." Her voice trailed off.

"Darlene! *Darlene!*" he screamed into the phone.

"Take it easy, John!"

Hands on his shoulders—

—Darlene's voice suddenly gone, replaced by Jane Mazek's concerned tones. "Cap? Are you okay? It's me, Cap, Mazek, on switchboard?"

He turned to see Henderson behind him, pushing him gently into the desk chair. John suddenly realized the lights were on. Henderson took the receiver from his hand and put it to his ear.

"Mazek? It's okay. It's me, Lieutenant Henderson. I've got Thompson. Call HSU on the landline and tell the doc to get over here, stat."

"Roger!" Jane Mazek quickly replied. Henderson returned the receiver to its cradle. "Everything's going to be okay, John. Don't try to get up. The doc's on his way."

What the hell is going on? John Thompson felt like he'd just stepped off a dizzyingly fast merry-go-round. He was light-headed, and his queasy stomach was slowly rolling over on itself. *How could Darlene be on* that *phone just now? What the hell is happening to me?*

"Jim!" he said, trying to tell Henderson what had just happened, but after the first word he was suddenly breathless. He tried to speak again, and a sharp pain traversed his chest. He sat back and tried to breathe through it.

"It's okay, John, the doc's coming. Stay calm. Breathe deep. That's it."

Approaching footsteps outside the door heralded the arrival of Doctor Feldman, the same puny guy he'd seen sleeping in the break room in HSU. He came through the open door and hurried over to Thompson and Henderson.

"I don't know what's wrong with him, Doc," Henderson said, quickly. "I think he's wiggin' out."

Dr. Feldman knelt next to John and put his fingers to John's throat, feeling his pulse while looking into John's eyes. "It's okay. Try to relax." He glanced at his watch and pulled a stethoscope from his pocket. "Unbutton his shirt," he told Henderson as he put the stethoscope on. Henderson bent over and ripped the front of John's shirt open, revealing his dark blue T-shirt beneath. Buttons flew, clattering on the floor around them.

"I said *unbutton* it, not rip it off him," Feldman reproached. He put the receiving end of the stethoscope to John's chest and told him to take a deep breath. John wheezed and gasped, attempting to breathe. After listening for a few moments, Feldman took the stethoscope from his ears and returned it to his coat pocket. From his breast pocket, he now pulled a penlight. He thumbed it on and shined it into John's eyes, flipping from one to the other and back again, watching his pupils.

"Are you having chest pains?" he asked.

John nodded.

"Is it constant pain?"

John nodded, looking scared.

"Is either arm numb?"

John shook his head, no.

"Good." Doctor Feldman pulled his radio from his belt. "MD-3 calling HSU. Over," he said into it, using the prison radio code.

"Go ahead, MD-3. Over," came Sheila Donner's voice in reply.

"I'm going to need a wheelchair here, Nurse Donner. Over."

"I can't leave my post right now. Over," she returned.

Doctor Feldman remembered they had two inmates in the ward, one with a toothache, the other with stomach pains, and no help on the unit.

"I'll go get it," Henderson offered.

"Good. Thanks." Feldman spoke into the radio again. "I'm sending someone to get the wheelchair. Over."

"Roger, MD-3. Over."

Henderson hurried off. Doctor Feldman removed a plastic bag from his pocket. In it was a plastic inhaler like the ones used by asthmatics. Feldman opened the bag and held the device to John's lips. He opened his mouth and Feldman slipped the inhaler in. He depressed the pump. John jerked a little as the medicine penetrated his lungs, but it brought relief. His panting, gasping, *desperate* breathing slowed, returning to normal as his airways opened up. A few deep breaths later, the pain in his chest loosened, softened, and subsided.

"Better?" Feldman asked.

John nodded.

"I thought so. Just relax and we'll get you back to the unit, but I think you're going to be fine. Just a little asthma attack. Has this ever happened before?"

"No," John whispered.

"So you didn't know you have asthma? You're not taking anything for it?"

John shook his head. *Asthma?* This was news to him.

"Interesting," Feldman said.

"Why?" John wanted to know.

"It appears you've had an asthmatic panic attack. It's common for people who have severe asthma; it happens during periods of severe stress or panic, or in emergency situations."

"So, I've got asthma?" John asked.

"It would appear so," Feldman told him. "It's not uncommon for someone your age to develop it. People don't notice it until they get stressed or have a panic attack, then boom— can't breathe. Are you a smoker?"

"Used to be."

From outside the door, they could hear the squeaky trundling of the wheelchair coming down the hall.

"What happened, anyway?" Feldman asked. "What caused you to panic?"

"I didn't panic," John said quickly and stood.

"Please don't get up, sir," Feldman said.

"I'm fine. I'm fine now." John walked to the door and met Henderson with the wheelchair, coming the other way.

"John! You okay?" He looked shocked to see John on his feet. He had been sure Thompson was having a complete nervous breakdown.

"Just great!" John said, abruptly. "I haven't wigged out yet," he added sarcastically, and walked away.

Peanut butter and jelly again?

Dave Stirling sighed, wrapped his sandwich back in its aluminum foil and tossed it into the brown paper bag standing open on the watch desk.

That damned Ellen. . . . How many friggin' times had he told her lately that he was sick to death of friggin' peanut butter and jelly?

"It's all we have in the house," had been her general complaint.

But if she would get off her fat ass and go shopping there would be more *in the house!*

Dave sighed again and slouched in his chair. No use getting all worked up about it. He had to watch his blood pressure. Besides, this was nothing new with Ellen—she'd always been a lazy couch potato and he had known it when he'd married her. But then, five years ago, he hadn't cared. She'd been slim, gorgeous, and perpetually horny with a taste for kinky sex. For the first two years Dave hadn't cared, or even noticed, what she gave him to eat; his sexual appetite (which was considerable) having been more than satisfied had made up for the lack of edible cuisine. But then she'd got laid off from her job as a molding machine operator at Starby Plastics in Leominburg, and Dave had made the mistake of not pushing her to get another job, telling her he made enough to support them. And he did. And he *hadn't* minded, until she went from a sexy 105 pounds to a grotesque 230 in less than two years. At five feet, six inches, with all that poundage—making her face bloated and her arms and legs thick and lumpy with cellulite—she was no longer a pretty sight. And as her appetite for food (and her weight) had increased, her appetite for sex (and Dave's, too) had decreased proportionately. Now they were lucky to get it on once a month, and even then Dave had to do a *lot* of fantasizing to even get an erection, much less achieve an orgasm.

He closed his eyes and massaged his temples with his fingers. No use dwelling on that either. He became aware of the clock ticking and opened his eyes. It was 3:00 A.M. His break didn't come for another half hour, and then he'd be able to get something, probably candy and peanuts from the machine in the break room. At least it wouldn't be PB&J.

He yawned, stretched, and stood, pushing the wooden chair back with a loud scraping sound on the hardwood floor that startled him. Usually, he enjoyed the quiet of the eleven-to-seven shift, but since the incident with Tobi Dowry, it wasn't so. He found himself jumping at every little noise, like when the captain came over the radio from the observation room at the other end of Digbee, and he had nearly jumped out of his skin. He was unable to sleep most of the shift away as he had normally done when he had worked in the towers last year. Now all he could think about was that crazy night when Tobi had her breakdown.

"*Breakdown!*" he muttered disdainfully. That was the official word for it, but Dave didn't think she'd had a breakdown. He *knew* what a breakdown was—his mother had had one when he was five and he remembered it vividly—and he knew a person didn't just lose it with no warning, just like that. He'd heard his father over the years lament that he hadn't paid more attention and attributed more significance to the warning signs from Dave's mother. His dad always blamed himself for her suicide.

But Tobi Dowry had given no warning signs. At least not that he had seen, or any of her friends. He knew Jane Mazek and Judy Bennett; knew they hung out with Tobi and neither of them thought anything was wrong with Tobi before she flipped out. Certainly, neither had thought she was heading for a breakdown. Even more convincing was Tobi herself. That night, after Dave found her, hysterical and stinking from having soiled herself, and calmed her down, she had told him what had happened. Though it was a crazy story, Dave was convinced it was true, but a dream, a very vivid one—a dream so real that Tobi wasn't able to tell the difference. Though he had never had a dream like that, he'd heard another guard mention having weird dreams when he had worked the Can on night shift.

Since then, thinking about her story had become something of an obsession for Dave, especially when he was at work, until he had become a nervous wreck. Never mind the regular stress of working in a unit that housed the 20 percent of the prison population that had been incarcerated for homicides committed before or since imprisonment, now he had to deal with all the imaginings Tobi's story churned up too. And he had a *good* imagination.

Another thing was that Tobi wasn't alone in being freaked out by the Can. The place was just damned *creepy*! The Can, which made up the north wing of Digbee Hall, had a basement level and the first two floors with twelve cells per floor, or *tiers* as they were called, one inmate per cell on each tier. The basement had housed the morgue, where the hospital had stored bodies because of the room's natural coolness, and the upstairs four floors had been doctor's offices. Now the third and fourth floors were empty. He'd been down to the basement once and it was a lot colder than cool, and it was anything but a *natural* cool; it was the kind of chill you feel when you're running a fever.

The rest of the building was only slightly warmer.

Transferring there in the dead of winter, Dave, at first, hadn't thought much of it, assuming it was an old structure, built back before the turn of the twentieth century. But as spring had come on, then early summer, and the place hadn't warmed up at all, he got to wondering about it. One morning, he'd hung around talking to the day watch commander and had learned that when the place was converted to a prison, the building had been fully insulated with new, double-paned wire mesh windows; foam insulation had been pumped into the attic and window casings, and a brand new furnace and heating system were installed. Dave had asked, "Then why is it so friggin' cold?" and the watch commander had laughed dryly and commented, " 'Cuz the fuckin' place is haunted!" Dave had laughed, too, but uneasily. There had been something in the watch commander's tone. . . . After hearing Tobi tell her story, he recognized that same something in her voice—*conviction!*

Dave shivered and rubbed his arms. Here it was June and it felt like February in the Can. All the other prison buildings had air conditioning, but SIU had never needed it. He retrieved his baton and flashlight from the desk where he'd laid them before sitting and slid them onto his equipment belt. It was time to make the rounds; make sure there was a living, breathing body in each of the cells. He took the watch log, which was on a clipboard hung on a hook above the desk, checked the time on his watch with the time on the wall clock, and wrote *3:06 A.M.* in the appropriate slot.

A noise from the cellblock—a door opening—froze him. Placing the clipboard quietly on the desk and grabbing his nightstick from his belt, he turned to the door. It was too early for his relief, and all the cell doors were locked after 9:00 P.M.—there shouldn't be anyone out there. Slowly he craned his neck and looked through the small, square, wire-mesh observation window set high in the door to the guard's station and couldn't believe his eyes.

There was an old woman—rose-patterned pink housecoat, matching fuzzy slippers, hairnet over short, steely gray curls—going from one cell to the other. Dave reached for the door handle and, at that moment, the woman looked up, smiled, and waved—

Dave woke with a start, sitting up straight in his chair.

A friggin' dream!

He shivered, looked at the clock.

3:06 A.M.

That was weird. It had seemed so *real*! Dave shook his head. It must have been because he couldn't stop thinking about Tobi. He laughed weakly at himself; *now* he knew what that guard, and Tobi, had meant when they spoke of their dreams in the Can being so real. He stood and picked up his nightstick and flashlight, slid them into their holders on his belt, and reached for the watch log, glancing at the observation window as he did so. Movement in the outside corridor caught his eye, freezing his arm in midreach.

There she was *again*! Dave was *sure* he wasn't dreaming now. It was the same old woman with her old-lady housecoat, slippers, and hairnet, only now she wasn't going from cell to cell; she was coming down the hall, straight for the guard's station. And she was no longer smiling or waving, for in her hand she clutched a bloody carpenter's hammer with which she cut the air in front of her with short, jerking swipes—

Dave woke again, his breath shrieking from his lungs with shock. He was still sitting at his desk, his nightstick and flashlight still on the desktop, the watch log still hanging on the wall, the clock still reading 3:06 A.M. Not wanting to, but unable to stop himself, he turned in the chair and looked up at the observation window.

The back of his head went numb with cold; the old woman's leering face—eyes red and wild, teeth bared, blood streaming from her nose over her lips and staining her savage grin red—was framed in the window, bloody hammer head resting against the glass next to her chin.

"The end is near. *He* is coming home!" Her whispering voice echoed inside Dave's head.

He let out a shout of fear and leaped from the chair, staggering back away from the door. The old woman's face disappeared, but the hammerhead drew back only momentarily, then smashed against the glass, fracturing it in a spiderweb pattern. Dave Stirling screamed—

—and woke for real. He was standing against the back wall, his entire body shaking with fear. There was no face in the observation window; the glass was undamaged. At his feet lay his shattered coffee mug, the dregs of his last cup splattered all over his normally shiny black boots. The room was even colder than normal; so cold, in fact, that he could actually see his breath. He blew out steam and looked at the clock—*3:06.*

"Am I awake?" he asked aloud, and felt foolish. He glanced again quickly at the observation window. Still empty. He listened intently—no sound except the adrenalin-pumped rapid beating of his own heart and his coarse, ragged breathing. He rubbed his arms briskly with both hands and then ran them over his face. There was something hot and wet there. At first he thought it was fear sweat, but when he looked at his hands, they were covered with blood. He turned quickly to stare in the small shaving mirror over the equally small sink basin in the corner of the room.

Blood was gushing from his nose, but that wasn't what caught his eye. What did was written in blood on the wall above the mirror and fading fast from view:

He's coming home!

5

John Thompson sat on the edge of the bed while his wife, Bella, packed her clothes. He found it a frightening thing to watch, her calm deliberation, her lack of emotion. She, of course, had heard about his latest "Darlene Episode," as she called it, from one of her friends who phoned to give her all the juicy info. Though Bella wouldn't tell him, John figured the "friend" who enjoyed telling his wife all about his exploits at work, was the wife of someone he worked with. There was a good chance it was Bill Capello's wife. He and Capello went back a long way—all the way to the Sarge's platoon in Nam, and further back, to high school and earlier. Their wives had known each other for a long time; though they'd never been close, they were friendly enough to each other that John could see Roberta Capello being the one. That and the fact that he'd always felt that Roberta didn't like him.

He supposed it didn't really matter who had told Bella, it wouldn't change anything—she was leaving; she'd had enough.

"I'm leaving," she'd said, a few moments after getting off the phone. They had been in the kitchen, he standing in front of the open fridge, looking for something to eat but finding nothing; Bella hadn't gone shopping since learning of his affair with Darlene. She was on the phone for a while, taking it on its extra-long cord into the bathroom off the kitchen and closing the door. This had got his suspicions up, and when he heard her crying at one point, that clinched it. He was expecting trouble. When she followed her first comment with, "I've had enough," (said in such a calm, matter-of-fact manner it gave John the chills) it wasn't much of a surprise to him. Since he had not replied, and did not offer any explanation, or try to stop her, she was left to go.

Bella wasn't the only one upset with John. Superintendent Capello was especially pissed off. John heard that Henderson had submitted a twelve-page incident report to the superintendent, and John was sure that it must paint him as a lunatic. Though he, too, was supposed to submit an incident report, he had failed to do so, which got him in even more hot water with Capello. He had tried, but he just couldn't put into words, didn't want to actualize, what had happened by writing it down. And how would it look if he did? It would look like Henderson was right; he *was* losing his mind.

John's meeting with Capello two days after the incident had gone badly. He hadn't been able to think of any way to explain to Bill what had happened that night; he still had no explanation for himself. He knew the superintendent well enough to know that he would think John crazy if he tried to tell him what really happened that night. Instead, he pleaded fatigue and not feeling well. He told Bill he had been sleepwalking and had a nightmare. He apologized profusely.

The look Bill had given him then had told him the super wasn't buying it, which made his next comment so surprising. "That doesn't excuse you from filling out an incident report. Do it before you leave today." John had smiled at his friend, but before he could say thanks, Bill went on.

"You need some time off, John," Bill told him. He took a cigar from his pocket and put it, unlit, into his mouth. John knew he always did that when he was truly angry. State regulations prohibited him from lighting it, but he could chomp on it, and chomp he did. "I want you to go on paid leave for two weeks—"

"But what about my command?" John interrupted.

Superintendent Capello chomped hard on his unlit cigar. "Henderson can handle it. You *are* going to take two weeks sick leave, then you *are* going to come back here to orient and schedule the new CO recruits we're getting from the academy.

"Please, Bill, I'll take the time off but don't stick me with rookie duty," John had pleaded.

"*That's* where I need you and *that's* where you need to be, *Lieutenant* Thompson."

Chomp! Chomp!

With the latter emphasis Bill put on his new, lower rank, John knew he had a less-than-zero chance of changing his boss's mind.

"It won't be that bad," the superintendent said, his tone softening a bit. "The Sarge's kid is one of the new recruits. Name's Tim. I was just talking to Joe and he said you met the kid; went to his academy graduation party?"

John nodded and forced a smile. That information was no consolation to him. It wasn't like he and the Sarge had ever been *good* friends; they had more or less shared a friendship with Bill Capello. That was why he'd been surprised when Joe Saget called him out of the blue after not seeing him for a good ten years. When he found out it was for a party cele- brating his son's graduation from the correction officers training academy, and that he'd been posted to New Rome, John had understood—it was just like the Sarge to play all the angles. He had gone, mostly to get away from Bella's angry, accusing silence, and had met Tim, but he had been more interested in keeping his glass of Southern Comfort full. Considering he was the Sarge's kid, John wasn't all that eager to work with him. If he turned out to be anything like the Sarge, John doubted he'd enjoy it at all.

Bella closed her suitcase and put a leather carry-on on

top of it and zipped it closed. "I'm going now," she said. Without another word, she left. He remained on the bed, listening to her heavy footsteps descending the stairs, the front door creaking open and then banging shut, the muffled *whump!* of her car door closing, the cough of her ignition, and the hum of the tires as she pulled away. When he couldn't hear her car anymore, he went into the office and pulled out a pint bottle of Southern Comfort that he kept in the drawer. He sat in the chair and put his feet up next to the computer keyboard. He took a long pull from the whiskey bottle and tried to decide how he felt about Bella's leaving. Surprisingly, he found that he really didn't give a damn.

It was funny; he had gone from not caring about Bella when he was with Darlene, to caring about her when she found out about Darlene, and now had come full circle again. If Bella had only been willing to forgive him when he *cared* about her, about saving their marriage, then he would have spent the rest of his life making it up to her. Or so he told himself.

Maybe this is for the best, he thought. After all, if he *was* going crazy . . . . *Maybe having a couple of weeks off will be a good thing.*

The phone rang, startling him. He pulled his feet from the computer table and leaned over to read the caller ID on the phone. "Out of area." He let the machine pick it up. After the beep to leave a message, there was nothing. For a moment, John thought he heard breathing and had the distinct feeling that whoever was on the phone was *listening* for *him.* He knew that was impossible; he knew it didn't make sense, but he could *feel* it nonetheless. His chest became constricted; his breathing labored. He remained perfectly quiet until the line disconnected.

The first day after his graduation party—his first day of vacation before starting at the prison—Tim slept in 'til noon. He would have slept longer if his father hadn't called to tell him he needed a tux for his and Millie's wedding, a week away. He didn't know why they had to get married so fast; some apprehension on her mother's part that she be married before she started to show, but the Sarge was on top of it. Now he wanted to take Tim down to Mr. Tux and get him fitted.

For Tim, this was getting scary. Never had he been subjected to such a level of interest, of respect, of . . . of *caring* from his father. He wasn't sure he could handle it; he wasn't sure he *wanted* to. He managed to beg off by telling the Sarge that Millie wanted to go with them to look at wedding dresses to rent. Practical Millie had upset her mother with that statement and Tim knew that her mother was secretly having a dress made for her, but he wasn't supposed to know that, and he knew the Sarge knew he wasn't supposed to know. Surprisingly, the Sarge didn't give him a hard time. Other than making him promise to go that night with him, Millie in tow, he wasn't as pushy as normal.

The rest of the day Tim spent eating junk food and lying on the couch, playing Madden NFL 2003 video football on his GameCube. Forty-five minutes before Millie was due to get home from work, he cleaned everything up, got dressed, and left her a note saying he had gone to the store. He left and drove to O'Brien's Pub, in nearby Fitchminster, where he spent four hours playing pool and drinking beer with his friends Kevin and Randy. During that time, the thought crossed his mind repeatedly that he should call Millie and tell her where he was.

But he didn't.

And at seven o'clock when Kevin and Randy suggested they go to the Other Door strip club in Leominburg, he thought about calling her again.

But he didn't.

The thought surfaced several more times that night with the same result until, by midnight, he decided it was too late to call her anyway. He got home at 1:30 A.M. to find no lights on, the apartment quiet. Strangely, he was disappointed. He had been expecting Millie to be sitting up, waiting for him, perhaps with the Sarge by her side, back to his disapproving glare. Tim lay awake a long time, unable to sleep, pondering what this meant. He didn't know what to do; he had never been in a relationship where the woman hadn't been judgmental about everything he did. Generally following that was where the woman tried to change him. Except for the night she'd found out she was pregnant and he had lost his job, staying out until three in the morning, she had never yelled at him for drinking or partying with his friends. Now that he thought of it, that was a big reason why he hadn't really minded her subtle move in. Maybe being married to her and spending the rest of his life with her wouldn't be so bad.

He felt like a jerk for having stayed out late; for not calling. The feeling grew in him that things were going to be okay; that everything was going to be all right. Millie was a great girl. Her body was incredible, her face pretty. Her large, dark eyes, small nose, and full lips were framed by long, curly hair so black it shone. When she smiled, dimples lit up her face.

But do I really want to be tied down to one woman for the rest of my life? He had seen a comic on HBO who'd described his situation well: Being married is like having cable television, and you got 105 stations, but you can only watch one. All the time!

If it was anyone *other* than Millie that he had fucked up with and got pregnant—any of the previous women he had known in his life—he would have said *No!* Unequivocally. But, when all was said and done, he decided Millie was worth a chance.

In truth, the prospect of marriage and fatherhood did not worry Tim half as much as his future job did. When he was a kid, he had played cops and robbers and had even wanted to be a cop, too, just like the Sarge, but he had never thought that he would one day end up as a *prison guard*.

He'd enjoyed the academy, the training and the camaraderie with the other cadets, but now, thinking about working *every day* with criminals, always on your guard, literally and figuratively, having to be this macho tough guy all the time worried him. He wasn't a wimp, but he was no tough guy either. He'd got in shape during his training and had dropped down to 200 pounds. He was solid, broad-shouldered, thick-legged. He was in good shape; ran two miles a day. He thought he could hold his own in a fight, but he hated violence. The only fight he'd been in since childhood scuffles in the playground had been eleven years ago when he was twenty and out at a nightclub trying to pick up chicks. Some girl's boyfriend took a swing at him for hitting on her. He hadn't wanted to fight; he hadn't known she was with someone, but the guy was determined and swung first, hitting Tim in the side of the head. Tim had the guy on the floor and was sitting on his chest, telling him to calm down when the cops arrived and arrested them both. Two hours later, they both got free, thanks to the Sarge.

Tim wished he could just not show up for work at the prison in two weeks. He could find other work. Even as he thought of it, he could hear the Sarge saying, "But you won't find nothin' that pays as good, has such good benefits, or such a good retirement package." He could imagine more of the Sarge's reaction, especially after the old man had pulled strings for Tim to get the job. It wouldn't be pretty. He could easily imagine the disapproving scowl, absent these past two months, returning to the Sarge's face. It would be the all-time biggest fuck-up for Tim. The Sarge would never forgive him; he would treat it as the ultimate betrayal.

Tim was surprised to realize he couldn't do it to him. Though he harbored a lot of resentment toward his father for giving him a less-than-stellar childhood in terms of love and caring, he couldn't help but love his father much more than he ever deserved. In truth, the only reason he was going to work at the prison was because of the look of pride in the Sarge's face when he had graduated. There had been a time, when he was younger, that Tim would have quit just to spite the old man, but not now, no more. Besides, everything the

Sarge would say about the pay and the benefits of working at the prison was true. He'd be able to retire when he was fifty-eight. All he had to do was forfeit the next twenty-five years and he would be set for life.

Twenty-five years.

Fifty-eight years old. That wasn't bad, but how many years to live would he have left after that?

Twenty-five years, on the other hand, that was something. Twenty-five wasn't much of a number when it came to cents, but in terms of years—in terms of his *life*—it was staggering. *Twenty-five years* in that place. Twenty-five years watching over murderers, robbers, rapists, drug dealers, child molesters, *perverts*!

Twenty-five years.

It was as good as a life sentence.

John Thompson spent his two weeks off drinking, watching TV, and trying not to think about what had happened at the prison his last day of work. Bella came back a few days later but only for some more of her things. His second Monday off, a young man in a business suit knocked on the front door and served him with divorce papers. He threw them in the trash and had a bad asthma attack that sent him running for the inhaler Dr. Feldman had given him. He didn't let that slow his drinking, though.

By the end of the first week of pretty heavy drinking, he had figured out that he could keep himself at a steady level of drunkenness by having a drink every twenty minutes to a half hour. The system worked well until he passed out, but that was okay. Nothing more could bother him. He started right back in drinking again as soon as he came to. On the Friday before he was supposed to go back to work, Superintendent Capello called to see how he was doing. John managed to fake sobriety over the phone and reassure Bill that he'd be there on Monday.

He stopped drinking that very night. The next day, Saturday, he cleaned the house, every room. Anything of Bella's he put in a cardboard box that had once held their bedroom TV set. When the box got filled, he started stuffing her things into trash bags. He left the box and four full trash bags on the front porch. The next morning they were gone; he assumed she'd come back and taken them, but he didn't really give a shit if homeless people had taken it all.

By Monday, John Thompson was ready to go back to work. He was more than ready; he felt *compelled* to return. The one good thing to have come out of his two-week suspension was that he had come to the realization that he was fine; he was not losing his mind. If he accepted that to be true, which he had—it was the *only* thing he had—then what happened at the prison had to have truly happened. And if it had happened, there had to be an explanation. He was going to find that explanation, even if it cost him his job. That was the only thing he had left to lose, and he was willing to lose it if it meant he found out what happened to Darlene Hampton.

Tim Saget was the model future husband during the week leading up to his marriage. He went with his father and Millie to Mr. Tux and let the Sarge rent him a black tux with tails. He even helped dissuade Millie from renting a wedding gown, knowing that her mother was having one made for her as a surprise. He was home every afternoon when Millie got home from work, and even cooked supper on two evenings. On Friday night, they had the wedding rehearsal at the Unitarian Church. Afterwards, the wedding party, which consisted of Mary, Millie's maid of honor, and Randy, Tim's closest drinking buddy and best man, plus Millie's parents and the Sergeant, went out to dinner at Longhorn's. The bill for the entire party came to over $300 and the Sarge picked up the tab.

The wedding went off with no problems. To Tim, the ceremony went by extremely fast. It seemed as soon as he got to the altar the reverend was giving him the ring. Millie read a poem she had written for the occasion, titled "I Will Always Do You Right." Tim could've sworn a couple of the lines had been lifted from rock songs, but he couldn't put his finger on which ones. He almost started giggling at that point, and if he had, he would have lost it. He'd heard of a guy who laughed during his vows and his girlfriend walked out, refused to marry him. Of course, there was that part of him that said: "Perfect! That's the way to get out of this," but he ignored it; he had resigned himself to the choices that were being forced on him. Getting married was just the first door being closed and locked against him. This was what "growing up" meant—loss of freedom.

He tried, and succeeded, in not thinking about his impending start, Monday morning, at the prison. He tried, and had less success, not thinking about the endless years that lay ahead of him. His ace in the hole was always to ask himself: What would you do with your life if you weren't in this situation? He couldn't think of an answer to that, and that not knowing told him the job at the prison was probably the best place for him.

The wedding reception was held at the British-American Club. Millie and her mom had arranged for catering and a DJ. Though Millie's dad had been against the idea, the Sarge and Millie's mom split the cost of the reception between them. Some of Millie's friends decorated the hall, which was adjacent to a large horseshoe-shaped bar. He drank and ate antipasto, ziti, and meatballs and drank some more. He danced with Millie and his mother-in-law; Millie danced with the Sarge and then her father, to the tune of "Daddy's Little Girl." They cut the cake and did all the wedding-y things. Throughout it all he played his part, and drank. At ten, he and Millie left for their honeymoon—a weekend, courtesy of the Sarge, at the Mount Washington Hotel in New Hampshire. It was while piling all the gifts into Millie's mother's van that it struck him; he and Millie had received $920 cash, plus a pile of typical wedding gifts—three toaster ovens, two blenders, and a bread maker, to name a few. Looking at this pile of domestic goods, it sunk in like a lead weight that he was *married*. It left him with a knot firmly seated in his stomach.

Jim Henderson stood at his locker, looking in the mirror at the new captain's bars he'd just pinned on his shirt collar. Being promoted to sole watch commander of eleven-to-seven also meant going up a step in rank. Not to be slighted was also a raise in pay, though the money wasn't the most important thing to Jim Henderson. The most important thing for Jim Henderson was right there in the mirror—those captain's bars. It gave him an erection just to look at them. Remembering where he was—an erection in the CO men's locker room might be taken the wrong way—he looked around, readjusted his package, and saluted himself.

He strolled with pride across the east yard to Digbee Hall. At the Inner Control command desk he stood surveying his domain. Life can't get much better than this, he thought. He picked up the duty roster, and saw that everyone was at his or her posts on time. He checked the eleven o'clock head count; all prisoners were accounted for. He checked the ten monitors, arranged five over five against the back wall with a console and chair below. From the console, an operator could control all the indoor closed-circuit TVs in the facility. Every screen showed him things as they should be. All was quiet on *his* watch, and always would be.

He swelled with satisfaction and nodded his approval to the air. "All right then," he said expansively, "every thing is ship-shape here." To Officer Seneca, who Jim knew had bid for the second-in-command position, which hadn't been given yet, he said, "I'll be in the head. Radio if you need me."

Henderson headed for the staff bathroom in C building; it was the only one where he could sit on the throne and, if he propped the stall door open, see himself in the tall, tilted wide mirror on the wall over the sink. Though it was a two-stall bathroom, he locked the outside door to insure his complete privacy, then grabbed the small, metal wastebasket and used it to prop open the first stall door. He unzipped and dropped his pants. He sat, legs apart, on the toilet and admired himself and his new captain's bars. Soon he was enjoying his favorite pastime.

Dr. Louis Feldman sat up in darkness, unsure for several panicky moments where he was. Gradually it came back to him as shapes in the room—the breakfast table with its six rickety aluminum-and-vinyl chairs, the counter, the cabinets, the disgustingly dirty filter coffee maker, the Coke machine by the door, the refrigerator—came clear, identifying the place as the staff lounge in the Health Services Unit of the prison.

He stretched and yawned. He started to look at his watch, then stopped himself, closed his eyes and concentrated. Priding himself on an infallible inner clock, he knew automatically, that it was midnight, or shortly before. But of what day? That was the question that brought confusion. Between the ten- to twelve-hour shifts at Hayman Memorial and another seven here at the prison four nights a week, he found himself going longer and longer periods of time where he had only a vague idea of the current day of the week. It bothered him.

He concentrated harder.

Sunday . . . Sunday night heading into Monday morning!

The chiming wall clock in the break room began to beat out the hour. He counted twelve and smiled with satisfaction. It confirmed his estimate of the time dead on. He checked his watch—he was right on the day, too. He felt very tired suddenly, thinking about the long hours ahead of him. He had to be back at the hospital by 8:00 A.M. for morning rounds, then another grueling ten- or twelve-hour shift, then back here again at 11:00 P.M. for the night shift.

Actually, the prison practice was the one he looked forward to; it meant *sleep,* blessed, uninterrupted sleep—sometimes a whole six hours of it. Even on a busy night at the prison he managed to grab a couple of hours of deep, undisturbed sleep.

So why was he awake now when there were some serious Z's to catch up on? Something had woken him, but what, he didn't know and didn't care. He lay down to resume his slumber. There was the sound of a door opening and foot-steps coming toward him. He sighed. Sleep would have to wait. He sat up, opening his eyes, expecting to see Nurse Donner ready to gently wake him to examine one of the in-mates or a guard, but the room was empty. He was alone.

He got up and went to the door, opened it, and peered into the hallway. The wide second-floor corridor that ran the length of Digbee Hall, from the Can past HSU to the obser-vation room over the inmates' day room and library, was empty. He was about to return to the couch when a loud, electrical, staticky buzzing sound reached his ears. It seemed to be coming from the CO's observation room at the end of the hall. Dr. Feldman stepped into the corridor and heard the buzzing again, a little louder. He heard something else, too—the faint sound of screaming.

"Nurse Donner?" he called, looking to the right, toward the HSU reception desk. There was no response. The sound came again, crackling, static electric buzzing and the now distinct sound of screaming.

It was definitely coming from the left end of the hall—the CO's observation room over the day room/library on the first floor. Dr. Feldman walked slowly toward it, fumbling in the pocket of his lab coat for the small two-way radio he carried while on duty. He pushed the button and spoke.

"Uh, this is, uh, MD-3 calling the, uh, office, no, not the office, the uh . . . control? Over," he stammered and felt foolish. He could never remember the correct terminology and names for things at the prison and was always embarrassed when he had to use the radio to speak to anyone other than the nurse.

"Inner Control here, MD-3," the radio crackled back. "What can I do you for, Doc? Over."

"I think there's something going on in the room over the library, you know, the observation room down the hall from HSU," Feldman said into the radio, then remembered to add, "Oh! Over!"

"I got nothin' showin' on the monitors in there, Doc. You sure? Where are you? Over."

"I'm right outside the staff break room at HSU." The crackling, air-skewering sound came again, so loud and sudden it made him jump. It was a familiar sound, but hard to name. Someone let out an awful guttural moaning. It sent a chill down his spine.

"There's definitely something going on, over." Feldman said. He had walked down the corridor as he spoke to Inner Control and was now at the observation room door. He put his ear to it and could hear a muffled voice say: "Up the wattage. I want to fry his wiener."

"Okay, Doc. You sit tight and I'll tell the watch commander."

Dr. Feldman could tell by the tone of his voice that the man didn't believe him. He doubted the watch commander would be along any time soon. In the meantime, it sounded like someone was being killed in there. Dr. Feldman pressed his ear harder to the door. The voices were speaking again and he tried to catch their words. He gripped the doorknob as he did and it turned, the latch clicked, and the door opened.

Frightened, Dr. Feldman took a step back. This door was supposed to be locked at night. He reached out, tapped the door, and it swung silently inward, revealing the dark and quite empty observation room.

"Hello?" he called. There was no one in there. He reached for the handle to close the door when the noise and the screaming resounded again, filling him with cold fear. The sound was coming from the room, but not the observation deck. It was coming from below. Louis stepped into the room. Slowly, hesitantly, like a moth reluctant to the flame, he crossed to the wall of glass overlooking the prisoners' day room. Only it wasn't the prisoners' day room any longer.

When Louis Feldman had first started at the prison, Nurse Donner had given him a tour of Digbee Hall and he had immediately recognized the circular inmates' day room with its second-story observation deck as an operating theater, such as they had in teaching hospitals and medical schools. Now, as he looked down, the inmates' day room had returned to its original function—that of a sterile operating room. But it wasn't an operation that was going on.

Two male attendants and a muscular, blonde female nurse had a very overweight, naked man strapped to a tilted operating table. Feldman's throat went dry at what he saw next to the table—an ancient electroshock therapy machine, the kind that had been banned because it was more instrument of torture than of healing.

Before Feldman could react, the nurse shoved a rubber bit in the fat man's mouth; the attendant set the conducting clamp on his temples and yelled, "Clear!" The other attendant threw a switch.

"No!" Louis yelled, banging on the glass and feeling a moment of panicky imbalance.

"No *what,* Doctor Feldman?" It was Nurse Donner. Feldman looked at her then back at the operating theater below, but now it was a drab inmate day room again, replete with grungy chairs, plastic tables, and all the other accouterments of an institutional living room.

Jim Henderson paused from his nightly routine and listened to the exchange between the HSU doc and Inner Control and decided it was nothing urgent. He gladly went back to the business at hand.

"*Captain* Jim Henderson. *Captain* James A. Henderson. *Captain* James Andrew Henderson," he whispered fervently. With each title he admired the bars on his collar, listened to the sound of his rank echoing in the bathroom, and stroked his flesh. He was building, getting close.

"*Captain* Henderson. 'Yes, sir, Captain Henderson. Yes, sir! Yes, sir!' " On the verge of orgasm, he closed his eyes for a moment; when he reopened them he couldn't believe what he was seeing. There was a woman on her knees in front of him, her head buried between his legs. He could suddenly feel her hot, wet tongue sliding around him, her mouth sucking at him. Over her stood another woman, tall, blonde, and muscular. She was so muscular, in fact, that if she hadn't had huge breasts, Jim might have wondered about her gender. The muscular blonde wore a tiny leather thong and knee-high black riding boots. In her left hand she had a wooden yardstick. She raised the stick and brought it down on the buttocks of the woman pleasuring him. Again. Again. The blows rained on her back, her legs, her ass, raising welts and bruises and making the woman jump with each *smack!* of the ruler. But she never lost her oral grip on Jim; not once did he feel her teeth.

The blonde dominatrix unhooked a coiled whip from her belt and let it unfurl. She let it slither slowly over the slave's naked back before she cracked it. The slave buried her face and her scream of pain in Jim's crotch. The dominatrix leered at Jim and gathered up the end of the whip. Deftly, she tied a slipknot in the end of it. She straddled the slave, her knees digging into the submissive woman's ribs. Jim felt the first tingles of impending orgasm as the slave increased the speed of her fellatio.

The dominatrix leaned forward and kissed Jim, shoving her long, metal-studded tongue into his mouth. He reached for her, but she thrust his arm away and slipped the whip-noose around his neck, pulling it tight enough to cut off his air. The tighter she pulled on the noose, the more Jim Henderson's orgasm built.

The dominatrix leered at him as he reached the precipice of orgasm, groaning loudly. The woman on the floor sucked hungrily on him. The dominatrix pulled on the noose. Jim threw his head back and felt consciousness slipping away. The slave between his legs went down all the way and stayed there. This was it. He was on the extreme edge of the best, most powerful orgasm he'd ever had.

The radio crackled.

"Outer Control to One-twelve. Over."

He opened his eyes. He was lying on the bathroom floor, his pants around his ankles, his own leather belt cinched tightly around his neck, choking him.

What the hell just happened?

"Outer Control to One-twelve. Over," came Jane Mazek's voice again.

Henderson untied the belt from his neck and pulled up his pants. On the floor a few feet away lay his radio. He picked it up. "One-twelve here. Over."

"Your wife's on the phone, Jim. Let me know where you are and I'll put it through on the closest landline. Over."

Jim frowned. He didn't like Mazek using his first name. It had been okay when he was just a lieutenant, and had wanted to encourage camaraderie with the other COs, but now that he was *captain, watch commander,* that would not be acceptable. He'd have to speak to Mazek later, and the last thing he needed right now was to talk to his wife.

"Ah, you tell her . . . tell her I'll have to call her back as soon as I can. Over."

"Roger. Over and out."

Jim Henderson struggled to his feet. His neck hurt and his balls ached; he still had a raging erection. Frustration added to his confusion. *What the hell just happened?* Had he put the belt around his *own* neck? Had he been dreaming? Hallucinating?

"I wasn't dreaming," he said to his reflection in the mirror. "I was wide awake."

* * *

Jane Mazek relayed the message to Henderson's wife and went back to her own call.

"Tobi? You still there?"

Tobi Dowry's voice came back listless and small. "Yeah, I'm here."

"Sorry. Henderson's wife calling her new *captain*. You remember Henderson, don't you? He used to work in Inner Control. GI Joe type with a stick so far up his ass he can't bend over."

Tobi didn't laugh. Jane was *always* able to get her friend laughing, but not lately. Since she quit the prison, Tobi had changed and not for the better. It made Jane angry that her best friend—Tobi had been her closest friend since fourth grade—could be so self-indulgent. She just wouldn't let go of that cockamamie dream she'd had. She wouldn't admit that it *was* just a dream—a fucked-up nightmare that she could *easily* get over if she would just *try*. But all she seemed to want to do now was hide in her apartment and sleep.

She was letting it destroy her life. Her boyfriend, who was, granted, an asshole, left her because of it. Lately, she'd been so depressed, Jane was afraid she was going to let it kill her. Jane and her lover, Judy Bennett, had tried to help Tobi; tried to take her out for drinks, dinner, and to the movies. In the past two and a half months since she'd flipped out at work, they'd been able to lure her out of her apartment three times. Once for a night of boozing at O'Brien's Pub in nearby Fitchminster, once for a movie, and once to go to a gay nightclub in Worcester. She had managed the drinking and movie nights, though she went home right after the movie, when normally she would have wanted to go to the pub for a nightcap. But the night they went to Worcester, she snuck out of the club and drove home while Jane and Judy were dancing and left them stranded there without a ride.

Judy, who hadn't known Tobi as long as Jane, had wanted to cut her loose then. Being abandoned in Worcester had really pissed her off, but Jane wouldn't do it. Tobi was her old-est friend, and the only straight friend she'd ever had who had never judged her for being a lesbian, who had always ac-cepted her for who she was. That meant a lot to Jane. She couldn't desert her friend and leave her to go through what-ever she was going through alone.

"How about you come over for dinner Wednesday night?" Jane asked. Wednesdays and Thursdays were hers and Judy's days off. "We'll make strawberry daiquiris and get loaded. How about it?"

Tobi didn't answer for so long Jane thought she had hung up.

"You there?"

"Yeah," came her voice finally. "I don't think I can make it, Jane."

Jane had to nearly bite her tongue to keep from swearing at Tobi; she suddenly wasn't sure if her friend was respond-ing to the dinner invitation or making a statement about her life. She wanted to scream at Tobi: "Snap out of it!" She wanted to slap her and shake her and make her get over this.

It was maddeningly frustrating.

"I'm going to bed now," Tobi said. "I guess I'll talk to you soon." She hung up.

Jane hit the disconnect button and sat back. She sighed heavily. She was at the end of ideas of what to do about Tobi. She had hoped to talk her into coming back to work instead of quitting, but Tobi would not give the thought a chance. When her sick leave ran out, she was done; she was quitting. Luckily, because this had happened at work, she was cov-ered under the state worker's comp and disability insurance programs. If she couldn't go back to work, she could file for disability. Yet, even the news that this might all have been a good thing in a way; that she was set for life and didn't have to quit, *or* go back to work at the prison, wouldn't change Tobi's mind. She'd had enough of the prison. She didn't want anything to do with it or anything from it.

Jane couldn't understand how her friend could give up a

free ride, but there were a lot of things about Tobi that Jane didn't understand.

Captain Jim Henderson zipped up his pants, adjusted his still semihard package so that it didn't bulge so much, and left the staff bathroom on the first floor of C building. He looked around outside the bathroom, checked the visitors' area, the back stairs. One of the officers from the Outer Control monitor board was getting a Coke from the machine outside the visitors' area, heard him and came to investigate.

"You lookin' for somethin', Captain?"

Jim smiled. He didn't think he'd ever get tired of hearing his new rank. "No, no," he replied. He couldn't remember the officer's name and had to squint at his tag. "Officer Dennison?"

The young man nodded. Jim started to ask him if he'd seen anyone in the building, but thought better of it. Of course he'd seen no one, because no one had been in there. It was the middle of the night; there was no way anyone could have got in there—certainly not a topless, muscular blonde dominatrix and her naked sex slave—without being noticed and reported. There was no way he was going to start asking questions and have everyone think he had gone as loony as John Thompson.

"Just making sure everything's as it should be," he said to Dennison and turned, going up the stairs to Outer Control. Either he had been dreaming, which meant he had fallen asleep *in the middle of masturbating,* or he was starting to hallucinate, just like John Thompson. Maybe Thompson had some kind of weird disease that caused hallucinations and he had caught it from him. What that disease could be, Jim Henderson had no idea, but it was the only reasonable explanation he had and he *needed* a reasonable explanation. *He* was *not* going *crazy*! *He* was *not* like *John Thompson!*

He was Captain James Andrew Henderson.

Jim Henderson returned to the staff bathroom several

times that night and tried to repeat what had happened, but unsuccessfully. These attempts were likewise unsuccessful in the orgasm department. He came away from each one more frustrated than the last. Less than three hours into the shift he was walking around with an erection that just wouldn't quit. After his fifth unsuccessful attempt at finding any trace of the dominatrix and her slave, Jim gave up and decided the whole thing had been a fluke, a mirage, *anything* but him going crazy.

He decided he only had two choices available. He could blather on about what happened, like John Thompson had, and suffer the same fate—demotion, loss of command. There was no way he was giving up his captain's rank; he'd already set his sights on making deputy. His other choice was to just forget it had ever happened. Just forget.

He could do that.

He hoped.

While Jim Henderson convinced himself he could have a selective memory, Tim Saget couldn't sleep that Sunday night before his first day at the prison. He and Millie got back from their honeymoon around five, unpacked, and had pizza delivered for supper. Tim kissed Millie off to bed at ten and stayed up to watch the Red Sox playing the Athletics in Oakland. He was too wired to sleep. Millie had wanted him to come to bed with her but he declined.

"I'm too stressed," he told her. "I just need some space to get my head in the right place to be able to do this job."

Millie didn't say anything, but Tim could tell she was annoyed. "Whatever," she said and went upstairs. Tim shrugged. It wasn't like she wanted him in bed so they could make love. She'd made it very clear this weekend that sex was too uncomfortable while she was pregnant. What was supposed to have been their honeymoon had turned into thirty-six hours of discomfort and frustration. Tim had been completely miffed by her all weekend. This sweet girl he had lived with and about whom he had thought that if anyone could settle him down and make him happy it was her, had been kidnapped and replaced with an evil Stepford wife who now criticized everything he did, wanted nothing to do with him physically, and expected him to jump at her every beck and call.

It was astounding. Tim was mortified by it. He'd heard of this before, of women changing after getting married, but he'd thought it was a joke, or something that happened gradually over the years, not *overnight!* Maybe it was because she was pregnant, he reasoned. He'd heard pregnancy could make women even wackier than PMS. If it was that, she'd get better after the baby was born, he hoped, though doubtfully.

The thought of spending the next fifty to sixty years with the bitch Millie frightened and sickened Tim. He pushed it away and tried to concentrate on watching the Red Sox do what they do every summer—*lose.* By the end of the first inning, the score was five to nothing, Oakland. He drank a couple of beers, stared at the game, and wondered what tomorrow would be like. He couldn't help but think in terms of his only frame of reference—movies. In all of those prison movies he had seen, none showed prison as being a good place to be or a good place to work in. Granted, his frame of reference was limited to *The Green Mile, The Shawshank Redemption, The Longest Yard*, and *Cool Hand Luke*. He figured the reality had to be much worse than anything in those movies. He figured, at best, it would be like the worst of the prison movie scenes, only without the charismatic, quirky, heroic and engaging despite-being-criminal characters. Instead there were dangerous, demented, sickos there who would just as soon stick a shiv in his back as look at him. Yet, he was supposed to guard these criminals. *Him*! He was supposed to control them; command them!

For the next twenty-five years!

He went to bed shortly after 1:30 and lay staring at the ceiling illuminated by the street light outside. He felt as he

had when he was a kid and had done something bad; waiting
for the Sergeant to pronounce his punishment—that intensity of anxiety; that sense of impending doom.

Bleak was the word for it. If ever something could be described as *bleak,* Tim Saget figured his future was it.

John Thompson had trouble sleeping also. Like Tim
Saget, he, too, sat up watching the Red Sox lose to the A's.
He drank iced tea instead of beer, but he, too, was contemplating what the next day would be like. In one way, he was
glad he was going to be working day shift; he could avoid
Jim Henderson. He couldn't believe Henderson had made
captain, and did *not* want to see him so he could gloat about
it. The biggest problem with breaking in new recruits was
the boredom; there just wasn't that much to do once he gave
the tour and saw that the recruits got their shadow assignments. And it lasted for eight days. Normally, he would have
been dreading the long days, but for his purposes it couldn't
have been better. It would give him time to find Darlene
Hampton.

Monday would be the hardest day; he had to deal with a
lot of paperwork. He had to meet with each recruit and give
them their shadow assignments for the next eight days. He
also had to give the new recruits the full tour of the prison,
which would take close to three hours, including stopping
for lunch in the officers' mess. This was the day he had to do
a lot of talking and explaining—a lot of gung-ho "Brotherhood
of the Screws" song and dance, blah, blah, blah.

He wasn't looking forward to it. He wasn't going to have
any time to look for Darlene. By Tuesday afternoon, he figured he might be able to slip away and check a couple of
places. He had to be careful, though. Word was out, he was
sure, on what had happened to him that night at the observation desk over the prisoners' day room. Jim Henderson was
enough to ensure that happening; add Sheila Donner, Dr.

Feldman, and Jane Mazek, and he was bound to still be the topic of conversation for a few days, at least, upon his return. If there was one thing he had learned in his many years working in the prison system it was that it was like being in a television soap opera. And that was just based on the correction officers' interactions with each other, never mind what went on between the officers and inmates and among the inmates themselves. Among the COs, everyone knew everyone else's business. Every divorce, addiction, affair, breakup and breakdown was common knowledge. If you told anyone anything juicy enough on any of the three shifts, you had to be prepared for all personnel on all shifts to know it within forty-eight hours.

John had a feeling that if he got caught in another "Darlene Episode," Bill Capello would force him to retire for medical reasons. Unless he found her, of course.

Tobi Dowry just wanted to be able to sleep, peacefully, restfully, without dreaming. Just *one* night, one *hour* of dreamless sleep would be a godsend.

But *they* wouldn't let her.

"What's left?" she asked her mirror reflection. Her face was gaunt and haggard. Dark circles encompassed her eyes, giving her a ghostly, haunted look.

It was how she felt.

"What's left?" She didn't know. When the escape of sleep was taken away, what else was there to help mend a damaged psyche? She'd never been much of a drinker; one night a week was almost more than she could handle, and she'd never been interested in drugs. Besides, she had the feeling that alcohol or drugs, or a combination of both, would only make matters worse; would only make *them* stronger.

They were already too strong; so strong she was beginning to hear them calling to her even when she was awake. Like now, faintly, as though there were tiny voices deep in her head, yet coming from far away. She could hear them telling her what they'd been telling her in her dreams for weeks—telling her what she must do.

She was tired of resisting. She was tired of being empty. She agreed. She gave in.

A half hour later, in the wee hours of Monday morning, Tobi Dowry was traveling along Route 140. She turned at the sign for New Rome Prison and drove up the winding road that climbed Windigger Hill and led to the prison. She glanced at the dash clock—1:45 A.M. She shut off her lights and drove by moonlight. Twenty yards before the main gate, she took a right turn onto a narrow dirt road and drove into the woods, risking her headlights again to see. Shortly, those lights showed a small graveyard up ahead. She stopped, left the engine running, and walked to the graves. She checked the headstones, seemed satisfied with what she found, and went back to her car, reaching in to pop the trunk. She took out a garden hose and a fat roll of gray duct tape she'd brought from home and got to work. After several burns to her hands, she managed to get one end of the hose taped securely, as air-tight as possible, to the exhaust pipe. She unrolled the hose and fed the other end through the open driver's-side window. She slid into the driver's seat, rolled up the window until it was open only enough to hold the hose, and turned up the radio. The Rolling Stones' Mick Jagger was singing: "You can't always get what you want, but sometimes, you get what you need."

Tobi stepped on the gas, revved the engine, and sang along as she breathed deeply of the gray cloud filling her car.

6

"Gentlemen, welcome to the New Rome Correctional Institute of the Commonwealth of Massachusetts; locally known as Windigger Hill—and if you spend any time outside up here in the winter you'll know why it's called that—or just the 'Hill.' This is a combined-security facility. The majority of our population—85 percent—is medium security, but we also have minimum- and maximum-security inmates on the premises."

Tim Saget recognized John Thompson from his graduation party, but he wasn't listening. He and the other recruits—eight in all—were standing at the edge of the employee parking lot, which sat atop a small, flat ridge overlooking the prison, lying nestled in a level hollow just below the crest of the hill. An intense, almost overwhelming sense of déjà vu had hold of Tim, distracting him and befuddling his concentration.

I've seen this before, he thought. *But where? Pictures, maybe?* He knew he had never been to the prison before.

"All right, now we're going to move down to the front gate and begin the orientation tour," Lieutenant Thompson said. He had already explained that he was one of sixteen lieutenants in a chain of command that started with the superintendent, then went down to three deputies, eight captains, sixteen lieutenants, and over 200 corrections officers, more commonly called COs.

Tim was jostled from his thoughts by the recruits following Lieutenant Thompson as he led them single file to the edge of the parking lot and down a set of steps made from railroad ties dug into the sloping earth. Like ducks following their mother, Tim and the other recruits followed Thompson across the entrance road to the main gate, which was set into a massive, thirty-foot-high chain-link fence that made up the outer perimeter of the prison.

"This is the main entrance through which all visitors must enter the facility," the lieutenant explained, pointing to a six-foot gate set into the towering fence. "The only other entrance is in the rear of the complex and is used for trucks delivering food and supplies, delivery of new prisoners, transferring prisoners in and out of the facility, and for prisoners being transported to and from court appearances. As you will notice, there is a large empty causeway between the outer perimeter fence and the inner—this is called the 'Dead Zone.' Any prisoner managing to get into this area has one chance, upon command, to drop to the ground, hands and arms outstretched, or they will be shot." Lieutenant Thompson pointed to the towers at the corners of the fence.

"We will now enter the prison proper, proceeding to C building, which houses 'Outer Control.' Outer Control is responsible for operating the pedestrian trap, which is where all visitors are processed and checked before being allowed access to the visiting room. Outer Control is also responsible for all incoming and outgoing telephone communications from the facility. It also houses one of the two main radio communication consoles within the facility. Outer control also has a monitoring station, which covers the inner and outer perimeters of the prison, the power station, the prisoner visiting room, and various other spots. The facility's tactical units are also housed here, in the basement, and are deployed from C building in the case of an emergency in the yard, a riot, or a full facility lockdown. Due to security reasons, you will not be allowed into the tactical unit area today. After two years service you may bid to attend training for a position on the tactical unit if one comes open."

The lieutenant opened the outside gate and led the way through a fenced-in corridor spanning the width of the Dead Zone to a second, similar gate. Tim noticed twin security cameras over this gate and an intercom box next to it. Above the intercom was a sign in Spanish, English, and Chinese instructing visitors to press the button and state their name and that of the inmate they wished to visit. Unlike the outside gate, this one had a thick metal lockbox set into it and no handle. Thompson pressed the TALK button on the intercom and barked: "New recruits coming in." There was a loud buzzing sound and the inner gate clicked open. Tim and the rest of the new guards filed through, down a short concrete walkway enclosed by a twelve-foot-high chain link fence on either side, and up a short flight of granite stairs to a small brick building that reminded Tim of his old grade school, Hosmer Elementary.

"We will now enter C building and what is called the 'pedestrian trap,' where all incoming visitors are checked for contraband, drugs, hidden weapons, and the like." The lieutenant opened the door and led the way into a large open hall. To the right were a reception desk and an electronic switchboard housing the outside intercom and remote gate locks behind a Plexiglas shield wall that extended all the way to the ceiling. A sliding metal drawer was centered in it for the transfer of the register book for visitors signing in. The rest of the hall was cordoned off with equally high Plexiglas around a square doorframe that resembled an airport metal detector. Next to it, Tim recognized the familiar conveyor belt and X-ray machine that airports use to examine carry-on luggage.

"This is the Pedestrian Trap," Thompson continued. "Visitors must sign in at the reception desk. The form they sign is a sworn statement that they carry no illegal contraband and lists the materials that are considered such. The form also warns of the resultant prosecution that will be pursued should they violate any of the facility's visitation policies."

The metal drawer slid open and the captain pulled out a stack of papers that he began distributing among the new men. "These are the rules of visitation in English on one side, Spanish on the other. Translations are also available in Hmong, Chinese, Vietnamese, Korean, and French. Since you should already have reviewed these during your training at the academy—the same rules and restrictions apply to all Massachusetts correctional facilities regardless of their security level—we will not waste time doing so now."

Thompson turned to the metal detector. "After signing the registration book and the visitor's agreement form, visitors are directed through here, a standard full body metal detector. Before doing so they are directed to empty everything from their pockets into the receptacles here." He pointed to a large plastic bucket sitting on the table next to the metal detector. "Any packages, pocketbooks, briefcases, whatnot, must also be placed on the examination table at this time. These are then passed through a standard security X-ray machine. Once visitors pass through the metal detector, they may be further checked with a metal detecting wand, or subjected to a full-body pat-down and an oral cavity search if the officers have reasonable suspicion that such action is warranted." The lieutenant stepped through the doorway, setting off a buzzing alarm, and stood with his arms outstretched, crucifixion-style, while a guard checked him with the wand, asked him to open his mouth for a visual check, and then demonstrated a standard police pat-down. "Any visitor refusing to comply is escorted from the premises and denied visitation. When you come on duty and enter the facility, you will bypass all this and use the door directly opposite me, next to the sign in drawer. An officer on duty will buzz you in. Follow me."

Lieutenant Thompson walked on and Tim and the rest of the recruits went single file through the metal detector, creating a constant buzz from their badges, belt buckles, watches, and any other metallic personals they wore. Thompson was standing outside a doorway to the left and the eight recruits clustered around him.

"This is the visiting area. To the right is the observation cage. As you can see it is elevated to allow for a full view of the room. The room is also manned by three corrections officers placed strategically around the room. Note the security cameras in each corner of the ceiling. These are monitored during visiting hours by officers in the Outer Control Command Post, which is on the second floor, this way." Lieutenant Thompson led them further along the hall to a stairway at the rear of the building next to a pair of double metal doors leading outside.

Before following, Tim glanced in at the visitation room. There were four long rows of tables with low, hard aluminum benches on both sides of each table. It reminded Tim of his high school cafeteria. He glanced down at the visitation rules paper he still held in his hand—*No conjugal visits; embracing allowed for 15 seconds at the beginning and end of visit; mouth kissing not allowed; hands must be in view on the table at all times*. The list went on, but Tim had fallen behind and had to hurry to catch the others, who were now ascending the stairs to the second floor.

"This is the Outer Control Command Post," Tim heard Thompson saying as he caught up, but he was stuck on the stairs behind the others crowding the doorway, and so couldn't see. He stood on tiptoes to get a glimpse of the lieutenant. "From here, surveillance of the entire perimeter of the facility is maintained twenty-four/seven. As you can see"—he paused to point to a row of TV monitors suspended from the near wall—"closed-circuit video cameras provide observation of the front entrance, the Pedestrian Trap, the visiting room downstairs, the Dead Zone, the rear delivery entrance, the parking lots and emergency power station, which are situated outside the facility's perimeter, and the outside entrance to every building in the facility. In fact, the only building not surveyed from this room is the K-9 headquarters, where the kennels are."

Lieutenant Thompson led the throng through the room to another door marked EXIT and Tim was able to get his first clear look at the Outer Control Command Post. It was a long, rectangular room with industrial green painted walls and a high plaster ceiling that was stained brown in two corners from water damage. Along the right wall were two large windows with wire-mesh glass panes that overlooked the fences of the Dead Zone and the front gate. Between them was a table with a grimy Mr. Coffee machine on it. On the opposite wall was the switchboard—an old-fashioned wire type. To its right was a large radio. A bored-looking young woman sat at the console and smiled thinly at him, as if weary beyond words. Next to that ran a countertop under a bank of eight monitors with three swivel chairs placed at three-foot intervals. Only two of those chairs were occupied. Both guards ignored him. Tim noticed that each monitor had a label on its pedestal identifying the view represented. The far wall held the exit door through which the rest of the recruits were now filing. Following them through the exit door, which led to an outside fire escape that would take the group to the yard, Tim looked back and saw the two guards manning the monitors had taken out a deck of cards and a cribbage board.

"Now we are in the east prison yard. All administrative buildings are in the east yard, also the Segregated Inmate Unit in Digbee Hall. The SIU has its own secure, fenced-in rec yard for its prisoners. Since we are a combined-security facility, only the minimum-security inmates are allowed unsupervised in this area of the yard so close to the Dead Zone and the front gate, and that is generally only for clean-up and maintenance details during times when all other prisoners are inside. After 3:30 P.M., unless they are going to the Health Services Unit or have a visitor, all medium-security inmates are restricted to the west yard, which we'll get to later. Digbee Hall is our next stop."

Walking away from C building across the beautifully manicured lawn, Tim couldn't help but think that without the tall fences topped with barbed wire surrounding the place, it could easily be a college campus. The buildings were all brick, Victorian-style, with granite cornices and tall arched windows of the New England type that are so familiar to anyone who's spent time in the area. The walkways were concrete squares, many of them lined with flowers and small, decorative evergreen bushes. He knew the prison had been a state hospital once, and he thought it must have been a nice place to visit back then.

"This is Digbee Hall, constituting the Segregated Inmate Unit, or SIU, which is the maximum-security housing section of the New Rome Correctional Institute." Lieutenant Thompson's booming voice brought Tim's attention back from its wandering. He looked up at the large building before him. It was a long, four-story brick building, with one end—the closest to Tim and the others—rounded, giving it a faint castlelike appearance. Scaffolding was set up all along the face of the building and on the roof, which was covered with a massive blue tarpaulin that flapped at the edges where it was secured to the roof. Workers were busy all over the structure. Again, Tim had that feeling of déjà vu looking at the building. Something—movement in one of the fourth-floor windows—caught his eye and he looked up, squinting against the sun.

There was an old lady standing in the window, looking down. She was waving and blowing kisses . . . at *him*.

John Thompson checked his watch. It was only eight o'clock and the tour wasn't even half over. He groaned to himself; this was going to be a long day.

"Excuse me, Lieutenant?"

He turned. It was the Sarge's kid, Tim. The kid pointed at the top of Digbee Hall. "Who's that, sir?"

John squinted up and frowned. He hated stupid questions. "Obviously, they're workers fixing the roof. It was damaged by a bad snowstorm last winter and it caused significant damage. They're almost finished. The first and second floors house this facility's Inner Control and Health Services Unit—HSU for short. The round section on the end here houses the prison library, which is also the inmates' day room. Above it is a glassed-in observation deck for officers to keep an eye the cons. On the far end, there, is the Segregated Inmates Unit, also known as 'the Can.' It's where we also keep inmates awaiting transfers and a cooler for inmates who are being punished for crimes committed within the facility." He was about to lead them inside when he heard the Sarge's kid ask another recruit, "Did you see that lady up there?"

"What did you say?" he asked, turning and addressing Tim Saget so abruptly several of the recruits took a startled step backwards.

"Uh, I asked him if he saw the lady up there, sir."

"Where?" John asked. The Saget kid pointed at Digbee Hall. "Up there. In one of the top floor windows. That's who I was asking you about. She looked like a cleaning lady or something. She waved."

"Was she black or white?" John asked, anxiously.

"What, sir?"

"Was she a black woman or a white woman?" John said, his voice rising. Several recruits looked questioningly at each other, their eyebrows raised as they cast wary looks in Thompson's direction.

"Um, she was white and she had gray hair, sir. She looked kind of old," Tim Saget replied nervously.

"You're sure?" John Thompson asked, looking back at the top floors of Digbee. They were the first places he wanted to look for Darlene Hampton. Though they had supposedly been searched when she disappeared, he figured it had been merely a walk-through. Though the fourth floor was being renovated, the third floor was empty, used for storage, making it the perfect place for someone to hide out or hold someone hostage.

"Yes, sir. I'm sure."

The recruits around Tim Saget were mumbling to each other. John Thompson realized he was wheezing and caught the looks they were giving him. He quickly decided he had better calm down. Whatever the Saget kid had seen, it wasn't Darlene Hampton. He had to be careful. At least half the new recruits were related to officers working at the prison. He couldn't afford to have them go yapping about him acting strangely. Capello would get wind of it and John would be gone. He made a mental note to talk to Tim Saget later, in private.

Billy Dee Washington put his ID chit on the work wall, hanging it on the hook for the optical shop, and got in line for the first movement of the day. He took a deep breath; there was something in the air today, something different. He felt it—an excitement, an energy and sense of expectation that he thought he could actually see in the eyes of his fellow inmates. He thought the guards could sense it, too; they looked unsure of themselves.

Billy Dee tugged at the front of his pants and did a little dance to resettle his testicles. They were sore. He smiled remembering how they got that way. The doctor had visited him again last night with that black guard bitch in chains. Oh! What fun they'd had with her! Finally, the doctor had let him consummate all his desires concerning that bitch screw. She had always thought she was so *black* and *bad*. He had really shown her what it was like to be black and bad. He had shown her *good*. He had beat her, whipped her, bit her, and fucked every hole she had, several times, until she could not even moan with pain. And all the while the doctor had been right there, watching, helping, making suggestions—always good ones. There were others around also, followers of the doctor's, who held the bitch's chains and who positioned her for him. They were vague shapes in his mind, mere bodies that had done his bidding, but he vividly remembered their voices, their giggling and groaning pleasure as they watched and, Billy Dee was quite sure, had an orgy all around him. He had several flash memories of piles of bodies writhing in pain and ecstasy.

He felt pressure on the front of his pants and looked down. He had an enormous erection pushing out the fabric of his jeans, but the pressure was from the short black guy next to him who was rubbing Billy Dee's crotch.

"I can meet you in the bathroom if you want me to help you with that," whispered the man, Julian, whom Billy Dee had let service him before, and on more than one occasion. He brushed the man's hand roughly away now, though.

"Back off, faggot," Billy Dee growled. "I don' need yo' help no mo'."

The guy put his fingers in his mouth, sucked on them, and spoke around them. "Why? You got a hot babe stashed away in here somewhere?"

Billy Dee Washington just smiled.

Billy Dee Washington was not the only inmate to feel a change in the air on Tim Saget's first day at the prison. Throughout the facility, the half-remembered recent dreams of many of the inmates suddenly returned, pressing strongly upon their memories with scenes of abominable gratifications. One inmate, who sensed the change more than others and who was one of the few untouched by slumber's seductive dreams, stood on the steps of D building, watching the new recruits following their leader like schoolchildren. On the lower step stood two companions, much younger.

Like Tim Saget, the oldest of the three was new to the prison and had been there only a few days. Sometimes called "Chief" since he claimed to be three-quarters Mohican, he'd come in during the night, transferred from Springfield because of threats against his life. He was a harmless, if odd-looking, man. Not more than five foot four, he was hunch-shouldered and completely bald. His head displayed a connect-the-dots illustration of brown liver spots. His head was large, but it had to be to support its nose, a large, disfigured thing covered with fleshy mushroom-like growths, moles, and carbuncles. The rest of his face was hairless and rough-textured; a collection of wrinkles had collected around his eyes and at the creases of his grotesque nostrils. The corners of his mouth drooped when he wasn't smiling, giving him a perpetual frown.

His younger companions, who also claimed Indian blood, wore their hair long, tied with colorful bandanas the way they thought Indians would wear them. If either of them had any true Native American blood in them, it was minimal and the Chief knew it, but still they were eager and helpful and he liked to talk.

"This is one fucked-up place you got here," he said, his voice an incongruous high-pitched nasal whine, pausing on the stairs to watch the recruits. He had been called to the administration building to speak to a counselor. His companions had tagged along on their way to their jobs in the woodshop.

"Ah, it ain't so bad, Chief. I just wish they hadn't taken away our smokin' privileges. Hey, ain't that like sacred to us? You know, tobacco?"

"Yeah, and so's cancer," the chief muttered and turned to go into D building. "No I mean this *place* is really fucked up and we are in for a world of shit here."

The two acolytes looked confused. "Whattya mean, Chief?"

He puts his hands in their faces and wiggled his fingers. "Heap bad medicine," he said and laughed at the looks on their faces. But as he turned to go inside, he looked back at the new recruits and the worry in his eyes was real.

Jim Henderson couldn't get it out of his head. Everywhere he went, every thing he did, eventually the image rose, bringing with it an erection. Sometimes the memory was so real he could almost feel the hot, wet tongue working on him; hear the *crack!* of the yardstick on soft, bare flesh; sense the whip-noose tightening around his neck.

He fantasized about it when he masturbated—on average two to three times a day—at work, at home. He couldn't get those two women, dominatrix and slave, out of his mind. It was the only thing that could get him off anymore.

Because of the incident in the prison bathroom, Jim Henderson had discovered a new sexual experience that he had begun to explore whenever possible. A sex addict since he'd had his first orgasm at age ten, Jim had always led a mirror life; on one side of the mirror he was a normal man, the upstanding corrections officer, Captain Jim Henderson, by the book, who did his job better than anyone else. Take a step through to the secret side of the glass, and he was a sexually unquenchable dynamo. Oddly, he never saw how much he was like the convicts he guarded; his needs were normal—sex with a woman whenever possible, but masturbation and a good fantasy were fine, too. But the fantasies were all about women; Jim Henderson wasn't a perv like the skinners and diddlers at the prison. Yes, he loved pornography and had quite a large hidden stash, but he would never rape a woman (though he had fantasized about it) and the thought of anyone having sex with a child turned his stomach.

Jim Henderson's wife knew nothing of Jim's secret side. Her sexual appetite was normal in every way: she liked to make love no more than twice a week; she preferred one of two sexual positions, missionary, or her on top. Though he had tried to get her to explore, she had denied him every fantasy he had ever wanted to pursue, and she never gave oral. The sad thing was that he really loved her. Thus, instead of leaving her, he found escape in hookers, pornography, and an overactive fantasy life. He could have taken a mistress, but in his mind that would have been *cheating,* where as being with a hooker purely for sex was not. Lately, even his lust for hookers had been replaced by his desire for the noose around his neck and fantasies of the blonde and her slave.

Like now.

He had just got home from work. The wife was at her job for the day and wouldn't be home for hours. It was a perfect time. He had found the perfect spot for his latest fetish. He locked the front door and went upstairs to the master bedroom, where he opened the closet door. He undressed, letting his clothes lie where they fell. The only article he kept was his belt, which he removed from his pants before letting them drop. When he was naked, he pushed aside the row of Mary's dresses hanging in the closet and looped the belt through its buckle before tying the other end to the clothing bar in the closet. He put the looped end over his head and around his neck. He leaned forward, tightening the leather noose around his neck, cutting off his air. With his left hand he held the end of the belt to keep it from sliding off the clothing rack. With his right hand, he fondled and stroked himself, fantasizing that it was the blonde dominatrix that had her leather whip wrapped around his neck while her slave knelt at his feet, ready to service him.

Tim Saget sat in the cafeteria with the seven other recruits at 10:45. The tour was over. He'd been in every building in use by the prison system, inside and outside the prison fence. The tour had taken him from C building to Digbee Hall, where'd he'd seen the woman and which held the Health Services Unit (HSU), Inner Control Command Station, the inmates' day room/library, and the Segregated Inmates Unit (SIU, also known as the "Can") which was the maximum-security section of the prison. Next they'd gone to D—the administration building, which also held the school and the prison chapel.

After D building, they went through the garden/agricultural area, which included a vast greenhouse at the end of three-quarters of an acre planted with vegetables from corn to tomatoes. From there it was a short walk to the woodshop where inmates made dollhouses and butcher blocks, then beyond to a large, low, square building that housed the laundry and the optical shop. Tim had found the optical shop interesting. The inmates working there learned real skills in making eyeglass lenses and frames, plus industrial lenses for telescopes and microscopes. All the laundry for the prison, including guards' uniforms if officers wished to use it, was washed in the prison laundry room.

To the left of the optical shop and the laundry was the north gate in the tall fence that divided the prison right down the middle. Tim and the others had passed through it, going from the east yard to the west yard, while Lieutenant Thompson explained that the dividing fence was twenty-five feet tall, topped with barbed wire, and ran the entire length of the prison, from the back fence to the front near C building. The reason for this was for population control; it gave them the ability to section off parts of the prison whenever they needed to. The west yard held all the inmate dormitories, the kitchen, another garden, the gym, and outdoor basketball courts. The east yard held all administrative and industrial buildings, plus Digbee Hall and the rear gate building. Inmates were only allowed in the east yard between 7:00 A.M. and 3:30 P.M., when all the workshops and the school closed for the day, unless they had a visitor. In case of a riot, which experience had shown was most likely to happen in the dorms or the cafeteria, prisoners could be contained in the west yard without access to any weapons, communications, or the outside. The dorms in the west yard were all in a row, along the outside western fence and the Dead Zone, from the front of the prison to the rear. They were designated A dorm, B dorm, G dorm, and E dorm. I and F dorms were parallel to each other and the rear gate of the prison so that all the dorms formed an upside-down **L**. Opposite the dorms were the gymnasium, a splendid flower garden, and the kitchen/prisoner mess hall. Next to A dorm, directly under the corner tower, were three basketball courts.

Throughout the tour Tim had been struck by what a nice place the prison was, considering that it *was* a prison. The Victorian-styled brick and granite buildings with their green copper roofs were surrounded by immaculately kept flower beds, trimmed with perfect deep green narrow strips of grass in the east yard and with lush lawns bordered with narrow flower beds in the west yard. Lieutenant Thompson had explained how the care and upkeep of the grounds in the east yard was handled by inmates in the minimum-security section, whose dorm was outside the front gate, across the road leading to the parking lots. The minimum security dorms were three large Victorian houses that could house up to twenty-five inmates total for all three houses. Right now there were twenty inmates in minimum security. Doing time there was like being in a halfway house. Groundskeeping in the west yard was handled by a detail of medium-security prisoners under the direction of one of the COs who also ran a landscaping business part time.

The last step of the tour was where he sat now, the building that housed the COs' barracks and mess hall. Meals were transported from the kitchen in the west yard through the tunnels to the buildings over in the east yard. Lieutenant Thompson came strolling in and took off his dark blue baseball cap with the Massachusetts Department of Corrections logo emblazoned on it in gold. He wiped his forehead and let out a deep sigh before speaking.

"That's it, officers. You'll get to learn the layout better and familiarize yourself with the facility in general during the next eight days when you will make the rounds shadowing officers from every station this facility maintains, except for the towers. You have to work here two years before you can become tower eligible. For the next six days, your on-site training will consist of you shadowing at various positions. The seventh and eighth days you will be shadowing at the position you will be working full time. When I call your name, come up and get your schedule for the next six days. Please note that you will be working a swing shift. You are on days today and tomorrow, 7:00 A.M. to 3:00 P.M. Wednesday and Thursday, you will be on 3:00 to 11:00 P.M. Friday and Saturday, 11:00 P.M. to 7:00 A.M. You will receive your permanent assignments on Saturday. There will be *no* deviations or any excuse from this schedule. After you get your shadow assignments, you will have twenty-four minutes for lunch before you report to D building for paper processing, then back here for your locker assignments. Today you will all go home at 3:00 P.M. Tomorrow you will show up at 6:45 A.M. I, too, will be working swing shift and will be observing and helping out as much as possible."

The metal shutter closing off the officer's mess from the small serving kitchen suddenly rattled up as an inmate opened it. The smell of tomato sauce and garlic wafted out over the new men.

"All in all," Tim said to himself, "this might not be as bad as I thought."

She is tall and wide, strong and perfect. She is the most perfect woman he has ever seen. She towers over him as he kneels in front of her, offering his neck to her studded collar. She puts it on, threads the buckle, and pulls it tight.

Tighter.

Her sex slave is on the floor, under him. Her head comes up; her mouth latches on to him.

The collar tightens; the mouth tightens. More.

The leather burns; the tongue burns.

The buckle bites; the teeth bite.

Harder.

Tighter.

Tighter.

There was an explosion of light in his head, matched by an explosion of sperm from his other head. Jim Henderson convulsed into consciousness on his bedroom floor. The leather belt was still tight around his neck, but it had let go at the other end when he'd become unconscious and had released it from his hand, as it was supposed to. If it hadn't, he would have strangled himself.

He pulled the belt off and gasped for air. He looked down; his drying come had spotted the carpet in front of the closet door. Swearing softly, he got to his feet and hurried to the bathroom where he grabbed a face cloth, wet it, rubbed it on the bar of soap in the soap dish, and ran back to the bedroom. He dropped to his knees and scrubbed the rug. Standing afterward, looking down to see if he had missed any spots, he saw something that made his heart skip a beat and his breath vacate his lungs in a loud gasp.

There were fading teeth marks on his penis.

"What did you see up there, son?"

Startled, Tim dropped his fork and turned to Lieutenant Thompson, who had managed to sit at the table next to him without Tim seeing him coming.

"What?"

"What did you see up there? The top of Digbee Hall?"

"Oh," Tim answered. He shrugged. "I told you. There was a woman up there. She was waving at us."

Lieutenant Thompson looked around the officer's mess like a man afraid someone might overhear. "What did she look like?"

"I told you. She was an old woman, like maybe sixty or seventy."

"You said before that she was white?"

"Yeah."

"You're absolutely sure? She was old and white?"

Tim looked around also, but he was hoping someone *would* be overhearing; the lieutenant was making him nervous. "Yeah, I'm sure, Lieutenant. Why? I don't understand what's wrong. Was she not supposed to be up there?"

Lieutenant Thompson sat staring at the floor, seemingly

lost in thought. Tim didn't think he had heard and was about to repeat himself when the lieutenant got up and walked away.

"John Thompson is a weird duck," the Sarge said effusively when Tim asked about him. Tim had decided to stop by and see the Sarge when he got out of the prison at three to get the lowdown on Lieutenant Thompson. The rest of his day after the incident in the officer's mess had been uneventful, spent in the administration building where there was a mix-up on his CORI sheet, which shows criminal records. His had come back with several felonies on it. He waited around for over an hour until one of the secretaries noticed the record was for a Timothy Saget, with no middle initial, and he was Timothy *J.* Saget. From there he had gone to the CO barracks to claim his locker and get and store his gear, consisting of two uniforms (he had to buy the boots himself) his badge, baseball style–cap with the DOC badge on it, a flashlight, his two-way radio, a Colt M-13/PR-24 V6 military combat baton and a Smith and Wesson .38 revolver. Finally, he got a utility belt for carrying all the above. He felt a little like Batman. By the time he had finished that, it was time to go home. He hadn't seen Lieutenant Thompson again that afternoon, and he had been glad of it.

The more he thought about his encounter with Thompson earlier in the day, the more it bothered him. It bothered him so much it led him to do something he had never done before—confide in the Sarge and seek his advice. After all, Thompson was an old friend of the Sarge; maybe the Sarge could enlighten him concerning the lieutenant. He wasn't wrong.

"I didn't become friends with either Bill Capello or John until they ended up in my squad in Nam. Bill Capello and John were best friends; grew up together right next door to each other in New Rome. I grew up there, too, but I was seven or eight years older than them and I grew up in the Turkey Hill section. They lived down by the railroad tracks in 'The Patch.' When they got assigned to my squad in Nam—purely by chance—and we discovered that we were all from New Rome, we became friends.

"Anyway, we had been in Nam for two months when Thompson started acting weird. He was fine until the first time he saw someone get fragged. He got religion then. That's how some guys handled it. Some drank, some did drugs, some got religion, and some of us didn't need anything to get through it. But most did.

"John started wearing rosary beads around his neck. We had all got pocket bibles with our first issue of boot camp equipment, but most of the guys chucked them. John kept his and half a dozen others he must have got from guys or he dug them out of the trash. He kept one in each of his pockets and tucked one into his shorts. 'To stop bullets,' he told me once. When I saw those bibles I realized he must have got those back in boot camp, and that's when I started to suspect that he'd had something wrong with him long before he ever got to Nam. I've never met anyone as superstitious as him.

"Bill and me used to laugh at him behind his back. Sometimes he'd go off on these religious tangents, talking about some way-out stuff. Everyone called him 'Preacher' when he wasn't around." The Sarge paused, smiled, and shook his head. "The strangest thing about him, though, was what happened after we came back from Nam. He completely changed—we never heard another religious word from his lips; he never went to church and hasn't said or done another religious thing since. He got married, had a kid, joined the Department of Corrections. He went back to normal. Weird."

The Sarge mused for a long moment then added, "I'll talk to Bill Capello, find out what's going on with Thompson. He seemed okay when he was here for your graduation party. I'll do it in a subtle way, of course. I won't mention you."

Tim shrugged in unsure agreement.

* * *

At 3:45 P.M. Billy Dee Washington was at the universal gym, pumping 500 pounds with his legs. He had just come from the optical shop for his daily workout. It hadn't taken him long to get a good sweat going. He put everything into it: every fiber of his being, every thought in his mind. Weekends and weekday afternoons, Billy Dee spent all his time in the weight room. It made the days fly by. That's the way it was for him; he had a good system for doing time. He kept busy and never looked forward to anything and never looked at a calendar or a clock. He was a man who did well with routine. He lived life in the moment, taking joy in the time he had to improve his body without thinking about what was going to happen next. This had worked fine for him until he met the doctor. Now he found himself charging through each day, trying to push each second to a minute, each minute to an hour, each hour to a day as quickly as possible. He couldn't wait for the night; he *lived* only for the night. Even working on his body couldn't take his mind off it.

He paused from his leg presses and wiped his face, arms and legs with his towel. On the rowing machine opposite him, the fag bitch, Julian, who had grabbed him that morning, sat staring at him.

"What?" Billy Dee asked, shrugging slightly while tilting his head menacingly.

Julian shook his head and smirked. "You got somethin' goin' on, man. I seen it in your face." He looked around and leaned forward. "Lemme in on it, man. I won' tell no one."

Billy Dee smiled and shook his head.

"Aw, come on, *homey*! You can trust me!"

Billy Dee was about to tell the little faggot to fuck off when he remembered what the doctor had said, just before daybreak that morning, as their session was coming to an end: "We need more meat." Yeah. Billy Dee could dig that. The doc never said what kind of meat he needed, but as every con knew, fag meat was the next best thing to pussy.

* * *

John Thompson sat back in the swivel chair in his home office and took a long pull from the twelve-ounce bottle of Schaeffer he held in his right hand. It had been a long first day back, and as far as his search for Darlene Hampton went, a fruitless one. He hadn't had any time to do any looking for her. The incident with the Sarge's kid was weird. John couldn't help but think he'd been mistaken about what he saw. It was worth checking out. Then there was the news that Tobi Dowry, who'd been the Can's tier two CO on eleven-to-seven when John had first transferred to New Rome, had killed herself, and on the Hill no less, not far from the front gate.

It was weird. He remembered the night she had freaked out on duty and then quit. It had been his first night on duty, and he had never got the whole story on what had happened; she had been reticent about discussing it—she just wanted to quit and never set foot in the prison again, which made it seem strange that she would drive all the way to the prison to kill herself.

When he first heard about her suicide that day, he had wondered if it had any connection to Darlene Hampton, but he couldn't see how. Tobi had quit his first night on duty as watch commander, before he and Darlene had even hooked up. He doubted whether Tobi Dowry and Darlene Hampton had even known each other.

He took another pull from the beer, placed it and his head on the desk and closed his eyes.

God, he was tired.

Jim Henderson had a sore throat. He also had a sore neck and a sore dick. He sat up in bed, swallowed painfully, and rubbed his neck with his left hand, his dick with his right. There was a note on the night table on his side. It was from Mary.

Went to bingo with Kim and Melissa. Dinner is in the fridge. See you in the morning.

Jim crumpled the note and looked at the digital clock by the bedside. It read 7:00 P.M. He usually didn't get up until nine to eat and get ready for work, but he was wide awake. He knew he wouldn't be able to get back to sleep again. Grunting, he pushed himself out of bed and went into the bathroom. His reflection in the medicine cabinet mirror made him flinch—there was a band of dark, purplish bruises, right where he'd had his belt, around his neck. He touched them gingerly and wondered if Mary had seen them while he was sleeping. From the matter-of-fact tone of her note, he guessed she hadn't. He felt a panicky thrill at the thought that Mary might have seen his bruises. The biggest pleasure inherent in his new erotic pastime was its danger, both of getting caught and of being on the edge of life and death. Keeping it secret and performing it alone increased the dangers and thus the thrill.

He felt a stirring in his loins at the thought of Mary walking in on him and debated doing it again. Looking at the dark bruises on his neck dissuaded him. He had to give it a rest. He'd been doing it too often; this was the first time he'd bruised. He went back to bed and lay on top of the covers, masturbating while watching the porn channel on cable, but try as he might he could not reach a climax. Frustrated, he gave up and took a hot shower, where soap and water did nothing to cool his lust.

Julian James and Billy Dee Washington sat on Billy Dee's cot, in identical positions, legs apart, heads down, arms resting on knees, hands clasped in front of them as if they were praying together. But they were talking in low voices, with frequent looks around to see if anyone was eavesdropping.

"I don't exactly know how we're going to do this," Billy Dee said. For the past forty-five minutes he had been describing to Julian his sexploits under the tutelage of the doctor. When he started, Billy Dee had been unsure as to how he could explain and describe everything that had been happening to him every night when he went to sleep, without sounding like he was crazy. But then a funny thing happened. Billy Dee had never been good with words, neither writing nor speaking them. As usual, he started haltingly, stuttering and mumbling along, but the more he talked, the easier the words came until they were flowing, and he was describing everything with an eloquence that was far beyond his education and unlike any way he had ever been able to speak before.

His descriptions were so good they both soon had erections. And he was *convincing*! Not once did he sense that Julian thought he was crazy. Just the opposite—he *listened* with rapt attention, smiling dreamily. He *believed* every word unflinchingly. He was *eager* to join in the fun.

There was one problem.

Billy Dee didn't know how he was supposed to do that. But once again, the words came to him as if someone else were speaking through him, using his mouth and voice to tell Julian James what to do.

"First," Billy Dee heard himself say, "you must sleep . . . ."

But it was an excruciatingly long wait for sleep. They lay on their separate cots early, an hour before lights out, in the hopes that they might slip into somnolence sooner. Miraculously eloquent, Billy Dee had explained to Julian what he had to do. It was simple, really; just go to sleep with a thought of the doctor in his head, and he would soon awake in that other world, much like a dream and yet somehow more real than reality.

The trick was getting to sleep.

The dorm was noisy and smelly at night. Forty cons slept in one vast room. The beds were within a few feet of each other in four rows of ten. At the end of each bed was a four-and-a-half-foot-high TV stand with shelves for books or personal toiletries and mementos such as photos. Atop nearly every stand was a television, all of them with nineteen-inch screens, the largest prisoners were allowed to have. Near the double doors to the stairs sat the CO's desk, upon which was a VCR that all the televisions on the floor were hooked into. If a prisoner wanted to watch a movie there had to be a majority of inmates on the floor who wanted to see it, too. Needless to say, this led to a lot of arguments, but the cons had learned to police themselves, for the punishment for arguing over televisions was to have them all turned off. Even when all was calm and every inmate on the floor was watching the same movie or TV channel, the floor was noisy. When the TVs were tuned to different channels—a pick from what the cable company called "Industrial Basic," namely twelve stations, most of them local—even with the volume down low, the cacophony was anything but conducive to sleep. Add to the noise the stench of forty male bodies, sweating, burping, farting, and the dorms could be unpleasant. The Department of Corrections was considering requiring headphones for all televisions, but they knew if they did some con would sue them for infringing on his rights. The DOC's lawyers were researching the legality of it.

It was easier for Billy Dee to reach the shores of sleep than it was for Julian. He had been practicing blocking out all the noise for a lot longer. He'd become quite adept at doing so, finding it easier each night to get to sleep, and to the doc and his promised pleasures, sooner. In no time he was nodding off, heading down that long, descending corridor toward that strange flickering light, reminiscent of a campfire, casting long strobing shadows and illuminating writhing flesh. While Julian James was still struggling against the distracting noises around him, Billy Dee Washington was knee deep in bodies—a regular warmup before the doctor brought in Darlene Hampton for the real fun.

"I invited someone like you tol' me to, Doc!" Billy Dee said eagerly when the doctor finally arrived at the party.

"Good! Good!" the doctor cooed. "We need more men of your caliber, Billy. And you are going to bring them to us, for which you will be richly rewarded." The doctor smiled and snapped his fingers. Two orderlies brought forth a naked, bound, and struggling Darlene Hampton. Billy Dee grinned with satisfaction at the fear burning in her eyes.

Julian James felt like a kid on Christmas Eve; he couldn't wait to get to sleep so he could wake up. Of course, such anxiousness precluded any hope of sleep. It was a vicious circle. The more he wanted to sleep, the more awake he became. The fact that he was horny as hell didn't help either. Listening to Billy Dee tell him about his perverted dream life had reminded Julian of nights in his Uncle Armando's bed. Uncle Armando had liked to describe everything he was going to do to Julian before he did it, and he had a way of making it sound like *so much fun!* Julian's earliest memories were of his mother passed out drunk in the living room and her younger brother, Armando, taking him into his room so they could "play."

Julian had liked every moment of it right from the start. Neglected and physically and emotionally abused by his mother—he never knew his father—Julian latched onto the attention from Uncle Armando and it soon became everything to him. The "fun" continued, with Julian a more-than-willing partner, for the rest of Armando's life. He died from a drug overdose when Julian was fifteen. Since then Julian had taken on his uncle's role with as many young boys as he could get his hooks into. First sent to Juvenile Hall when he was sixteen for raping his five-year-old next-door neighbor, he had been in and out of jails and mental institutions ever since, for thirteen years. A dozen or more fat-assed, white and black therapists, counselors, and doctors had told him that the root of all his problems was the abuse he had suffered at the hands of Uncle Armando. Always one to sense an advantage, he had agreed and played the victim as long as it kept him out of jail. Deep down, however, he knew it wasn't true; he had loved every minute with Uncle Armando and he had loved every minute with his young friends after Uncle Armando died. Only one person had ever come close to figuring Julian out, and that had been the chaplain at the first reform school he'd been sent to. The chaplain had told him he was possessed by the demon of lust, giving him an unquenchable hunger for sex—and Julian had immediately recognized himself. Of course, that had done nothing to "cure" him. If he weren't in prison now, he'd be out humping some young kid. As soon as he got out, the first thing he would do is find some sweet young thing.

In the meantime, Julian had spent his time in prison doing just about anyone who wanted to be done and fantasizing about what he would do when he got out. Just as living moment to moment was Billy Dee Washington's method of coping with incarceration, Julian James's escape was through sex and fantasy. Every moment he could spare was spent fantasizing, usually sexually oriented fantasies, but not always. Sometimes the fantasies started out as sports dreams where he was a famous NBA player or in the NFL, but eventually even those fantasies wound up being about sex as he imagined how easy it would be to coax idolizing young male fans into bed with him.

With the rich fantasy life came a lot of masturbation. Whenever possible he jerked off. He poked holes in the right-hand pocket of all his pants and never wore underwear so he could play pocket pool no matter where he was. He had played the gang bitch for a while to the Latin Knights, the dominant gang in the prison, until they had tired of him, and now he spent as much time as he could get away with in the dorm bathroom offering beejays to anyone who came in, and getting lucky more often than not. Once in a while he even got a fellow con who wanted to bend him over the sink and really give it to him. Julian preferred prepubescent boys, but he was not averse to accepting and seeking out sex of any kind, and he was not above any act. At last count, he reckoned he'd had sex with at least a eighteen boys under age thirteen, and a dozen more fourteen- and fifteen-year-olds. Older than that and he didn't keep count.

All in all, prison was actually a good environment for someone like Julian. He judged no one, threatened no one, and offered sexual services—generally for free and at which he was unusually adept—to other cons, straight and gay alike. The only place he could have been happier was if the prison were combined with a boy's reform school, or an orphanage (one of his favorite fantasies). As it was, prison was a veritable paradise for someone like Julian. He had sex at least a couple times a day—mostly with straight guys—and that did not count self-abuse.

When Billy Dee Washington had started telling him about his sleepwalking adventures, Julian had thought he was joking, but then the strangest thing happened. Billy Dee's voice had started to change. It was like listening to a stereo, then putting headphones on; his voice became richer, thicker, deeper and clearer. Even his tone and dialect changed; he no longer sounded like a young black man, his voice was cultured, eloquent. It was not Billy Dee's voice at all but that of someone else. At first Julian wasn't fazed; a kid at juvey hall had had a split personality. He had met crazier people in some of his stints at clinics and mental hospitals.

Then everything changed.

Suddenly, he was *seeing* what the voice coming out of Billy Dee was describing. The dormitory room around him just faded away and he was suddenly in a strangely lit room, watching a pile of writhing bodies entwined in enough different sexual acts to constitute a visual sex manual. Julian hadn't been able to believe his eyes.

"Welcome, Julian," the voice coming out of Billy Dee said. Julian turned toward him, but Billy Dee wasn't there anymore; a white guy, with long hair and a hippie mustache, dressed in doctor's whites, had replaced him.

"Are you the doctor?" Julian asked.

"That's right. I know what ails you, Julian." His eyes grew larger and larger until Julian was falling into them, while at the same time every fantasy, every perversion, every dirty thought he'd ever had or done danced before his eyes and he relived them in moments, as if at the speed of light. His breath was literally knocked out of him by the all-encompassing vision. At the last, he had ended back in a room much like the prison dorm room, where a rumble of bodies orgied on the floor, and he wondered if he was losing his mind, going stir crazy. He didn't feel any crazier than usual. He realized at that moment that if he wasn't crazy then Billy Dee Washington had tapped into something incredible. The more he had listened and watched, the more he wanted to go to the place that the doctor offered him.

Then came the clincher.

At the foot of the pile of naked adults involved in every form of copulation, fornication, sodomy, fellatio, and cunnilingus known to man, there suddenly appeared a young boy. Not more than seven years old. He had blond hair and big blue eyes and he was completely naked.

Julian's favorite dream come true.

That clinched it for him. It was crazy and it was impossible, and though a part of his mind recognized that, a stronger part didn't care. A stronger part of him wanted to believe and so he did. If it was real; if it was true, it was the answer to all of Julian's hopes and desires.

"Lights out!"

The sound of the CO's voice brought him back to consciousness from the edge of sleep again.

"Lights out! Let's go!"

Julian cursed softly under his breath and rolled over. Slowly, the large room grew quiet as TVs were turned off and inmates retired. The squeaking of bedsprings, the coughing, the sneezing and clearing of throats, all died down. The CO hit the light switch and the overhead fluorescents went out, leaving only the emergency exit light over the main double doors, the light from the bathroom, which was kept on all night, and a small lamp on the CO's desk to illuminate the dorm room.

Julian settled in with a sigh, ready to embrace sleep and

the promise of Billy Dee Washington's words, but almost immediately, the fat guy in the cot next to his started snoring. Julian snaked out a foot from under the sheets and nudged the edge of his cot. The fat guy, whose name was Henrique, snorted a couple of times then kept on snoring. Julian kicked his cot again. Henrique said something in Spanish and rolled over. His snoring subsided.

Julian relaxed again after a quick look over at Billy Dee Washington's cot. He appeared to be asleep. Julian closed his eyes and listened to the sound of bedsprings squeaking as inmates settled, the sound of the CO's chair scraping on the wood floor as he sat at his desk. A moment of quiet.

Sliding . . .

Into darkness wet like mud.

Sinking . . .

Under a thick veil, a bubble of blackness.

Sucking him down, slipping sideways falling and suddenly—

Light!

He was in a room. In many ways it was the same room he had just come from, the same room in which his body slept. In far too many other ways to count, it was a different room. Mostly, it was the *feeling* of the room; the atmosphere created by the flickering light which cast such grotesque, gigantic shadows, as if a giant candle were lit somewhere nearby.

Julian took a tentative step forward. The light danced; the scene shifted and suddenly he was in a chair, leather sticking to his naked flesh. There was a chair opposite him in which sat the man he'd met earlier during Billy Dee's hypnotic oratory. He sat cross-legged, his long hair very dark and shiny in the light, his gaucho mustache neatly combed, his eyes smiling. He had happy eyes.

"Welcome back, Julian. I'm glad you decided to join us."

Julian smiled and nodded. This was incredible! This was going to be the best dream he'd ever had; he could *feel* it.

"You don't think this is real? You think this is a dream?" the man in white asked, as if reading Julian's mind.

Julian smirked, something he did when he was embarrassed and on the spot. He also shrugged a lot, which he did now.

The man in white leaned forward. Julian felt compelled to lean forward also until their heads were nearly touching.

"This place is more *real* than *real*! Let me show you."

The doctor put his hand on Julian's knee and the scene shifted again. Now he was no longer sitting, but kneeling. He looked up and gasped. The doctor was standing a few feet away, up to his crotch in naked boys. In his sleep, Julian got out of bed, pulled his shorts and T-shirt off, and walked, trancelike, seemingly led by his erect penis, through the rows of sleeping cons.

"Any fantasy, any perversion can be yours here," the doctor said, smiling. "Come with me, there's someone I want you to meet." He led Julian over by the window where a skinny young man stood over a sleeping boy. The man turned and looked Julian in the eye and suddenly Julian was *inside* the man. He looked down at the naked boy sleeping beneath him, and couldn't believe his eyes, his senses. He became afraid that if he moved too fast, grabbed too greedily, it would all disappear, and he would wake up.

"I told you, sleep is but the doorway," the man in white said.

In the dream, Julian grabbed the boy and forced himself on the tender young flesh. Somnambulating in A dorm, he did the same with the new con, a nineteen-year-old punk three rows over from his bed. Julian reveled in the pleasure of the boy's flesh. It *was* real. Julian almost wept he was so happy

"You can have it all," the doctor said. "I don't ask much in return," he added as Julian continued his violation of the young boy, too busy with the flesh to pay much attention to those last words.

* * *

Jimmy Delilah was unlucky and had been all his life. "Born under a bad sign!" his mother used to sing to him when he was a kid. It had proven true too many times just to be a coincidence. For example, his most recent arrest had come one day after he turned eighteen. Tried as an adult, found guilty of rape of a minor, he'd been sentenced to the prison at New Rome rather than Juvenile Hall in Worcester. At juvey hall he would have been a hitter, a *playa*; at New Rome he was just new meat. He'd only been there a week and a half and already he'd been groped in the bathroom twice. He had no doubts that he would have been raped if it hadn't been for the dorm officer coming in. Jimmy did not recognize this as good luck; it meant only that the inevitable was postponed for a little while. Someone would rape him sooner or later. But God help them when they did.

His first night at New Rome, he had lain on his bed with just his boxers on and had seen the pervs, like vultures eyeing a carcass, checking him out, so now he slept with his pants on, the sheet pulled up to his chin and tucked in as tightly as he could make it around his body, despite the humidity of the summer nights. He knew this was probably a needless precaution; lying in bed in full view of the dorm officer was probably one of the safest spots for him—but it made him feel better and helped him sleep. He never expected to be woken by a terrible stabbing pain in his rectum. In the grogginess of sleep he first thought there was something seriously wrong with him, until he came fully awake and realized he was being sodomized.

He tried to turn over, reaching up with his right arm to knock the con off, but for a small guy, the rapist was surprisingly strong. He grabbed Jimmy's arm and twisted it behind his back while clamping his hand down hard on the back of Jimmy's neck, pushing his face into the pillow, nearly suffocating him.

Jimmy tried to yell; call for help, but all that came out was a muffled grunt. He fought back, squirming, his butt aching with the worst pain imaginable with every thrust into it. The pain was too much, ripping him open. He finally got his face free of the pillow, gasped for air and let out a scream.

Jack Roy was sound asleep when Jimmy Delilah's scream woke him. He still hadn't adjusted to the dorm watch station and had been catnapping regularly. He much preferred to be out in the yard, at his old station, where he could move around, get some air and stay awake. Being inside for a full shift was too boring. He liked to read, but he could only do that for so long before he fell asleep as he had this evening.

Another thing was the quiet. Out in the yard, at least he had the other yard officer to talk to, and the watch commander, who was always coming and going. Inside, there were only sleeping cons. The drone of their snores, the collective prolonged sigh of their breathing, the hum of the exit light behind him, the stuffy air, all combined to create an irresistible sleeping pill. As though weighted with lead, his eyelids had slowly closed despite his struggling last-ditch efforts to keep them open.

Jimmy Delilah's screams pulled him from sleep like a drowning man abruptly pulled from the surf. He was disoriented, confused. For a moment he thought he was in a movie theater with his wife, and he had just dozed, as he often did when she dragged him to see the latest release.

He stood abruptly, knocking his chair to the floor. He was not the only one awakened by Jimmy Delilah's screams. Nearly every con on the floor was awakened by his painful cries. The noise was a catalyst—like the starter bell for a horse race—causing the inmates to bolt into action. Henrique, the large, snoring con in the bed to the left of Julian, let out a high-pitched shriek and leaped upon an elderly con in the bed to his right. The fifty-five-year-old con, in for forging bad checks, had barely woken when Henrique's 365 pounds of flabby flesh crushed him into his mattress and meaty fists began pummeling him.

In the bed to the right of Jimmy Delilah, a Chinese con, Yang, tore his boxers off, stood on his bed, and began jumping up and down, his privates flopping about, while demanding a blowjob in Mandarin Chinese. Another con threw a sneaker at him, bouncing it off his testicles and knocking Yang to the floor where he lay in a fetal position, moaning and cupping his balls.

Jack Roy was unable to move, unable to respond. It was bad enough that the con in bed number seventeen, a short black guy whose name Jack didn't know, was raping the new meat in bed number thirty-eight, but all around them—and the circle was widening like a blast wave from a nuclear explosion—cons were fighting, freaking out, and committing violent sexual acts upon each other. The only one not caught up in the riot was the little bald-headed guy with the big nose; the one they called the Chief. He sat on his bunk, holding something in his hands and mumbling to himself while he calmly watched the commotion around him. Cots were overturned, TVs smashed. As the disruption grew, Jack Roy realized he was going to need help. He picked up his radio while simultaneously hitting the body alarm button on his belt.

Jim Henderson stood before his locker looking at his neck. He was not admiring his captain's bars again, but checking to see if his bruises were showing. He had spent forty-five minutes applying Mary's make-up to his neck to cover the bruises and wanted to make sure it hadn't rubbed off. There was a small make-up smudge on his collar but not enough to notice unless someone was really looking closely.

He closed his locker, put on his captain's hat, and left the barracks, crossing the east yard to Digbee Hall and Inner Control to check the duty rosters and make sure everything was running smoothly for the start of the shift. He couldn't help but make a quick stop in C building to check the bathroom in the hopes the dominatrix and slave had returned, but no luck. Already he was itching with desire, barely able to hide the bulge that wouldn't go away. He had found it impossible to forget the incident with the dominatrix. It was never far from his mind when he was away from the prison, keeping him on the edge of constant arousal, but when he was at work, she dominated his thoughts as much as he wanted her to dominate his flesh. At the prison, his arousal was constant, driving him to distraction. He thought he had been a horny guy before, but he was redefining that description daily.

Everything was fine at the Inner Control command desk. All personnel were on duty and things were running smoothly. Jim gave it all a cursory glance. The fun had gone out of his captain's routine. Since the visitation in the bathroom, he no longer felt the thrill of his command as he used to—all he wanted was another moment with *her*. She was the answer to every prayer and fantasy he'd harbored during these many long years with *normal* Mary.

"Hey Jim! You hear 'bout Thompson?" Lieutenant Pete Seneca, his new second-in-command, asked.

Henderson absent-mindedly shook his head.

"He almost freaked out again while giving the new meat the tour. He thought he saw Darlene Hampton on the third floor here, upstairs." He pointed at the ceiling with his thumb.

Henderson asked, "Who told you that?"

"My cousin. He works the day shift. Actually, he said one of the new recruits claimed he saw a woman up there and Thompson started pumpin' the kid with questions: How old was she? Was she black? You know," he laughed. "Did she look like a complete maniac and was she carrying a gun? Who *else* was he askin' about?"

Jim Henderson leaned forward, interested now. "One of the recruits saw a woman on the third floor, here in Digbee?"

"I guess. They were outside. He saw her in the window. It was probably one of the roofing guys."

"And it *wasn't* Darlene Hampton?"

"I don't know, he—"

"Was she white?" Henderson asked eagerly.

"Uh, I guess . . . ," Pete said weakly, taken aback by Henderson's enthusiasm. "I'm not really s—"

"Was she a blonde?" Henderson interrupted again.

"What?" Pete asked, confused.

"Was she a blonde?" Henderson asked anxiously. "A blonde! Blond hair, you know?"

"Yeah, yeah. I know what blond is," Pete said defensively.

"Was she?" Henderson persisted.

"I don't know!"

Henderson looked up at the ceiling and headed for the elevator, leaving Pete Seneca behind to wonder as much about Henderson's sanity as he had about John Thompson's. In the elevator, Jim Henderson took out his massive key ring that would allow him access to the third and fourth floors of Digbee Hall. The crackling of the radio at the Inner Control desk prevented him from inserting the access key into the panel.

"Inner Control! This is A dorm. I've got a ten thirty-three here. Over."

"Roger that. Over," Seneca said into the console microphone and looked at Henderson. A *ten thirty-three* was the code for officer in need of assistance. Looking at the monitors for A dorm, the problem was obvious. Henderson swore under his breath and put his key ring back on his belt.

"SOP," Henderson shouted at Seneca. "Mobilize the tact team and get the K-9 unit inside, ASAP!"

Running across the yard, Jim Henderson glanced back at the top row of windows in Digbee Hall. They were black squares in the face of the building—empty shadows.

Jimmy Delilah lay on a bed in the Health Services Unit, listening to the nurse out at the receptionist's desk, singing to herself. Jimmy's pillow was wet with hot, angry tears. He hated crying, being weak—but then, he berated himself, he *was* weak. After all, he had not been able to stop puny *Julian* from raping him, had he? Jimmy shuddered at the memory; at the pain he still felt in his rectum; at the humiliation that made him bite the pillow or scream.

More tears came and he wiped them furiously away. "I'm gonna get you, you black bastard," he vowed, fervently. "I'm gonna get you good!"

I can help.

Startled, Jimmy flinched at the voice. He looked around the infirmary room, which contained a dozen beds like his, side by side, all of them empty. He was alone. He sat up and leaned out of the bed to get a view of the nurses' station. The nurse was reading *Cosmopolitan* and softly singing a song he didn't recognize. The CO who'd brought him to the HSU sat just outside the ward, reading a newspaper. Jimmy turned to lie down, and nearly leapt from the bed.

Suddenly standing next to his bed was a doctor. "Who are you?"

"Call me Doctor Stone, Jimmy," he said. His voice, when he said Jimmy's name, conveyed so much sympathy, empathy, and understanding that it seemed to Jimmy the doctor knew all the pain he was feeling.

"Yes, Jimmy, I *can* help," the doctor continued softly. Jimmy looked into his eyes and felt for the first time in his life that here was someone he could trust. Doctor Stone smiled, showing white teeth under the black mustache shrouding his lips.

"How?" Jimmy asked.

"Let me show you," the doctor said and held out his hand.

At the nurses' station, Sheila Donner finished taking a sex IQ test in the latest edition of *Cosmo* and started adding up her score. The sound of someone talking caught her attention and she looked up. She and the CO guarding the patient looked at each other. It was coming from the ward. Sheila pushed her chair back and stood. Quietly, she and the guard stepped over to the open doorway and peered around the edge.

The voice was coming from the only patient in the HSU—the poor guy who'd been sodomized. Sheila watched the guy—a kid, really—talking in his sleep, in *different voices*. She and the CO looked at each other and burst into laughter.

7

Tim Saget was feeling a lot better about his new job, and even about being thrust into his new role as husband and parent-to-be. The prison was nothing like what he had expected. He couldn't get over the fact that walking in the prison yard felt like he was on a college campus. Of course, the front gate, thirty-foot outer fences and the twenty-five-foot inside dividing fence between the east and west yards, the towers, the cons in work denims, were all reminders of the reality of the place, but there was still that campus feeling.

During his first five days there, which included the Fourth of July, he moved from job to job according to the schedule Lieutenant Thompson had given him. The lieutenant had become more reserved, something Tim was glad of. On the first day of shadowing, Tuesday, Tim had the day shift in the woodshop and the greenhouses, spending the morning in one listening to the COs recount the A dorm rape and brawl the night before and the afternoon in the other. On Wednesday, he worked seven-to-three in C building with the officers in the Pedestrian Trap and visiting area. One to four

P.M. daily were the visiting hours during the week. On weekends, inmates could have visitors from one to five on Saturday and ten to four on Sunday. The latter part of Wednesday's shift Tim spent in Outer Control, watching the visitor's area on a monitor and getting a rundown on how to use the switchboard and the radio. Thursday was another three-to-eleven shift, first shadowing the guards in the optical shop, then the COs working the gym and weight room until supper, then he followed the yard officers around until 10:45.

During the first half hour of that shift, spent in the optical shop, Tim became a little unnerved by a con who wouldn't stop staring at him. He had been the focus of brief attention in each of the stations he'd shadowed, especially from the cons, but the guy in the optical shop wouldn't give it a rest; he just kept staring. Every time Tim looked in his direction, the guy, a tall, muscular black man with long cornrowed hair, was looking at him. Several times he appeared to be talking to himself as he stared.

Tim asked the shop officer, a big red-headed bruiser named Jake O'Malley, what the con's problem was, and O'Malley tapped the side of his head with his forefinger. "That's Billy Dee Washington, in for aggravated rape and assault and battery. He's losin' it. I've noticed it the past couple of weeks. He gets worse every day; talks to himself. Sometimes he just stands there, staring into space for minutes on end. I let him alone as long as he's not buggin' anybody. This happens to cons sometimes; they go slowly and quietly bonkers. Stir crazy. Then one day—*boom!*—they explode and someone gets seriously hurt or killed. Usually another con, but sometimes a screw. Sometimes they off themselves."

O'Malley looked over at Washington and shook his head. "That's what I hope happens with this one. I really don't want to mess with him. He spends every afternoon in the weight room working out. Last I heard he could bench press seven hundred pounds."

Tim was glad when that half hour was up, but then the con was in the weight room, too. On Friday he worked three-to-eleven again, this time outside the prison walls, shadowing the K-9 officer for five hours and spending the other three in the minimum-security houses watching TV with the guards stationed there. The K-9 part of the shift was fine, but went by far too quickly compared with the other stations he had worked. At every position he worked, after the routine duty of taking attendance, there wasn't much to do. The K-9 unit, at least, was out of doors, and the care and upkeep of the dogs kept officers busy. He had the sneaking suspicion that the best job in the prison was probably on the K-9 unit.

The unit was situated in an old barn, which sat on a flat ridge to the northwest of the prison proper but within sight of the fences. Next to it were two tall grain silos that were in severe disrepair. Inside the barn, twelve horse stalls and animal pens had been converted to kennels covered with chicken wire and locking wooden gates. There were twelve dogs in the unit, working two per shift. Most of the dogs were German shepherds, but two were Dobermans and one appeared to be the largest Rottweiler Tim had ever seen. The kennel officer he was shadowing, Officer Lou Lefregna, explained that he was a mutt, part Great Dane.

Tim thought the K-9 officers' duties, cleaning the kennels, washing the dogs, patrolling the prison perimeter and all adjacent buildings on the Hill, were great. It was the only station he'd shadowed where he hadn't been eventually bored. Even in the three minimum-security houses, where the COs watched television or movies on the second and third shifts, he had been more bored than he was in the kennels. He was supposed to receive his permanent duty assignment on Saturday, but he'd already been told it would not be on the K-9 unit. Whenever jobs came open with K-9, a lot of COs bid for them. Since all jobs were assigned according to seniority, he knew he'd have to wait a while to get posted there.

Saturday was his first graveyard shift, leading into Sunday, which was the Fourth of July. His station was the Segregated Inmates Unit—the Can. This was the only part of the prison where inmates were kept in locked cells. These were the criminals convicted of serious crimes and who were doing hard time. They were the most dangerous cons in the place; some of them had nothing to lose. Tim had thought working the Can might be a bit more exciting, but he was wrong; it was just as boring as any of the other stations. He worked the first floor, tier one, from 11 P.M. to 3 A.M. with a white-haired CO, Bob Welch, who kept reminding Tim that he was only six months away from full retirement benefits. He had been working days for the past thirty years, mostly at Walpole State Prison before transferring to New Rome. He had begun experiencing insomnia just after his transfer and had put in for the switch to eleven to seven; the pay was better and he was up anyway, so why not make some money?

The second four hours of the shift Tim spent on tier two, on the second floor of the SIU wing, working with CO Dave Stirling. Stirling was the first CO Tim shadowed who seemed actually excited, even grateful, to have him around. He looked haggard, worn, as if he hadn't been sleeping well, and he had a flurry of nervous gestures, like jiggling his leg on the ball of his foot and clicking his fingernails together. He was a talker and barely let Tim get a word in edgewise. He started out by giving Tim a little personal history on each of the cons on the block.

"In Two-A we've got Hiram Pena. He's doing thirty years for killing his girlfriend's baby. Shaken infant syndrome. He was so wasted when it happened, he tried to get rid of the body by stuffing it into a sewer outside her apartment. The cops drove by while he was out there and caught him in the act. He's a bad-ass, though. Real attitude. Likes to brag that he's a baby killer. Likes to brag how he used to beat up on his girlfriend, too. He's a real sadistic bastard.

"In Two-B is Elwin Patoire, one of the meanest guys you'd ever want to meet. He robbed and raped a seventy-year-old woman and *bit* her to death! I kid you not. He bit her nipples clean off and tore open her jugular with his bare teeth. He's a transfer from Walpole where the Crips, one of the black gangs that are in just about *every* prison in the state, had a contract out on him. They sent him here because we're about the only prison in the state that ain't dominated by the Bloods and the Crips. We got the Latin Knights. And Elwin is a member of Aryan Nations, the neo-Nazi gang—skinheads. Elwin is in for life and a day, which means no parole. At no time are you to go into his cell alone. Usually we call in the K-9 unit when we want to roust him and search his cell. He's scared shitless of dogs.

"In Two-C is Marty Miller, a serial rapist who, according to him, accidentally killed his last two victims. Of course, he won't tell you that they were ten- and twelve-year-old nieces of his visiting from California. He's a weasely little scumbag. He probably doesn't need to be in the Can—he's not a threat to anyone over the age of twelve—but if he was in general population he'd be dead already. He was beat up a lot at Green Mountain Prison, out in Springfield, before he was moved here.

"Two-D holds Ivan the Russian; that's what everyone calls him. He's one of the biggest guys you'd ever want to see. His real name is Ivan White. I don't think he's Russian at all, but he seems to like the name—he hasn't killed anyone over it. He's in for kidnapping and child rape. Don't really know much more than that; there wasn't much in his file. Oh, you know about the inmate files, right?"

Tim shrugged. He knew each con had a file, and he knew from the academy that as a CO he had access to them, but beyond that he was unsure what Stirling meant. The lieutenant might have mentioned it; he doubted he could remember everything he'd been told over the past few days.

"In D building—the administrative offices—are all the inmate files. You can go in there and read them. I suggest you do that when you find out where your post is going to be. Go and read about the cons you'll be watching; it might save your life someday.

"So, where was I? Oh yeah! Two-E is another scary guy, Tou Xiong—spelled T-O-U X-I-O-N-G, but pronounced *two-zshung*. He's what they call, *Hmong*-Chinese or something. He killed a family of five out in Orange. Cut them up and fed them to their dog because he said they were starving the animal. He's off the deep end. He's got evil eyes—I hate it when he looks at me. It's like he's visualizing all the nasty things he'd like to do to you. His smile gives me the creeps. Thank God I don't have to deal with him much on this shift.

"Two F, G, and H are the awaiting-action cells and the cooler for general-population prisoners being punished, but we may need to use them soon. We're supposed to get three transfers from Walpole next week. There's a couple cells open down on tier one. That's what we mostly get here, a lot of lifers from other prisons who have caused trouble there or whose lives are in danger from other cons.

"The last two cells on this block, I and J, hold a couple of real scumbags. Lester Dublois and Kevin Gomes. You'd think they were nice, normal guys if you met 'em on the street. Smart. Friendly. Helpful. I remember when I transferred to the Can I had to train on each shift. I was working three-to-eleven on this block and got talking to Dublois. Seemed like a real nice guy. The CO I was working with—he's retired now, Jeff Dolman—reamed me out good afterward. He said, 'Don't you ever talk to any of these scumbags like they were human.' When we got off work, he took me over to D building and showed me the files on these guys.

"Dublois was a teacher in Worcester. They got him on child pornography charges initially, then discovered he had been trafficking in young boys from South America for a group called NAMBLA. Ever hear of them?"

Tim shook his head no.

"It stands for *North American Man-Boy Love Association*. They're a bunch of pervert child molesters who think it's good for boys to be molested by men. And the sickest part of it is these guys are all professionals—doctors, teachers, lawyers, accountants, business executives. Lester would travel to South America two, sometimes three times a year, during school vacations, and pick up boys, mostly homeless, living on the streets and in the slums. He got forged passports for them and brought them back into this country to be *sold* to NAMBLA members. It was a slave trade. He got three consecutive twenty-year sentences for the three kids they finally caught him trying to sneak into the country. He'll be eligible for parole in thirty years. That's another good thing to know. You want to watch out for cons who have no hope of parole or who have a long way to go for parole.

"Next to Lester the Molester, in J cell, is Kevin Gomes. He came here from Worcester County Jail. He's a drug dealer, caught selling Ecstasy and LSD to seventh graders. One of the kids had a bad trip, flipped out, and killed himself. When the cops raided Gomes's home, they found a ton of kiddie porn and a drug lab where he was making his own drugs. When he got caught, kids started coming forward, boys *and* girls, telling how Gomes had drugged and raped them in his apartment. They threw the book at him. Gave him twenty to life."

With barely a pause for air, Stirling then launched into his personal history, starting with his days as a motorhead in high school, leading up to how he got the job with the prison (his father, too, had connections, since he was a former mayor of New Rome) and to his marriage to Ellen and his subsequent misery. It was far too much for Tim. He barely knew the guy, and here he was telling Tim details about his sex life and how gross his wife's body had become. He must have picked up on Tim's discomfort because he suddenly changed topics, practically in midsentence, and stopped talking about his wife's stretch marks, switching to: "This place is haunted, you know."

The statement took Tim by surprise, but he was glad for the change of subject. "No, I didn't know that." Actually, one of the other guards Tim had shadowed had mentioned it, but the guy didn't believe it and hadn't said much more than that.

"Yeah. It used to be a state hospital. You know, an insane asylum. Something happened, a fire or something like that and a bunch of doctors and patients got toasted. They closed it down for a while before converting it into this place." Stirling leaned over his desk and spoke in a quiet voice. "My former partner—she was on tier one, downstairs—something happened to her that freaked her out so bad she had to quit. Then she committed suicide just last week. Right up here on the hill."

Tim had heard about the suicide—and that she was crazy, always had been, according to the COs he'd heard talking about her.

"I'm not kidding! And she's not the only one. There was another woman guard over in A dorm who freaked out, too, and she's *disappeared!* Left her car in the parking lot and just took off. The powers that be are trying to keep it quiet; we were told not to talk about it, but it's just too damn weird." He paused a moment and quietly added, "I've seen some weird shit, too." He became unexpectedly silent.

Tim waited for him to go on, but Stirling became suddenly busy with paperwork on his desk. The bit about the place being haunted and his partner "seeing" something gave Tim an idea.

"Hey! You ever see an old lady up in the fourth-floor windows of this building?" he asked.

The look Dave Stirling shot him was frightening. "What woman?" he asked, sitting up straight so quickly there was a loud pop from his lower back.

Tim told him about the woman he'd seen his first day at the prison. Stirling pumped him for a detailed description in much the same way as Lieutenant Thompson had.

"Why is everyone so curious about this woman?" Tim asked finally in exasperation. "Does she work here, or did I see a ghost?"

After a moment's reflection in which Dave Stirling seemed to make a decision with himself, he said, "Yes, I think you did. I've seen her, too. In *here*."

Tim was puzzled. "What do you mean, 'in here'?"

"On the cell block. Outside that door," he said, pointing to the door to the cells. "My partner told me she heard voices the night she quit. I think it was the old lady. It scared the shit out of her so bad she quit, then last week, like I said, she killed herself."

"Why?" Tim wanted to know. "What's so scary about an old lady? She looked harmless. She waved to me, for Christ's sake."

"*Really*. Well, when *I* saw her she was at that door, a bloody hammer in her hand, covered in blood. *And* she was trying to get in!"

"What?" Tim didn't buy it and his tone and expression said so.

"Don't believe me, but it's true," Dave Stirling claimed. "She looked like a homicidal maniac. Scared the shit outta me, I can tell ya."

Tim thought Stirling actually believed what he was saying, but he still didn't buy it. "You must have been dreaming or something," he said.

The look on Stirling's face told him he had hit upon something.

"You were! You *were* dreaming! You were *asleep* when this happened, *weren't* you!"

"I don't know!" Stirling finally admitted. "At first I thought so, but there've been other things."

"Like what?" Tim asked skeptically.

"You know," Stirling said with a sudden tone of exasperation in his voice, "this is why I didn't want to talk about this."

"You brought it up," Tim said shrugging.

"I know. I know. I don't know what I was thinking. Forget I said anything."

"No!" Tim said quickly. "I don't think you're nuts. Tell me. I won't scoff. Promise."

Dave Stirling looked at Tim doubtfully, then around the empty room cagily. "I . . . I've heard voices a couple of times coming out of the air vent. And I *wasn't* asleep!"

"So? This is a big building. You were probably hearing someone in another area."

"At three in the morning? It sounded like a friggin' party goin' on!"

"Maybe you were picking up someone's radio or television or something. We're on a hill overlooking the city, you know. You could be getting some kind of weird-ass reception up here."

"I don't think the radio or television would call me by name," Stirling said in a dead-calm voice.

"Voices out of the air vent called you by *name*?" Tim asked, incredulously.

"Now you think I'm crazy again!"

"No! No!" Tim said. "Well, maybe a little," he joked, laughing, but Stirling didn't join him. "But seriously. You're telling me you heard a voice coming out of *that*"—he pointed to it—"air vent and it called you by name. Was it a man or a woman?"

"The first time it was her—the old lady. Sometimes it's both men and women's voices."

"What do they . . . want?"

Stirling looked away. "Nothing."

"Nothing? Whattya mean nothing?"

"I mean *nothing*! I leave the room—in a hurry! And don't come back all night! It happened again just last week. I went downstairs and got Bob Welch and brought him up, but it was gone. This office is directly over his. We share the same air vent shaft, but he didn't hear anything downstairs. But Tobi Dowry did. The same thing happened to her. She told me; it's what drove her out. And when she heard shit from the vent, I didn't hear anything up here."

Stirling looked genuinely scared and Tim couldn't help but feel sorry for him.

"Actually, I don't stay alone in here too much if I can help it. I sit down at the other end of the tier in the day chair by the stairs, or I go downstairs to talk to Bob. The watch commander comes by at least twice a night, too. It used to be John Thompson, who was a good egg, but he got demoted from captain to lieutenant when he freaked out after Darlene Hampton disappeared. Everyone says they were having an affair. I don't know. But the new guy, Henderson, is a dickhead. He's by-the-book. I think I could have talked to Captain Thompson about this and he would have helped me, but Henderson, he'd just write up a psych referral on me." Stirling looked at the window in the door and added, "Speak of the devil."

Tim looked up just as the door opened and a tall officer came in.

"Good evening, men," the watch commander said, entering the room.

Tim stood and saluted, and the commander returned his salute, then shook his hand. Dave Stirling remained seated. The watch commander frowned at him.

"I'm Captain Henderson, the eleven-to-seven watch commander."

"Tim Saget, sir."

"It looks like we're going to be working together, Saget. I have your shift assignment. You're going to be in A dorm, eleven to seven, on my watch, starting tomorrow. Your days off are Tuesdays and Wednesdays. You'll shadow Jack Roy tomorrow night and Monday, then start on your own after your days off on Thursday. You'll like A dorm. It's pretty quiet."

Dave Stirling snickered. "Except when they're having a riot."

Henderson shot Stirling a warning glance. "Officer Stirling is referring to a minor incident—hardly a riot—that happened earlier in the week, which you may have heard about. I'm sure the details of it have been grossly exaggerated, like every other bit of gossip around here." Captain Henderson smiled at Tim. "You'll soon learn that anything and everything is grist for the gossip mill in this place. Believe me, there is no problem with A dorm."

Tim couldn't help but notice Stirling rolling his eyes at that, but Henderson either didn't see or was ignoring him.

"I'll see you in A dorm, second floor, tomorrow night," Henderson said to him. "Good to have you on board."

He left. As soon as he was gone, Dave Stirling farted. "That's what I think of that!"

"What's wrong with A dorm?" Tim asked.

"You mean besides the fact that there have been like three near-riots there since May? Or that Darlene Hampton was working there when she was raped, either by one of the cons in her dorm or one of the guards? I don't know which is worse. I wasn't working the night she disappeared, but I heard she tried to kill a couple of officers in A dorm that night. Give me the Can any day. There's something fucked up going on over in A dorm."

Tim mused over Stirling's words. Both men lapsed into silence and remained so for the rest of the night.

In the stairwell to tier two in the Can, Jim Henderson looked at his watch and wondered if he had enough time to check out the top two floors of Digbee Hall. It was 5:30 A.M. and everything was quiet, not like every other night this week. It seemed there had been some minor emergency on each shift lately, from the rape in A dorm last Sunday to a flood in the kitchen on Monday, a power outage on Tuesday, a brush fire outside the north fence on Wednesday. Thursday and Friday saw three of his officers out sick and he had to scramble to get coverage. He had ended up working Inner Control by himself, stuck in Digbee Hall all night.

Deciding it was now or never, Henderson turned around and went up the stairs, heading for the third floor.

John Thompson went through the main gate with barely a nod and wave at the surveillance camera and waited impatiently to be buzzed in. He hurried through the officer's entrance in C building, which avoided the Pedestrian Trap, and ran the length of the first floor and the rear stairs to the short tunnel that would take him to the officer's barracks. He quickly dressed and strapped on his belt, making sure his flashlight was charged. He crossed back over to C building and checked in at Outer Control, where he also got a radio. He had a legitimate reason for being there—to check on the new guys who were shadowing on the eleven-to-seven shift—but his real reason was to check out the third and fourth floors of Digbee Hall.

He was going to have to be very careful how he did that, especially with Henderson now the watch commander. John had to make sure he did everything by the book, but he thought he could get up to the top of Digbee now. The watch commander was supposed to be making rounds of the dorms at this time, preparing for the upcoming 6:00 A.M. head count before the 7:00 A.M. breakfast movement, so Henderson should be over in the west yard, and John figured he had at least thirty minutes to check things out before Henderson got back to Inner Control.

John strode purposefully along the walkway from C building to Digbee Hall. He sprinted up the steps and through the doors. Just as expected, Pete Seneca was working the Inner Control command station with one of the rookies. Jim Henderson was nowhere to be seen.

"Captain Thompson!" Seneca hailed him, smiling.

"Better not let Henderson hear you call me captain; he'll probably write you up. I'm just a lowly lieutenant now, like yourself."

"Aw! You just missed his majesty," Seneca replied and laughed, but then turned serious. "Please tell me you are coming back as watch commander."

"I wish I could," John said. "No. I'm here to check on the rookies, like Mr. Torres there." The recruit nodded.

"He's doin' fine," Seneca reported. "He just got his work assignment—three-to-eleven in A dorm."

"What?" John was puzzled; *he* was supposed to hand out the work assignments tonight. "How do you know that?"

"King Henderson just gave it to him, about fifteen minutes before you arrived."

John swallowed hard and tried to suppress his rage. Henderson *knew* that handing out the rookies' assignments was *his* job. He'd usurped him deliberately. *Forget it,* he told himself. It wasn't important. Let Henderson play his little power games; John had bigger fish to fry—namely, proving to himself and Bill Capello that he was not crazy and Darlene Hampton was still in the prison somewhere.

"I'm going over to the Can to check on another rookie over there," John told Seneca and headed down the corridor. "I'll be moving around a lot, so radio me if you need me," he called back. At the end of the hall he unlocked and went through the heavy metal fire door, which led to the short hallway to the wing of Digbee Hall that held the Segregated Inmates Unit. Another double steel door waited at the other end, which led to tier one and the stairs. He stopped by the guards' office on tier one and spoke briefly to Bob Welch, who had taken the position after Tobi Dowry quit.

"You see the rookie, Saget, yet?" John asked.

Welch nodded.

"Everything okay?"

"Yep," Welch replied. "He's upstairs now, with Stirling."

"Okay, thanks." John went through the exit door to the stairwell and started up quietly. The stairs would take him all the way up to the third and fourth floors of Digbee. He just had to be quiet and not attract the attention of Stirling and Saget when he went by tier two. At the second-floor landing he stopped. He was breathing hard. He fished out his inhaler, took a blast and another and breathed deeply. To his right were the stairs leading up to the third and fourth floors. They were in shadows, leading up into total blackness, but even in the dim light John could see footprints in the dust on the floor before him. He chanced his flashlight, shining the beam on the stairs. The footprints led up, and were fresh. Someone had recently gone this way.

I knew it! John thought. "Someone's been up here," he mused, whispering. He clicked off his light, but kept it in his left hand, ready to use. He put his inhaler away and turned his radio off before unclipping and holding his baton. Slowly, he started up the stairs.

Jim Henderson moved quietly along the third-floor corridor, just above and to the right of John Thompson. There wasn't much to see. The third floor was a maze of empty cubicle-type offices whose off-white corkboard walls did not reach to the ceiling. The cubicles stretched the length of the building on both sides with a narrow hallway between. A door at the end where John Thompson was ascending led to the section over tier two of the Can where the offices were more spacious and had whole, solid walls. Most of the rooms were filled with boxes, files, and records from the prison's past seventeen years of operation, since its opening in 1986. Even though computer records and files were now in use, state law required that the prison system keep hard-copy files on inmates incarcerated before 1995 for twenty years after the inmate was released. After that, paper files could be destroyed. Jim remembered Superintendent Capello had mentioned at the last captain's meeting the need to organize a work crew to go through and clean out all the twenty-year-old files so that the third floor of Digbee could be renovated like the fourth floor and used for much-needed dorm space. The prison was overcrowded by at least 300 inmates. A lot of crowding would be relieved when the prison made better use of Digbee Hall. The fourth floor was scheduled to open sometime in January.

There was no sign that anyone had been up there recently. Dust lay thick on everything. There was certainly no sign of the blond dominatrix and her sex slave. He didn't know what he had been thinking, what he had been hoping. Of course she wasn't up there—*she wasn't real!* None of it was real—it had been a dream, a hallucination, a figment of his over-sexed imagination.

He could accept that and just forget it—he longed to do so—but for the fact that it had seemed *so damn real!* Why was he so obsessed with it? Why couldn't he just let it go? He didn't know, really, except to say that it had been the most exciting, satisfying, and *real* sexual experience he'd ever had.

He reached the end of the corridor and put his key in the lock of the exit door leading to the stairs at the far end of the building. At that precise moment, at the opposite end of the hallway, John Thompson was unlocking the opposite door and stepping onto the third floor just as Jim Henderson was leaving it. In the stairwell, Henderson hesitated, looking up into the darkness leading to the fourth floor. Was there really any point in checking up there? With workers up there every day he didn't think so, but he found himself mounting the stairs anyway, an excited little lump of anticipation swelling in his chest and loins despite his knowledge that hope was futile.

Below Jim Henderson, on the third floor, John Thompson was also excited and hopeful, but he thought he had good reason to be. The footprints all along the third-floor corridor were *fresh.* He was certain now that he had been right—Darlene Hampton was up here somewhere, most likely being held against her will. There had to be a phone up here that wasn't listed on the system, and that's how she had called him. One thing was certain, whoever was keeping her was going to be sorry.

The prints led straight along the corridor with minor deviations toward each office door along the way, as if whoever had been there had checked each room, on both sides, as they walked down the hallway. John followed the prints, looking into each office, trying to take in every detail, trying to find some indication that Darlene Hampton was near, or had been there, but he found nothing, just shoeprints in the floor dust.

He knelt, turned on his flashlight, and examined the prints more closely. He flashed the light behind him and looked over his shoulder at the prints he had made—the two were exactly the same type, but slightly different sizes. That meant that the guy who was keeping Darlene wore the exact same type of shoe Thompson—and every other corrections officer in the prison—wore. It was the standard-issue black military combat boot.

A creaking sound overhead made John look up quickly. Someone was on the fourth floor, walking around. John turned off his light and hurried back to the exit door and up the stairs. As carefully and quietly as possible, he slid his key into the door lock, twisted it, and pushed the door open just enough to put his eye to the crack and scan the floor. Unlike the third floor, the fourth was a vast open space, much like the sleeping areas in the dorms. It smelled of fresh paint and polyurethane.

There!

A dark silhouette was moving through the shadows in the middle of the hall, looking for something—*or someone!*

Darlene must have escaped! John Thompson thought.

The dark figure moved closer to the windows, and light from one of the tower floodlights, spilled in, illuminating . . . Jim Henderson?

What the hell is he doing here? John wondered, and quick on its heels: *Is he the one holding Darlene captive?* Henderson went past, not more than ten feet away. The door, which John had not dared to risk opening more than a crack, hid Henderson as he went by. A moment later he reemerged. He looked around, shook his head, and went back through the hall to the exit door at the other end. He unlocked the door, took a last look around, and left the floor.

Quickly, John Thompson opened the door and went through the hall, checking out every corner and spot where he'd seen Henderson. He had been hoping (expecting) to find Darlene Hampton (or at least some trace of her) there, but he found nothing. There were no clues, no indication of why Jim Henderson had been up there or what he was looking for, but somehow—John Thompson was *sure* of it—he had something to do with Darlene Hampton's disappearance.

That's it! I'm done! It's over! It was nothing but a dream, or . . . or a weird hallucination! Whatever it was, it's over! O-V-E-R—over!

Jim Henderson mentally repeated those words as if they were his mantra. He descended the stairs at the south end of Digbee Hall, passing the observation deck for the inmates' day room. At the first floor, he quietly unlocked the door and slipped through, after making sure no one was around. He checked his watch—his shift was almost done. He just had to check prisoner tallies at Inner Control, sign off on them, and he was finished.

Walking along the first-floor corridor that ran from Inner Control to the inmates' day room/library, Jim Henderson felt a growing sense of relief. He had proven to himself that the incident in the bathroom had been a dream, or a hallucination brought on by who knows what. He had proven she wasn't real; that's all that mattered. Now he could go on. Yes, the more he thought about it the better he felt.

"Hey! Jim! Did you run into Thompson?" Pete Seneca asked, smirking. Next to him, Alex Torres, the recruit shadowing the position, gave Seneca a look of disgust. The kid said something soundlessly that looked to Jim to be: *Asshole!*

Henderson shook his head by way of answer. He had known Thompson would be observing the new officers tonight—it was the reason he had made sure to intercept the job postings for the new guys and hand them out. Just sending his former superior a little message—a little *dig*. Henderson smiled to himself as he checked the end of the shift tally. He was about to leave and head for the COs' barracks when he noticed a brown envelope in the interoffice mail tray on Seneca's desk.

"What's that?" he asked.

Seneca pushed his chair over and snatched up the envelope. "Dunno. We been here all shift and no one came in. It must have been there since we came on duty and we just didn't notice it, I guess." He read the front of the envelope. "It's addressed to you." He tossed it to his watch commander.

Henderson frowned. He knew that the tray had been empty at the start of the shift; checking that tray was part of his regular routine, and he was as anal about his work routine as he was about his sex. He turned the envelope over and looked at it. *Captain Henderson* was written in a tight scrawl in green ink on the envelope. Jim caught a faint scent of perfume and lifted the brown paper to his nose. *He knew that smell.* The aroma immediately brought to his mind's eye the image of the blond dominatrix and her kneeling slave. He tore open the envelope, releasing a stronger whiff of scent from within, and pulled out the notepaper, crumpling it badly in his haste.

I saw you on the third floor. You just missed me. Meet me there when you get off your shift this morning.

It was signed: *Madame Q.*

John Thompson hurried down the stairs, following Henderson as quietly as he could. He stopped and listened when he heard Henderson reach the bottom and unlock the first-floor fire door. When he was certain Henderson was no longer in the stairwell, he ran the rest of the way down, nearly stumbling and falling at the bottom. He leaned against the fire door, catching his wheezing breath and counting to sixty before he opened the door and stuck his head out to check the corridor. It was clear. He slid through, letting the door click closed, then headed for Inner Control.

Henderson wasn't there. Pete Seneca was just leaving, having turned the Inner Control Command Console over to the day shift relief officer.

"Where's Jim?" John called to Pete before he could walk out the door.

"Just left," Seneca tossed back. Thompson followed him out of Digbee Hall and down the steps, running past the befuddled Seneca on the sidewalk. He ran all the way to the barracks and up the two flights of stairs to the locker room, reaching it out of breath. Henderson was not there either, and no one had seen him.

John looked at his watch. It was 7:05. Henderson wasn't the type to run off right after his shift was up. Usually he showered and shaved, and often he'd sit in the watch commander's office—which was shared by all shift commanders—and write up reports on the guys on his command. So why was he rushing off so early?

It was more weight added to the growing sense John Thompson had that Jim Henderson had something to do with Darlene Hampton's disappearance.

At the moment that John Thompson was adding another tally to his list of Jim Henderson's guilt, Henderson was back on the third floor of Digbee Hall. He was trembling with anticipation and excitement. A part of him feverishly tried to find some explanation, while another couldn't stop fantasizing over what he hoped was about to happen.

Who was this *Madame Q*?

The only plausible answer he could come up with was that she worked at the prison. She had to. It was the only thing that made sense. He thought he knew everyone who worked there, but maybe she was a new secretary in administration during the day—if she was a new guard, he would have known her and recognized her.

Confounded in his attempts to rationally explain it, he

gave up as the scent of Madame Q—the same scent that permeated her letter—wafted up to him, and the back of his neck began to tingle.

"Hello?" he called in a quiet voice. It sounded like a gunshot, and added to the growing atmosphere of trepidation.

"Shhh! In here," came the whispered reply.

Henderson turned. The voice had come from one of the offices at the SIU end of the floor, which he'd just passed. The door was closed. There was a flickering light visible beneath the bottom edge of the door. His breath held nervously in check, Jim Henderson put one hand on the door—it felt strangely hot—and the other on the knob, which turned in his hand of its own volition.

The door opened.

The room before him was filled with wavering shadows, larger than life, dancing over the walls and leaping to the ceiling. They distracted him for a moment, until he heard *her* voice again.

"At last!" she breathed. "I'm so glad you could make it."

Henderson looked around, and there she was, standing with her legs apart, hands on hips, whip wrapped around naked thigh and trailing to her jackbooted feet where her sex slave cowered, timidly licking the sides of those knee-high black leather stiletto-heeled turn-ons. The slave cast a shy, furtive, yet sexually *hungry* glance at Jim, licking her lips. She received a knee to her head for it.

Henderson let out a gasp of delight. She was even more magnificent than he remembered. Her long platinum blond hair cascaded around her neck and over her shoulders, falling to the tops of her massive breasts jutting out like two torpedoes in their firmness. Her leather thong was so tight it creased the skin of her abdomen and cut into her wide hips. He could see wiry wisps of black hair curling around the edges of the triangular piece of leather covering her privates. To a man who had for too long held his desires in check, who for too long had been a prisoner of his wife's sexual mundanity, she was a vision of heaven.

Henderson gave out a soft moan. His erection was so large it hurt. It felt like it could literally explode.

Madame Q looked at the bulging front of his pants and asked coyly, "Are you glad to see me or is that your baton in your pocket?" She laughed a sexy, throaty laugh.

Henderson tried to speak. His mouth opened, closed, opened again, but no words came forth.

"What's the matter? *Pussy* got your tongue?" Madame Q asked. She put one booted foot on her kneeling slave's back and spread her legs, exposing the thin strap of leather thong cutting through her groin, separating her labia into two swollen purple lips before disappearing up the crack of her ass.

Time seemed to shift to another speed at that moment for Jim Henderson. He stared with wonder and lust at so much moist flesh—within the blink of an eye he was on his knees in front of that thin strap of leather; that incredible flesh mere inches from his face.

"You're a cruel man," Madame Q said softly. "And cruel men must be dealt with in cruel ways." She grabbed the back of his head, filling her hand with a fistful of his hair, and pulled his face closer. But just as he was about to snake out his tongue and delve into the nether regions surrounding that delicious strap of leather, she pulled his head back and wrapped her whip around his neck with a quick flick of her wrist.

"Not so fast, *Captain*!"

Henderson shivered with the thrill of hearing her use that word when addressing him. The whip tightened in exquisite slow motion. He could feel every millimeter of its coarse surface as it slid over his skin, scraping up cells, exposing epidermal capillaries, bringing drops of blood, which trickled down to his collarbone where they puddled in the hollow of his clavicle.

He realized he was suddenly naked.

He felt a warm sucking mouth envelop his erection; it was like sliding into a hot mud bath. He breathed in sharply, the leather whip tightened around his neck; every second of air rushing through his clenched teeth, down his throat, and into his lungs was stretched out until it became a minute, then an hour. His breathing became windstorms, spilling and falling over each other as they tumbled in and out of his lungs.

Madame Q was bending over—time stretched—he was amid a pile of bodies, flesh in his mouth, mouths on his flesh, *everywhere,* flesh *in* his flesh. He moaned with pleasure and the moan took minutes, days, years. One moment he was whipping a naked, bloody woman who begged for more, and the next he was rubbing his face against Madame Q's breasts as she persistently tightened the noose.

John Thompson was walking through the COs' parking lot on the way to his car when he noticed Jim Henderson's blue Cadillac parked in its usual spot in the corner of the lot away from the pine trees and their falling sap. He stopped and stared at the car, then back at the prison.

That bastard's off duty, he thought, *and he's still in the facility!* John had a real good idea *where.* He turned and ran back to the front gate, through the COs' entrance into the barracks and out the other side, heading for Digbee Hall. There was a lot of activity around the Inner Control command desk, with construction workers going in and out and using the elevator to go up to the fourth floor, which allowed him to slip by as if he were on his way to the inmate day room. At the end of the corridor, he gave a quick look around before pulling out his keys and swiftly unlocking the fire door.

He took the stairs two at a time and stopped to catch his breath and take a gulp from his inhaler at the second-floor landing. He knelt, inspecting the stairs leading up to the third floor. There was a new set of footprints in addition to the ones from last night disturbing the dust on the stairs. It was obvious someone had just come this way, and John was pretty sure it hadn't been one of the workers. Preferring the elevator, they *never* walked up or down the stairs from the fourth floor. To John Thompson, that meant only one person could have made those prints.

"I've got you now, you rat bastard," he muttered and headed up the stairs.

Jim Henderson was in ecstasy. Every nerve ending in his body was tingling and buzzing with either pain or pleasure until the two began to merge into one orgasmic vibration that literally had him trembling under its force. His breath squeaked laboriously in and out of his lungs, rasping against the choking constriction of the leather whip wound around his throat. His face was a dark red, bordering on purple; his tongue protruded from between his slightly parted lips. His eyes were rolling, ready to disappear into his head, leaving only the whites showing.

Madame Q grabbed his jaw firmly in her left hand and squeezed his face while letting up on the whip-noose. Slowly, Henderson returned from a place where he was bathing with a host of naked beauties who couldn't keep their sucking mouths off his flesh.

"Take this," Madame Q whispered into Henderson's ear. She placed a slim book in his hand and closed his fingers around it before jerking the whip tighter than it had been, cutting off all air and making his face erupt with dark blotches of purple. His eyes bulged from their sockets and his tongue protruded from his mouth.

The last thing Jim Henderson felt, as the leather of the whip cut into the skin of his throat and the teeth of Madame Q's slave bit into the flesh of his erection, was an orgasm better than any he'd ever experienced.

He died ejaculating.

*   *   *

John Thompson stopped outside the third-floor fire door and listened. Above, on the fourth floor, he could hear the work crews starting their day. Henderson wouldn't be up there. Carefully, quietly, John opened the door, saw no one in the hallway and slipped through, closing the door soundlessly behind him. The sounds from above were immediately muffled, except for the occasional thump on the ceiling as a piece of equipment was placed or dropped. He saw no indication beyond the fresh footprints in the floor dust that anyone might be up there. Thompson squatted, looking at the footprints, and followed them with his eyes. They led down to one of the larger offices over the segregated unit.

Cautiously, head held slightly to the left, listening, John Thompson walked to the office. A creaking sound froze him before the door, breath held, listening. There it was again, softer, and again a moment after that. In fact, the sound was repeating and had a certain rhythm to it. At first Thompson thought it was the creak of approaching footsteps—perhaps someone attempting to sneak up on him. But as he listened and looked around, seeing no one, he realized the sound was too regular, too rhythmic for that. He'd heard this sound before; it was not an uncommon one. It sounded like—the sound a child's rope swing would make as it swung back and forth, straining under the weight of a kid.

The sound was coming from behind the door in front of him, open just a crack. He leaned forward and pushed it with his outstretched finger. The door silently swung open. John Thompson blinked, rubbed his eyes, and blinked again. He squinted; what he was looking at was not at first believable to him. It took several moments to sink in that he was staring at a naked Jim Henderson—a naked *dead* Jim Henderson, on his knees, a leather belt tied around his neck, the other, buckle end snagged on a coat hook on the wall. Henderson's face was hideous. His eyes bulged from dark purple sockets nearly as far as his bloated tongue from his swollen purple lips. His right hand still held his erect penis, from which hung a long strand of milky fluid stretching all the way to the floor. In his left hand, Henderson held what appeared to be a book. He was on his knees, leaning forward, the weight of his body keeping the belt taut in the air behind him. His entire body was swaying slightly, as if someone had just bumped it, causing the leather belt to produce the soft creaking John had heard.

The full weight of what he was looking at finally hit John.

"Holy shit!" he gasped and found no air. He fumbled out his inhaler and recovered the breath shock had stolen. He stepped into the room, taking in Henderson's clothes strewn about the floor, and focused on the book in the dead man's hand. It was a small, slim book, like a daybook used for keeping appointments. From the look of things, John assumed Henderson had committed suicide. If that were true, it seemed to John that the book might contain a suicide note, maybe even a *confession,* as to what he had done with Darlene Hampton.

Gingerly, John reached out and took the corner of the book between his thumb and forefinger, being careful not to touch Henderson's dead digits. The book slid from Henderson's hand, but not before the action caused his body to sway even more. John Thompson jumped back, watching with fascinated horror.

I'd better radio Inner Control, John thought, but first he had to look in the book. It had a black simulated-leather cover and was less than an inch thick. The edges of the paper were embossed in gold. He opened the cover and read what was scrawled on the first page:

If this book is found, please return to:
Dr. Jason Stone
New Rome State Mental Hospital
Room 313, Digbee Hall
New Rome, MA 01420

John looked at the door to the office—he was in room 313.

*   *   *

Jim Henderson opened his eyes and let out a long, slow breath. With it came a soft moan of complete and utter satisfaction. He couldn't believe it. That had been the best orgasm he had *ever* had. He had thought he would never stop coming. He had achieved something he had previously thought only women could have—*multiple orgasms*. In the warm afterglow of so much intense pleasure, he realized that for nearly all of his life he had been seeking sexual satisfaction of this kind, of this intensity. He felt like a man who has been stranded in the desert, searching for water, who suddenly falls into a pool of the clearest, cleanest, coolest, sweetest water on Earth.

Dazed and dizzy with delight, Jim Henderson looked around vaguely, like a dreamer suddenly awakened. He wasn't sure where he was or what time it was, and he didn't particularly care. None of that mattered very much anymore, and he wasn't sure why. He swallowed hard. His throat hurt and he had a camel's thirst. He got off his knees, stood, and looked around for something to drink. There was nothing in the small office other than boxes stacked in the corner near the door.

Where is Madame Q? he wondered. He turned and nearly fell down in shock.

What the hell is going on here?

His euphoric dizziness was replaced with a wave of nausea so strong it blurred his vision. He felt as though he might faint.

Is that . . . me?

It *looked* like him, except that he seemed to be . . . *dead.*

"That's not me," he said softly. He didn't feel dead. It had to be a joke.

"That's not me," he repeated, as if doing so would make it true. "That's *not me!*"

"Oh, but it is, lover."

Jim Henderson whirled around. Madame Q was walking toward him *through the office wall.* In fact, everything around him, including his dead body, was fading, becoming transparent. A vast, poorly lit space stretched out around him, giving him the disconcerting feeling that he was moving, gliding away from the real world as it slowly disappeared before him. His last glimpse of mortal reality was that of John Thompson pushing open the office door and looking aghast at his dead body. A moment later, John Thompson, the office, Digbee Hall, and the prison itself were all gone, melted away, replaced by this gloomy, cavernous place.

Frightened, Henderson turned to Madame Q. "What's happening?"

"It's okay," she said, smiling. "There's someone I want you to meet." From behind her stepped a tall man dressed all in white. Henderson recognized him but could not place exactly where he knew him.

"Lover," Madame Q said to Jim, "This is Doctor Stone."

Stone. Now Henderson remembered. *Dr. Jason Stone.* He was in the picture hanging in the Health Services Unit. This was the guy Thompson had claimed to see on A dorm that night.

"You . . . you're a doctor?" Henderson asked.

"That's right," replied the man, smiling.

"Am I dead, Doc? Am I . . . dead?"

The doctor's smile broadened. "Let's say evolved, shall we? *Dead* is such a disturbing, misleading word."

"I'm evolved?" Henderson asked, noticing there were throngs of people milling about in the gloom around him, coming closer. As they came into the light, he could see that they were all naked.

"Oh yes," the doctor said. Around him the naked crowd sidled closer, touching and stroking each other and eyeing Jim Henderson with lust and desire.

Watching them, Jim felt himself getting erect again. "Is this Heaven?"

"Heaven?" Dr. Jason Stone chuckled. "No, not quite."

Tim Saget was tired; the eleven-to-seven shift didn't agree with him. He couldn't believe he had been assigned to it full time. He walked into the apartment at 7:30 A.M., just as Millie was getting out of the shower. He was feeling a little frisky and tried to coax her into bed but—big surprise—she refused; she was going to breakfast and the Fourth of July parade with her mother and she was late. She reminded him that her parents' cookout was at 3:00 just so he could be there—so he'd better be there. She went on about how her family *always* had their Fourth of July cookout at noon, but her mother had insisted on changing it so Tim could get his rest and still go. Millie had only reminded him of this at every opportunity the past few days, so when she started in again now, he just tuned her out until she left.

After she was gone, Tim made toast for himself and washed it down with orange juice. He went to bed, setting the alarm clock for 2:30. Though he was tired, he couldn't get to sleep. He tossed and turned until nine, then gave up and turned on the TV, flipping through the Sunday morning fare of news programs and infomercials. He settled on ESPN, which was showing an Australian rules football game.

With the television on, acting as a kind of white noise, Tim eventually slipped into a fitful sleep where his dreams were vague but left him with an intense feeling of edginess, like a kid who's done wrong; he knows he is going to be punished for it, and is waiting for the hammer to fall. At one point Tim woke in a cold sweat and didn't know why. The day had turned into a scorcher and the room had become quite warm. He flipped the switch for the ceiling fan and lay back, staring blankly at the TV—a sports talk show—and almost immediately fell asleep again, sliding into a dream where he thought he was still awake, lying in bed, watching television. A commercial came on in which an attractive young woman was running along what looked like a dank, dark alleyway. Everything in the commercial was black and white except for a blood-red silk kerchief the woman wore over her head, tied under her chin. At first, Tim thought it was one of those weird perfume commercials, like for *Obsession,* that try to be so artsy-fartsy and which make no sense.

The woman, looking frightened and bewildered, ran toward the camera until her face was in a tight close-up, framed in the television screen.

"Tim!" she said.

In the dream, Tim sat up on the bed. "What?" he said to the screen as if it were a normal, everyday occurrence to have a conversation with an actor on the television.

"Don't go back there," the woman on the screen said.

"Where?" Tim said aloud in his sleep. The sound of his own voice woke him and he sat up, startled to realize he had been asleep and dreaming. He looked at the television, half expecting to see the woman with the red scarf staring back at him, but there was a soccer game on.

"*That* was fucking *weird*," he muttered sitting up.

Don't go back there, she'd said.

Tim couldn't help feeling she was talking about the prison.

PART TWO

8

When John Thompson slipped the journal of Doctor Jason Stone into his pocket, he had every intention of looking at it as soon as possible. He didn't know that would translate into several months. Within minutes of his radio call, the fourth floor was swarming with corrections officers, within an hour it was overrun with deputies from the county sheriff's department, local New Rome cops, and detectives from the state police CSI unit. The prison population was put into lockdown for forty-eight hours. During the first week or so, bigwigs from the Department of Corrections showed up in droves. John was interviewed more than two dozen times by various local police detectives, deputies from the DOC and the county sheriff's department, committees from the DOC, fact-finding politicians from legislative committees, the media—some all the way from Boston—and the state police investigators, not to mention the numerous meetings with Superintendent Capello.

To John's delight, the official verdict handed down in late September was that Jim Henderson appeared to be connected to the disappearance of Darlene Hampton and had

committed suicide when he had become aware that John
Thompson was onto him. Bill Capello reinstated John as full
captain and sole commander of the eleven-to-seven watch.
Jim Henderson's wife and brothers protested the official verdict, but they were quickly silenced by the revelation that
investigators had discovered an abundant amount of pornographic material, mainly dealing with sadomasochism, bond-
age, and fetishes, that Jim Henderson had in his locker at
work and in his computer files at home. Three days after the
DOC released its findings, something happened that wrapped
it all up for John Thompson and put an end, or so he thought,
to the "Darlene Fiasco."

The K-9 unit's drug-sniffing dog had been called inside
the prison for a search in A dorm, where it was suspected
that several inmates had marijuana and cocaine, but the dogs
found nothing. The K-9 officer was coming down the stairs
outside A dorm when the animal began to sniff the air and
whine, tugging on his leash wildly. The officer tried to keep
the dog on the main walk, but the canine, named Turbo, kept
pulling him toward B dorm, next door. Finally the officer
gave up trying to coerce the dog and let it lead him. Turbo set
off at a lunge, tugging the CO behind him to the narrow
alley that ran between A and B dorms, then around the back
of B to an old abandoned basement door at the rear of the
building.

"Stupid dog! Get the hell away from there! There's nothing there, you idiot," the CO, one Dave Magden, yelled at
the dog. Turbo would not be pulled away. The dog scratched
at the door and tried to dig under it. He whined and barked
furiously in that high, whining, irritating way that dogs do
when they are excited or nervous about something. The dog
grew more and more frantic until Dave Magden stepped
closer to the door to inspect it and something strange happened. The crosspieces of wood that had been nailed over
the door to keep it from being opened suddenly faded and
disappeared. A doorknob appeared where there had been

none, and he noticed the door was slightly ajar when he was *sure* it had just been closed tight. He caught a smell he recognized from his days in Vietnam—the stench of decomposing flesh. He grabbed the knob and pulled on it, but the door was stuck and wouldn't budge either way.

He radioed the watch commander, who came to check out the door and was at a loss to explain how it could be open like that when it had always been boarded up. Dave Magden didn't tell his superior how it had changed right before his eyes—he had done enough LSD as a teenager to think it had been a flashback, and he didn't want to get into that. The captain left the K-9 officer guarding the door and came back a few minutes later with a crowbar, which he used to try and open the door. Swollen with age and disuse, its hinges rusted solid, the door did not want to open easily. They managed to get the edge of the door open another half-inch and then had to walk away, as the ensuing stink was too much for them. The door couldn't be budged any further until the captain sent Dave Magden to get two of the strongest inmates and hammers, saws, and chisels to remove the hinges and get the door off in pieces if necessary.

Billy Dee Washington and a six-foot-five Venezuelan, Ricki Valdez, who was built like a linebacker, were sent. The hinges of the door had too many layers of paint, rust, and grime for the two to be able to remove them. They ended up using a reciprocating saw with which they carved the door into three triangular pieces and removed it. The odor emanating from the stairway leading down into darkness was now so overpowering that Ricki Valdez got one nose full of it and had to walk away, gagging. Billy Dee Washington pulled his T-shirt up over his mouth and backed away, coughing. With the full scent released, Turbo barked and whined more frantically than ever. The watch commander ordered Dave Magden to escort the two prisoners back to the woodshop just as Superintendent Capello arrived on the scene. He and the watch commander held handkerchiefs over their mouths and, with the watch commander leading the way with his flashlight, went down into the dark basement of B building.

Walking back to the woodshop, Billy Dee Washington wondered what could have been down there, making such a stink. A moment later, he found out when he heard the voice of the prison superintendent over the K-9 officer's radio.

"Fifty to Outer Control and Inner Control. Over."

"This is Outer Control, Fifty. Over."

"Inner Control here, Sir. Over."

"Inner Control, I want the entire facility to go to full lockdown immediately. Outer Control, we're going to need the coroner up here again and the state police. We just found Darlene Hampton."

For Tim Saget, the hoopla surrounding Jim Henderson's death and the discovery of Darlene Hampton's corpse remained distant. Working the eleven-to-seven shift was far removed from the investigative activity going on during the day for the past three months, but he'd heard bits and pieces. One night, as he was getting changed in the officers' barracks to go on duty, Dave Stirling informed him that Jim Henderson's death had *not* been a suicide. Stirling's locker was two down from Tim's.

"If he committed suicide, then I'm fucking Madonna," Dave exclaimed as he donned his uniform. "What he did wasn't suicide," Stirling explained. "It was *perversion*. Had to do with all that porn they found. He was getting his rocks off, not killing himself. He just fucked up is all."

Tim had no idea what he was talking about.

"It's called *autoerotic asphyxiation*. A bunch of famous people have croaked that way. You see," Stirling went on, "you put a noose around your neck and tie off the other end loosely, so that it will come undone real easy if you tug on it.

Then you jack off while choking yourself. If you do it right, you have an orgasm just as you're passing out. Supposedly it's an awesome orgasm, too. But when you pass out and fall, the weight of your body is supposed to cause the rope to come undone, so if you tie the rope too tight at either end . . . you end up dead.

"Captain Thompson told me when he found Henderson, Henderson was naked with his belt tied round his neck and come all over the floor around him. When he told me that, I knew it wasn't suicide—*autoerotic asphyxiation*."

"So how do you know so much about this?" Tim asked, eyebrows raised.

"Ha! Ha! Very funny. I know about it 'cause I read."

"Read? What's that?"

Later, when Darlene Hampton was found, the first-floor guard in A dorm told Tim that John Thompson had been the one to find her and that he had flipped out; had to be taken away in an ambulance. But that night, Thompson came by on his usual rounds and he seemed fine. In fact, he was more than fine; he was downright exuberant. After that, Tim didn't put much stock in rumors that came his way.

The first four months of Tim's employment at the prison were a quiet contrast to the events going on at the time. Except for an uncomfortable beginning caused by the huge black con, Billy Dee Washington, Tim found that the worst thing about the prison was working the graveyard shift. He was finding it difficult to adjust to sleeping in the day and staying up all night. Combined with the intense boredom of the job, it was very difficult for him to keep alert at work.

He wasn't happy when he saw that Washington, who had eyeballed him weirdly in the optical shop during Tim's observation shift there, was one of his charges on the second floor of A dorm. As he had the first time they'd seen each other, Washington stared at Tim intently, all the while muttering to himself. Tim was glad that on his first night he had

Jack Roy with him. When he told Roy about what had happened with Washington in the optical shop and that it was happening again, Jack Roy acted immediately.

Roy, who was by no means a small man himself, was a good seven inches shorter than the six-foot-seven Billy Dee Washington, but he went right over, spoke quietly to him, and came back to the command desk.

"You won't have any more problems with him," Roy said to Tim. Tim glanced over at Washington and, sure enough, he had his back to Tim.

"Jake O'Malley in the optical shop told me he thinks the guy is going stir crazy," Tim whispered.

Jack Roy thought about that for a moment and shrugged. "Three-quarters of the guys in here are certifiable," he said with a laugh. "And not all of them are inmates," he added with a knowing nod and wink. "Washington may be nuts, but I don't think he'll bother you anymore."

"Why not?"

"He's got to go before the parole board sometime. He knows he's got to be a model prisoner and not fuck up in any way, especially since he just did time in the Can about six months ago. I just reminded him of that. I told him that if he messed with you we'd both file reports with the parole board and he'll be doing his full time."

"How long is that?" Tim asked.

"I have no idea."

"Do you know what he's in for? I think O'Malley told me but I forgot."

Roy shook his head. "I figure he's a skinner, but this isn't my regular station. I was just fillin' in until they hired someone—you! I'm usually out in the west yard on eleven-to-seven. We've been operating with only one yard officer at night since that crazy bitch, Hampton, disappeared. You know about all that, right?" Roy asked eagerly; he enjoyed telling the story.

Tim shrugged and nodded; he didn't care about Darlene Hampton. He was more worried about six-foot-seven, 260-

pound Billy Dee Washington. "Why did Washington get put in the Can six months ago?" Tim asked.

Jack Roy frowned with disappointment that Tim didn't want to hear all the juicy, dirty details about Darlene Hampton, but then he suddenly brightened. "He got thrown in there '*cuz* of Darlene Hampton," he exclaimed, smiling broadly. "The night she went nuts in here, she incited these guys"—he nodded toward the room full of cons—"to riot. Washington attacked her and ripped her blouse open. When I got up here her boob was hangin' out and everything. She had a nice lookin' rack, too. She was a good lookin' woman. Washington tried to fuck her, but she wasn't anyone to fuck *with*. She was a strong girl. She put Washington on his knees, and he wasn't able to stand straight, or piss regular, for about a week after. The guys in the Can said you could hear him moanin' in his cell when he tried to go. You know, for him, the best thing that could have happened was Darlene Hampton disappearing. Everyone seems to have forgotten about him. If she hadn't, you can bet he'd be facing assault charges, but I don't think they want to drag all that Hampton/Henderson shit up again. He's gonna get away with doin' a month in the Can; that's it. They just want it to go away. It's been too much of a black eye for the prison."

Tim mused over that and Jack Roy grew quiet. He took out a paperback novel while Tim found an issue of *Popular Mechanics* in the desk drawer. It was over a year old, but he didn't care. After his initial talkativeness, Jack Roy settled down to reading for the rest of the shift with intermittent breaks from which he came back smelling like a cigarette. Tim knew there was no smoking anywhere on the prison grounds, as was the rule in Massachusetts for all state property and buildings, but he also knew from Dave Stirling that all the COs who smoked broke the rule, including Superintendent Capello himself. Tim didn't smoke, but he was glad to be able to get outside for some fresh air on his breaks. Jack Roy recommended he use the tunnels if he wanted to get to the kitchen quickly for a snack—the supper crew always left sandwiches for the eleven-to-seven guards—but Tim just nodded and didn't tell Jack that the thought of going into the tunnels left him in a cold sweat. He didn't like tight, dark places—never had.

His first night on duty alone, Tim was extremely nervous. He didn't know what to expect from Billy Dee Washington. He was relieved to find that Jack Roy was right; Washington barely looked at him all night. Tim brought a book with him that first night, but it was one of Mickey Spillane's Mike Hammer novels, less than 200 pages long. He was halfway through it before he even got to work and was finished with it before his lunch break. He ended up playing solitaire for the last four hours of his shift. About halfway through his solitaire marathon, Tim got the feeling of being watched. He immediately looked over toward Billy Dee Washington, but he was in his cot, his back to Tim at the watch desk. Tim turned slowly and saw who it was—the little bald guy with the freakish nose whom everyone called the Chief. His cot was in the middle of the first row, almost directly in front of the CO's watch station. He was lying on his stomach, his chin on his folded hands, and staring at Tim. Tim tried to ignore him but the guy wouldn't let up. Finally, Tim had enough.

"You got a problem, Chief?" Tim asked, trying to put an air of authority into his voice and completely clueless as to whether he pulled it off.

The Chief's head came up like a squirrel's peeping out of a tree hole.

"Me?" he asked in his whiny, nasal voice, his face wide-eyed with feigned innocence.

"Yeah. You could just take a picture, it'd last longer." Tim inwardly winced the moment he uttered the immature response.

The Chief chuckled and sat up, swinging his legs through the head bars of his cot and sitting on his pillow, facing Tim. "Those are pretty strong words, Pilgrim," he said, his voice deepening to a dead-on John Wayne impersonation.

It was so unexpected that Tim laughed, but he immediately remembered what Dave Stirling had said about being too friendly and wondered what the Chief was in for.

As if reading his mind, the Chief said, "I was transferred here a few days before you started, back in June. I noticed you outside Digbee Hall when I was going in D building. I got sent here 'cuzza religion." He paused and Tim couldn't help but look at him questioningly. "It's true," the Chief went on in his whiny twang. "A Jehovah's Witness wanted to kill me. He said I was in league with the Devil. He said I had a black heart." The Chief looked at his chest and laughed softly. "He may be right. I know there's *some* African blood in me somewhere." He looked around the dorm. "Ever hear of the punishment that don't fit the crime?"

Tim shrugged.

"Well, that's me. I got caught with an ounce of marijuana—which was strictly for religious purposes—and I got ten years because I was arrested within two miles of a school. So then they throw me in Belchertown Prison, where they keep the criminally insane, and this guy sees me doing my morning sun-greeting ritual and decides I'm a Satan worshiper. So, to keep me safe, they send me here where there's nothin' but perverts." He shook his head and looked at Tim through narrowed eyes. "I'll bet you've smoked some weed in your time."

Tim couldn't help but smile, though he shrugged noncommittally.

The Chief grew suddenly serious. "I know that all this has happened to me for a reason, but do you know why *you* are here?" he asked in a softer tone than before. He was leaning eagerly against the cot's head bar.

Tim looked at him curiously. What a strange question. Surely he was asking *why* Tim was working in a prison. "No choice," Tim muttered, wary of saying anything about his personal life.

"There's always a choice," the Chief said. "If you think about it, that's the only difference between my incarceration here and yours: You have the choice of walking away. If you did it now, soon, I think you'd maybe save a lot of lives; maybe even your own."

Tim looked keenly at the Chief. Was that a veiled threat?

"I don't think you understand me," the Chief said carefully, perceiving a threat in Tim's face and posture. "I meant, are you aware that you were brought here for a reason; that powers beyond us have arranged that we be here at the same time, and for the same basic reason?"

Tim's expression boldly told the Chief what he thought of that.

"Don't look at me like I'm crazy. There are more things in heaven and earth than are dreamt of—"

"Yeah, yeah," Tim said, getting up. "I've heard that one. You should be getting some sleep. Six A.M. comes early." Tim walked through the cots to the bathroom in the back of the hall. The Chief watched him go and shrugged. He slid under his covers and lay down, muttering, "White people! They think they know everything."

Tim relieved his bladder and washed his hands. He glanced at his wristwatch—only 4:45, still a long way to go until shift's end, and he was out of reading material. *You could always chat with the Chief some more.* He laughed at himself. What a weirdo that guy was. It served Tim right for talking to him, though if what he said about his crime was true, at least he wasn't a pervert. Even so, Tim was glad to see him asleep, or faking it, when he returned to the watch desk.

After that first night, Tim armed himself with better reading material, but he soon realized he was losing the battle of boredom. He began to wish he had been given a swing-shift position; at least then it wouldn't be the same thing night after night. He envied the three-to-eleven guards who got to watch TV until ten o'clock and lights out. He bought several weeks' worth of good diversion time when he bought a GameBoy Advance handheld video game system. Armed with Tetris and a sword-and-sorcery role-playing game called Golden Sun, he was able to while away nearly all of each shift for close to a month.

A problem eventually arose; playing the game for hours on end bothered his eyes and started to give him excruciating headaches. He started restricting himself to playing forty-five minutes at a time and still ended up with a headache by the end of the shift. From then on, each night he was presented with the challenge of trying to occupy his mind enough to stay awake.

It didn't help that he wasn't sleeping well during the day. He was having trouble adjusting going to bed with the sun out. He found himself tossing and turning daily, eventually putting on the tube and lying there like a zombie watching vacuous morning television. He would doze off around noon, sleep fitfully, and awake again two and half hours later, when the school bus pulled up outside and let loose a herd of yelling, chattering children. He usually stayed awake then until Millie got home at five. After dinner, he'd lie down again and would sometimes be able to sleep, but he usually woke feeling more tired than if he hadn't slept at all. More often than not, he tossed and turned until 9:30, then just as he would start to fall asleep, it would be time to get up and get ready for work. His days off were spent trying to catch up on sleep, but after the first couple of weeks, his internal clock was so off that he often slept less on his days off than when he was working.

It took Tim over two months to just *begin* to adjust to the graveyard shift to a point where he didn't feel like he was sleepwalking all the time. Almost comical was the fact that one of the hardest things to adjust to was the *smell* of the dorm at night. With the mix of so many bodies, the odor was so downright rancid at times that it should have kept him awake. Eventually he got used to it and barely noticed it; the lack of sleep, however, was something else. Each shift was still a struggle against boredom and a battle against sleep. By October, it was a battle that Tim Saget was losing. He began to fall asleep every night at work, sometimes dozing while sitting up and waking when his head would slump and his chin would hit his chest or he'd feel like he was falling. The first few nights he dozed, he had a strange dream of a vast cavern filled with people. They were calling to him, but then someone took his hand and he turned to see the woman with the red headscarf leading him away. She was saying something, but he couldn't hear her because of the wind howling in his ears. In another dream, he and the woman were running through a dark passageway, and she turned to face whatever was chasing them and shouted: "No! You cannot steal him this way!" Each time he awoke with the vague feeling he had escaped some injury or, at the very least, some sort of personal disaster.

Tim Saget didn't know it, but during those first four months of his employment, the Chief, whose real name was Tom Laughing Crow, kept a close eye on him. After that first time, the Chief didn't try to speak to the new CO anymore; he knew the time for that would come and the young man would not believe anything he had to tell him until that time. He just hoped it wouldn't be too late. So he watched and waited and became more convinced with each passing day that he was right about the prison.

Tim Saget wasn't the only one Chief Tom Laughing Crow kept an eye on. Billy Dee Washington also earned that honor, but for a different reason. From the first moment he had laid eyes on him, the Chief had sensed something about the large black man. After observing him for a while, the Chief confirmed his feeling. Unlike the other cons who did as cons have always done—try to get through each day— Billy Dee Washington seemed to have a purpose and a goal beyond just doing his time and toward which he worked diligently. This purpose consisted of talking to other cons, sometimes one on one, sometimes in groups. At first the Chief hadn't thought anything of it, until he happened to overhear his conversation one day and heard the seductive, hypnotic eloquence that was Washington's voice. The Chief had heard Billy Dee speak before and this mellifluous, convincing instrument was *not his voice*!

Slowly, over the days, weeks, months, the Chief watched Billy Dee work a difference in the cons he spoke to. One by one, they took on that same faraway look, as though they lived elsewhere and were sleepwalking through this world. Even the Chief's two young followers succumbed; the Chief saw Billy Dee talking to them in the gym one day, and after that, they ignored him as if he were a stranger. They stopped tying bandannas in their hair and seemed to have lost all interest in expressing their heritage.

By October, the Chief estimated three-quarters of the prison's inmate population had succumbed to Billy Dee's oratorical powers. In response, the Chief petitioned the Department of Corrections, through the ACLU, to allow him to build a sacred sweat lodge in the garden across from A dorm for religious purposes. While the DOC and the ACLU lawyers bandied that about, the Chief kept watching. With each passing day he grew more frightened.

9

Jimmy Delilah lay on his cot, covers pulled to the bridge of his nose, peering out at the cons getting ready for bed around him. Jimmy had been in bed for over an hour, slipping under the covers fully clothed and then undressing so no one could see him. Since being sodomized by that scum Julian, this had become Jimmy's regular routine: Morning and night he dressed and undressed under the covers of his bed, watching, waiting, biding his time.

When he'd first come to New Rome Correctional, Jimmy had been a cocky, outgoing *punk*. But being forcibly raped in front of the entire dorm had changed him and he knew it. He could see the change every morning when he looked in the mirror, could see the change in the hollow stare of his eyes, the sick pallor of his skin, and the grim thin line his lips always seemed to be set to these days.

Jimmy cringed and pulled the covers over his head at the sound of Julian's voice nearby. He and the big black guy Julian was always hanging out with were cloistered with a group of cons, talking secretively again. He forced their voices from his ears, humming loudly to himself. *Not long now,* he thought. *Not long now, you bastard!* Jimmy almost smiled under the covers. He'd been waiting a long time for Julian to finish his punishment of solitary confinement in the Can and come back to the dorm. His plan was on the verge of fruition. Soon, that fucking pervert would pay, and Jimmy had the doctor to thank.

Jimmy remained still under the covers and stayed like that until lights out. Even then he did not move. He lay trembling, unconsciously emitting soft mewling noises from his throat. He lay, eyes open in the darkness, his body as rigid as frozen rope, listening intently to every sound, eyes furtive at every flickering shadow. All the while he kept one thought in his head—*This is the night.* Soon, under the weight of so much wide-eyed vigilance, his lids grew heavy and began to droop. His body twitched a couple of times as he dozed, bringing him briefly back to wakefulness, but he soon slipped off again.

From midnight to three Jimmy dozed lightly, dancing at the edge of deep sleep, dreamless and unaware that he was asleep. He didn't want to sleep past his window of opportunity, and at 4:30 A.M., as if in response to some silent alarm clock, Jimmy opened his eyes, threw back the covers, and got out of bed. He slipped his feet into his shoes and made his way amid the maze of cots to the CO's station.

He approached the desk and stood before it quietly waiting for the new CO to look up from the GameBoy Advance video game he was playing. Jimmy cleared his throat after a minute to get the officer's attention.

"What's the matter?" asked the CO, whose nametag read *Officer Saget.*

"I've been put on breakfast detail in the kitchen, Officer Saget. They told me to be there at 4:45."

The CO picked up a clipboard and asked, "What's your name?"

"Jimmy Delilah."

The CO ran a pencil down the margin of the top page on the clipboard, then flipped to the next page, stopping halfway down. "Delilah, James. Yeah, here it is. Okay. Get your chit and sign out on the board." As Jimmy did the former and latter, the CO got on his radio to notify the yard officers that an inmate would be en route from A dorm to the kitchen. The radio crackled with the same message from several of the other dorms as the rest of the kitchen staff reported to work.

Jimmy had been assigned to lunch duty when he first came to the prison, but the doctor had seen to it that he got switched to breakfast, just like he'd seen to it that Jimmy and Julian stayed in the same dorm when it was standard operating procedure to transfer one or the other after an incident such as rape. Monday, the kitchen supervisor just came over and told him he was switched, just like the doctor had said he would. That night, he and the doctor had finalized his plans for revenge.

Jimmy went down the stairs and outside into the chill early morning November air. Passing by the south gate, he murmured good morning to the yard officer, who ignored him, and joined several other inmates making their way opposite the row of dorms along the path to the rear of the building that held the inmate cafeteria and the kitchen. Once inside, he went to work immediately, filling a five-gallon pot with four one-gallon jugs of vegetable oil. He put it on the stove to boil and covered the pot to make the oil boil more quickly.

While he waited, he helped one of the other inmates empty two 250-pound sacks of oatmeal into three massive pressure cookers. He then helped haul cases of milk cartons from the walk-in freezer out to the stainless steel coolers in the inmate cafeteria meal line. By the time he was finished, he was happy to see the lid on his pot of oil rattling and puffs of steam escaping as it boiled.

Jimmy looked around. The civilian supervisor and all the cons were busy getting the morning meal ready for the nearly 2,000 inmates. No one was paying any attention to him. He grabbed two large, quilted mitten pot-holders from their hooks on the wall near the oven and slipped them on. He lifted the lid and smiled into the cloud of steam that licked his face and left it oily.

Perfect!

Now came the hardest part. Now came the part where he had to trust Doctor Stone. He replaced the lid and shut off the flame. Grasping the pot's handles with his mittened hands, he lifted the four gallons of boiling oil from the stove. He grunted once, hunched over with the weight of the pot, but then he straightened, bringing the steaming container up to waist level and holding it out in front of him. With one more look around—all clear—he walked out of the kitchen, right past the supervisor, and out the rear door.

He walked along the back of the building, marveling at how light the pot of oil had become. Jimmy had always had more *attitude* than strength to back it up with, and could never have carried a four-gallon pot of boiling oil like this, so far, without feeling any strain, before . . . before . . . meeting the doctor.

He must have given me a hypnotic suggestion.

Approaching the south gate, he began to get nervous. The doctor had told him not to worry, that he would take care of it, but Jimmy couldn't help it. He had left the kitchen without permission; he didn't know how he was going to get by the yard officer. Jimmy looked up at the towers, wondering if the officers there were watching him and wondering where he was going, maybe aiming their guns on him at that very moment. Had there been a message about him on the radio? He tensed as he walked, expecting the glare of multiple spotlights to trap him in their exposing beams, but he kept walking, getting closer to the gate, and the tower lights continued on their normal route, even passing over him as if he wasn't there.

Ahead, he spotted the yard officer, Roy, and took a deep breath. This was it. This was where he got caught; he was sure of it. He didn't even know what to say. Officer Roy was standing to the left of the gate, hands on hips, staring at the stars. As Jimmy approached, Officer Roy barely acknowledged him and *he walked by without incident!*

Doctor Stone must have bribed him, Jimmy thought. He couldn't believe it; this was actually going to happen. Whistling softly to himself, Jimmy carried his boiling load toward A dorm.

Julian James was in his favorite place—crotch deep in naked prepubescent boys. On his cot, he ground his hips into the thin mattress, breathing deeply and loudly as he dreamed of pleasures that were usually beyond his reach in prison. At the watch station, Tim Saget, too, dozed, his elbows on the desktop, head in his hands, leaning forward slightly in his chair. He snored softly, a breathy, gurgling sound that joined with the wide assortment of other snores in a sleep symphony that filled the vast hall. Faintly at first, growing louder by the second, a new noise joined the slumber sonata—footsteps. Coming up the stairs. Entering the dorm.

At the watch desk, Tim Saget frowned in his sleep. He was dreaming that he was sitting at his desk, hearing the footsteps approach. In his sleep he grunted and snorted; in the dream he turned to see the lady with the red headscarf entering the dorm. She looked concerned. Behind her, the con who had left for the kitchen a little while ago was carrying a large pot with the help of two cons dressed in white whom Tim didn't recognize. The lady with the red scarf looked from the cons to Tim.

In his cot, Julian James was just about to climax. He humped his mattress furiously, drooling into his pillow, moaning softly in orgasmic ecstasy. Through the rows of beds, Jimmy Delilah carried his pot of boiling oil to Julian's bed, where he stopped and stood watching Julian's gyrations and grinned. He quietly placed the pot of boiling oil on the floor and, without a sound, lifted the lid and placed it on the floor next to the pot. Then he waited for Julian to turn over. Clouds of steam rose around him from the pot.

You're in danger, the dream lady said to Tim.

"How did you get in here?" Tim asked but the end of his question was drowned out by a scream. The lady with the red scarf disappeared and Tim woke.

Twenty yards away, Julian had finished coming into his bed sheets and had rolled over. He woke as he did and saw someone standing over him. It was the last thing he saw as a cascade of steaming oil hit his eyes.

Screams mixed with howling laughter split the night. Every inmate sleeping on the second floor of A dorm, and most of those on the first floor, woke at the same moment. The cons nearest Julian James's cot watched in mute horror as Julian leapt from his bed, lungs bellowing out his pain, hot oil spraying from his mouth. His face was bright red, the color of cooked lobster. He put his hands to his face and screamed louder as great swatches of his skin stuck to his fingers and came off in his hands like clumps of wet cardboard. He lost his nose and both cheekbones, which slid from his hands and dripped to the floor with a bloody *plop!* Julian took two steps forward and collapsed face down on the floor. He twitched twice. Great clouds of steam rose from him and his oil-soaked cot.

Jimmy Delilah stood, laughing hysterically, holding the now empty five-gallon stainless steel pot by one handle in his mittened hand, over Julian's twitching form. He swung the pot up and over his head and brought it down in a crushing blow to the back of Julian's skull. He swung the pot again, bringing it down on top of Julian's head. Julian sluggishly tried to crawl away but moved less than an inch before Jimmy crushed his skull completely with repeated blows from the pot. Julian stopped twitching long before Jimmy stopped hitting him.

"How do you like that, you fuckin' turd-burglar? You fuckin' *faggot?*" Jimmy screamed as he pummeled Julian with the pot. "Huh? I can't *hear* you!"

The dorm was silent. Everyone in it, including Tim Saget, watched in mute astonishment. Tim was the first to break the trance. He pulled out his radio, while at the same time thumbing the body alarm on his belt.

"Two-oh-three to Inner Control—I have a ten thirty-three," he said as calmly as he could into the radio. He heard his words and realized he didn't sound calm at all. Looking around, he thought he saw looks of disdain from some of the inmates.

Now is not a good time to show fear, he silently intoned.

"Roger Two-oh-three. Help is on the way," came the radio reply. The squawk of the radio transmission broke the general spell in the room and distracted Jimmy Delilah from hitting Julian James any more. He turned and faced Tim, dropping the pot as he did. He walked down the aisle between the beds and the cons parted like a biblical miracle.

Tim's radio squawked with transmissions calling help to A dorm. Tim tensed, hoping it would arrive in time. He put his hand to his baton and unbuckled it from his belt.

"I don't want no trouble, " Jimmy Delilah said quickly upon seeing Tim reaching for his club. "I don't want to hurt any *people*," he said and pointed back at the prone body of Julian lying on the floor next to his bed, a pool of blood spreading out from around his head. "*That's* not a person." He looked up at the other inmates in the room. "You all saw what he did to me! He *deserved* this! *Nobody* fucks with me! I got the *doctor* on my side! Nobody fucks with *me!*" he shouted. Many inmates cheered, shouting: "All right!" and "The doctor's fuckin' A!" Their enthusiasm was immediately curbed by the sound of many men coming up the stairs.

Jimmy Delilah calmly lay on the floor, face down, and put his hands behind his head.

* * *

Sheila Donner reached for the phone to call her best friend, Darlene, before she remembered Darlene was dead. She rubbed her eyes and sat back. *Why do I do that to myself?* The only answer she could some up with was *guilt*. She'd been on vacation, visiting her husband's family in Chicago, when Darlene was raped and when she disappeared. Sheila had spoken to her on the phone several times during that period and had known what was going on; she should have flown back to be with her friend as soon as Darlene told her she'd been raped. The poor kid had no family in the area—just some snotty sister down South somewhere who Darlene didn't get on with. Maybe if Sheila had been there for her; if Darlene had not been alone, she'd still be around. She'd still be *alive*.

Sheila's biggest reason for guilt, though, was that she had found it hard to believe Darlene had been raped when her friend told her. Anyone who knew her would have agreed; she had far too much strength, training, and just all-out *attitude* to ever let anyone do that to her. On the other hand, Sheila had initially entertained the notion that Darlene had participated willingly in the sex and was crying rape after the fact. Hearing Darlene tell her that her rapist had looked like Captain John Thompson, Darlene's lover, Sheila had been convinced of it. She had dismissed it as just another one of Darlene's scams she was always trying to run on the system. She'd mentioned doing this before; luring some prison higher-up into sex then crying rape to sue the state. But when she disappeared and then turned up dead, Sheila had to accept that what Darlene had told her was true, and the guy who had raped her had got rid of her.

She glanced over at the photograph on the wall, showing the medical staff that had worked there when it was the state mental hospital. She looked in particular at the guy in the second row, the one John Thompson had seemed to recognize. She had never got a satisfactory answer on what that was all about. Then Thompson had to flip out and get taken off eleven-to-seven. She didn't believe Henderson had had anything to do with Darlene. Thompson was the one who'd had a near breakdown, raving about Darlene calling him on the phone, still being in the prison somewhere. Sheila was convinced he was dealing with even more guilt than she was.

"I'm going to find out why you been feeling so guilty, Triscuit," she said to the picture on the wall as if she were talking to John Thompson.

She smiled. Yes, that's what she'd do. Looking at Dr. Jason Stone's kind, smiling face, she felt reassured.

She was doing the right thing.

From her pocket she pulled out a slip of paper with a phone number on it. She dialed the number, listened to John Thompson's voice telling her to leave a message after the beep. She did, mimicking the light southern accent of Darlene Hampton's voice, and doing a good job of it.

John Thompson closed his front door and let out a sigh.
What a night!

Just when it had seemed things were quieting down at the prison, more shit had to hit the fan.

Murder, no less.

There was going to be some hell to pay for someone—the only bright spot for John was that it wouldn't be *his* ass in the sling this time. For a change, he was covered—he had put in an order to have Julian James transferred to another dorm and somehow that order had not been carried out. Whoever had overlooked that order in administration was going to be in deep shit.

He glanced at the hall clock: 11:00 A.M. He was so tired; he was bone-weary, but not sleepy. His brain was wide awake—wired, in fact. He'd just come from Superintendent Capello's office, where he and Bill had spent the past two hours going over what had happened and the last half hour dealing with the media in a press conference. One prisoner assaulting and murdering another inmate was a serious matter and didn't happen as frequently as one might think. In all of John Thompson's twenty-odd years of being a corrections officer, this was the first time it had happened on his shift. Still, it did happen and was one of the aspects of prison life—for guards and prisoners alike—that had to be dealt with. Normally the perpetrator would immediately be shipped out to the county jail or another prison for holding until arraignment. It was always a good idea to get a murderer out of the prison population, especially if the victim was a member of a prison gang. Luckily, New Rome Correctional didn't have much of a gang problem. The usual big gangs like the Crips and the Bloods weren't present in large numbers like in other prisons. There were about a dozen white cons who belonged to the Aryan Nations, but the largest group was the Latin Knights, primarily because Hispanics made up a majority of the prison population. They did not have enough of a majority, though, to rule the population effectively. They could stir up trouble, but Julian James did not belong to the Latin Knights or any other gang, so they didn't care.

But this case was different. In most assaults the weapon of choice was a shiv the inmate managed to make in one of the shops. But to have an inmate kill another with a pot of boiling oil that he *carried across* the prison compound from the kitchen without anyone questioning what he was doing— that was crazy. John and Bill Capello hadn't been able to figure out how Jimmy Delilah had managed to leave the kitchen, pass by the south gate, and go into A dorm without any of the guards on the ground or in the towers stopping him for questioning. It should have been impossible, yet the con had done it.

John and Superintendent Capello had interviewed the kitchen supervisor, the yard officers, the tower COs, and the two COs working A dorm, and none of them had seen Jimmy Delilah and his five-gallon pot of boiling death. That was another thing that bothered John Thompson: How did scrawny Jimmy Delilah carry that five-gallon pot of scalding hot oil all the way from the kitchen to A dorm by himself?

238 R. Patrick Gates

Jack Roy, the west yard officer, had no explanation for how the perp had got by him at the south gate, and when they'd questioned Jimmy Delilah, he had refused to talk.

Tim Saget, though, had said something interesting, something that had caught John Thompson's attention. He'd said Jimmy Delilah had claimed to have a *doctor* on his side. That was all. But it was enough to make John immediately think of the journal in his possession.

He realized he'd been standing there in the hall, trance like with his thoughts. He shook himself out of it and took off his coat and hung it on the hook next to the front door. His hat followed. He went down the front hall to the kitchen and opened the fridge. He grabbed a beer, popped the top, and sat at the kitchen table. He drank slowly, listening to the sounds of the empty house around him, the furnace turning on, the ticking of the clock on the wall, the hum of the refrigerator, the clanking and hissing of the radiators as they filled with steam.

He wondered briefly what Bella was doing. He'd seen her sister at the grocery store and she'd told him gleefully that Bella had gone to California and was living with their daughter, Kathy. Much to the sister's disappointment, John had shrugged and replied, "That's nice." But it wasn't, and the knowledge tore at him. He tried not to dwell on it and turned his mind back to recent events at the prison. Could the doctor Tim Saget had heard the perp mention be the author of the diary he had found in Jim Henderson's hand, and the same doctor whose picture was hanging in the HSU? With all the excitement of finding Henderson and then Darlene Hampton's corpse, John had all but forgotten about the journal. He didn't know what the connection could be, or how, but he had a gut feeling there was one.

He finished his beer, crumpled the can, and tossed it into the overflowing trash can in the corner of the kitchen. He yawned loudly and rubbed his close-cropped hair with his left hand.

"I'm too tired to think about this anymore," he said to the

kitchen table. He pushed his chair back, rose, and was lumbering into the front hall, heading for the stairs and up to bed, when he noticed the message light blinking on his phone on the hall table. He took several steps backward and hit the *play* button.

"John? Why did you kill me, John? Give yourself up."

It sounded like Darlene Hampton's voice. A queasy, cold, liquid panic immediately squirmed through John Thompson's intestines. His mouth went dry; his throat closed up; his breathing stuck in his chest. He had to use his inhaler three times before he could breathe comfortably again.

"Son of a bitch!" John swore. This had to be someone's idea of a sick joke. "Sick fucking bastard!" John muttered and turned the machine off. He stood, shaking with anger and more than a little fear, staring at the phone for several moments.

That had to be a joke, he told himself. But it had sounded just like Darlene. Did someone have a recording of her? A thought occurred to John: Maybe Jim Henderson hadn't killed Darlene. After all, there had been no proof that he had; the commission had determined it was likely, but that was based solely on John's testimony. If that call was a recording of Darlene, made under duress before she was murdered, then her killer was still out there, and it seemed he wanted to pin Darlene's murder on John.

John Thompson went back to the kitchen and grabbed a fifth of Southern Comfort out of the cabinet. He took it into the living room, cracked it, and took a long pull from it. He repeated that process several times until he started to feel the heavy-headed effects of the liquor. His head drooped, his chin touched his chest. He jerked awake, his head snapping up. He yawned, widened his eyes, and rubbed his face with his hands. He knew he should go up to bed but he was too tired to move. He'd been working the graveyard shift for his entire career, most of it spent in Walpole before transferring to New Rome. Some guys never got used to it, but not John Thompson. In fact, he preferred it.

Until recently.

In the past few weeks he'd found it harder and harder to stay awake and alert on duty. At first he'd thought he was coming down with something; then he'd just attributed it to age. But lately, he'd been having disturbing dreams.

Like just now, for instance. He dreamt he was in Outer Control when the switchboard, radio console, and the monitor station that made up the room melted away, replaced by a plush office with a leather couch, mahogany desk, plants everywhere, and tasteful, lurid pop art prints by Peter Max decorating the walls. Sitting behind the mahogany desk was Dr. Jason Stone, the guy in the picture in Health Services; the guy whom John Thompson had seen on the monitor in A dorm—the guy who was his first suspect in the rape and disappearance of Darlene Hampton until Jim Henderson had given himself away.

"You got the wrong guy, Cousin," Dr. Stone said, smiling at John.

He woke, sitting bolt upright. He looked around at his living room, perplexed for a moment, like a man who doesn't know where he is.

Tim Saget got home at about the same time John Thompson did after dodging reporters waiting outside the prison. Before that he had been questioned by the captain, the superintendent, and the state police detectives. He had spent over an hour filling out the incident report. In his sessions with Captain Thompson and Superintendent Capello, and on the incident report, Tim had lied about what he was doing when the assault took place. He said he had been in the bathroom when Jimmy Delilah came onto the floor, instead of sleeping at his desk as he had been. Now he was worried about that lie. On the way home, it had occurred to Tim that Captain Thompson and the super would be checking the surveillance video and would see that he had been at his desk, sleeping.

Tim wondered what he should do. He wondered if he'd get fired for sleeping on duty and lying about it. A feeling of dread overcame him. He wanted to call the Sarge and ask him what to do, but he was afraid to reveal to his father that he had fucked up again.

He'll know soon enough if I get fired, he thought ruefully.

He grabbed a six-pack of Budweiser from the refrigerator and took it into the living room with him. He lay on the couch, the six-pack on the floor next to him, and guzzled two cans quickly in succession before settling down to a more leisurely pace of drinking. Twice he got up to call the Sarge, but both times he had second thoughts and returned to the couch and another beer. By one, the six-pack was finished and Tim was passed out, snoring.

He dreamed:

A farm. A summer's day; the sun beating hot upon his back. There are people all around him, bending over, working the earth with hoes and hand spades; pulling vegetables from the ground and placing them in large wicker baskets.

"Gypsy, bring me some water," a gray-haired, middle-aged woman calls out, pointing at him. Tim looks around, but he is alone at the edge of the field. Next to him is a large plastic water jug with a pull-out spout and a stack of small paper drinking cups.

Tim looks back at the woman, who is nodding at him and motioning frantically with her hand for him to hurry up. Tim reaches for the jug and marvels at how slim his hands are.

The dream shifted:

He has a feeling similar to taking the first step off a rapidly spinning amusement ride and the earth feels like it's still moving underfoot—a blurring slide and suddenly he is standing on a ridge overlooking Digbee Hall and the rest of the prison, only it isn't the prison. There is no perimeter fence of steel and barbed wire, no guard towers, no search lights, and many of the newer prison structures, like the gym and I dorm, are missing. It's the landscape of his nightmare, only in daylight. He recognizes Digbee Hall, with a white cupola on top, right away as the building of his dream. More than ever, the area resembles a small, snowbound college campus.

He is standing and is aware that there is someone next to him. He turns and is surprised to see the lady in the red headscarf sitting on a long sleigh.

She is obviously very pregnant. She strokes her belly and coos: "Is my little man kicking?" A shadow passes over the scene and the woman looks up, frightened.

The dream shifted again:

The sleigh scene spins away. The green grass and blue sky swirl together, darken, and become night. He is standing in almost the exact same spot, only now it is snowing, bitterly cold, and dismal. Below him, Digbee Hall is on fire. He watches in horror as a section of the roof collapses and smoke and vague flying black shapes pour out, one indistinguishable from the other.

John Thompson took the journal of Dr. Stone out of his locker, where it had sat since he'd found Jim Henderson's body. He put it in his inside jacket pocket. He figured he'd have time to look at it later, after he had a chance to speak to Tim Saget again. After having that dream about Dr. Stone, John Thompson decided to try and find out about him, see if he was still around. Though he hadn't admitted it to Sheila Donner, or Jim Henderson at the time, John had known Stone was the guy he'd seen on the monitor in A dorm that night, standing near the windows. John knew he hadn't been seeing things; he had *seen* the guy, and if he had seen him then that meant he was *there*. John clung to that thought with determination and would not let any other possibility reach the light of his reasoning.

John tried to figure out how Dr. Stone could have got into the prison without being seen, but other than the lame supposition that Stone had kept a master key from the hospital days, he could not explain it. He tried very hard to convince himself of the master key theory; the truth was that most of the doors and locks in the prison were the same ones that had been there when the place had been a state mental hospital. So it wasn't that far-fetched that someone who had worked in the hospital could gain access to many places inside the prison. But how the doctor had got through the *main gate,* or even the yard gates, which were new gates and locks, was beyond him. Stone could have found a secret way in through the tunnels. If he had managed that, it would only get him by the front gate and maybe the yard officers if he knew their routine, but not the dorm guards. As far as John was concerned, there was only one way to find out—find Dr. Jason Stone and ask him.

He went into work at 3:00 P.M. to check with the personnel office, looking for proof that Stone might have worked at the prison in its early years, but found nothing. He then checked the phone book but found no Stones listed in the New Rome area. He was at a loss until, on his way out to a nearby Dunkin' Donuts for a break, he noticed Farmer Jones, the former hospital caretaker, and the guy who'd found Tobi Dowry, unloading produce from his pickup truck onto his roadside stand to the left of the exit for the prison on Route 140. John pulled over and spoke to the old guy, who stood about five foot one, was completely bald, and whose every inch of skin that John could see was more wrinkled than a raisin.

"You still live up on the Hill?" he asked, trying to break the ice with small talk.

Old Jones looked at him as though John had suddenly grown an extra head. "Ain't *never* lived on that hill. I've worked there. I've tilled my land up there, growed my food, but I never *lived* up there, Never have, never will. Couldn't make me. Queer place. Always has been, always will be."

"But you worked at the old hospital, right?"

"Yep. I was the groundskeeper for fifty years. Retired just a couple years afore they closed the place down."

"Did you know Dr. Jason Stone?"

"Yeah, I knew Dr. Stone, a little. You see, I worked days; he was the head honcho on the graveyard shift. Why?" Joe Jones had a voice like gravel and a suspicious nature. He looked John up and down like a state cop who smells liquor on the breath of a driver.

"Do you know where I can find him?" John had asked.

Again, Jones regarded him with suspicion. "You family? You his son?"

"No," John replied. "I just need to see him."

Joe Jones smiled and laughed throatily, his already wrinkled face cracking into hundreds more small, deep lines. "Yeah, sure. I know where you can find him. He's still on the Hill, don't you know."

I knew it! John thought. "Where?" he asked Jones.

"Just before the main gate, take a right onto that dirt road—not more'n a cow path really—and go down there 'bout a mile. You'll find Stone at the end of the road; you can't miss him. He's the last one on the left."

So excited to be finally able to get some answers, John Thompson hadn't questioned Joe Jones any further. He jumped in his car, turned around, and sped back up the hill. On his way, though, he'd wondered what Jones meant by "He's the last on the left." As far as John knew there were no houses or structures on the hill other than Jones's farm buildings—a barn and a shack John had thought was the old guy's house—and the abandoned bungalows. Driving down the dirt road, he had an inkling of what he might find at the end of it. He found he was right.

It was a cemetery, and Dr. Jason Stone was right where Jones had said he'd be—last grave on the left in a row of ten stones, all marking the graves of doctors and nurses. There were three more rows of stones behind it, all with what John assumed were patients' names on them. On Dr. Stone's headstone, John read the year, *1973,* that he died.

Back on Route 140, Jones was waiting for him, hands on hips, smiling like the proverbial canary-eating cat. "Found him, did ya?" he asked, winking.

"Yeah," Thompson replied, trying to be angry with the man, but Jones's joy at his little joke was infectious. "Why didn't you tell me he was dead?"

"You didn't ask," Jones replied, his grin widening.

"Is that marker correct? He died in '73? Thirty years ago?"

"Yep. Died in the big fire in Digbee Hall—you still call it that?"

John nodded.

"All of 'em did; there's a marker for every staff member and patient who died in the fire. Course, not all of 'em are buried there, just them that had no family to bury 'em, like Stone and a couple others. That was the nail in the coffin for the state hospital, so to speak. The state closed the place within a year of the fire—"

John cut him off. "You mentioned a son. What about him? Is he still around?"

"Oh, I ain't even sure he had a son. There was a rumor goin' around after the fire that he'd knocked up one of the lady patients, who had his son, but where they got to when the place closed, I wouldn't know. Why you so interested?"

John had started to tell him, but didn't. He thanked Jones and drove off, contemplating the fact that Dr. Stone was dead. And if he was dead, then whatever John had seen in A dorm that night, it could not have been Dr. Stone.

After his chat with Joe Jones, John spent six of the next seven hours in Bill Capello's office. Capello had to leave to attend a convention in Virginia. Since the deputy superintendent was sick, Capello was leaving John Thompson, his senior captain, in charge of the Inner Perimeter Security Squad's investigation into the murder of Julian Jones. All the time he was with the superintendent John tried to stay focused and not think about Dr. Jason Stone, but it was impossible.

So Stone was dead. Big deal.

It *was* a big deal.

I know *I saw him in A dorm. I* know *it.*

A big deal.

But I also know *he's* dead! *I saw his gravestone.*

A very big deal.

I must be losing it. That or I'm seeing ghosts. And if I think I'm seeing ghosts, then I really am losing it.

He pushed the thought away and tried to concentrate on the reports, interviews, and procedures he was to file, conduct, and follow while Bill Capello was away. It wasn't until Capello was gone that John finally got to the most important piece of evidence—the surveillance tapes. They perplexed John. It was clear on the tapes from both Inner Control and Outer Control that Jimmy Delilah had been in places he shouldn't have been, and was in plain view of his superiors when he was. The kitchen cameras had caught him leaving there with his load and walking right past the kitchen supervisor. Minutes later, he showed up on the yard surveillance tape. The yard cameras used at night had infrared lenses and everything appeared gray, but Jimmy Delilah was clearly visible, carrying his pot of boiling death openly along the walkway, as if he had every right to be there at four in the morning. The camera over the south gate caught him passing by and Officer Jack Roy nodding at him as he did.

That was the part John found incredible. Jack Roy had sworn he'd never seen Jimmy Delilah, and John had believed him. Yet, there it was on tape: Jack Roy's back was to the camera as he stood by the gate, but he could clearly be seen nodding to Jimmy Delilah. Then came the taped images of Jimmy entering A dorm, where he walked right past the first-floor CO, Chris Frieburg, and headed up the stairs with nary a glance from Frieburg. Next, Jimmy appeared on the second-floor camera, walking past a sleeping Tim Saget, and going about his gruesome task.

John shook his head. This was too weird—Jimmy Delilah had moved unimpeded through what was supposed to be tight security. It was as though he was invisible, as though he were a ghost. Of course, that thought brought him around again to Dr. Jason Stone.

At one time, anyone asking him if he believed in ghosts would have got dismissive laughter as a response. Even after coming to this prison, which he'd heard from day one was haunted, he had never accepted the existence of ghosts. And there was a very simple reason for it: He'd never seen one.

Until Dr. Jason Stone, that is.

He tried once again to get his mind around it. He supposed he could accept the reality of ghosts, but what about what happened to Darlene? Could he accept a ghost who could rape and kill a woman and cause her to disappear? He fervently wished the doctor were still alive; it would make everything so much simpler. It would all be so much more *sane* if the doctor were just sneaking into the hospital somehow. He tried grabbing at the straw that it *could* be Stone's son, but that, too, was unlikely. According to Jones, the son was only a rumor. Even if he was real, John doubted he could track him down. Even if he could, he doubted the kid, who must be in his thirties by now, would even remember his father, much less be inclined to dress like him, find some way to sneak into the prison and rape and kill a corrections officer. To what purpose?

John wasn't sure what he was going to do. If *one* officer had missed Jimmy Delilah, the guy would have been severely reprimanded, maybe even fired. But John couldn't fire half the night shift. Either they were all lying, or they had truly been unaware of Jimmy Delilah and their own actions in regard to him. The similarity to how he had seen Dr. Stone in A dorm, seemingly unnoticed by anyone else, was not lost on him. Even so, it served only to make him more confused.

What the hell is going on?

He crossed the yard to Digbee Hall and checked in at Inner Control, going through his regular duties of roster checks and population counts. As soon as he could, he excused himself and headed out to the yard to talk to Jack Roy about the discrepancy between his story and the surveillance tapes.

"Hey, Cap," Jack Roy said a little wanly. He looked tired;

he, too, had been kept late at the prison, being interviewed and filling out reports.

"Jack," John said, nodding. "I need to talk to you, Jack, about what happened last night."

"Sure, Cap," Jack Roy said nervously, "but I don't know what else I can tell you. My brain was picked pretty clean today."

"I know," John replied, "but we've got a problem. What you *said* you did, and what the surveillance tape *shows* you did, are two different things."

"What do you mean?"

"You said you never saw Jimmy Delilah cross the yard and you didn't know how he got by you at the south gate, but the videotape shows you *nodding* to him as he walked by, like it happened every night."

Jack Roy stared, dumbfounded, at John for several moments. "*What?*" he said finally.

"You don't remember Jimmy Delilah going by you at the south gate last night? You don't remember nodding at him?"

"It's not a matter of *remembering,* Cap, I didn't do it!" Jack Roy said vehemently.

"The videotapes don't lie, Jack."

Officer Roy looked flabbergasted and was unable to respond for several moments. "Th-that can't be!" he stammered. "I swear somebody must have messed with the tape!"

John shook his head. "No. I don't think so."

"I'm not lying, Cap. You know me better'n that!" Roy was becoming agitated.

"Calm down, Jack," John Thompson soothed. "I'm not calling you a liar. In fact, I believe you. You're not the only one whose story is different from what the video shows. I don't know how that skinny rat, Delilah, did it—hypnosis maybe—but I'm going to find out."

"So what happens to me?" Jack Roy wanted to know. "Am I in trouble?"

"No. Not yet, anyway. It all depends on what happens next. Jimmy Delilah isn't talking—we've got him in the

Can. You're lucky in that the super left today and he'll be gone for a week, and he *hasn't* seen the security tapes. The supe put me in charge of the internal investigation team on this. Unless the victim has a family member who makes a stink, you shouldn't have any problems. But I am worried about the family making trouble. I smell a lawsuit in this. The vic—Julian James—has only one living relative, a sister who lives in Dorchester. I tried to contact her earlier today, but I only got her answering machine. If she doesn't cause problems, the only thing you have to worry about is the state police CSI unit, but they usually let us handle our own messes. The super doesn't want them called in unless absolutely necessary. So . . . keep your fingers crossed."

Jack Roy did not look reassured.

John Thompson left him at the south gate and crossed the west yard to A dorm. He stopped on the first floor to speak to Chris Frieburg, who reiterated what he'd said when questioned earlier: He never saw Jimmy Delilah enter A building and go by him. Unlike with Jack Roy and Tim Saget, the videotape agreed with what he said. He wasn't asleep and he wasn't doing something he shouldn't have been doing. He was just sitting there reading when Delilah walked by, and he never looked up. John Thompson could not prod his memory to recall anything about seeing the perp enter A dorm and go up the stairs. John didn't bother to tell him the video showed Delilah walking past him less than two feet away. He headed upstairs to talk to Tim Saget.

"Captain Thompson! I was hoping to see you tonight. I've got something to tell you," Tim Saget said before John Thompson could say a word. "I didn't tell you the truth today. I wasn't in the bathroom when the attack occurred. I fell asleep at my desk; that's why I didn't see Jimmy Delilah come on the floor. I'm sorry I lied to you."

John Thompson sized Tim up. He had to admit he liked the kid—much more than he thought he would, knowing he was the Sarge's son. It took balls for him to do what he'd just done, and John respected and admired him for it.

"I know, kid," John said. "I watched the surveillance tape." He smiled at the expression of worry on Tim Saget's face. "Don't worry, Tim. It seems we had an epidemic of people fucking up. I appreciate your honesty. It's weird, but you're the only one on duty who seems to actually know what you were doing when all this went down. The other guys are either lying—in the face of video proof, no less— or something really strange is going on around here."

"This whole fucking place is strange," Tim muttered in agreement.

John Thompson looked at him curiously just as his radio squawked to life with Jane Mazek's voice: "Outer Control to One hundred, over.

"One hundred here. Go ahead, over." John Thompson replied.

"Cap, I got a Mrs. Hendrix on the phone. Says she's the sister of the vic who got wasted last night. Over."

"Okay," John said hastily. "Keep her on the line. I want to take this in my office. I'm on my way."

"Look, kid," John Thompson said to Tim Saget, "don't sweat it. I'm glad you told me the truth. I'll talk to you later, okay?"

Relieved, Tim Saget smiled and nodded.

Billy Dee Washington lay awake in bed, listening to the conversation between the two screws—the watch commander and the new one, Saget. Lately, since the arrival of Saget as the new CO in A dorm, Billy Dee lay awake often, secretly watching him while pretending to be asleep. Billy Dee wanted to sleep; he wanted to get back to the doctor's delights and all the new friends he'd introduced to the doctor, but he felt compelled to stay awake and watch, just as he had done last night when Jimmy Delilah had made a lobster out of Julian. Billy Dee had seen the whole thing; he had known it was coming. He had seen Jimmy enter the second-floor dorm carrying the pot of scalding oil. What Billy Dee saw that the camera didn't record was two of the doctor's cohorts helping Jimmy Delilah with the weight of all that boiling oil. And following just behind, observing, smiling, encouraging, had been the doctor himself.

After the watch commander left, CO Saget returned to his desk, moving out of Billy Dee's sight line. Finally, he could close his eyes and keep them closed. Finally, he could go over to the other side and have some fun. He yearned to pass over completely and stay there all the time, the way Julian had done, but Doctor Stone wouldn't let him. Soon, he and all the other cons he had spoken to and brought to the delights of the other side would be able to cross over forever. But in the meantime, the doctors needed him right where he was, continuing to convert inmates, continuing to keep an eye on the screw, Saget.

"But why don't you just go to him in his dreams? He sleeps every night at his desk," Billy Dee had asked. The doctor had frowned and muttered, "*She* protects him." Billy Dee didn't know what that meant. The next moment the doctor added, "I need you, Billy Dee. You are my *eyes,* as well as my voice."

10

October 19

Three nights after killing Julian James, Jimmy Delilah sat in the cell called the "cooler" on tier two of the Can. It was a room no bigger than the average walk-in closet, eight by five feet, with a stainless steel toilet tucked into the corner next to a stainless steel sink not much bigger than a kid's lunch box. Against the opposite wall was his narrow bed, the mattress so thin it felt as though he were lying on cardboard. He could go from the bed to the toilet and sink in one step. There was just enough space lengthwise in the cell that he could pace three steps from the sink to the cell door and three back. Since being put in there, he'd traversed the cell 1,069 times.

Jimmy didn't mind the cramped cell. He felt good—better than he could ever remember feeling. Killing Julian James had been the single greatest moment in his life, and he was basking in the afterglow. Even the backbreaking cot he was lying on couldn't wipe the goofy smile from his face. Wallowing in the feeling of righteous satisfaction, Jimmy Delilah dozed and fell asleep, still smiling. He dreamt and didn't know he was dreaming. The cell door opened and Doctor Stone stepped in.

"Hello, Jimmy. Feeling better?"

"Yeah, Doc! How'd you do that? I couldn't believe it. I owe you, man," Jimmy replied.

"Yes . . . yes, you do. And there's someone here who is going to help us collect." The doctor stepped completely into the room and a shadow filled the doorway behind him. The backlight from the corridor made it impossible for Jimmy to see right away who was there. The shadow stepped into the room just as several hands grabbed hold of Jimmy's arms and legs. He looked around. There were suddenly several people on the cot with him, holding him down. He looked up, got a good look finally at the person entering the cell, and wanted to scream.

It was Julian James, his face half melted away, the slimy raw bone of his cheeks peeking through the shreds of bloody tissue hanging from what was left of his boiled red skin. A gaping triangular black hole where his nose used to be leaked bloody mucus, while his eyes, which had been poached by the oil, bulged from their sockets like boiled eggs straining to give up their bloody yolks. What was left of his mouth—just ragged shreds of his top lip, hanging over his broken teeth—smiled. When he spoke, it was in a lisping, gurgling, barely articulate voice.

"You know, I was just telling the doctor that I'd *die* to get into your ass again. And *voila!* Here I am!" He laughed, and steaming blood bubbled from his mouth and ran down his chin like a small waterfall.

Jimmy looked frantically to the doctor for help, but Doctor Stone was leering at him, his face distorting and changing, the eyes growing huge, the pupils changing to milky white orbs devoid of emotion. A shadow blacker than night exhaled from the doctor. Like an inky cloud it surrounded him, shrouding him in its dark tentacles. It filled the room.

The hands on Jimmy tightened, picked him up, turned him over. He was suddenly naked, on all fours on his cot, his head jammed against the wall. Hands tightly gripped his arms and ankles, keeping his legs apart. He felt the dead, cold hands of Julian James caress his buttocks and reach between his legs to cup his testicles.

"Oh, please no!" Jimmy whimpered. "Help me, Doc. Please! Don't let him do it to me again."

The only sound from the thing the doctor had become was heavy breathing.

Julian reached up to the back of his own skull, where Jimmy had laid it open with the pot, exposing his brains, and dug his fingers into the mess, scooping out a wad of slimy, bloody gray matter, which he promptly used to lubricate Jimmy with.

"Open up the tunnel!" Julian crowed. "The train's coming!"

Jimmy Delilah screamed.

In the COs' office on the second floor of the Can, Officer Dave Stirling jumped at the sound of the screams. He immediately grabbed his baton and ran out of the office. The screams were coming from cooler cell Two-H, holding the new guy. Dave ran to the door and opened the small square observation window in it. He couldn't believe what he saw—the guy was asleep! He was *screaming* in his *sleep*! Dave couldn't help but laugh. The guy was down on all fours on his cot, screaming and crying like a woman being raped.

The humor of the situation wore off quickly as Jimmy Delilah's screams became more intense and pained and his tears more pathetic. Suddenly, he started rocking back and forth on the bed, banging his head against the back wall. Faster and harder and harder and faster he rocked until he was smashing his head into the wall with such violence Dave Stirling felt the cell door shake each time his head hit the wall. A smear of blood appeared on the wall and still he kept rocking, kept plowing his skull into concrete. The blood began to splatter, droplets flying in all directions.

"Hey!" Stirling shouted through the observation window. "Hey! Wake up! Cut it out!" he screamed as loudly as he could, but to no avail. Jimmy Delilah's head pounding into the wall had become a booming bass drumbeat now, waking other cons on the floor, who began yelling and banging on their cell doors. In the cell, blood dotted the corner like some giant spin art painting with tendrils of red running out in spidery webs from the point of impact.

Dave Stirling fumbled with his keys and pressed his body alarm button. His hands shook as he tried to slip the key into the door lock. Delilah's rocking and head butting was slowing, the blood splattering less and less. Finally, Dave got the key in the lock and opened the door just as Jimmy came to a halt and collapsed onto his side on the bed. Dave Stirling stepped into the cell and stood over the body. The guy lay unmoving. Blood was everywhere, dripping down the walls and from the ceiling, falling into his hair. It soaked into the blanket and sheets on the cot. Dave could feel it on the floor, causing the soles of his boots to stick. He could see it had even speckled the sink, the toilet, and the far walls of the cell. Fearful of getting any blood on him, Dave Stirling gingerly leaned over the body to check for any signs of life. He realized he could hear breathing, heavy, yet faint, and it wasn't coming from Jimmy Delilah or himself. Dave turned around and his eyes widened. Melting into the wall, as if it were slowly backing away, was a shadowy figure with a face so hideously frightening it immediately brought a cold sweat to Dave's scalp and an urge to defecate to his bowels. The face and figure quickly dissolved, receding into the concrete, leaving the wall as unmarked as it had been before. But the eyes lingered a moment or two longer than the rest and burned into Dave Stirling with an intensity that made his eyes roll up into his head as he fainted.

* * *

John Thompson put his head down on his desk and let out a long sigh. Not for the last time he had to question the air: "What the hell is going on?" He had been in the middle of finishing up paperwork on the Julian James incident. Luckily, his sister, Dorothy Hendrix, had been uninterested in the fact that her brother was dead, which made things a lot easier for John Thompson. He was in the office in Digbee Hall that all the watch commanders shared when Inner Control informed him of Dave Stirling's body alarm going off. He had immediately called an emergency code, bringing all available personnel, plus the K-9 unit, to the second floor of the Can. Being already in Digbee Hall, John had been the first on the scene.

He had found Dave Stirling unconscious on the floor. With all the blood everywhere, John's first impression had been that it was Dave's and he had been attacked, but after closer examination he realized Dave was just out cold. The blood had obviously come from Jimmy Delilah on the cot. John looked at the large splotch of blood and brains on the wall over the cot, then at Jimmy Delilah's head. It looked to John like Dave Stirling had repeatedly smashed Jimmy Delilah's head into the wall until his skull was as crushed as Julian James's had been. Maybe Delilah *had* attacked Dave, but even an attack wouldn't warrant this.

His radio squawked, bringing his mind back to the office. "Outer Control to One-hundred. The coroner's wagon is leaving the facility. Over."

"Roger. Over," he replied. John sat back. Two inmate deaths in one week. This was not good. He could imagine the hell he was going to catch when Superintendent Capello came back. It was bad enough when one inmate killed another, but it was a disaster when a *guard* killed an inmate, even if he did it to save his own life. With everything else that had happened lately, the press was going to have a field day with this. Already many politicians were calling for an investigation, not only of the prison, but the entire DOC.

Dave Stirling was still unconscious and had been taken to

Hayman Memorial Hospital under heavy guard by the state police. John looked at his watch. It was 6:00 A.M. Stirling had been taken away fifteen minutes ago. John had Lecuyer, the other yard officer working with Jack Roy, cover tier two on the SIU until the day officer got in. He also had Jane Mazek call in as many extra officers as she could get hold of; word of Delilah's murder by a guard would travel fast and he would need the extra men for population control. He had ordered the prison go into lockdown, with all inmates restricted to their dorms and cells until further notice.

There was a knock on the door. It was Lieutenant Seneca, John's second in command. "I've got tier two's surveillance tape for you, Cap."

"Thanks, Pete," John said, taking the black plastic cassette. He waited until Seneca was gone before going over to the small television that sat on top of a VCR in the corner of the office so that watch commanders could review tapes at their discretion. He put the tape into the machine and flicked on the TV, punching up channel three on the remote to get the brilliant blue screen that preceded *play*.

He wasn't sure the surveillance tape was going to do anything to help Dave Stirling, but he was hoping. It was a violation of prisoners' rights to have cameras in their cells or in any spot that would allow a view into any cell. The only position that didn't violate their rights was hanging from the ceiling at the end of the corridor, near the exit door. Cameras were allowed in the dorms, since it was assumed that just being in a forty-bed room precluded any chance at privacy that cameras might infringe upon. In the dorms, with one guard for forty, sometimes more, inmates, cameras were a necessity.

John rewound the tape to the beginning and pressed *play*. The blue screen went black. The screen blipped, a picture appeared, rolled upward, then steadied. John frowned. He wasn't sure what he was looking at but it wasn't tier two in the Can. It looked like a dungeon or cellar, and the picture quality was grainy and blurry. Suddenly the camera swung around, and a naked black woman, chained to the wall, came into view. A huge black man was whipping her breasts with a small cat-o'-nine-tails. The woman appeared to be howling in pain with every stroke, but there was no sound. It was so blurry, focusing in and out rapidly, that John couldn't make out much else.

As if in answer to his thought, the camera moved in closer, the lighting grew stronger, the quality of the video clearer. The scene came into steady focus. A close-up revealed the woman's breasts criss-crossed with bloody stripes. Tiny rivers of red ran down over her stomach and thighs, and perfectly formed scarlet droplets fell from her nipples like dark liquid bombs.

John Thompson had seen enough. He didn't know where this tape had come from but it obviously wasn't the SIU's tier two surveillance. Someone's head was going to roll for this. He was reaching for the remote when the camera panned up, revealing the silently screaming face of Darlene Hampton.

John froze; felt his heart pause then come thudding back so hard it made him gasp. His eyes bulged.

"John, help me!"

John stared at the screen, horrified. She was looking *right at him*! She was talking *right to him*! He grabbed the remote, hit the stop button, but it didn't work.

"Help me, *please,* John!"

He jabbed at the mute button with his thumb.

"Please, John. I can't stand it any more."

Still her voice came through the set; still her eyes bore into his, filled with pain, suffering and pleading.

"John! Oh God! Help me!"

The whip cracked across her chest and she let out a deep, grunting, moaning scream that gave John Thompson chills and made the hair on his arms and scalp bristle.

"You're dead," John mumbled, staring at the screen, a sick feeling invading his body. His chest got tight and he grabbed for his inhaler, remembering as he did that he had left it in his car. He tried to take slow, deep breaths.

"You're the only one who can help me, John," Darlene managed to choke out before fainting from the flogging her chest was receiving. The huge, naked black man, whose face was obscured, threw down his whip and grabbed her ankles, spreading them.

The screen went black.

Someone is trying to mess with my head. John didn't know how they had done it, but someone had made this tape to mess with his head. Whoever it was, they were going to wish they hadn't before he got through with them. He pulled out his radio and gulped in air before calling Lieutenant Seneca to his office on the double.

"Where did you get this tape, Pete?" John asked him as soon as he walked through the door. He held up the cassette.

"From the video console at Inner Control, you know that."

"And you're sure this is the same tape that had been in there for last night's eleven-to-seven shift?"

"Yeah, it was last changed at midnight. You know, that's when I change all the tapes. They have six hours of recording time so I change them again at six. Why?"

John ignored the question. "Could someone have switched tapes on you?"

Pete Seneca laughed, but it was weak. He looked confused. "Why? I don't know what you mean, Cap. There was no one else around. What's on that tape?"

John leaned over and pushed the cassette into the VCR and pressed rewind. After a few moments he hit *stop,* then *play.* The blue screen went to black before a picture appeared. John Thompson gaped at the television. The screen showed not the dungeon scene with Darlene Hampton chained to the wall, but what it should have shown in the first place—the corridor of tier two in the Can.

Confused, John pressed *fast forward* until Dave Stirling

emerged from his office and walked, Chaplinesque, to cell Two-H. John hit the button to slow the motion down to normal and watched, dumbfounded, as Dave Stirling opened the observation window in the cell door, looked in, and started laughing. He continued to watch as Dave's laughter ended and he began shouting into the cell. With no audio on the tapes, John couldn't tell what he was saying, but he was upset and shouting. Next he began hammering on the door and then he hit his body alarm before fumbling out his keys to open the door. As he opened the cell door and rushed inside, John Thompson hit *fast forward* again and ran nearly all the way through the tape, but it was all SIU surveillance—including him and a long parade of officials: local, prison, and state police, marching in and out of cell Two-H— but no sign of Darlene and the dungeon.

"Where is it?" John wondered out loud, completely unmindful now of Pete Seneca's presence.

"Where's what, John?" Seneca asked.

"The tape you gave me. This isn't it."

Pete Seneca reached over, hit the *stop* button on the VCR, then *eject*. He took the tape out and showed it to John. "Sure it is. It's got the log sticker right on it."

John looked at the sticker with the last entry, today's date, and *12:00 A.M. to 6:00 A.M.* marked clearly on it next to: *Tier 2—SIU.*

"You feel okay, John? You're looking kind of pale."

John put his head down, hand on forehead. "No, actually, I don't."

"Can I get you anything?" Pete Seneca asked.

"No, I'll be okay."

"What's this all about, Cap? What was on that tape?"

"Uh, nothing," John said hastily. "It was blank, but I guess I forgot to rewind it before I watched it."

Pete Seneca looked at him doubtfully—he knew he had rewound the tape before bringing it to John—but said nothing.

"Look Pete, do me a favor and call Captain Skovic of the

State Police at Hayman Hospital and tell him to notify me as soon as Stirling comes to."

"Sure John, I'll do that right now."

After Pete left, John sat in front of the TV with the tape in his lap. *Dear God, please tell me what is going on,* he silently pleaded. He'd thought that when Darlene Hampton's body had been discovered, all the weird shit was at an end. Of course the coroner's report that she had been dead for several months—probably since the night she disappeared— hadn't jibed with John's theory that she had been alive and in contact with him while being held captive in the prison by Jim Henderson, but at the time he hadn't cared that there were discrepancies. He'd just wanted to put it all behind him. The whole Darlene fiasco was at an end and he thought— *hoped*—he was going to be able to get his life (his work life, at least) back to normal.

It seemed he had guessed wrong.

He put the tape down on the TV and stood. He had quit smoking three years ago, but now he felt the urge to light up. From force of habit, he felt the breast pocket of his jacket and shirt looking for a pack, and felt instead the lump of Dr. Stone's journal in his jacket. He took it out, looked at it, and then opened it to the first entry: January 22nd, 1972.

The last journal I kept was for tenth grade English class with Mrs. Stephens. I'm not sure why I feel the need to keep one now—maybe it's because I'm starting my first residency; maybe it's because Dr. Lauricella, my advisor at Harvard Medical School, always said: "A psychiatrist who does not keep a daily personal log is going to miss key patient insights."

I started today at the New Rome State Mental Hospital, as the night shift medical supervisor and psychiatric resident. I suppose I should be grateful for the position, since I barely made it through med school and my internship at McDonald Psychiatric in Boston, but I'm finding it difficult. Maybe if I hadn't

*grown up in New Rome I wouldn't mind it now, but my
dream was always to get away from here. It's why I became a doctor—a psychiatrist—in the first place. I
thought I'd work in Boston or Worcester; or maybe
even go to New York or the West Coast. I always
thought I'd make some great discovery that would
make everyone sit up and take notice. I never thought
I'd end up working at New Rome, within a couple of
miles of where I grew up.*

*I've got to remember: this is just one rung in the
ladder. That shall be my mantra.*

John flipped through the log, skimming the pages, frowning at some of the things he read, until he came to the six-
teenth or seventeenth entry, which started with the line:
There is something weird going on around here. Before John
could read any further, the door to his office opened and
Fred Milardo, the day shift commander, came in.

"I hear we got more trouble!" he said, closing the door
behind him.

"Trouble? That's an understatement," John told him. He
folded the corner of the page in the journal and slipped it
back into his jacket pocket before settling down to fill in
Fred on the events of the past night.

Tim Saget felt like the proverbial guy in the electric chair
who has just received a last-minute reprieve from the gover-
nor. He had convinced himself that he was going to get fired
for lying to Captain Thompson. He had to laugh. Things always seemed to go that way for him; just when he became
certain one thing was going to happen, the exact opposite
usually did. From what the Sarge had told him about John
Thompson, Tim had thought it was all over for him.

"I wouldn't trust him if I were you," the Sarge had told
him after his chat with his friend Bill Capello, the prison's
superintendent. "Bill tells me John's started acting weird

again. Got caught fucking around with a female guard. He's basically still on probation right now."

That had been before Captain Henderson's suicide and the finding of Darlene Hampton's body. Shortly after those events, the Sarge told him that John Thompson had been exonerated in the superintendent's eyes, but the Sarge had still warned: "Don't trust him as far as you can throw him." Whatever that meant; it had bothered Tim that his father wasn't more supportive of his old friend. After tonight and the way Thompson had treated him, Tim decided the Sarge was all wrong about Captain Thompson. As far as Tim was concerned, the Cap was okay.

Tim got up and walked around his desk, stretching his legs. Stressing over what was going to happen tonight had kept him from sleeping decently at home. He'd been running on adrenalin and nerves since getting to work and right up until Captain Thompson let him off the hook. As soon as that had happened, it was as though an energy switch had been turned off inside him and he became so suddenly tired that he felt he could fall asleep standing on one leg. But now that everything was okay, the last thing he wanted to have happen was to fall asleep again on duty and have Captain Thompson walk in and catch him this time.

Tim walked around the nearest row of beds and headed for the bathroom to wash his face. With his job safe, a new worry occurred to Tim: What if the con with the pot of boiling oil had been after *him*?

You are in danger here.

The words and image of the woman in the red headscarf flashed in his memory. Along with them came the recollection of Julian Jones's face as it literally melted away in his hands.

If the woman in his dreams hadn't been warning him about Jimmy Delilah, then what had she meant? Tim wondered.

He went into the bathroom and ran cold water in the middle sink, splashing it on his face and the back of his neck.

Instead of wiping the excess water off, he let it trickle down his neck to his back and chest. The cool liquid helped, and he exited the bathroom feeling more awake than when he went in. He started back to the COs' desk when one of the shades on the tall front windows suddenly rattled up all the way to the top. Light from the full moon descended into the room in a narrow beam and fell on the last cot at the end of the fourth row. The con sleeping there suddenly sat bolt upright, as if jerked into a sitting position by a jolt of electricity. His eyelids popped open wide, but his pupils were rolling into his head, showing only the whites of his eyes. He spoke, but his lips and jaw barely moved.

"We're going to get you, Jason."

A soft, sighing moan followed these words, and the con flopped back onto the bed, closed his eyes, and began to snore. Tim quickly put a hand over his own mouth to stifle a nervous explosion of laughter. *That scared the shit out of me!* he thought. *That was weird.* He went over to the con's bed and leaned over him. He was sound asleep, snoring deeply.

"What the hell was that all about?" Tim wondered aloud in a soft whisper. Moving between the cots, Tim made his way across the room to the window where he started to pull down the shade. Movement outside caught his eye and stopped him. He put his head close to the glass, shading his reflection with one hand above his forehead like a visor.

There were *people* down in the garden area across from A dorm next to the kitchen. That would be odd enough at 3:20 A.M., but these people did not look like cons or prison staff. They looked like . . . *farmers,* just like in his dream! And there were men *and* women out there with rakes and shovels, hoes and baskets. The men, at least three of them, were working with the tools, tilling the earth, while the women knelt amid the rows of produce, picking the veggies and filling the straw baskets by their sides.

"What the hell?" Tim muttered to himself. He reached for his radio but it would not come free of its holster. He looked down, unsnapped the holding strap, and removed the radio, bringing it to his lips. He was just about to call Inner Control and tell them about the "farmers," but now they were gone. The garden was empty. In fact, it didn't even look like the same garden he had just seen. This was a flower garden, as it always had been for at least as long as Tim had been working at the prison. But what he had seen moments ago had been a *vegetable* garden.

At that moment the emergency code for the tact team to report to the SIU came over the radio. Tim ran to the stairs. Chris Frieburg, the first-floor guard, was halfway up the stairs.

"You heard the call?"

Tim nodded.

"I gotta go then."

"Right," Tim answered. He followed Frieburg to the front door of A dorm and locked it after him. It was now Tim's duty to patrol both floors of A dorm, which meant he didn't have to worry about falling asleep on the job tonight, anyway. He walked through the first floor of the dorm, which was a mirror image of the second floor in the way everything was laid out. All was quiet. A few cons had been awakened by the emergency radio broadcast, and a couple of them got up to use the bathroom. Tim waited until they were back in their beds before returning to the second floor. He spent the rest of his shift that way, fluctuating between the first and second floors, wondering what the emergency was and what the hell that was that he had seen out in the yard.

All the while, Tim Saget was unaware of Billy Dee Washington at one end of the dorm, watching his every move, and Chief Tom Laughing Crow watching them both.

11

October 26

Tim was in the COs' barracks getting ready to go on duty when Captain Thompson stopped at his locker.

"I need to talk to you tonight," he said, speaking in a low, conspiratorial voice.

"Sure thing," Tim replied, caught off guard, then the captain was gone. Tim's inner worrywart came alive and tormented him with possibilities as to why the captain *needed* to talk to him. The worst he could imagine was that Julian James's sister had changed her mind and was going to sue after all and Tim was going to be fired as a result. He fretted away the first two hours of his shift, pacing around the edge of the vast second-floor array of beds. When Captain Thompson didn't come by at his regular time of 3:00 A.M., Tim settled down a little, figuring it couldn't be so urgent if the captain couldn't come when he was supposed to. Then again, what if he was sequestered with the superintendent and maybe lawyers for the victim's family and they were discussing charges to be brought against Tim and the other guards? He could easily imagine himself and the others being made scapegoats to save the prison face and money.

Such thinking got him all worked up again. The only benefit of all that stress was that he was not in any danger of nodding off to sleep. He was mulling over the possibilities yet again when Captain Thompson tapped him on the shoulder. Tim was startled but made a quick recovery; he didn't want the captain to think he was easy to sneak up on.

"Hey! Captain Thompson! I was wondering when you were going to come by. What did you want to talk to me about?"

Captain Thompson sat on a corner of Tim's desk and bit at a fingernail on his left hand. He looked over the room of sleeping inmates and seemed lost in thought. Tim waited for him to speak, but the captain remained silent, staring at the cons, but in such a way as to make Tim think he wasn't really *seeing* them.

"Uh . . . Cap? What'd you want to see me about?"

The captain looked around at Tim as if noticing him for the first time. "Huh?" he asked.

"Earlier you said you needed to talk to me about something?"

The captain continued to stare for a moment, then came out of it. "Yeah, right," he said. "I wanted to ask you about something you reported that Jimmy Delilah said after he killed Jones. You reported he said something about a doctor, that he had a doctor 'on his side'?"

"Uh, yeah," Tim said, perplexed at this line of questioning. "He said there was a doctor helping him. His exact words were: '*The* doctor is on my side.' "

"Was there anything else odd that you remember?" Captain Thompson asked.

Tim looked at him and thought about the dream he'd had the night of the murder of seeing Jimmy Delilah carrying the pot with helpers he'd never seen before and the lady with the red scarf and her warning. But that had been a dream . . . hadn't it? He wasn't so sure anymore. "I . . . I . . . I had a . . ." Tim started to tell the captain about the dream, then thought better of it, but the captain finished the sentence for him.

"You had a weird dream that seemed real?"

Tim was astonished. "How did you know that?"

John Thompson smiled. "Welcome to the club. I was just talking to the night doc over in the infirmary, and he's been having weird dreams, too. So has Jack Roy and a couple other guys. So, what was your dream?"

After a moment's hesitation, Tim told him about dreaming that he was awake and on duty and seeing the woman in the red scarf. He repeated the warning she had given him. Captain Thompson took a photocopy of a picture from his clipboard and showed it to Tim, pointing at a man in the photo.

"You recognize this guy? Ever see him in the facility?"

Tim looked at the photo and read the caption: *Doctors and Nurses of New Rome State Mental Hospital—1972.* Captain Thompson was pointing to a young doctor with long black hair and a gaucho mustache worn in the hippie style of the early 70s.

"He looks familiar," Tim said, "but I don't think I've ever seen him around here. Who is he?"

"His name is Dr. Jason Stone and he used to be a doctor here when this place was a state loony bin."

"Jason? That's weird," Tim mused.

"Why?"

"Earlier, one of the cons said that name in his sleep. I thought maybe he was talking to me—my middle name is Jason."

"What did he say?"

"It was weird and kind of spooky. The shade over there suddenly went flapping up—scared the shit out of me—and moonlight came in through the window in a single beam that fell directly on the face of the con lying over there at the end of the last row. He sat bolt upright and said: 'We're gonna get you, Jason!' It had me worried at first; I thought he was threatening me. But when I checked the guy, he was sound asleep—I mean really out cold. I realized it was stupid to think he was talking to me; I mean how could he know my middle name?"

Captain Thompson didn't answer. He was lost in thought again, seemingly oblivious to his surroundings.

"What's going on, Captain?" Tim asked. "What's this all about?"

Captain Thompson turned and leaned toward Tim. "Have you seen anything else strange around here?"

Tim didn't have to ask what he meant. "Yeah. When I went to pull the shade down, I saw people—farmers—working crops outside where the flower gardens are, next to the kitchen. There were six or seven of them—men and women; I dreamed about them before, too. And you already know about the lady I saw on the fourth floor of Digbee Hall. Dave Stirling told me he's seen her, too, on his cellblock. He was afraid of her, I think. Also, I've been having this dream about a building on fire that was familiar but I couldn't quite place it at first. Tell me, did Digbee Hall used to have a cupola on top?"

"Yeah, it was destroyed in a blizzard last winter that caused a lot of roof damage. That's when the super decided to convert the fourth floor to another dorm. They're supposed to be putting the new cupola up soon."

"I thought so. It was the building in my dream. I saw it burning and the roof collapsing."

John Thompson mulled that over for several moments before saying, "Yeah, well, Dave Stirling has got a lot to be afraid of these days. To tell the truth, kid, I don't know what the hell is going on. I'm not one to believe in hocus-pocus bullshit, but I think this prison is haunted, and I don't mean just *haunted* like people seeing a spook on occasion, I mean *haunted* like in *possessed* by something evil."

Thompson paused and looked at Tim to see if he understood. Caught off guard, Tim politely nodded, which was all the encouragement John Thompson needed to go on. "I think this Doctor Stone might be that evil. I found his journal—it was clenched in the dead fist of Jim Henderson. You knew Henderson, right?"

Tim nodded.

"When I found Jim, he had Doctor Stone's personal daily journal held out in his hand, as though he knew I was going to find him and he was just waiting to give it to me. I think Doctor Stone *wanted* me to find it."

Tim was bewildered. "What? This guy is still around?"

"His *spirit* is."

Tim looked doubtful. He noticed that many of the cons' heads were up, listening.

"No, no, no! Hear me out!" Thompson said quickly. "I did some investigating into Doctor Stone. He used to work here back in the 70s. He was the head night shrink when the place was the state mental hospital. For therapy, patients used to grow crops and farm—during the day, anyway. That's what you saw. But at night, when Doctor Jason Stone was in charge, a very different kind of therapy went on." Captain Thompson reached into his jacket pocket and pulled out a half-inch thick, five-by-seven-inch black book. "This is Doctor Stone's daily log. It's full of his notes on how he *changed* while he was here."

"What do you mean?" Tim asked.

"From what I've read in here, he started having weird dreams, too, and found himself doing things he would never normally do—sadistic, sick things. He began carrying out therapies that went far beyond the bounds of normal psychiatric treatment. It seems working here brought out an evil side in Jason Stone. I just started reading this, but already I can see this guy was sick. He writes about administering shock therapy as punishment and subjecting two female patients, who had been severely sexually molested and abused as children, to gang rape at the hands of the male patients. In the next sentence he writes about how guilty he feels and how it is as if he's not in control of his mind and body anymore."

Tim shrugged.

"There's more. He started getting into some sick stuff and he didn't know why, and he couldn't stop himself. He *murdered* patients, and . . . I think he *ate* them. I think that fire he died in was no accident. I'm willing to bet he was murdered by the patients he was abusing."

"And you think he's haunting this place?" Tim asked.

John Thompson looked at Tim through narrowed eyes. "Yeah. Somehow, he's come back. I think he's continuing his perverted therapies on the inmates." Thompson paused and looked around, before adding in a quieter voice, "And I think I have a connection to this guy somehow, though I don't know what. But the first time I heard his name it rang a bell . . . for some reason, I think he's after *me*."

12

Dave Stirling sat quietly in the hard green leather upholstered armchair in his hospital room on the fifth floor of Crocker Hospital in nearby Fitchminster. Since Crocker Hospital was the only one in the area operating a psychiatric ward, Dave Stirling had been transferred there from Hayman Memorial Hospital in New Rome once doctors there had determined there was nothing physically wrong with him. A week after arriving at Crocker's fifth floor, Dave suddenly came out of his shock-induced coma. The last thing he remembered was sitting in his office on tier two and wondering what crap his wife had packed for his lunch again. Since then, his memory was a blank, leaving him with an irrational feeling of fear. He felt like a man who has fallen asleep in his own bed, only to wake somewhere else. It was a disconcerting, uncomfortable sensation, that of losing a chunk of time from his life. What had happened? Why was he in the hospital? Why was there a state trooper outside his door?

He went to the door and asked these questions of the state police officer in the hall but the guy, Lieutenant Colich, would tell him only that Captain Thompson was on his way over and he would answer all of Dave's questions. He sat on the bed, staring at the floor, trying to remember what had happened. The most that came to him was a scream; he remembered hearing a scream, but then nothing. He was glad when the door opened and in walked Captain Thompson. Dave had never been so happy to see someone in his entire life, and nearly hugged his watch commander in his excitement.

"Dave, I need to ask you some questions," Captain Thompson said after sitting on the edge of the chair to face Dave.

"Sure, Cap! What the heck is going on anyway? Why am I here?"

"You don't remember *anything* about your last shift last week?"

Dave looked bewildered. "I've been here a week?"

John nodded. "Think, Dave, what do you remember?"

Dave shrugged. "I remember a little. I remember being in the office and looking at the clock—it was just after three. Then, I . . . I . . . think I remember hearing someone scream."

"Yeah! That's right! What else do you remember?"

Dave Stirling concentrated; looked at his hands, the floor, out the window. "I don't know," he said, his face troubled.

"You said you heard a scream . . . ?" John Thompson prompted.

Dave Stirling scrunched up his face and closed his eyes. After a few moments he let out a sigh, relaxed, and spoke in a low voice: "I know what I said but I can't remember anything beyond that. I'm sorry, Cap," he added, distraught. "What's this about?"

Thompson ignored the question. "Let me ask you something else. Tell me about the old lady you've seen on tier two."

"Who told you about that?" Dave wanted to know.

"It doesn't matter," Thompson answered. He added, "You're not the only one who's seen her."

"Oh," Stirling said immediately. "You've been talking to the new guy, Saget."

"It doesn't matter who told me; you've seen her, right?"

Dave Stirling's face clouded. "Is that what this is about? Did she do something to me or one of the cons?"

"What do you mean? What could she do?" Captain Thompson asked, leaning forward anxiously.

Stirling looked away.

"Why are you so afraid of her?" the captain persisted.

Dave laughed weakly. "I'm not *afraid* of her," he said, and added softly, "I'm *terrified*."

John Thompson waited for him to go on. Dave Stirling went over to the tray table by the bed and poured himself a glass of water from the beige plastic picher there. He drank it down and poured another.

"I think she wants to kill me," he said, quietly.

"What makes you say that?"

Speaking slowly and so softly at times that John Thompson had to tell him to talk louder, Dave Stirling stumblingly told John about his encounters with the gray-haired lady in pajamas who wielded a bloody hammer and the voices in the vents. John Thompson listened attentively, nodding occasionally. "Ever since that night, I've been dreaming about *her*—horrible dreams. They're so horrible I can't remember them when I wake up screaming—all I know is they're about her and I wake up scared shitless, one time, *literally*."

John asked, "Did you see her the last night you worked?"

Dave Stirling thought for a moment and a strange expression crossed his face. "No, not her. But there was something *in the cell*! Something *awful*." He shuddered at the memory.

"What?" John Thompson urged.

"I'm not sure . . . it was something . . . *something* . . ." His voice trailed off. Suddenly he sat up straight. "I remember now! I heard Jimmy Delilah screaming and I ran to his cell window. He was naked, kneeling on the bed, and he was sound asleep! It was funny at first, until he started ramming his head against the wall. When I saw blood fly, I hit my body alarm and tried to wake him up by yelling through the observation window, but he wouldn't wake up. I got my keys out as fast as I could, but I couldn't seem to do it fast enough; my hands were numb. I finally did open the door, and there was blood everywhere. By then the guy was dead.

"It was weird. I heard a noise behind me and I turned. There was . . . something . . . in the wall . . ."

"The wall?" John Thompson asked.

"Yeah, I thought it was someone come to help . . . but it wasn't." He shuddered. " It was, like, *really* dark, like a shadow if a shadow could be solid. It was melting into the wall and . . ." Dave Stirling's face screwed up tightly and he began to cry.

John Thompson was completely nonplussed. He fumbled in his pocket awkwardly for a tissue but found none. Stirling quickly regained his composure, and John took out a photocopy of the group photo of the mental hospital staff, circa 1972, that had been hanging in the HSU. He had made a copy and enlarged the section with Doctor Stone in it until he had a good-sized, if somewhat grainy, headshot of the man. He showed it to Dave. "Is this who you saw?"

Dave Stirling looked at the photo and shook his head. "No. This . . . this wasn't a man . . . this wasn't human . . ." He looked at John with such helpless despair and fear in his eyes. "That place is haunted, Cap, by somethin' *bad*. Tobi Dowry knew it—it got to her. It drove her crazy and she killed herself rather than deal with it. The place is crawlin' with fuckin' ghosts and they don't just jump out and go 'Boo!' or rattle chains, they fuckin' slam your head into a wall until you're dead and they come after you with a hammer and they turn into somethin' so fuckin' horrible you shit your pants if it . . . if it . . . just . . . just *looks* at you!" He broke down, sobbing: "Oh God, Cap. It *looked at me*!"

* * *

"First, Darlene gets raped by someone who looks like me, but isn't; isn't even *there*. He's *dead*." John Thompson looked into his own eyes in the rearview mirror and nodded. He agreed with the look of incredulity there. He took a wheezing breath. "Second—wait a minute." He paused, eyes back on the road. He was driving along Route 2, heading for New Rome after his visit with Dave Stirling. "Maybe," he continued, thinking aloud, "Tobi Dowry was first. What did Stirling say? What she saw drove her to kill herself? Okay. So she was first, then Darlene, then Jim Henderson, then Julian James, and now Jimmy Delilah, not to mention Dave Stirling being reduced to a simpering coward on the verge of a breakdown." John hadn't seen a look of impending madness on someone's face like that since his days in Nam, and then, it had been his own.

Whatever is going on, he thought, *it's spreading, getting stronger.*

Little did John Thompson know the extent to which he was correct. All across the prison a darkness was growing like a virus, spread by Billy Dee Washington's power of speech and through dreams, and it was infecting the inmate population until nearly every con in the place succumbed to its exotic, violent, and often perverted spell.

Even into solitary confinement, the darkness reached. In cell Two-A, Hiram Pena waited, lying on his bed naked, erection in hand. Since late summer Hiram had been enjoying a new and delicious diversion from life in the Can. In the fall months, the extreme pleasures of the flesh he experienced in sleep with the doctor and others came to dominate every waking thought, and he spent all his time trying to remain asleep.

His dream world had at first been one of simplicity where he had his way with supermodels and movie stars, until he realized the *power* he had in that world. From then on, he had let his sick mind fester with perversions and he experienced every taboo he had ever imagined and some he had never thought of before. For the previous two weeks he'd been enjoying the same dream, only eight nights ago, it had stopped being a dream—it had become more; it had become real—it had become a *visitation*.

He tensed. It was starting. He could feel it—a tingling sensation in his balls, like someone had just put a cold metal vibrator to them. Tiny white sparks danced at the edges of his vision, but disappeared if he tried to look at them directly. He had learned not to; it interrupted the process. He stared straight ahead, eyes focusing so hard on the dark spot within the swirls of light that the rest of the room blurred away, and he was left with those whirling sparks that were now forming long bands of pure white light, spinning around and around him. Slowly, like ice forming on glass, these bands of light sent out irregularly fan-shaped tendrils of fog that began to expand and fill up his vision. The darkness in the middle got darker, and at the same time, deeper and wider, as if the spot before his eyes were a frost-encrusted porthole looking into a vast, shadow-filled space behind. If he looked close enough, concentrated hard enough, he could see a dark landscape, swarming with bodies, naked and bound; fleshy, thin, bloodied, tortured, all of the sick forbidden fantasies he'd always been ashamed of; women and children, raped, mutilated, and murdered.

And in the midst of it all, wallowing in the gore, reveling in the pain and torture, in the sadistic sexual gratification, was Hiram Pena.

He looked back at himself, winked, and grabbed a fresh victim.

On the bed, the other Hiram began to masturbate in his sleep.

Two cells down from Hiram Pena, another inmate was having a sexual experience also, but not one of torture, blood, or sadistic pleasure. Like Hiram Pena, since meeting the doctor, Marty Miller thought his dreams had become reality. He lay on his stomach, grinding his pelvis into the thin cot mattress, churning up the dingy, yellowing bedsheets beneath him.

In Marty's dream, he was still in general population, in the prisoners' day room, only it had been reimagined the way *he* wanted. There were no bars on the high, arched windows along the walls, allowing beautiful sunlight to spill into the room without casting long striped shadows over everything. Instead of rows of cheap plastic tables and chairs, the room was decorated with furniture, *real* furniture, like couches, rocking chairs, and plush, cushioned armchairs. There was a Ping-Pong table and a pool table. In the corner of the room, beneath one of the high windows, was a children's play area, complete with rocking horses, piles of building blocks and a sandbox.

In Marty's dream, he was in the sandbox, surrounded by children of both sexes, all under the age of ten, all naked, just as he was; all climbing over him and rolling around him and rubbing against him. Touching them and kissing them and doing whatever he wanted; it was Marty's idea of heaven.

"I've taken good care of you, haven't I, Marty?"

Marty looked up from under a three-year-old boy with the face of an angel. The doctor in white stood near the rocking horse, beaming down at him.

"How can I ever repay you, Doc?" Marty asked, his voice muffled by boy flesh.

"Don't worry, Marty. I'll think of something," the doctor replied, smiling.

In every dorm in the prison, more than a few cons embraced this new world of anything goes, just as Hiram Pena, Marty Miller, Billy Dee Washington and others had. In it they found not only sexual freedom but escape from the crushing loneliness of their lives.

One such con, living in E dorm, was Walter Holstrom. Walter was sixty-six years old, serving life and a day for killing his wife, her lover, and the man's two brothers. Walter wasn't a violent criminal; in fact, he had never broken a law, had never even been in a serious fistfight before he came home early from his job at the Worcester Public Library one day and found his wife of five months in bed with three brothers!

Walter had grown up a lonely boy, friendless, sans siblings, and had thought when he met Lucy that his most fervent wish had been granted—he had found someone to love and care for who would do the same in return; someone who actually *liked* him. To see her cheating on him in such a vile, disgusting, *pornographic* way had just brought all those years of loneliness and self-loathing back on him like a crushing stone, and he snapped. In his closet he had kept an old Civil War four-shot revolver in mint condition with ammo that his grandfather had given him. Walter loaded that gun and put a bullet in each member of the ménage a quatre.

That was forty years ago, when he was just twenty-six. He'd been in prison since, first at Worcester County Jail, then at Concord Maximum, and finally at New Rome. He'd been here for two years. Forty years was a long time, seeming more like eighty to Walter. Every day of the past 14,610 days had felt like a month dragging by. If he'd had any courage at all, he would have killed himself long ago, but he was a coward, and a self-pitying one at that, reveling in reliving Lucy's betrayal and wallowing in the loneliness and despair of prison life.

Walter Holstrom was ripe for picking and Billy Dee Washington was ready to harvest, telling him about the "dream doctor"—as he was coming to be called among the cons—one day at lunch. That night, the doctor had paid him the first of many visits, bringing the gift of renewed and endless vengeance against those who had cut him so deeply. At twenty-six, Walter Holstrom may not have been a violent man, but forty years in prison changes a man. It festers in him and makes him calloused until he is hard and nasty and capable of doing anything against anyone. In the "dream

doctor" Walter sensed a kindred spirit and more, something
greater and darker, *more* lonely and despairing than even he
was or could ever hope to be.

Walter Holstrom longed to embrace it.

13

Thanksgiving

John Thompson sat up in bed and looked at the alarm clock on the nightstand. 8:25 P.M. As usual, he had woken fifteen minutes before his alarm was set to go off. He did this with such regularity that he knew he didn't really need to set his alarm; he just did it out of habit. Since developing asthma he'd also developed the habit of coughing and spitting up phlegm when he got out of bed every morning, which he did now, spitting into the small wastebasket next to the bed. Another thing he did out of habit was to sniff the air to see what Bella had made him for breakfast. It took a moment before the memory of her leaving resurfaced.

He pushed the unpleasant reminder from his thoughts and headed for the bathroom. He turned on the shower and automatically reached to lift the toilet seat before he urinated, but it was already up—another reminder of Bella's absence and the fact that he no longer had to be mindful of her. He could leave the seat up, throw his clothes on the floor, leave dishes in the sink, put his feet on the furniture, and watch whatever he wanted, whenever he wanted, on television.

So why was he so miserable?

He stepped into the shower and stuck his head under the soothing, steaming water, breathing it deep into his sore bronchial tubes. He closed his eyes as the hot rivulets ran down his face. He was tired, and the hot water made him want to sleep again. Once again he'd had a restless day of trying to get some shut-eye while his sleep was disturbed by outside noise, acid reflux, and more weird, unpleasant dreams. Standing in the shower now, he remembered snatches of disturbing images—a long, dark hole, wet and foul-smelling, full of fleeting shadows with eyes. Despite the steaming shower, he felt a chill, remembering.

He finished washing and rinsing and got out of the shower. He was getting dressed when the phone rang. He pulled his pants up and sat on the bed, staring at the phone, a cold fear tightening his sphincter. He panicked a moment, then remembered that he had disconnected the answering machine. He relaxed only a little, though; the phone kept ringing. He began to get nervous—maybe it *wasn't* what he was afraid of; maybe it was the prison calling; maybe it was the *super*! Worry got the best of him, and he reached for the receiver just as the phone ceased ringing. He snatched up the receiver and punched in *star 69* to see who had called but got the recording: *"The number of your last incoming call cannot be reached by this method."*

John frowned. It wasn't the prison. The dread and tightness in his chest returned. He finished dressing quickly, grabbed his keys and inhaler, and headed for the front door. He paused, turned back, and went up to his office. He opened the closet door and dug around on the overhead storage shelves until he found what he was looking for—a pocket Bible from his days in Nam. He slipped it into his jacket with Doctor Stone's diary and left the house. Starting his car, he thought he heard the phone ringing again.

*   *   *

Sheila Donner put down the phone and frowned. That chicken-shit Triscuit John Thompson had shut off his answering machine. She must really be getting to him; she had seen the raw look on his face at work whenever he'd come by. She got up and began dressing for work, contemplating how to up the pressure on John Thompson. She latched onto the idea of sending a letter made out of cutout words, like a ransom note, accusing him of killing Darlene and seeing if it flushed him out any further. Yeah. The more she thought about it, the more she liked the idea.

Before leaving for work, she filled a plastic shopping bag with all the magazines she could find in the house. She hoped it was going to be a quiet night; she had a lot of work to do.

Dave Stirling pulled into the COs' parking lot and sat in his car with the engine idling. This was his first night back at work since Jimmy Delilah had taken *head banging* beyond reason. After a thorough investigation by the prison's Inner Perimeter Security Squad, part of which consisted of a grueling interrogation while hooked up to a lie detector, Dave had been cleared of any wrongdoing in Jimmy Delilah's death.

He had taken some vacation time at the suggestion of Captain Thompson but he didn't feel ready to come back. He was just expected to go back to work like nothing had happened. Of course, no one other than Captain Thompson knew what he had really seen in the Can. On the Cap's advice, he had kept quiet about certain things he had seen that night.

Dave looked at his dashboard clock—ten minutes before he had to go in. He looked around the lot but didn't see Captain Thompson's car. He really wanted—*needed*—to talk to the captain before he went on duty. If it hadn't been for Captain Thompson, Dave wasn't sure he would have survived remembering what had happened that night. But he hadn't seen, nor spoken to, the captain in over two days. He'd tried calling the captain's house while he was out the past couple of days, but there was never any answer.

Dave leaned forward, shut the heater and the ignition off, and got out of the car. He walked slowly across the entrance road to the main gate, all the while keeping a hopeful eye out for Captain Thompson's car. In the locker room of the COs' barracks there was no sign of the captain. Dave lingered at his locker as long as possible, but to no avail. Signing in at Inner Control, he asked Pete Seneca if Thompson was in yet.

"Yeah, he came in early. Said somethin' about goin' down to check out somethin' in the tunnels. Why?"

"Tell him I need to speak to him ASAP, okay?" Dave asked.

"Sure," Pete remarked. "By the way, the kitchen left turkey and all the fixins for us in warming trays in the officers' mess. You can get some on break."

Dave thanked him, but food was the farthest thing from his mind.

Tim Saget was trying to walk off the feeling of fullness he still had from eating Thanksgiving dinner with Millie's parents and the Sarge at the Arpanos' house when Captain Thompson came up the stairs to the second floor of A dorm.

"There's something I want to show you. I think you'll find it interesting." He took Doctor Stone's journal from his pocket and began flipping through the pages. "He mentions a new patient—name of Lena *Saget*." He stopped flipping pages and looked at Tim. "Any relation?"

Tim shrugged; she was no one he'd ever heard mentioned by his father or aunts.

"Here it is," Thompson said and read from the page. " 'A new patient arrived today. She is a local New Rome girl. Her name is Lena Saget and she is the most beautiful woman I have ever laid eyes on. According to her medical records she suffers from acute schizophrenia and has had episodes of personality fracturing in which she has manifested new personalities for short periods of time.' It goes on; I haven't finished it yet," Captain Thompson said, looking up from the page. "I just thought it was interesting. What do you think? A long-lost relative? A skeleton in the closet? You know, the weird stuff has gotten worse since you started working here; maybe you have some connection to this Lena Saget."

Tim balked. "What, you're saying *I'm* the reason weird stuff has been happening?" Before the captain could answer, Tim went on. "The last time I talked to you, you were saying you thought *you* were the cause of this. You thought *you* were the target."

"Easy, kid. I think we're *both* targets here; this may explain why *you* are. You need to ask the Sarge about this Lena Saget. Maybe he knows something. If he don't, we could ask the old guy, Jones, who used to work at the hospital. He's down on the highway every day selling his produce."

Tim shrugged. Though he did not know of anyone in his family by that name, the more he heard it, the more it had an uncomfortable familiarity about it. He felt he'd heard the name recently. Had it been in a dream? He couldn't quite remember. "I will ask my father," Tim replied. "Speaking of interesting things, I've got something, too; an article in the *New Rome Telegram*. The three-to-eleven guy left the paper. I was flipping through when I saw it." Tim went back to his desk, grabbed a folded newspaper from the desktop, and brought it back to the captain. He pointed at an article near the bottom of page six as he handed the paper to Thompson.

New Exhibit at New Rome Library

A new historical exhibit recalls the history of New Rome's Windigger Hill, also known as Stone's Hill, where today the New Rome Correctional Institute stands. The exhibit recounts through pictures and newspaper articles the history of the prison's prior

*function, that of a state hospital for the insane, until a
Christmas Eve fire thirty years ago killed two doctors,
eight nurses, the night custodian, and twenty patients.
The cause of the fire was never discovered.*

John Thompson looked up from the newspaper. "You
think this has something to do with what's going on?"

"I don't know, but keep reading, further down, the stuff
about 300 years ago."

"Oh, okay, let's see. Here it is: 'The exhibit also tells the
story of how, three hundred years ago next month, the property of New Rome founding father Elijah Stone was found
abandoned. The farm, situated on what is now the site of the
New Rome Correctional Institute, was the first settlement in
the area, which at that time was an unforgiving, brutal
wilderness. Elijah Stone and his wife disappeared from their
farm sometime in late December and were never found or
heard from again. Within fifty years, the same thing would
happen again to Elijah Stone's only surviving son, Parson
Stone. A full account of the mysteries surrounding the Stone
family settlement were recorded in the 1800s in the locally
produced and published book *Fireside Legends and Tales of
New Rome,* an original, handwritten copy of which will be
part of the exhibit.' Wow! Elijah *Stone*! You know, since I
first saw the doctor's name it's been nagging at me—where
have I heard it before? Now I know why it sounded so familiar." The captain frowned. "Oh, my God!" he gasped. "This
is all starting to make sense now," Thompson went on. "I
think *I* might be related to our Doctor Stone."

"What?" Tim was confused.

"I remember my daddy always used to say we were related to the founding father of New Rome, Elijah Stone. I
never connected him with Doctor Jason Stone, though. I'd
love to get a look at that book at the exhibit."

"Why?" Tim asked. "What's that got to do with anything?"

"A lot," the captain answered emphatically. "I've been

jumping around in Stone's journal and the last few entries are really strange, then there's a big chunk missing—torn out. He also mentions several patients disappearing. And he thinks he and the other patients may have *eaten* them, but he can't remember."

"So?"

"So, Elijah Stone *disappeared*; his kid *disappeared*; patients from the hospital *disappeared*, three cons *disappeared* from here before I got transferred. They supposedly escaped but were never caught, and we never found out how they got out. In his journal, Stone wrote about the feeling that something was after him." He opened the diary and skimmed pages until he found what he was looking for. "Here. Listen to this: 'I continued to feel an irresistible urge to explore the tunnels that were discovered last week under Digbee Hall. They are not on any of the hospital's building plans for tunnels. Doctor Digbee thinks they may be so old as to have been dug by Indians; but to what purpose is not known. Since I first heard of their discovery, I have felt this pull to go and explore these artifact structures.

" 'So this morning, just before the day shift came on, I went down there to look around. There was a huge pile of stone off to the side of the entrance to the cavern. The wall was collapsed, revealing the cavern, but it looked as though the wall had been *constructed*. It was mortared together and wasn't a natural solid stone wall. I think it had been built to block off the cavern deliberately. Doctor Digbee thinks it might have been part of a cellar to one of the original colonial-era structures and was walled up when the tunnels were built.

" 'The tunnels are not a comfortable place to be. A feeling of trepidation always accompanies me down there, but once inside that cavern, it grew until it was a force of terror. Something kept pulling me on, but the feeling of unrelenting terror, of something horrible about to happen any second, made me turn back.' " John Thompson flipped the pages. "Then he says: '*Something* has followed me out of the tunnels.' "

Tim was perplexed and showed it, shaking his head and shrugging his shoulders. "So what does that mean?"

"I don't know; the journal ends there. The rest of the pages have been torn out," Thompson replied. "But when I get off duty, I'm going to go and try to find this cavern he writes about. To my knowledge the prison has never used the tunnels under Digbee, and I never heard about a cave down there."

"I can come with you," Tim offered.

"Good," the captain said, then waffled. "On second thought, you could do me a bigger favor."

"What's that?"

"Go to the New Rome Library exhibit and see if you can get a look at that book about Elijah Stone."

"Uh, yeah. Sure. I can't go until my day off, though," Tim answered.

"Great. I'll let you know if I find anything in the tunnels and you can fill me in on the book at the library. The spirits here want something from us and we've got to find out what that is."

As John Thompson walked to the top of the stairs, a voice from the rows of supposedly sleeping cons broke into song:

"When there's something strange in your neighborhood, who you gonna call?"

More than half the dorm room of cons shouted out the answer: "John Thompson!" and burst into mocking hilarity.

John stopped, looked back, but all the cons were lying down and laughing; he could see none of their faces. He had no idea who had sung out. His face burning hot with embarrassment, he turned on his heel and left.

Chief Tom Laughing Crow couldn't help but laugh along with the other cons. It was, after all, funny. He had always thought it strange that evil should have the best sense of humor, while good is generally witless and boring. The chief snuck a peek at Tim Saget, who had tried to hide his own smirk from his superior. He was now settling down with his handheld video game. The chief thought about what he'd just overheard. The captain knew something was going on but he was a fool. And Saget was just going along to please his boss. He didn't really buy anything the captain was selling; the chief could see it in his face.

Too bad, the chief thought. Day by day the situation at the prison was worsening. He could see it in the eyes of the cons—they were all connected and they were all waiting.

The chief was worried, more worried than he could ever remember being. He had spent the major part of his adult life playing at being an Indian—a con game, pretending to be a medicine man, a shaman, selling useless potions and amulets and magic feathers at his shop in Williamstown on the scenic Mohawk Trail, which bisects Massachusetts from Boston to the New York State border. His great-grandfather had been a real shaman, and a lot of the stuff Tom had he had inherited from his great-grandfather.

One of the more important things he had got from the old shaman was *knowledge* that helped him to recognize what was really happening in the prison, and this knowledge made him very *afraid*.

14

December 1–December 2

On his day off, Tim drove to New Rome, turning onto Main Street, which ran along a ridge between the two smallest of New Rome's seven hills, and concentrated on finding the library, not having been there before. At the third red light—he couldn't believe how many traffic lights this short Main Street had—he spotted the sign for the library. He went through the green light and turned into the small parking lot. There were plenty of spots and he pulled into the one closest to the street.

He was a little taken aback. He had thought all small New England towns and cities had antiquated, architecturally interesting libraries, usually built in brick and granite, but from the outside New Rome's library looked like an ordinary concrete-and-stucco office building, low and rectangular, and like a converted supermarket on the inside.

"May I help you?" the librarian at the front desk asked him. As far as he could see, the library was otherwise empty.

"Has this always been New Rome's library?" he asked.

The woman, fiftyish with large, bright brown eyes, short,

salt-and-pepper hair, and an attractive figure, blushed. "No. The original library was *much* nicer than this. A work of art! It was destroyed about ten years ago. We lost nearly all our entire inventory in the fire and had to start over in this building." She looked around, a scowl on her face. "This place was built to be a Victory Supermarket!"

Tim laughed. "I thought so." She laughed with him. "Tell me, is the exhibit still on about the history of Windigger Hill?"

"Oh, yes! We were lucky not to lose some of those things in the fire. The old library had an incredible book vault that was as good as any bank vault in town. We kept all our valuable manuscripts and books in there. That's what saved them. We had quite a collection, but most of them have been shipped to the New Rome Historical Society and the library at Montachusett Community College. But we still keep copies of the old books that pertain to local history, like Lord Cleghorn's *Fireside Legends and Tales of New Rome*. We have the original here for display only, but you can look at a copy of it if you like."

"That's great," Tim said, relieved. "May I?"

"Certainly," the woman replied. "Follow me." She went back to her desk, opened a drawer, and removed a large key ring. Tim followed her down the main aisle of the library, between rows of now empty Dewey Decimal System card catalog cabinets, which had been replaced by and were now topped with three computer stations, then past tall racks of books. She led him to a large adjacent room where the exhibit had been set up on four long tables, with photo collages displayed on several easels.

The librarian went to a side cabinet, unlocked its door, and opened it. "All our local history books and books by local authors are normally kept in this room. Though you can't take them out, there is a copy machine right around the corner behind the last row of books. You can make as many copies as you want; they're twenty-five cents apiece. The exhibit starts at that end of the room with the early days of Windigger Hill."

Tim stepped into the room. It smelled of musty paper and old book leather. The two side walls and the rear wall were covered with books stacked on industrial-type metal racks that extended from floor to ceiling. The librarian went to the rear wall, ran her fingers along the spines of the books on the fifth shelf and pulled out a large, thin black vinyl notebook. There was no title on its cover or spine.

"This is it, *Fireside Legends*." She placed the book on the table. "This is a copy. The original is in that glass case on the first table. We don't let that out any more. It is nearly two hundred years old and brittle in spots. We're trying to raise money to have it preserved and restored, but you'd be surprised at how much that costs. So we've been forced to use this photocopy."

"Thank you," Tim said. "It'll be fine."

The librarian started out of the room but paused at the door. "If you don't mind my asking, you don't look like a student. Do you have some connection to the Hill? What's your interest, if you don't mind my asking, that is."

Tim hesitated, feeling awkward. He didn't know what to say; he couldn't tell her any of Captain Thompson's theories, and wouldn't know how to begin to make anything that had happened at the prison sound rational. Truth be told, he wasn't really sure what he was supposed to find out.

His reluctance was apparent on his face, causing the librarian to bow out. "I'm sorry. Of course, it's none of my business." She lingered in the doorway a moment longer, hoping Tim would give in, but he turned his attention to the exhibit and began walking around, looking at the photos. After she left, he carefully opened the book. The first page was blank; the second was the title page. The photocopy was slightly askew and read:

Fireside Legends and Tales of New Rome
By
Lord Cleghorn

The story started on the next page, headed:

The Legend of Windigger Hill

Elijah Stone considered himself to be a man apart. If ever there was a contradiction to the well-known dictum "No man is an island," it was Elijah Stone. He did not suffer fools lightly, and he thought most men to be fools. His great-grandfather had come to New England in 1638, at the age of sixteen, on the HMS Diligent, *landing at Hingham Village in the colony known by the Indian name of Massachusetts. Finding that sparse hamlet to be too crowded for his liking, Ezekial Stone had set out for parts less populated. He settled his family on the uninhabited shores of Lake Algonquin, in what would later become the town, then city, of Worcester.*

Elijah was a lot like his great-grandfather. At age twenty-seven, his father died and left him the family farm. After his great-grandfather settled the area, more families had followed until a bustling community was thriving. Such crowding was something Elijah Stone could not abide. He chose instead to turn the homestead over to his younger brother, Larkin, and set out for a place of solitude with his wife, Lucy, and their 12-year-old daughter, Sarah.

They moved around often for two years, living out of doors and off the land; Elijah was a good marksman with his father's English-made musket. They first followed the winding path of the Merrimac River, then headed cross-country until they hit the banks of the Nashoba River. With child during this time, Lucy bore

Elijah a son, Parson, on the banks of that mighty river. Here also it was that Elijah Stone first heard of the place the Indians called "The Land of the Seven Hills." It was the highest arable ground—part of the Central Massachusetts Plateau, which makes up the foothills of Mount Wachusett—for hundreds of miles around. Having read of ancient Rome in his father's meager but well-rounded library, Elijah was drawn to the area. High ground in New England was not generally good farmland, but that meant he would not have to worry about being encroached upon by other settlers. It also meant it would be difficult for anyone to approach his homestead without his knowing about it.

Being the solitary type that he was, Elijah shunned the hills of the west and north for their close proximity to each other, and instead founded his homestead on the solitary hill to the east. He built a stockade home, after the fashion of New England pioneers, and tried to till the land. He spent hundreds of backbreaking hours digging up rocks and building walls to section off and enclose his fields and pastures, but no matter how many stones he pulled from the earth, there were always more. Due to this, his crops went in late that first spring.

There is a story told whose veracity is doubtful, but which I will recount here for the reader to judge. It is said that several Indians of the Mohegan tribe visited him one day in early summer, speaking loudly and expressively, waving their arms and pointing at the summit of the hill. Elijah smiled and nodded, most likely silently cursing himself for leaving his musket back at the stockade. But the Indians were not hostile, nor aggressive. When they realized the bearded, dirty white man did not understand what they were saying, they shrugged, regarded him with pity, and moved on. In their minds, he was either stupid or crazy. If he was the latter, perhaps the spirits would protect him; if he was the former, he was doomed. For according to Indian legend, the hill Elijah Stone settled on was a haunted place; a place to be shunned. But for better communication, disaster might not have befallen poor Elijah Stone.

The facts that are verifiable are that the first summer on what has come to be known variously as "Windigger Hill" or "Stone's Hill" passed uneventfully, except for the marriage of his daughter to one Jonathan Thompson. Even this was a nonevent in that there was no wedding, no feast nor party. The young man, twelve years older than the 14-year-old Sarah, had known the family back in the Worcester settlement. He had contracted with Elijah for Sarah's hand upon her fourteenth birthday, which was November 11. Two weeks later, the young man dutifully appeared at the Stone stockade and, after receiving his meager dowry of a bushel of rabbit, beaver, and raccoon pelts, plus five gold coins, Sarah left with him, not knowing she would never again set foot on Stone's Hill, nor see her parents.

One month later, on Christmas, a trapper traveling south from Canada stopped at the Stone farm, looking to trade for a meal and provisions, and found the farm abandoned. Legend has it that the trapper found human bones in the kettle over the fire, but there are no actual records to that effect. Writings of the day record that the only unusual thing the trapper found, other than the desolation of the farm, was a word carved into the inside of the front door: Windigger, hence the name "Windigger Hill." This story became so well known that the hill is called by two names: "Stone's Hill" and "Windigger Hill." The origin and meaning of the latter word and why it was carved into the door of the Stone farmhouse remain a mystery.

As for the Stones' only son, Parson, as the trapper was leaving the abandoned Stone farm, on his way to

*the Worcester settlement, he found two-year-old Parson
Stone wandering in the woods, naked, freezing, starving,
and unable to speak. The trapper fed him, swaddled
him in furs, and carried him to the Worcester
settlement, where he was claimed by his sister, Sarah
Thompson. Parson's ability to speak eventually returned,
but for the rest of his life he claimed to have no
knowledge of what had happened to his mother and
father.*

*When Parson was twenty, he returned to Stone's
Hill and reclaimed the family property. He was a successful
farmer and raised a large family, siring seven
boys and five girls, all but one of whom survived to
adulthood in a time when such survival rates were not
common. Normalcy, unfortunately, was not to be poor
Parson Stone's lot in life. Like his father and mother,
Parson and his wife, Elizabeth, disappeared at Christmas
in 1750. A week later, the children, led by the oldest
boy, Oliver Cromwell Stone, aged fourteen, walked into
town with the story of how, on Christmas Eve, their
parents had gone off into the woods and not returned.
A search was made of Windigger Hill and the surrounding
area, but no trace of Parson or Elizabeth was ever
found. The eldest son tried to make a go of the farm,
but sold it ten years later to a neighbor who used the
land as pasture for his sheep.*

Tim took the book to the copy machine and made two
prints of the page that had John Thompson's name on it. He
could imagine what the captain would make of this—even
he had to admit it seemed to fit everything Thompson had
said to him earlier. He went back to the small exhibit to look
at the stuff about the old state mental hospital. He was looking
at the photos of patients farming, stunned to realize the
scenes were so similar to what he'd seen outside A dorm that
night and in his dream. The door opened behind him and an
elderly, white-haired, stooped woman entered.

"Hello," she said in a high, soft voice. "June told me you were interested in the history of Stone's Hill. I'm Dottie LeBlanc; I run the New Rome Historical Society. I set up this exhibit. Perhaps I can help with any questions?"

"Actually," Tim said, "I was wondering if you have any books about the old state hospital."

She shook her head. "You'd think there would be, with all that happened up there before the place closed, but no. We do have a collection of newspaper articles about the fire and the inquest that followed displayed over here." She indicated the last table.

"Inquest?"

"About the fire."

"I thought it was an accident," Tim said.

"Oh no. The fire was supposedly set by a patient. There was more, too. A question of improprieties on the part of some of the hospital doctors and staff."

"Was . . . Doctor Jason Stone one of them?"

"So you *do* know some of the story. Yes, he was implicated, but of course it was after the fact, after he was dead."

"What did they find out?"

"Unfortunately, not much. The only surviving witness to the tragedy was a patient, but she had a severe breakdown before she could testify. So the cause of the fire was laid at the feet of one of the dead patients, a fellow known for being a pyromaniac. But questions lingered; still linger to this day."

Tim had a strange feeling, similar to what he felt when he had one of his prophetic dreams. "Do you . . . do you know the name of the woman patient?"

"No, not offhand, but I'm sure it's mentioned in one of the articles. She was a local girl, I think. Hold on." She went to the table she'd indicated before and opened a large red leatherbound photo album. Tim could see that its black pages were filled with yellowed newspaper clippings. Dottie LeBlanc flipped several pages and ran her finger down a couple of articles. "Here it is. *Lena Saget* was her name.

Bright girl—valedictorian of her high school before she had
her first breakdown."

Local girl, Tim thought. Didn't the Sarge tell him the
family was originally from New Rome?

It was time to talk to the Sarge.

When he got home, there was a phone message for him
from Millie, calling from work. Though she knew it was his
night off and their only chance to spend some "quality" time
together, she was going to dinner and a movie with her
friends from work that evening and wouldn't be home until
late. Tim listened to the message and tried to remember the
last time he and Millie had spent any *real* time together, or
made love. She froze up so bad with the anticipation of pain
every time he touched her that he had pretty much given up
trying.

Knowing his father would be up—he rose at five every
morning like clockwork—Tim called him on the phone, but
then thought better of it and hung up before the second ring.
He had a feeling he needed to ask the Sarge face-to-face
who Lena Saget was. He drove to his father's house and
parked in front. He went to the front door, found it locked,
and rang the bell. His father came to the door in his T-shirt
and boxer shorts—what he called his "skivvies"—and seemed
surprised, and pleased, to see Tim there.

"Hey! How's it goin'? Come on in. I was just making a
fresh pot of coffee. You want some or will it keep you up?"

"None for me, thanks," Tim replied.

"So, how's things on the Hill? Anything new up with my
weirdo buddy, John Thompson?"

Tim decided not to be truthful. "No, everything's cool.
Something did come up, though. There was an article in the
New Rome paper about the fire back in '73 at the old mental
hospital, you know, where the prison is now. You ever hear
about that?"

"No, no, can't say that I did, but I was still in the army in 1973. I'd just got back from Nam."

"Well, this article mentions a woman—a patient—who survived the fire, and her name was Lena *Saget*." Tim paused. All the time he'd been talking, the Sarge had been measuring coffee into the electric percolator. Tim was certain he'd seen a moment's hesitation, a wavering, even a *quivering* of the Sarge's hand when Tim mentioned the fire at the hospital, and again at Lena Saget's name.

"Hm. That's interesting," the Sarge replied but didn't look at Tim, occupying himself with putting the lid on the pot and plugging it in.

"Is she any relation?" Tim asked. The Sarge went to the sink, his back to Tim, and rinsed out a cup. He shrugged. "I doubt it. I know we had some distant cousins in the area; she might be one of them, but I'd hardly call that *related*."

Back at home, sitting on the couch, drinking a beer, Tim couldn't shake the feeling that the Sarge had been lying to him or, at the very least, had not told him everything he knew. Why would the Sarge do that? Who the hell was this Lena Saget?

He sat on the couch until noon, drinking beer, staring vacantly at the boob tube, and pondering all that he'd learned that morning. He fell asleep in front of the TV and was visited by restless, uncomfortable dreams that flitted through his slumber, leaving him with a growing sense of trepidation. All his dreams centered around Elijah Stone and the hospital fire; in one of them the two different events became mixed together so that Tim saw Elijah Stone setting the fire at the hospital. In the dream, Elijah smiled at Tim, showing green teeth, and said: "*Windigger!*"

He remembered only one other dream clearly—the rest were vague and fleeting, more residual sensation than memory. In the remembered dream, he was sitting by a fireplace, stirring a large kettle that hung over the flames. The room was lit only by the flames, but he could see log walls chinked with dried mud with bits of grass, leaves, and other forest debris sticking out of it. It was cold, and he clutched some sort of foul-smelling animal fur around his shoulders.

He stared at the kettle and wept, yet didn't know why; he only knew he was terrified. He became aware of the wind blowing like a tempest outside the cabin. It whistled through the loose mud chinks and became a voice calling him out into the night and the forest.

That was when he woke, nearly leaping from the couch, his heart pounding, his head and neck clammy with fear-sweat. Why? He couldn't remember. That voice . . . He couldn't remember what it had said, but he remembered the terror it made him feel.

15

Dave Stirling glanced at the clock on his desk. It was after 5:00 A.M. and, as on every other night since coming back, he had not sat down once since coming on duty at eleven. The door to his office was propped open with his desk chair, allowing him to keep an eye on the office and the tier and giving him an unimpeded runway for pacing. Normally he would walk the length of the tier to the exit door and back to his office a couple of times a night. Now he did it constantly, but every time he passed by Jimmy Delilah's cell, he kept his head down and looked at the floor.

"Where the hell is the Cap?" Dave muttered to himself. He had seen the captain only twice since starting back, and both times the captain had been called away by Inner Control. Dave really needed to talk to him; if the Cap signed off on Dave's disability claim, he could get out of there. He didn't know what he was going to do otherwise. He didn't know how much longer he could last at the prison.

There was a sudden sound from the air vent—was it a voice, or just the heat coming on? Dave didn't wait to find out. He turned around and walked down the tier.

* * *

Hiram Pena sat on his bed, legs crossed Indian style, leaning back, head resting against the wall. Out of the corner of his eye, he saw the CO's head go by in the small cell door window. A few moments later he went by again, going the other way. Hiram sat on the bed and smiled. The CO, Stirling, was nervous. That was good. Hiram stared at the opposite wall, and slowly his eyelids slid closed, but in his mind's eye, he still stared at the opposing wall.

The industrial green concrete blocks suddenly shifted to the right. A ripple passed over the surface for a moment, giving the rough stone the incongruous texture of water. Again it rippled, as if an invisible stone had been dropped into it. With each rippling wave emanating outward, the light in the cell grew brighter, then suddenly dimmed as the ripples faded. Shadows stretched across the narrow floor and over the ceiling. They crept up the walls and crawled across the dingy sheets to caress his feet. The concrete blocks across from him took on a strange luminescence of their own, as if tiny candles somehow burned deep within. The wall ceased being solid; it became a corridor, a tunnel. Shapes moved within the concrete, creating whispers of air that set the glowing lights to flickering—

—and in the beat of a strobe, the shapes jumped closer in jerky, rapid movements. A crack appeared in the wall and spread, weblike, over the entire surface. The blurred shape behind it stretched out a hand to touch the stone, and it shattered like glass, flinging thousands of shards outward like a driving hail. He put up his hands to protect his face, but the shards all dissolved in the air before they reached him.

The shadowy shapes in the wall flowed into his cell. There was a sound like steak sizzling, and the shapes coalesced into focused images, like amoeba caught under a microscope.

Hiram Pena smiled and welcomed the doctor and an elderly lady in a housecoat and slippers.

"This is Myrtle," the doctor said.

* * *

Dave Stirling returned gingerly to his office, breath held, ears straining. All was quiet. He glanced at the clock: 6:30 A.M. His relief would be there soon. As far as Dave was concerned, it couldn't be a moment *too* soon. He'd spent the past hour and a half sitting in the uncomfortable wooden chair set at the other end of the tier, near the exit door. Though nothing had happened—other than the voices he'd *thought* he'd heard a short time ago—there had been something in the air; an anticipation that Dave could feel as a liquid fear made his knees weak and his intestines tight. He was glad the shift was over. He quickly got his things together and then sat on the edge of the desk where he could see down the tier to the door his relief would be coming through.

"Come on!" he breathed, impatiently.

Hiram Pena stood and embraced the old lady, Myrtle. With a sound similar to that of a vacuum-packed can opening, the two merged and became one. Like a hologram, first one, then the other, surfaced in Hiram's skin. Walking to the cell door, he was Myrtle, then Hiram, before shifting back to Myrtle again. She looked over and smiled at the doctor.

"Ready?" Doctor Stone asked.

Myrtle looked hopefully at the door, then at her hands. She flexed them and looked at the doctor. "Where's my hammer?" she asked the doctor, and her image shifted to that of Hiram Pena.

"You won't need it. You have strong hands," the man in white told him. He nodded toward the door. As if by remote control, it unlocked and opened.

Now that his shift was seconds from being over, Dave Stirling finally let himself relax. He slumped against the desk and yawned. Tonight had been like every other night since returning: For the last eight hours he'd been running on fear and adrenalin. It was exhausting, but he couldn't remember the last time he had gone home after work and slept for more than a couple of hours without being awakened by those horrible nightmares.

He slumped further on the desk, his shoulders slouching, his left arm sliding off his lap to the desktop. He yawned again, and with the closing of his mouth also came the closing of his eyes. He dozed until the distinctive *bang* of one of the cell doors closing woke him. He bolted to his feet and gasped. He rubbed his eyes and patted his cheeks with both hands. Was he awake or asleep?

He hoped he was still sleeping, for down the tier, a malicious grin on her face, came the old lady of his nightmares. Dave Stirling didn't think he was still sleeping; in fact, the closer the old lady got, the more he was sure of it.

She means to hurt me, he knew. He could see her intention in her eyes and quivering, smirking lips.

She means to kill me.

The old lady nodded in answer to his thought and rushed at him. Reflexively, Dave scrambled back, sliding along the edge of the desk where his right hand came upon the landline phone. As the murderous old hag closed on him, Dave grabbed the phone receiver and base and brought them both up in a hard roundhouse right to her head, catching her on the temple with the corner edge of the base. She went down immediately. Blood, liberated from her head, ran down the side of her face as she fell, forming a crimson sideburn.

Dave dropped the phone and ran. He didn't stop when he passed his relief coming up the stairs, and he didn't stop when Pete Seneca, the new second in command on night shift, called to him as he ran past the Inner Control command post. He didn't stop running until he got to his car in the parking lot, and then only long enough to get out his keys and unlock the door.

In his wake, Dave Stirling left an angry Pete Seneca and a puzzled Corinne Macon, Stirling's day shift relief. Macon entered tier two of the Can and immediately went to the of-

fice. There she found Hiram Pena, unconscious on the floor,
a bloody gash to his left temple. CO Macon immediately
used her radio to call a ten thirty-three, then retrieved a first-
aid kit from the desk and set about tending to the prisoner's
wound.

In C building, Tim Saget was unaware of the commotion
going on inside the prison. He'd been relieved a little early
and was glad for it. He hadn't seen or heard from Captain
Thompson all shift, until Pete Seneca brought a message
over to him from the captain. He wanted Tim to meet with a
guy named Joe Jones, who was the former hospital caretaker
who still farmed on the hill. The captain had suggested to
Tim that he should ask the old guy about Lena Saget, see if
he remembered her, and Tim wondered if that's what this
was about. Jones had called the prison and left a message for
the captain to meet him outside the front gate in the morning. Eager to talk to this guy himself and maybe find out if
Lena Saget was related, Tim hurried to change in the barracks, not bothering to shower as he usually did.

Tim passed through the COs' exit, saying good-bye to the
two officers behind the reception glass. He stepped into the
chilly December air and pulled his coat tighter about him.
His breath steamed in the air, flitting away and dissolving in
a cloudy nimbus around his head. He stood on the high steps
of C building, peering over and through the several meshes of
fence and gates until he saw a truck parked across the road in
front of the minimum-security house. Standing next to it was
a grizzled old man whom Tim assumed was Joe Jones.

Tim went down the steps and through the first gate, not
noticing the approaching whine of an automobile engine
running at high speed.

Dave Stirling hurriedly got in his car, tried to jam the key
in the ignition and dropped the entire keyring. He fumbled

around awkwardly, reaching between his legs and bumping against the horn, before scraping his fingers over them. He inserted the key more carefully, started the car calmly, put the stick shift into reverse easily, and tromped on the gas pedal, making the tires spin on the frozen ground. They caught, and the car spun out into the center of the parking lot in a wide arc. Dave threw the shift into drive while barely stepping on the brake. He stomped on the gas again, peeling out of the parking lot as fast as he could.

He glanced back at the prison and let out a soft whimper. The old lady who'd attacked him was up in the new cupola on top of Digbee Hall, waving bye-bye to him. He felt sick with fear; he'd never been so frightened in his entire life.

What the fuck is happening?

A giggle came from the back seat. Dave whirled around, the car swerving with him—no one there—and turned back to the wheel, when suddenly *there she was* in the rearview mirror, leaning forward, reaching *for him.*

Her face *changed.*

It became the thing in the wall he'd seen in Jimmy Delilah's cell.

Dave Stirling screamed and let go of the wheel.

Tim Saget stepped through the last gate and started for the road and Joe Jones, who was leaning on the front left fender of his ancient pickup truck. The old guy looked at Tim, but his attention was abruptly drawn to the right. Suddenly, he turned, his arms raised in defense. At the same moment, Tim realized the growing hum he was hearing was an approaching car. In the next second, he saw it veering out of control, heading straight for old man Jones.

A moment before the car slammed into the truck, crushing Jones between the vehicles and sending the driver catapulting through his windshield, Tim thought he saw someone in the backseat—a face at the back window—just for an instant . . . and it was the face of the old lady he had seen in Digbee Hall.

She smiled at him and blew a kiss, then disappeared as the cars crashed.

John Thompson was tired—so tired he wanted to lie down *anywhere* and sleep. But he knew if he did that he'd be suddenly wide awake, his brain motoring away nonstop. He wished he could shut it off for just a little while, but he couldn't. Part of the problem was his asthma—he seemed to be struggling for breath and using his inhaler more, and it left him exhausted. Between that and the phone calls from Darlene wanting help, dead Darlene accusing him of killing her, the letters in the mail accusing him of the same, not to mention the weird shit with this Doctor Stone, John felt more confused and disconnected from reality than at any other time in his life, including the unreality of Nam. There, at least, he had known who the enemy was and what he wanted, even if he couldn't always see them. There, he had a specific course of action, dictated by military strategy, policy, and regulations—even if they were not always followed. Now, as he had in Nam when he had felt military discipline and security breaking down, he found himself turning more and more to the faith he'd been raised with.

His father had been an Episcopal minister and his mother a devout acolyte. John was raised in an atmosphere of daily prayer and religious solemnities until the age of sixteen, when he rebelled with booze and a dabbling in drugs, fast cars, and girls. Enlisting in the service upon graduation from high school had been the final step in his break away from his parents and their stifling devotion. Strangely, though, he'd always thought, when the going had got really rough and scary in Nam, it had been that stifling childhood faith that had saved him.

Lately, John had started carrying a pocket Bible with specific passages marked in red, their pages dog-eared. Both his parents had passed away in the early 90s—his father from a heart attack, his mother from a stroke one month later—and John had kept all of their religious bric-a-brac, knick-knacks, and icons in a box in the back of his office closet. He'd dug out his mother's favorite rosary beads and carried them with him at all times. He'd started wearing his father's cross and St. Christopher's medal around his neck. Three times a week, after work, he attended mass at the local Episcopal church. He'd made a practice of stopping by the prison chapel at least once per shift to offer up a few prayers and read from his handy pocket Bible.

It had been a quiet week since the suicide of Jimmy Delilah. He glanced at his watch—the shift was almost over. He had wanted to stop in and check on Dave Stirling, but he'd got held up nearly all night looking for paperwork on a new inmate and dealing with a lack of heat in F dorm. He hadn't made any of his normal rounds, hadn't had a chance to talk to Tim Saget, nor had he got the chance to look for the cavern mentioned in Doctor Stone's journal. A half hour ago, Jane Mazek had called him on the landline with the message from Joe Jones. He called Pete Seneca and asked him to make the last round of the night for him and ask Tim Saget to meet with Jones and get the message. That way, he figured, Tim could ask about Lena Saget. He regretted not checking on Stirling. There was something about him that had been bothering John since Dave returned to work, but he couldn't put his finger on it. He was going to have a long talk with him tomorrow. Right now, he had just enough time to quickly check the tunnels under Digbee Hall before the end of the shift.

He entered the tunnels by way of the kitchen, his mind churning with recent events. He spent forty-five minutes going back and forth in the cramped tunnels under Digbee Hall, exploring locked passageways that had not been used since the place had become a prison, and found nothing but a sense of uneasiness, of not being alone. It was almost a feeling of déjà vu after reading Doctor Stone's journal and his account of the same feeling. Several times in the narrow, dank tunnel he had felt someone or *something* lurking in the shadows, just out of sight, just out of reach. Once he stopped and turned quickly to try and catch whatever he sensed following him and could have sworn he saw a dark shape clinging to the shadows of the ceiling pipes. But when he flashed his light on it, there was nothing there except the feeling that the thing had somehow moved around behind him again. A moment later he distinctly heard a chorus of male voices cheering and laughing over the muffled screams of a woman. It sent chills running down his back and him running for the prison chapel.

Pausing at the entrance to the chapel, he shivered at the memory of the voices in the tunnel and the feeling of something watching and following him. He crossed himself with his right hand while taking off his cap with his left, and went in. The chapel was a good-sized room with seating for fifty in ten rows of wooden pews separated into two sections by a wide middle aisle. A small altar and lectern were at the front of the room. The prison didn't have a full-time chaplain. Religious professionals in New Rome shared Sunday duties at the prison on a rotating basis. On the first Sunday of every month the Catholic priest from Our Lady of the Lake said mass, heard confessions, and conducted catechism classes for a very small clientele. The second and third Sundays belonged to the Protestants from several of New Rome's churches. The last Sunday of the month was for the Seventh-day Adventists, the largest religious faction among the prisoners. Every other Saturday, Rabbi George Levi from Temple Bethlehem performed service in the chapel.

John went down the aisle to the altar, genuflected, and crossed himself again. He knelt at the altar railing and bowed his head in prayer, asking for the Lord's help and protection. Behind him, the floorboards creaked. Without lifting his head from his devotions, John turned slightly and looked behind him. The chapel was empty. Turning back, he noticed the rear left corner of the chapel was dark. A ceiling light must have burned out, he thought. He made a mental note to write a memo to maintenance to replace it.

He turned back to his prayer, finishing his pleas for help and protection with a recitation of the Lord's Prayer said three times, followed by three Hail Marys. There was another series of creaking sounds, much like footsteps, behind John again. This time he lifted his head and turned fully, expecting to see Pete Seneca or Jack Roy coming to get him.

Empty.

Only now he noticed another light had burned out near the first so that the last couple of pews were now in darkness. A cold breeze, like an expelled breath, washed over the back of his neck. He shivered. Another row of pews succumbed to darkness. In the growing shadows, something was moving. John Thompson strained to see, his forehead beading with cold sweat, the back of his neck suddenly clammy. The chapel went completely dark and suddenly filled with rustling sounds and unintelligible whisperings.

John rose from the altar just as a heavy black shadow rushed from the darkness, dealing him a heavy blow between his shoulder blades and driving him to his knees again. The whisperings, rustlings, and other half-heard sounds increased in number and volume. Something brushed past his face.

"Who's there?" John asked. A foul odor washed over him and a barely heard whisper reached his ears.

"Legion," it answered.

John struggled to his feet and pulled his Bible from his pocket and held it up to the darkness as if it were a dispelling light. "No!" he wheezed. "Be gone, demon! I command you in the name of Jesus Christ, Lord and Savior." He began to recite the Lord's Prayer, and the lights came back on. Continuing with his prayer—" . . . deliver us from evil . . ."— he looked around. The chapel was empty; he was alone. Shaking, he took a pull from his inhaler and glanced at his watch: 6:50 A.M. He had been in the chapel longer than he'd thought. It was almost past time for the shift change.

Suddenly his radio squawked to life: "Inner Control to One hundred. Cap, we got a problem. Can you call me on a landline, over?"

"Inner Control this is One hundred, will do. Over."

John left the chapel and headed for the check-in desk near the front door of D building, which also held the chapel and the school. He used the landline on that desk to call Pete Seneca.

"Cap! Dave Stirling's gone off the deep end. He left his post early, before his relief came on. The relief CO, Corinne Macon, found one of the Can's inmates, Hiram Pena, out cold in the COs' office. He's got a pretty nasty gash on his head."

John swore under his breath before answering. "Call the state and local police and give them his car description and license number. Have them pick him up. I'm on my way." As soon as John Thompson walked out of D building he knew there was more wrong than just Dave Stirling leaving his post and assaulting an inmate. Several corrections officers were running at full speed along the main walkway heading for C building.

"What's up?" he called to one of them.

"There's been an accident just outside the main gate," the man shouted back.

John ran down the steps and followed, sprinting to C building, then through it and the outside obstacle course of gates and fences to the road. There was a crowd of minimum-security prisoners and COs already gathered on the opposite side of the road. Crossing, John saw Tim Saget separate from the crowd and walk slowly away, head down.

"What happened?" John asked, running up to him.

"Joe Jones," Tim said. "He's dead."

"Oh, my God," John said softly.

"Dave Stirling, too," Tim added.

"What? How?"

"I don't know how it happened. I came out to meet Mr. Jones like you asked me to. I was hoping he could tell me

312   R. Patrick Gates

something about Lena Saget like you suggested—and Stirling just came careening along out of control and smashed into him, pinning him against his truck. Dave went through the windshield. I checked them both—dead. Probably instantly."

"Shit!"

"That's not all, Cap," Tim added and looked around to be certain no one could overhear. "Just before Stirling's car crashed into Jones, I could swear I saw the old lady Stirling was so afraid of, in his back seat, looking out the window at me."

The piercing wail of an approaching ambulance's siren caught their attention. The crowd of COs, minimum-security prisoners, and civilian prison staff parted to allow the ambulance to pull up to the scene. Close on the bumper of the ambulance was a large, red, square rescue truck.

John took Tim's arm and led him away from the commotion. "Look, this is getting very weird here. This is getting serious. This is getting *dangerous*. I just got attacked in the chapel and when I asked who was there, you know what answer I got?"

Tim shook his head.

"*Legion*. You know what that means? Do you know your Bible?"

"Something to do with Jesus and a possessed guy, wasn't it? And weren't there some pigs, too?"

"Right. But the important part is when Jesus asks the demon's name and it replies, '*Legion*.'" He raised his eyebrows and nodded his head slowly. "I think it's obvious what we're dealing with here. Pure evil. The Devil. Satan himself. Somehow, someway, he's gotten a foothold here." Thompson went on in a quiet voice as if talking to himself. "Maybe it was back when I first started and we caught those two guys sacrificing animals in the tunnels—some sort of occult ritual—I'll *bet* that's what started this." He stopped and looked Tim in the eye. "I think we're in danger unless we can do something about it." He looked back at the scene of wreckage and death. "This proves it."

The captain's words brought Tim's dream back to him. "You're in danger," the woman with the red headscarf had said. Tim's head was swimming. He didn't know what to think anymore. Before seeing Joe Jones and Dave Stirling killed in front of his eyes—not to mention seeing that old lady in the back seat—he would have thought John Thompson had finally flipped his lid the way he was talking. But now . . . ?

"What can *we* do?" he asked.

"A lot," Thompson answered. "I never told anyone this—not Bill Capello or your father—but when I got back from Nam I took a correspondence course to become a minister in the Church of the Savior's Blood. In Nam I learned that the Lord is a mighty power to have on your side in times of darkness and fear." He paused and looked around before looking Tim in the eye. "We're going to perform an exorcism on this place. And I know just when and where to do it; the anniversary of the fire that killed Stone and the others—Christmas, and we start in the tunnels where Stone first sensed the evil."

15

December 13

Tim Saget couldn't get over the feeling that the Sarge was lying to him about not knowing Lena Saget, so when he ran into his Aunt Rosie at the bank on his next day off, he lingered, waiting for her so they could walk out together. Watching her reaction carefully, he said: "I want to know about Lena Saget."

Rosie's reaction could not have been more telling; her face paled and her eyes widened with surprise. "Uh, you need to talk to your father," she said quickly.

"No," Tim said adamantly, grabbing her arm as she tried to hurry to her car and get away from him. "*You* tell me. I'm tired of the Sarge's games. I want to know."

She looked at Tim with sadness on her face, and in that moment, Tim knew what her answer would be even before the words left her mouth.

"She's my sister . . . and your real mother." Rosie looked around the parking lot as if everyone there had heard her. "This is no place to talk about his. I'm on my way over to your Aunt Sadie's for coffee. Why don't you follow me there?"

Thirty minutes later, after an equally surprised, shocked, emotional, and ashamed reaction from Aunt Sadie to the news that Tim knew about Lena Saget, he got the story of Rosie, Sadie, and the Sarge's baby sister, Lena Saget.

The three of them sat in Aunt Sadie's living room, which looked like it could have sprung straight from the pages of *Martha Stewart Living* with its collectibles of knick-knacks and country-homey crafts and decorations—only there was enough of the stuff to fill three of Martha's rooms.

"Lena was the youngest," Rosie started after an interchange of expressive glances with Sadie. "She was also the smartest and the prettiest."

"She was a genius—valedictorian of her class," Aunt Sadie chimed in. She and Rosie sat opposite Tim, nibbling on anisette waffle cookies and sipping coffee whenever the other was talking.

"But—" Sadie shrugged and looked at Rose.

"But she had problems. You know, like my daughter always says, she had *issues,* you know? It started right after high school. One day she came home from her summer job with the phone company as happy as a lark. She told us she had met someone and fallen in love. She was so happy!"

"Yeah," Sadie agreed, a dreamy look on her face.

"Well, of course we was all tickled pink for her. Mom and Dad—Pa and Nonna, remember them? They died when you were three—wanted to meet this guy. We all did. We all bugged her for about a week and finally she gave in and said she would call him." Rosie paused to take a sip of coffee and Sadie immediately picked up the slack.

"So she calls and the line is busy. She calls again and keeps on trying but it's always busy. This goes on for over an hour and Lena starts getting really upset. She starts talking about how he must have another woman with him and he's cheating on her. She started to act crazy, dialing his number over and over and talking to herself, saying stuff like how she would kill herself if she caught him cheating on her.

"We was all upset and tryin' to calm her down but we

couldn't. Then I was standin' next to her as she was dialin' the phone—it was the old kind with the spinning dial thing, you know? I was trying to get her to stop calling him and take it easy when I noticed the number she was dialing was *our* number!" Sadie shook her head, her eyes filling with tears.

"No wonder it was busy all the time," Rosie said with a sad smile. "We tried to tell her she was calling her own number but she wouldn't listen—she *couldn't* listen. She ran out of the house before anyone could stop her. She went to her girlfriend's apartment, locked herself in the bathroom and slit her wrists. Luckily the girl had a key and had to shower for work or Lena would've died then."

"Your dad was in the army at the time so he didn't see how bad she was; he didn't see her at her worst. The next couple of years was hell for our poor parents but most of all for Lena. She started hearing voices—"

Sadie cut in: "And the weird thing is sometimes the voices told her things that were *going* to happen, and then they *did*."

Rosie looked doubtful at that tidbit but held back comment and went on.

"Anyway, she got worse and worse. We took her to a bunch of doctors who said she was suffering everything from a nervous breakdown to dementia praecox—I'll always remember those words, they sound so *creepy*. We heard she was suffering from 'women's troubles' and manic-depression. One idiot even told us she had an 'Electra complex' and she wanted to kill her mother and marry her father and the guilt over that was driving her crazy."

"Bunch of quacks," Sadie said, offering Tim an anisette cookie for the eighth time, which he decided to accept to keep her from continually offering.

"We were at our wits' end. Mom and Dad were getting too old to deal with Lena's problems. Sadie and I had five kids between us under four years of age. We were no help. I remember it was a week after your father came home from the war. The doctors recommended we put Lena in the state mental hospital in New Rome. It was supposed to be very good for its day."

"A beautiful place," Sadie said, then frowned and looked sheepishly at Tim. "But you know that." She thought a moment then added, "Or is it still? I mean, can a *prison* be beautiful?"

Tim said, "Let's just say it's a nice place to visit but I wouldn't want to live there."

"Well, you almost did," Aunt Rosie said, eyebrows raised. "That's where your mother got pregnant, in the state hospital. We never did find out who the father was . . ." She paused, looking uncomfortable, as did Aunt Sadie. Neither of them would look at him or at each other.

"I'd like some more coffee," Rosie said, suddenly and stood, picking her cup from the table.

"Me, too," Sadie added quickly, doing the same.

"Wait a minute," Tim said stopping them. "You were going to say something. What?" Rosie still wouldn't look at him. He turned to Sadie. "Come on, tell me. Believe me, nothing else can shock me today. I'm all shocked out."

Sadie and Rosie exchanged another look and both sat down. Rosie's cup and saucer, which she still held in her lap, rattled from her hands trembling. "They told us she was raped," Sadie started, but became choked up.

"By more than one person," Rosie finished for her. "The hospital officials weren't sure who the father was and since he died in the fire she set anyway it didn't much matter."

"*She* set the fire?"

"That's what they told us," Sadie said softly, glumly. "They said she set the fire and locked them all in to get back at them for raping her—doctors and nurses, too, for letting it happen, I guess."

"What did *she* say?" Tim asked.

"Nothing. When they found her, nearly frozen to death outside in a snowdrift, she was catatonic. She stayed that way for two months, then came out of it, sort of, but she didn't remember anything, including us, her family. The Sarge paid for round-the-clock care for her so she wouldn't lose her baby, *you*. Two and a half months after the fire, you were born. She was doing pretty well up 'til then, but after the delivery she became catatonic again."

"When the hospital said they would put you in an orphanage, Joe said no. Him and Pauline couldn't have kids—Lord knows they tried! They adopted you, and Joe decided you should never know any of this—to protect you, you know? So you shouldn't be too hard on him. He really did all he could."

Tim ignored that and asked, "So what happened to her?" In his gut he knew the answer—she was dead, probably from suicide, but he had to know.

"Well, with her catatonic and Joe taking you in, the hospital bigwigs met with your father—the Sarge—and made a deal. They said they wouldn't press charges and put Lena and our family through the ordeal of a trial for arson if he would, as her legal guardian, commit her to the care of the state indefinitely. It was the same result we would have got, *maybe,* if she'd been tried. They would have had to find her insane and put her away. It was the same thing, and it was the best thing for Lena. The hospital blamed the fire on one of the dead patients and Joe agreed."

"So?" Tim asked, palms up.

"So they put her in Belchertown State Hospital, then Worcester State. Then in '85, when all the state mental hospitals closed and they turned out all the patients, Joe had her transferred to a private hospital near Boston called McDougal-Walker."

"And?"

"And what?" Sadie said. "That's where she lives."

An hour later Tim was speeding down Route 2, past the Concord rotary and the high-walled maximum-security prison there and on through Boston's boroughs to Storrow

Drive and downtown. Driving automatically, he mulled over all the incredible things he had learned that day. It seemed Captain Thompson was right in thinking Tim was involved in the weird shit at the prison; his own mother had set the fire that killed this Doctor Stone and probably the old lady he'd seen who seemed to be haunting the place.

He turned away from that unpleasant thought and fumed over the Sarge's subterfuge all these years. His aunts had said not to be hard on him; he had done all he could for Lena—but what about me? Tim thought. In light of all he'd learned, Tim wondered if that was why the Sarge had always kept him at such an emotional distance. It made Tim angry. Did the Sarge blame him for being born? Why didn't the hospital doctors just give her an abortion? he wondered. The way the Sarge had always treated him, Tim guessed he would have preferred that. But he remembered that the Sarge's wife, Pauline, the woman Tim had thought was his real mother, was against abortion. Tim remembered her fondly; she had loved him deeply. And, obviously, the Sarge had loved his baby sister deeply, but why couldn't he have shown some of that love for her baby? he wondered bitterly.

He saw a small, square blue sign with the McDougal-Walker logo of two doves bearing a caduceus aloft and an arrow pointing left. Ten minutes later he was parking the car in a lot that charged a dollar an hour.

Tim went into the massive concrete-and-glass structure and followed the signs to the psychiatric wing of the hospital. He stopped at the information kiosk in the lobby and was told that Lena Saget was in room 123, down the hall and to the left.

Tim found the room, right next to the nurses' station, and stood outside the door, suddenly uncertain of what he was doing or what he was going to say. Aunt Sadie and Aunt Rosie had said she had good days and bad days—coherent ones and ones when she lived in some other universe.

"Can I help you?" One of the nurses at the nearby station had noticed him standing there, waffling.

"Uh, is this Lena Saget's room?" Tim asked, feeling stupid and childlike.

"Yes," said the nurse, whose name tag read *Lucy Green, R.N.* "Are you a relative?"

Tim nodded and felt a strange tingle saying the words: "She's my mother."

"*Really?*" the nurse said, showing more than official interest. "Are you Jason?"

"No, no. I'm Tim," he said.

"Oh," the nurse frowned. "She often talks about, and sometimes *to*, a Jason. We were wondering who he might be. Her sisters didn't know. Do you have a brother?"

"Not that I know of," Tim said absently, thinking his *middle* name was Jason.

"Well, you can go right in," the nurse said, interrupting his thoughts. "She hasn't been that bad today. You haven't been here before, have you?"

"No," Tim said. He felt himself blushing at what kind of son Lucy Green, R.N., must think he was, and felt compelled to explain. "She gave me up for adoption. I just found out that she's my mother," and added, "and my middle name is Jason."

The nurse made a sympathetic face and touched his arm. "Oh! That's so sweet! You're going to finally meet her. Well, like I said I think you picked a good day for it—you know how she is, right? You know what to expect?"

Tim nodded.

Lucy Green squeezed his arm again, leaned close, and whispered, "Good luck."

Hesitantly, Tim stepped over the threshold. Afternoon shadows filled the small, nearly square room. Tim stood just inside the door and took it in. Directly across from him was a small window with lace curtains and a plastic suncatcher in a diamond within a diamond shape. It glowed red, blue and gold, catching the last rays of the setting winter sun and tossing them up to the ceiling where they danced like reflections off water. Next to the window was a narrow single bed covered in a pile of plush pillows on top of a fluffy blue quilt. The walls were hung with religious pictures—cheap prints of the Virgin Mary, Jesus in various scenes from the gospels, and a picture of John F. Kennedy. Other than the bed, the only furniture in the room was a narrow cabinet of drawers against the left wall next to the bed, and a thickly upholstered chair with a rose-patterned fabric that looked like it belonged in a fancy parlor instead of a hospital room. Immediately to his left was a small sink under a chrome-rimmed rectangular mirror hung on the wall. To the right of that was a door with a little red bulb over it. The red light was on, and since the room was empty, Tim figured it was the bathroom and the light indicated it was occupied. A moment later he heard a toilet flush and the door opened. The light went out.

A small, frail woman with long, stringy gray-and-black streaked hair that hung in her face, hiding her features, shuffled from the bathroom. She walked with the stilted, herky-jerky movement of the extremely elderly or someone who's had a brain injury. She was neither. She wore a flowered, long-sleeved dressing gown that hung to the floor. Even though it covered her body, Tim could tell she was the thinnest person he had ever seen. The gown hung on her as if she were a pole. What he could see of her neck looked to be no thicker than his forearm, which was not very big.

She held the bathroom door open with one hand and shuffled around it until clear, then let it swing closed, ruffling her nightgown as it passed. At that moment she looked up and saw Tim. She didn't react, just stood and stared at him. Tim could see one eye clearly through the hair hanging in her face, and it gleamed in the shadows.

"Jason," she said finally, her voice low, gruff, and mannish. "When are you going to leave me alone? Haven't I paid enough? Why do you want to keep dragging it up? Leave me be. Go back to that *thing;* go back to Hell for all I care." She waved a dismissive hand at Tim and crossed to her chair, moving more quickly and naturally now.

"Um, Ms. Saget, uh . . . I don't think you know who I am," Tim said and immediately wanted to take it back; it sounded so stupid.

Lena sat in the chair, barely filling half of it with her frail form, and peered at him. "You're right. *Is* it you, Jason, or is it your demon? Was it *ever* you?" She grimaced, bending over slightly with obvious pain in her midsection. Tim thought of getting the nurse, but Lena straightened again almost immediately. She ran a trembling hand through her hair, pushing it back, and Tim got his first good look at her face and eyes. Her face had thin, clawlike jagged scars running from above both eyebrows down over her eyelids and down both cheeks, disfiguring her entire face. Though his aunts had told him of this—how she had tried to claw her eyes out with a dinner fork back when she was at Belchertown State Hospital—it was still shocking to behold.

Lena looked at him as if she hadn't noticed him before. "Oh, hello. Do I know you?" she asked, squinting at him. Tim stepped closer.

"I'm Tim. Tim Saget."

At first she stared blankly at him, but then he saw understanding begin to dawn.

"I'm your son," he added.

Her hand went to her motuh and she bit at the gnawed ends of several fingernails, staring at him with wide eyes. Suddenly, something happened; another change came over her. Her gaze faltered for a moment and came back less clear. The trembling of her hands increased.

"You can't fool me, Jason. You couldn't have him then and you can't have him now. I'm sorry you died, but that's how you wanted it anyway. I'm sorry if it's not all you thought it would be."

Tim tried to think of something to say to snap her out of it, but she was becoming more agitated.

"Please leave now," she said and began rocking in her chair. "Please leave now. Please leave now. Please leave now. Go away. You're not real." Her voice was rising, the rocking motion of her body becoming more strenuous. Afraid she was going to have some sort of seizure or breakdown, Tim backed out of the room. The further he got from her, the quieter she became until he was in the hall and she was silently sitting and rocking in the shadows. Befuddled with conflicting emotions, Tim didn't know what to do. He decided there was nothing left to do but leave; this had been a waste of time. But what else had he been expecting? He didn't know, but this hadn't been it.

Halfway down the hall, he heard the nurse calling, "Sir? Sir?" He turned to see Lucy Green leaning over the counter of the nurses' station, pointing at Lena Saget, who was shuffling quickly after him. Tim went back to her. She shoved a sheaf of papers into his hands, turned, and shuffled just as quickly back to her room. Nurse Green shrugged and smiled at him.

Walking out of the hospital, Tim looked through the papers she had given him. They were small, blue-lined pages, like you'd find in a notebook or day planner. There were a dozen of them, filled with scrawled handwriting that Tim recognized; it was the same paper and handwriting that was in the journal of Doctor Jason Stone that Captain Thompson had.

Out in the parking lot, Tim sat in his car and blinked away hot tears. He didn't understand why he was being so emotional; it wasn't like him. He looked again at the notepapers Lena Saget had given him. About halfway through the pages, the handwriting changed to a lilting feminine scrawl. His interest piqued, Tim began to read, beginning with the first page, where the script was the same broad-lettered handwriting he had seen in Stone's journal.

Sept. 1, 1973: I know how this will sound, and I know how it looks as I write it, and I know how ridiculous it is but I have to write it anyway: I think I am losing my mind, going insane. But even as I finish that sentence, another pops to mind telling me that it is not insanity, but genius!

How clichéd is that?

Sometimes I feel like I'm trapped in a Frankenstein movie. When I'm away from the hospital I sometimes think that the path I'm on is madness, but then I come to work and it all becomes so crystal clear. I

September 2, 1973: I was interrupted while writing yesterday so I'll finish here. I have made an amazing discovery that could make me famous, maybe even bring immortality. I wrote in this journal before that I had sensed a presence in the newly discovered cavern below Digbee Hall and that it had followed me out of the tunnels. I was not wrong. The entity has made itself known to me as an intelligent being, mostly through dreams—I know how that will sound to my colleagues—but recently through a patient, Lena Saget, whom I mentioned before. It seems Miss Saget has some psychic abilities and can channel this entity, which should help a great deal in proving the existence of this thing.

Oct. 30: Oh, the things I have discovered! The power I have felt. This goes beyond science. I have begun an experiment in conjunction with the intelligent entity I discovered beneath the hospital and its results have been outstanding. I have discovered a way of increasing the life force of a human being.

Dec. 1st: Lena refuses to be my channel to the entity any longer. She says it is evil—so primitive! I thought she was smarter. Well, there are ways to get her to cooperate.

Dec. 13th: I'll show them all. Nobody knows what I've been through. I've been alone my entire life. I'll show them all. I get stronger by the day—whole lives stronger. Lena calls me a murderer but she is wrong. Those patients haven't died—they live on in me, stronger, saner, better.

Dec. 23rd: It all becomes crystal clear. The superior intelligence I have discovered here has shown me

the answer; it has shown me how to evolve. It is all so
perfect.

The large, sweeping handwriting of Jason Stone ended
there, and the lighter, tighter, prettier script that Tim assumed was Lena Saget's started:

I stole these pages from Dr. Stone to show Dr.
Digbee he's crazy. As crazy as anyone in here. I am
afraid something bad is going to happen soon, so I am
writing this now, in case I cannot later. I didn't get the
chance to steal these until today, Christmas Eve, and
Doctor Digbee is away until after New Year's. I don't
know who else I can give them to. I don't know who I
can trust; so many of the staff are under Jason's sway.
Dr. Stone is mad but it's not his fault. Something has
taken over his mind. I think he plans to do something
horrible, and I am afraid I have taken this too late to
stop him. I don't like the way he looks at me or my
pregnant belly.

The writing ended there, halfway down on the last page.

16

"Now it all becomes clear!" John Thompson said. He and Tim were standing near the tunnel door, as far away from the sleeping inmates as possible. Tim had just told him everything he'd learned at the library exhibit and in his visit to Lena Saget. "Weird shit started happening when I transferred here, and even *weirder* shit when *you* came. Whatever haunts this place is out for us, kiddo. Me, 'cuz I'm related to Stone and I think there's a curse on the Stone family; and you 'cuz your mother set the fire that killed him." He looked around the dorm, mindful of the past ridicule he'd suffered and continued in a whisper. "We've got to put these spirits to rest with an exorcism and it's got to be done on Christmas Eve, the anniversary of the fire your mother started *and* the anniversary of the disappearances up here over the centuries. Think about it! It's scary. So are you with me?"

Tim felt disoriented—had felt so since meeting with his aunts and going to see Lena Saget. All of his thoughts and movements seemed not a part of him. He found himself nodding and not sure what he was agreeing to; his head was still befogged with the aftermath of images and emotions from meeting his mother.

Great," the captain said. "I think we can trust Jack Roy in this, too." He looked around the dorm again and leaned closer to Tim. *"They"*—he indicated the cons with a nod of his head—"all know about this. They all *know* Doctor Stone. Keep an eye on them. Once we've cleansed the place, they'll be free of him." He shook Tim's hand and smiled. "So Christmas Eve it is." He left Tim to contemplate what he had got himself into.

PART THREE

17

December 24–December 25

When it was all over, the surprise blizzard that swept through New England on Christmas Eve and well into Christmas morning would be called "The Christmas Blindside" by the media. The National Weather Service and all the local meteorologists were caught with their pants down when a weak storm along the mid-Atlantic got sucked in by an east-moving front created by temperature shifts over the Great Lakes. The result: the forecast of a few flurries became the worst blizzard since 1978 slammed into a completely unprepared New England.

It started snowing around eleven, and by midnight it was a curtain of white. From southern Connecticut to northern Maine, from upstate New York to the Atlantic coast, heavy snow fell at a rate not seen in twenty-five years. On the Central Massachusetts Plateau, where the city of New Rome huddled amid its seven hills and where, because of its elevation, the wind was naturally strong, power went out in one town after another as those strong winds attained gale force and knocked down power lines.

On the Hill, the snow came down horizontally, each flake

like a tiny razor slicing through the air. As the snow thickened and the storm built, its clouds rolled in over the Hill, hit a blocking front created by Mount Wachusett, and rolled back over the Hill and the prison. Similar to the atmospheric inversion that causes the dense smog of Los Angeles, this brought about a thick, swirling and fast-moving cloud that rushed over and enveloped the Hill. Adding to the gray curtain, at exactly midnight, a low, rolling ground fog began to emanate from the many crevices and small holes and cracks between rocks that peppered the Hill. The blizzard winds blew it along and the mountain pushed it back until the fog joined the clouds racing over the Hill, dancing a mad dance with the snow.

Going on duty Christmas Eve, after having two days off, walking across the prison yard to A dorm, Tim Saget noticed it was starting to snow and a mist was moving in. He also noticed what looked like a large domed structure made from bowed and cut slender saplings with canvas stretched over it in the middle of the flower garden in what used to be a courtyard. The structure was impressive and familiar; Tim had seen a documentary about American Indians of New England and this structure resembled one of those he'd seen in the program. He remembered they were called "lodges" and not "teepees."

Inside A dorm, the three-to-eleven CO, Alex Torres, pointed at the Chief, sleeping in the first bed in the row of cots closest to the COs' station. "You see the teepee? The Chief calls it a 'sweat lodge.' "

Tim nodded. He'd figured the structure had something to do with Chief Tom Laughing Crow.

Alex Torres went on: "It seems the ol' Chief there has been busy since his arrival. I heard that through the ACLU he filed a petition to the state to let him put up the teepee to practice his religion. He says it's a 'sweat lodge' for cleansing evil spirits. Crock of shit, if you ask me—just a ploy so they can have a place to go smoke cigarettes or dope or whatever, since we can't disturb them when they're in their 'worship.' Not surprisingly, as soon as the ACLU got involved the Department of Corrections completely buckled on this one, but you can't blame them. They've lost too many of these lawsuits and wasted a shitload of money. Like three years ago this diddler sues the prison for serving unhealthy food after he develops high blood pressure. The older guards tell me the food here used to be pretty good—Salisbury steaks, fried chicken, burgers, fries, hot dogs, pizza. But this jerk sues and *wins,* so the state changes the menu in all the prisons and that's why we get the crap we get now."

Tim couldn't comment on the quality of the food; working eleven-to-seven, when the kitchen and cafeteria were closed, he didn't get the opportunity to eat the prison food. The one time he'd sampled it had been his first day and the meal had been pasta in tomato sauce. And while it wasn't Millie's mother's sauce and pasta, it had been okay for cafeteria food.

"Yeah, so the chief got word two days ago that the DOC was giving in so he started building that and finished it today. If you ask me, though, that thing won't last long. First good blizzard or windstorm we get and that thing'll be flying down the hill, scaring the shit out of drivers down on 140." Torres laughed at the image. He winked at Tim—something he did a lot of, as if perpetually letting you in on a little joke—and left.

Tim sat at the COs' desk and put his lunch bag, containing a peanut butter and butter sandwich and two boxes of nearly frozen Juicy-Juice berry fruit punch drink, into the large bottom drawer. He looked around, wondering how long it would be before the captain showed up to carry out his exorcism. The idea of doing such a thing had been bothering Tim since the captain had first mentioned it. The truth be told, Tim was scared of going into the tunnels, and worried; this seemed like the sort of thing he could lose his job over, and he couldn't afford that. It also seemed, for want of a better word, *crazy*. Wasn't the captain just overreacting? Were the deaths of Dave Stirling and Joe Jones really connected to the prison, or was it just a freak accident? Since then, Tim had spent a lot of time thinking about what he'd seen and had convinced himself that his eyes had been playing tricks on him when he thought he saw the old lady in the rear window of Stirling's car. The captain was probably right about the place being haunted, but them being in *danger*? Tim just couldn't buy it, especially after having visited Lena Saget. The whole story of her life and the others involved in it was just a sad tragedy; there were no vengeful spirits from beyond the grave seeking to make him pay for what she did. If that were the case, then Stirling's car should have crashed into him—he had as clear a shot at Tim as he did at Joe Jones. No. Captain Thompson, good guy that he was, had lost it on this.

From his back pocket he took a tattered, well-thumbed paperback novel he'd found lying on one of the locker room benches in the COs' barracks. Its cover touted that it was number six in the Assassin series of Mack Murdoch novels—a series Tim had never heard of. The book wasn't very long, but he only needed it to fill the time when he was taking a break from his GameBoy. He tried reading now, to take his mind off things, but it was no help. He switched over to his GameBoy, removing it from his coat pocket and turning it on when he heard footsteps coming up the stairs and recognized them as Captain Thompson's. He quickly put the video game in the drawer with his lunch. A moment later Captain Thompson entered the floor. Jack Roy, the west yard CO, was with him.

"Are you ready?" Thompson asked Tim. "I let Jack here in on what we're doing. He's had dreams and some weird shit happen to him, too. He's gonna relieve you so we can go through the tunnels and cleanse this place once and for all. I brought holy water, crucifixes, and communion wafers I made from unleavened hardtack."

The captain looked like such an eager—and desperate—kid, Tim hated to disappoint him.

"Uh, I been thinkin', Cap, and I . . . I can't do it. I'm sorry; I can't afford to lose this job. I just got married; my wife's pregnant—you know?"

Thompson looked crestfallen but recovered quickly. "I can guarantee you won't get in any trouble—I'll take all the flak if there is any."

Tim shrugged. "To tell the truth, Cap, I just don't feel *right* doing this. Please don't take offense. I don't know what's going on here, the place probably *is* haunted, but I really don't think that there's anyone after us, no matter what happened here thirty years ago."

"Not in danger? I was *attacked* in the chapel," Captain Thompson replied heatedly and looked at him for a long moment, but Tim avoided his eyes. "Okay. That's okay," the captain said quietly. He leaned over Tim, putting one hand on the corner of the desk, the other on the back of Tim's chair. "You know, you *are* in as much, maybe even *more* danger than me or anyone else here. *Your* mother set the fire that killed the people whose spirits now haunt this place, seeking revenge. You think you're not in danger? You think I'm overreacting? Try telling that to Dave Stirling and Joe Jones—*why* do you think Jones was killed *before* he could talk to you? Someone or something wanted to keep you from discovering that Lena Saget was your mother—I'm sure that's what he was going to tell us. What about Jim Henderson and Darlene Hampton and the two cons who are dead?" He stood and stepped back.

Tim kept his eyes averted and nodded. "I'm sorry, Cap. I just don't believe it."

Thompson looked at him for a long moment and shook his head. "All right, Jack, it's you and me. Let's go." He turned at a military clip and almost marched out of the dorm and down the stairs. An uncertain and bewildered Jack Roy looked to Tim for help, saw none, and reluctantly followed his captain.

* * *

Outside, John Thompson looked at the white sky. It was starting to snow. He didn't like the looks of it. The forecast was for flurries, but the sky looked more like blizzard weather. He noticed that the ground fog that often appeared at night was swelling more than normal. He turned to Jack Roy and put a hand on his shoulder. "We can do this, Jack. Are you ready?"

"I don't know, John. The kid's got a point."

"Look," John said angrily, "never mind what the kid said. You've been around long enough to know I'll cover your ass. Hell, no one other than the three of us even has to know about this. And remember how Jimmy Delilah got by you? And the weird, scary dreams you've been having—your words, Jack. Well, this'll stop them *and* we'll be saving countless lives—I'm convinced of it."

Jack Roy shrugged and looked at the ground.

"Listen, I went out on a limb for you and covered your screw-up in that whole Jimmy Delilah mess; now you can help me, goddammit," John shouted.

"Okay! Okay!" Jack Roy relented. "Sorry. Let's go."

Back in A dorm, Tim Saget slumped in his chair and let out a long sigh through puffed cheeks. Had he done the right thing? He realized there was someone standing at the desk in front of him. Startled, he lurched back in the chair, making it squeak loudly in the quiet dormitory and looked up. It was Chief Tom Laughing Crow.

"He's right, you know," the Chief said. He was of average height, but he had a habit of keeping his head cocked to the right, perhaps to keep that hideous nose in profile to lessen its effect. Because of this, he looked and talked out of the corners of his eyes and mouth. Tim had thought it before and he thought it again now: the Chief didn't look like any Indian he had ever seen.

"We *are* in danger here. Not just you and your captain. Me. Everyone. There is something really bad here; really *old* and really *bad*," the Chief said. His voice was high-pitched and whiny. "I can't get out; that's why I built the sweat lodge. You can get out."

"I don't fucking believe this," Tim said. "Maybe you should have gone with the captain," he said sarcastically. "Between you and him you'd think this place was a house of horrors."

The Chief looked him straight in the eye. "You have no idea," he said softly. Tim felt a chill run down his spine, but he shook it off and spoke with finality and authority.

"Go back to bed, Chief, and leave me be. It's Christmas Eve. If you're not asleep when Santa comes, he won't leave you any presents."

The Chief laughed. "Okay, Pilgrim, but I think you just dug your own grave. We'll see. You know where to find me if you need me."

John Thompson and Jack Roy entered the tunnels in C building after a visit to the armory for more powerful flashlights and their pistols, "Just in case," Thompson told Jack, who was too afraid to ask, "Just in case of what?"

"We need to go in here," Thompson explained as he unlocked the tunnel door in the basement of C building. "This is the main tunnel for the entire facility. It makes a loop under the entire compound. All the other tunnels connect to this one, eventually." He opened the door and stepped through. Jack Roy took a deep breath and followed. He was immediately surprised and encouraged to find the tunnel wasn't at all what he had expected. He had to go into the tunnels for checks every shift, but when he did he'd always entered through the kitchen in the west yard. There, nearly all the tunnels were hewn from solid rock and were tight, damp, low-ceilinged passageways that were no fun to maneuver in, especially if you were tall and/or had a substantial beer gut, and Jack Roy was guilty on both counts. But the tunnel here was wide and well lit; it was dry, with plenty of headroom. It was the largest and best maintained tunnel under the prison.

"We'll do this methodically, starting under D building, then going on under the greenhouse before cutting over to do Digbee Hall. Security doors have been put in place there, closing off access from Digbee and the Can, but I have the keys. We've just got to make sure we lock up behind us when we leave."

Twenty-five yards or so along the tunnel they came to a left offshoot marked with a small sign: ←D-BUILDING and a convex mirror on the ceiling to avoid collisions. It was an older, damper, rock-sided tunnel, curving slightly to the left for thirty or forty yards until it ended in the basement of D building.

John Thompson was carrying an old, beat-up leather gym bag that he placed on the stairs leading up to the first floor and opened. He withdrew a small Bible, a Ball jar filled with a clear liquid that appeared to be water, a clear plastic Baggie about half filled with broken pieces of hardtack, and a six-inch silver-and-gold crucifix.

Thompson kissed the crucifix and handed it to Jack Roy. "Hold this. It's very sacred, so it must not touch the ground, *ever.* Understand? Don't drop it."

Jack nodded and clenched the cross tightly. John picked up the Ball jar and unscrewed the lid. "This is holy water I *borrowed*"—he grinned sheepishly—"from the church I go to near my house." He dipped his fingers in the water and crossed himself with it. He then dipped his thumb in the jar and made the sign of the cross on Jack Roy's forehead. "In the name of the Father, Son, and Holy Ghost, amen," Thompson intoned.

"Amen," Jack Roy repeated softly.

Captain Thompson dipped the first two fingers of his right hand into the jar and flicked the water in the sign of the cross toward the stairs leading up to the first floor of D building. "In the name of Christ our Lord, I command any evil presence here to be gone! It is the power of Christ that commands you." He flicked holy water on each of the walls, the ceiling and the floor, repeating his chant each time he did.

He took the gold and silver crucifix from Roy, knelt at the base of the stairs, and prayed silently for several minutes.

Jack Roy stood awkwardly by. This was getting too weird for him. The captain was obviously losing it again. Shit, half the mumbo-jumbo the cap was saying came straight out of the movie *The Exorcist.* Who did he think he was kidding? Jack wanted to just say "Fuck it," and leave; what could the captain do if he did? He didn't know why he'd listened to Cap in the first place—if it hadn't been for that one night when Jimmy Delilah had got by him . . . and the dreams . . . he pushed the memories from his mind. So what if he was having weird dreams about the prison back when it was an insane asylum; it didn't mean the place was haunted or that he was in any danger like Cap would have him believe. The Saget kid was right; this was crazy. Deep down, Jack knew none of the stuff Captain Thompson had said to him had convinced him to go along; it was Jack's own love of spreading gossip that had brought him to this point. He already had a ton of juicy stuff to share with his comrades, and the lure of even more outrageous behavior on the part of the captain was too strong for Jack Roy to resist.

Getting to his feet, John took several pieces of hardtack from the baggie and placed a piece in each corner of the room, making the sign of the cross over each one as he did. "That should do it," he said, putting the Baggie, crucifix, and holy water into the gym bag and zipping it up. "Onward and upward, Christian soldiers," he said to Jack. "Or in this case, onward and downward," he added. He headed back the way they'd come, and Jack Roy followed.

They repeated the makeshift exorcism ritual in the basement of the greenhouse and headed for Digbee Hall. Just past the greenhouse passageway, the tunnel began to deteriorate in both size and comfort. The concrete walls were replaced by rough granite and shale that crumbled if you rubbed against it. The floor began to slant noticeably downward. The air became colder, the walls and floor clammy. They could hear water dripping somewhere. As the floor sloped, so did the ceiling, but at a steeper angle, so that they were soon forced to walk stooped over. They came to the intersection for Digbee Hall and turned right.

The passageway narrowed until they had to walk single file. Steam and water pipes became more frequent, jutting out of the walls and running the length of the ceiling, reducing headroom even more. At one point they had to suck in their guts and slide by a water main turn-off sticking out of the wall. Jack Roy had to crawl under it. A little further along, the tunnel widened again, and they came to a door that was half open.

"What the hell?" John Thompson wondered aloud. "This door is supposed to be locked. I know I locked it when I was down here recently." He pushed the door all the way open. The tunnel beyond was steeped in darkness. For a moment, Jack Roy thought he heard whispering coming from the tunnel, but when he listened more closely, there was nothing but silence and shadows.

They took out their flashlights and shined them into the tunnel. It seemed to Jack Roy that the darkness was hungry for the light and sucked it up greedily, leaving very little illuminated.

"Let's go." Captain Thompson led the way through, Jack following. The tunnel continued to narrow until it was a little wider than arms' length on both sides. The dim ceiling lights returned intermittently, giving rise to a shadowy gloom that promoted a dank and ominous air. There were long stretches with no light, and the darkness was thick and penetrating. Their flashlights were feeble in the face of such darkness. They dimly lit the way for barely a yard in front of them before gasping their last and dying in the gloom.

Jack squinted into the darkness ahead but could see no more glint of lights from the ceiling ahead. As if sensing his nervousness the captain said, "That's the last light until we get to the basement of Digbee. There are lights every ten yards or so, but they keep shorting out. An electrician told the super it's because water keeps leaking into the wiring down here, but after what's been happening lately, I'm not so sure. I think Digbee Hall might be the psychic heart of the prison."

Jack Roy rolled his eyes—more mumbo-jumbo. What movie was it from this time—*The Haunting of Hill House*? Yeah, that was it. He stumbled on something in the darkness and it squealed and moved. He pointed his light at it just in time to see a long, sleek rat disappearing into a ridiculously small hole in the base of the wall. Jack jumped back at the sight of it.

"Oh, fuck! I *hate* fucking rats," he complained. The light was fading rapidly. He looked up to see that the captain was getting too far ahead of him, rounding a corner, his light fading from view. A second later, Jack's flashlight died, and he was plunged into utter, impenetrable darkness.

"Cap? John? Wait up; there's something wrong with my light! I can't see!" There was no answer. He stood still and listened. He could not hear the captain in the tunnel in front of him. In fact, he couldn't hear anything. "Cap? Are you there?"

No answer.

Jack held his flashlight up and shook it. He clicked the button; it remained dark. He banged the heel of the flashlight against the palm of his hand. Nothing.

"Fucking great!" he muttered softly. "Cap! Goddammit, Cap! Where the fuck are you?" he shouted.

There was no reply.

Jack Roy felt the first twinge of fear. He took a few tentative steps forward and walked into the wall, bumping his nose and forehead. He stumbled back, bent over, and banged his tailbone hard against the opposite wall, dropping his flashlight in the process. He heard the *cra-a-ack* of shattered plastic at his feet.

"*Really* fucking great!" he muttered. "John!" he shouted as loud as he could. Being careful not to drop it, too, he took out his radio and tried calling the captain. "John, come in. I'm stuck—my light's out. Where the hell are you? Quit fucking around—I can't see a damn thing. *Over*!" His voice reverberated and came back to him muffled and weak, as though his echo had been bound and gagged, but there was no response, just a light static from the radio. He put it away and reached out with his right hand, feeling for the wall, and nearly lost his balance in the disorienting darkness.

"Where the hell is it?" he wondered aloud. He felt in his inside shirt pocket where he kept his cigarettes and lighter hidden for illegal smoke breaks. The lighter was a blue disposable Bic butane that he'd bought just that evening on his way to work, but when he flicked it, no flame erupted. He tried several times before finally getting a short green jet of flame that immediately went out, as if someone had blown on it like a birthday candle. He swore under his breath, shoved the lighter back in his pocket, and took a small step to the right, searching with yearning fingers but finding nothing but black air. He took a larger step, and another, but still nothing came in contact with his outstretched appendages. He began to sweat; the liquid chilled his already prickly skin and he shivered. He tried the left side, moving his arms wildly in the hopes of coming in contact with something—*anything*—other than empty air. The all-conquering darkness wreaked havoc with his sense of balance, and before he knew it, he was on the floor again, his knees throbbing with the impact, his palms burning from scraping on the hard stone floor.

He hung his head and let out a dry, pathetic sob. A waft of warm air reached him. He looked up. Far ahead in the darkness there was a faint pinpoint of light.

"Cap? Is that you?" he called. No answer came, but Jack didn't care. As long as he could see that light, he had an orientation point, something to help him. He struggled to his feet, reflexively putting out his hand to steady himself against the wall—and there it was, firm and solid to the touch. He reached out with his other arm and felt the opposite wall, right where it should be.

I must have been disoriented in the darkness and got

turned sideways somehow, Jack rationalized. The far light seemed brighter. At least I have a light at the end of the tunnel, Jack thought and smirked. He brushed off his knees and walked toward the light.

John Thompson walked steadily on, explaining his theory of what was going on in the prison, unaware that he had lost Jack Roy.

"When I found out I was related to Doctor Stone *and* Elijah Stone—when I learned about the history of the Stone family and the Hill, then heard what Saget learned about his mother setting the fire here thirty years ago—it all fell into place for me. I think there's some sort of curse on the Stone family and this land. It seems whenever a descendant of Elijah Stone's lives or works on this hill, bad things happen; they die a violent death or disappear."

He turned to gauge Jack Roy's reaction and realized he was alone in the tunnel.

"What the—? Jack?" he called. "Jack!" A seed of panic germinated in his chest, sending out roots of fear that constricted his lungs, making it suddenly hard to breathe. He took a few steps back the way he'd come, holding the light up in a futile attempt to pierce the near-impenetrable darkness and illuminate the tunnel for more than the few meager feet he could now see.

A woman's throaty, seductive laugh floated out of the darkness. In the distance he could hear voices—a crowd of people talking, both men and women. It sounded like a party; he could hear the tinkling of glasses mingling with spurts of laughter and the occasional strain of music—bits and pieces of the Eagles' "Desperado."

John turned around in the tunnel, trying to pinpoint where the noise was coming from. For a moment, he could have sworn he was standing in a vast room or cavern. He could sense space, an *immense* space, stretching out in the darkness around him. Even though he could play his light on the walls to either side or the low ceiling overhead, it felt as if they weren't there. The sound of voices, glasses, and laughter seemed to come from beyond them.

"Jack! Jack Roy!" John shouted. He pulled his radio from his belt and held it to his lips. "One hundred to One-six-nine. Come in, Jack. Over." Silence descended, and he had the uncomfortable feeling that the people who had been making the noise were now listening intently, the way a cat listens for a rodent in the walls, ready to pounce. John took a few more steps, stopped, turned, and went the other way a few steps before stopping again. He was confused; he couldn't be sure in which direction he had been going.

Like a low wind rising, the crowd noises returned, pulsing in an ebb and flow of snatches of conversations, short hiccups of laughter, and a strange intertwining melody that speeded up and slowed down and which reminded John of the Beatles' psychedelic symphony, "Revolution Number 9." John put a hand to his eyes and rubbed them. His breathing became raspy and thin. Disorientation and lack of air brought light-headedness. He felt dizzy, in danger of fainting. He took out his inhaler and used it, but it was weak. He tried again; it was empty. He reached out and steadied himself against the wall. Where the stone wall had felt cold and dank a moment ago, it now felt warm and soft. It was pulsating and felt like . . . living, breathing *flesh*.

John withdrew his hand in revulsion, his lungs restricting air even further.

More melodic laughter.

Something rushed past him from behind, spinning him around, knocking his flashlight from his hand, plunging him into darkness.

A gaggle of giggles swirled round him, followed by polite applause. Whispered words zipped past him in the dark, nicking his ears, leaving bits and pieces of words behind like drops of blood.

The smell of formaldehyde washed over him. Something scuttled between his feet.

"It's just a rat," he soundlessly told himself, but he still couldn't find the courage to crouch down and feel around on the floor for his flashlight.

"Kill him!"

The words, whispered by several voices at once, rushed out of the darkness at him. He flinched, staggering back as if from a physical blow. Fear chills rippled over the entire surface of his body, making each individual hair—long and short, thick and thin, gray and brown—stand on end, lie down, and stand up again. He shivered with such force that he wriggled like a wet dog.

Something licked the ice-cold sweat from the back of his neck. He whirled around, gasping for air, his arm striking out and finding only empty darkness.

"John?"

It was a familiar voice floating in the nothingness around him.

"John . . . *help me!*"

The light was definitely getting closer, brighter and clearer. Jack Roy took encouragement from that. He stumbled on, using his outstretched arms to keep in touch with either wall like a circus tightrope walker. The tunnel seemed to be getting less dark around him—another good sign, as far as Jack was concerned. He began to walk faster.

"Cap?" he called ahead to the light. He slowed. That wasn't a flashlight beam or a ceiling light he was seeing; it was unsteady, flickering, like a flame.

"Oh, shit," Jack Roy said softly. If there was a fire in the tunnel, he was in trouble. For a moment he thought about turning around and going back the other way, but the panic he'd just gone through still hung too heavily upon him; he couldn't face that darkness again.

He continued on toward the light.

A cool draft of air blew over him. Ahead, the flickering light danced as if touched by the same breeze. He thought he heard the rustling of movement just as the light jumped again.

"Captain Thompson?" Jack Roy called out. There was a muffled reply. "Cap? Is that you?" Jack called. "Of course it's him," he muttered. "Who else could it be?" Just as quickly as he said it, he regretted it. The question hung in the air, and he suddenly did *not* want to entertain any other possibilities as to who it might be. It *was* Captain Thompson!

It had to be.

"Cap?" he called again.

"Yeah!" came Thompson's voice, clear as a bell.

Thank God! Jack Roy felt like laughing and crying at the same time. He subdued both urges, his face warming with shame at having panicked so. He was just glad none of the guys had been around to witness it.

"Where the fuck did you go, Cap?" he said loudly, trying to keep his tone light, but his voice betrayed him with its slight quaver. "I dropped my flashlight and had a helluva time trying to find my way."

He kept on toward the light. The tunnel floor had been slanting downward, but now he could feel it begin to rise again. The light from ahead illuminated the tunnel well here, but it was definitely light from a flame and not electrical.

"Hey, John, are you holding a torch or an open flame?" He could clearly see the flame now, not far ahead, but could see nothing else illuminated around it. It appeared to be burning in midair.

"Cap?"

Why doesn't he answer? Jack slowed his pace.

"Yeah," the captain answered again. "Come on. Hurry up."

Jack sighed with relief. He could see well enough to run now and did so, sprinting up what was becoming a fair incline. He crested the rise and was astonished to see the tunnel widen into a vast cavern that stretched before him for a good thirty yards and whose ceiling had to be fifteen to twenty feet high, as high as forty feet in some places. In the middle of the cavern was the source of the flame: a large circular fire hemmed in by black stones. He realized he had only been seeing the very top of the fire, due to the incline of the tunnel floor, and that was why it had appeared to be floating. Sparkles of light glinted in the granite walls, floor, and ceiling, as tiny chips of mica caught and reflected the firelight. Jack Roy stood at the edge of the cave, transfixed by the sparkling display.

A shadowy form crossed behind the fire.

"Cap?" Jack called again and took a tentative step into the cavern. "I've never heard of this being here, have you? This is in-fucking-credible!"

The light shifted as he entered the cavern, and he had the sensation of everything stretching out away from him, yet at the same time becoming clearer and more detailed. He realized there were people in the cavern—a lot of people—beyond the campfire. He reached for his revolver; they had to be inmates. He noticed something that stayed his hand. They all appeared to be dressed the same, and it wasn't prison issue. They wore white hospital-issue johnnies. He realized there were women among them; one was dressed as a nurse. Two burly, dark-haired men were dressed all in whites, like hospital orderlies. Behind the ones in white, Jack could see more people coming forward into the light. They were dressed in coveralls and shabby handmade clothing that had the look of fashion from colonial days.

These aren't prisoners, he realized with a growing sense of dread.

All eyes were on him.

"Where do you people come from?" Jack asked.

An old woman in front smiled, showing toothless gums, and began nodding rapidly.

"What are you doing down here?" Jack asked. He liked this less and less. All the ghost stories he'd heard about the place since starting at the prison ran through his head.

A small, bald-headed man leapt upon a pretty young woman next to him and began humping her leg the way a horny dog would. "F-f-f-fucking!" he screamed. "F-f-f-f-ucking!"

Jack realized that all the while he had been talking to them they had been slowly moving toward him, only he couldn't see their legs or feet moving; they seemed to be *gliding* toward him.

"Oh, shit!" he said, lips moving, no sound forthcoming. The crowd on the opposite side of the fire was leering at him, sliding closer, closer. He fumbled for his revolver, but his arms and hands wouldn't work right. It was like trying to do something in a mirror; suddenly everything was reverse of where it should be.

They were gathering around the fire. He could now see that some of them were on their bellies, crawling on their hands and knees. Several of the men were openly masturbating as they glided along, looking at him lasciviously while two of the women hiked up their johnnies with one hand and diddled themselves with the other.

Jack Roy couldn't take his eyes from them; couldn't find his gun; couldn't move his legs; couldn't think straight. A shadow suddenly loomed from behind, rising around and over him. Abruptly, the clamoring throng ceased all movement and, as one, shrank back.

Jack felt something icier than any subzero winter's gale graze the back of his neck. It felt like . . . a *breath*.

He turned.

He screamed.

The tunnels were filled with echoing howls of derision and anguished cries of unspeakable horror and pain.

John Thompson heard the tumult as a faint roar that came to him like the sound of a faraway football game on a fall afternoon in any small town in America. The only difference was the distinct sound of someone screaming in unbearable pain mingled with the cheering. To John's ears, the screams were clearly, unmistakably, those of Darlene Hampton.

"I guess my exorcism has riled up the spirits," John said softly, his voice shaky. After several moments of concentrating just on his breathing, he was feeling better and less dizzy. He felt in his bag, found a book of matches and a holy candle he had "borrowed" from the church along with the holy water, just in case something like this happened. He left the candle in the bag and struck a match to life. He looked at the walls, the pipes, and thought he knew where he was—right where he should be, almost under Digbee Hall. Just a little further on was the huge wooden door that led to the actual basement of Digbee, which used to be the morgue for the state asylum. Where the hell Jack Roy was, John could only guess. The match got too hot and he dropped it. He tried the radio again but still couldn't raise anything on it. He had the sinking suspicion that Jack had chickened out on him and turned back, sneaking away while John ("like an idiot," he berated himself) had been going on and on about spooks and demons. John knew Jack probably thought he was full of bullshit.

"He'd just better keep his mouth shut," John muttered. He lit another match and searched for his flashlight, spotting it on the floor, a couple of feet away. He dropped the match and reached for the flashlight.

Out of the darkness came more pitiful cries for help.

"John, *please* help me. I can't stand it anymore! Please!"

John grabbed the flashlight and turned it on. It flickered and died. He banged it on the palm of his hand and it came back to light. John took a deep breath. Darlene's voice was coming from ahead, from Digbee Hall. He went on. Twenty yards later his sense of disorientation lifted when he saw the large arched wooden door that led to the basement of Digbee Hall. By the time he reached the door, Darlene's voice and the other sounds had faded and he was left in silence.

He pointed the flashlight at the ceiling light over the door.

The bulb was shattered inside its metal, bell-shaped hood. It had been intact last week when he'd been looking for Doctor Stone's cavern. He tucked the flashlight under his left arm while he got out his massive key ring and fingered through the keys to find the right one for the door.

The door creaked mournfully when he finally got it open. He stepped through a short passageway and felt along the inside wall, found the light switch, and turned it on. Fluorescent lights crackled and hummed to life on the ceiling. A stark, antiseptic room came to light. The walls were paneled in sound-absorbing white cork. There were several metal file cabinets under the stairs, but other than that the room was empty. There was another door opposite the stairs. From John's understanding of the layout of the basement, that door led to what had been the autopsy room and the freezer for storing bodies. Though it only worked with a key, John knew that the elevator panel in the Digbee Hall elevator could take riders directly to the autopsy lab in the basement.

John went to the stairs, placed his gym bag on the third stair, and unzipped it. He was about to remove the tools of his exorcism ritual but was stopped by a loud crash from above, followed by shouts, hysterical laughter, and the sound of a mob in full riot.

While John Thompson and Jack Roy lost each other in the tunnels, Hiram Pena lay in the infirmary, his eyes closed, waiting. He didn't need to look around to know where he was; he was acutely aware of the antiseptic smell of the place. To Hiram, all hospitals, whether they were private, prison, or public, smelled the same—of medicine, urine, and fear. Normally Hiram hated hospitals and doctors (though he wasn't averse to nurses) and would have nothing to do with them. So far in life he'd been lucky enough never to have been so sick or badly injured that he'd had to resort to seeking medical help. Until now, that is, but now he had a purpose for being there. He and Myrtle were on a mission for the doctor. Soon he knew, he would have help.

Hiram had been brought to the HSU after running head first into his cell door to open up the stitches on his head that he'd got after CO Stirling had clocked him. He lay on the soft hospital bed and listened to the nurse answer the land-line phone, then tell the yard officer, Lecuyer, who had brought him over from the Can, that he had to go back to SIU and get another lifer who was sick. Lecuyer came over and put the handcuffs on Hiram again, snaking the middle chain through the headboard's iron bars before leaving. Twenty minutes later, Lecuyer returned with Marty Miller, both of them covered in snow. Marty was moaning and groaning and holding his stomach. He had a snow-covered prison blanket wrapped around his shoulders.

The nurse pointed to the bed two over from Hiram and the guard led Marty to it. Hiram made eye contact with him once but that was all he needed—he knew Miller's illness was feigned; he was the help the doctor had promised him. Lecuyer left, going back to his chair just outside the ward, and Nurse Donner checked Marty Miller's vital signs before giving him a chalky green liquid to drink. He immediately stopped moaning, and she looked at him a little fishy, so he added another small groan and forced a loud burp.

"Hey, nurse," Hiram called, "can I get these cuffs off? I'm feeling kind of woozy. I think I'd just like to go to sleep if it's okay."

Nurse Donner considered him for a moment and shrugged. "Mike?" she called the guard in. "You know, with the weather the way it is, maybe Pena should stay here. That's a nasty head wound, and I'd like to keep an eye on him. I know the doctor wanted to check on him again before he left. He can sleep here and I'll send him back if he's doing better, so you can undo his cuffs. The other guy should be ready to go back in about a half hour or so." Lecuyer, who struck Hiram as being big and stupid, nodded at everything she said, then came over and obediently uncuffed him. He went back to sit on his chair and read a magazine.

Hiram looked at Marty. There was no need for talk. The time for action had come. They were only waiting for the right moment, and it came when the guard looked in to see both Marty and Hiram feigning sleep, and went downstairs to the break room to get some coffee. He wouldn't be back. He'd be taken care of by others; the doctor had told them so.

From between his mattress, Hiram fished out a flattened bottle cap, one side of which had been ground to a keen edge by Hiram against the bed frame in his cell whenever he had been able to get away with it. Now, with Marty keeping watch, he went to the window and used the sharpened edge of the bottle cap to cut the cord from the Venetian blind. He wrapped one end around each fist, leaving about a foot of cord between, and pulled it tight, making the rope snap. He nodded at Marty Miller who began groaning.

Sheila Donner was sitting at the reception desk pretending to read the latest issue of *Reader's Digest* but really thinking of what her next step would be in her campaign to force John Thompson to come clean about Darlene. She had seen the haggard look on his face and felt a surge of pride thinking it was due to her phone calls disguised as Darlene and the accusing pastiche letters she'd sent him. The rumors had started up about him again, that he was losing it, but this time the inmates had started it. Nearly all the cons, and some of the guards, had taken to calling him "Ghostbuster." It had become a running joke; *he* had become a running joke, which was more than he deserved.

Sheila felt she'd had a huge hand in bringing about all this. "And I ain't anywhere finished with you, Captain John Triscuit Ghostbuster, whatever-the-fuck-you're-called Thompson!" she whispered.

Hiram and Marty had other ideas.

Marty's loud moaning gave her a start, but she didn't respond immediately. She could tell from the sound of his voice that it was Marty Miller and, quite frankly, she was in no hurry to run to his aid. For some reason the little cracker creeped her out. She hoped he was just having a bad dream and would stop soon, but after a few seconds he began to call, "Nurse! I need you!" in between the moans. Sighing heavily, she put down her magazine and got up.

Marty Miller was lying on his side, his back to her as she entered the room. His head was hanging over the side of the bed and he began to retch. Sheila leaped into action, rushing forward to grab a bedpan off the empty bed next to Marty's and slide it under his head. In that moment she realized the mistake she'd made—the other bed was empty. It was too late. Hiram Pena stepped out from behind the door and gar-roted her throat with the window cord. Marty sat up and watched with delight until she was dead.

Taking her keys, they pushed her under one of the beds and unlocked the drug and medical equipment cabinets where they found and swallowed whatever pills they came across with no idea of what they were taking. They also found some nasty playthings like scalpels and syringes. Hiram took a scalpel and Marty helped himself to a huge syringe with a long thick needle on it. He regarded it with a mixture of admiration and fear, wondering what such a large needle would be used for. He knew what *he* would use it for, and he and Hiram went in search of a guinea pig.

They didn't have far to travel.

It was Doctor Louis Feldman's last night at the prison. His internship at Hayman Memorial Hospital in New Rome was over and he had been offered a residency at UMASS Medical in Worcester. He was excited about it and thus found it hard to sleep. He was scheduled to start at UMASS two days after Christmas, so that left him only one day, with the holiday, to find an apartment and move. He could com-mute from New Rome, but it was forty-five minutes one way and besides, he was sick of his roommate, another intern from Hayman, who gave new meaning to the word *slob*. He couldn't wait to move into his own place, and now he could afford to.

He was in the medical staff's lounge, looking through the apartment rentals section of the *Worcester Gazette* when he heard Marty Miller moaning in the infirmary next door. He started to get up, then relaxed. It was his last night; Nurse Donner would tend to him. If she needed help she'd call. A moment later, Miller's groans changed to retching, and Doctor Feldman looked up from the paper, listening. He was about to get up and go check on the man when it became quiet again, and he figured Nurse Donner had everything under control.

It was a crash in the infirmary that alerted Louis Feldman to something being wrong. He tossed the paper on the table and went to the door, sticking his head out into the corridor. The door immediately slammed back against his neck as Hiram Pena, who'd been waiting just outside the door, put all his weight against it and trapped Doctor Feldman there, with only his head sticking out. Before Feldman had a chance to even choke, Marty Miller shoved the extra-long, thick needle between his eyes and pushed it all the way in. Hiram Pena let the door go and he and Marty Miller ran down the hall to the exit door at the end of the building. Using Sheila Donner's keys, they left by the side exit, running out into the snow, unseen by the CO in Inner Control.

Doctor Louis Feldman fell to the floor as the gonging clock in the staff lounge struck midnight, drowning out his dying breath.

Outside, snow and fog swirled and the landscape slowly disappeared in the churning miasma of windblown ground clouds. The storm blasted the windows of the prison, ripping through the bars and rattling the panes of glass. The swirling, snowy air shook the towers, frosting the windows, seeping through any and every crack until being up there was like being exposed, thirty feet in the air.

In tower one, Officer Eduardo Isaacs, a Hispanic Jew originally from New York City, sat in the beat-up leather swivel chair, rocking back on its spring supports. The tower spotlight was out; there was nothing to see anyway. Ed had seen nights like this before on the Hill—the place was a haven for weird weather. Though he'd never seen fog in a blizzard, he'd seen it in every other kind of weather, including summer sunshine. The closest thing he'd seen to this storm was an ice storm two years ago that pelted the Hill with freezing rain and covered it in dense fog. The Hill seemed to produce its own fog, a low ground mist that covered everything by early morning most days, and in bad weather appeared to grow. Lately, in the last couple of months and even more so in the past week, the fog had been blanketing the prison every night, whatever the weather or temperature. It was weird.

Without the light to run, sweeping his section of the compound on a random basis, there wasn't much to do in the tower. Though guards were not allowed to watch television on duty in any part of the prison, each of the towers had a portable TV, mainly watched by the COs on the three-to-eleven and eleven-to-seven shifts, after the administration "suits" had left. A couple of the guys had rigged elaborate antenna contraptions to improve reception.

Ed Isaacs's television was not one of those. It was off and would remain so. It picked up only three channels, two from Boston and one from Worcester in the best of weather. On a night like tonight, forget it. If he wanted to watch snow, he could just look out the windows. He leaned back as far as possible in the chair without tipping it over and looked out at the storm. He could see nothing but swirls of mist flying by and spots of white slamming into the glass, immediately turning into droplets. The fog and snow were so thick they sporadically turned the night into a solid off-white wall that flickered with constant internal movement. Only during moments of clearness, when the wind was so strong it blew the fog away for a short period, could he see the light from A dorm to the left of his tower. The dorms beyond, and the other buildings in the compound that he could normally see well, were nothing but dark blobs in the snow-flecked night. The basketball court directly across from the tower was gone, covered in drifts. Then the fog/snow wall returned and the outside disappeared. Ed found that if he looked at it long enough, he noticed it began to have a strobe light effect on him, mesmerizing him, putting him to sleep.

He returned the chair abruptly to the floor and stood. He stretched and shook his arms and legs. He couldn't fall asleep out here tonight. The way the wind was blowing, he could feel it as though there was nothing around him. He had a small space heater, but it warmed him only if he sat right in front of it, which he had done on many a cold winter's night. He had fallen asleep away from the heater on one extremely cold night and had woken with chills and the worst pain in his side he'd ever experienced. Later, at home, he had begun peeing blood. That's when he had headed for the emergency room to discover he had a kidney infection. It might have been coincidental, but since then he tried to avoid sleeping on duty—during the winter anyway—as much as possible.

He picked his Thermos off the desk, opened it, and poured a cup of steaming black coffee. He warmed his hands around the cup and paced in the small space the tower afforded. He hated nights like this; he could see nothing down below and he was sure no one down there could see him. He could go home and it wouldn't make any difference. No one would ever know.

He put his face against the window, trying to see anything beyond the fast-moving gray-and-white streams flying by the tower windows, but could not. For a moment the mist and snow seemed to swirl in two circles that began to resemble eyes. For a second they seemed so real, then they were gone as the wind changed direction and the fog parted briefly. He stepped closer to the window. The wind, fog, and snow returned, the snow slamming against the tower glass with such force Ed could hear the *ping!* of every flake hitting it. He backed away. Had he really seen that? He shook his head. He'd heard about the weird shit going on at the prison lately. He had talked at length with Captain Thompson about it after he had seen the same midnight farmers Tim Saget saw. Lately, he'd been seeing other, more shadowy things in the night fog inside and outside the fence that, when investigated, turned up nothing. He had thought the tower was the best place to be, a place where he could observe the weird phenomena without being affected. He felt almost like a scientist.

Until tonight. Tonight, he felt like a sitting duck. He didn't feel so safe, so displaced from the prison. The tower shook with a fresh gust of wind. It hit the glass like a slap in the face and kept pushing. Instead of peaking and subsiding, the way the wind had all night, reminding Ed of the ebb and flow of ocean waves, the gusts continued growing stronger, pushing harder against the glass.

Ed stared in disbelief. The howling wind sounded like women screaming as it continued to slam into the window, throwing a steady stream of mist and snow against it like water from a high-pressure hose. A tiny crack appeared and began to grow. Ed Isaacs watched, helpless and unable to move, as the crack spread, forked, forked again, sent out branches and tendrils of cracks like a river seen from a great height. The cracks, thick and thin, began to run together, some of them doubling back and cracking in ways he had never seen glass crack—circles and rectangles and curves and—

It was a face. The cracks were creating a giant Etch-a-Sketch face in the window. But this wasn't just any face, this was the face of *evil,* a face to scare children to incontinence, pregnant women to miscarriage, and strong men to thinking twice about looking the wrong way at such a face. Taking in its awful countenance, Ed felt a trembling begin deep in his abdomen, just above his groin, and spread out. Soon his arms and legs were trembling, then his hands. His teeth began to chatter. For a moment it seemed the cracks were growing in time to the chattering of his teeth, then the window exploded. There was a sound like a train rushing by, and a thousand razor-sharp shards of glass flew straight at him—

And he woke, immediately jumping from the chair, which fell over backwards, banging to the floor. He looked around like a man madly searching for something, first to the left, then the right. He scuttled around the desk and went to the window that had been broken. It was whole now.

"Just a dream," he whispered and grinned sheepishly. The whole thing, the snow eyes, the face in the cracks; it had seemed so real.

He went over to the desk and started to reach for his Thermos but, remembering he had done that in his dream, decided he didn't need any right now. He pulled his swivel chair over to the heater and sat down, bending over to warm his hands. The wind outside was relentless. It blew the fog past the tower at such a speed Ed felt motion sickness if he looked at it too long. It crashed against the tower glass every few seconds, reminding Ed of one time he had been at the beach during a winter storm and the way the waves crashed against the sea wall. He imagined the storm like a giant white fog ocean, the snow carried along on waves of wind that crashed over any obstacle they encountered. It made him cold just to think about it. He hunched over closer to the heater.

There was a faint, yet distinct, cracking sound. He heard it for a moment, then it stopped. A few seconds later, it continued slowly for several moments and stopped again. For a moment, Ed thought it was his dream come to life. He jumped up and went around the tower, checking all the windows for cracks. Thankfully, there were none, and he took his finger off the panic button and relaxed.

But the cracking sound went on.

Looking at the window that faced the prison, Ed suddenly saw what was causing it. The moisture on the window, from snowflakes melting against the warmer-than-air glass, appeared to be freezing; the cracking sound was that of the ice forming on the glass, but it did so in the strangest way Ed had ever seen. Droplets of water ran together before freezing almost instantly, spreading out in clear streams from the bottom of the glass, the clear water turning white as it solidified into ice. Ed stared at the ice sheet forming and felt sick, getting sicker by the moment; the ice was taking the shape of the same face he'd seen in the window cracks of his dream.

"This is fucked up," Ed intoned softly. The entire glass, which was a good nine by nine feet, was three-quarters frozen, the face nearly complete. As in his dream, and with the wall of streaming gray and white behind it, the detail he could see was amazing. Wrinkles, eyebrow hairs, *pores,* every eyelash on the closed eyelids appeared real. He stepped back. Every line of the visage before him was a cruel line. Each crease in the skin sharpened the threat of evil the face exuded. It was a human face and yet it was not, it was more and it was less.

The wind outside took on the sound of a voice, or did he actually *hear* a voice? He couldn't tell. He couldn't take his eyes off the great sleeping face of evil on the tower glass. There it was again, only it was *voices* now; he was sure of it. Keeping an eye on the ice face, Ed stepped to the side window and tried to see out. He could see nothing—the snow and mist hid even the lights from A dorm, not more than thirty feet away. He rubbed at the window with the cuff of his sweater but it did no good.

The sound of voices came to him again, louder, closer. It sounded like people were right outside. Ed turned to go downstairs to see who was there and movement opposite caught his eye. He stared at the strange frozen face—had it moved? No, that was impossible. He wasn't dreaming now. Downstairs he heard the door blow open, bang against the wall. A blast of wind stronger than any before—reminiscent of his dream—shook the tower. Ed felt the entire structure sway and had to reach out and grab something to steady himself.

That was when the frozen face on his window opened its eyes and looked at him.

Ed inhaled with a shriek, muttered "Oh, fuck," and ran to the stairs. He was met there by Hiram Pena and Marty Miller. That was shocking enough, but what caught Eddy Isaacs off guard and gave Hiram Pena time to stick a scalpel in his Adam's apple was the sight of a throng of what looked like hospital patients in robes and loose, flapping johnnies, right behind the two escaped inmates.

Ed felt nothing more than a pinch as the scalpel went into his throat, then a hot throbbing sensation. A moment later he couldn't breathe. He staggered backward, away from a grinning Hiram Pena, his hands at his neck, fingers gingerly touching the thin metal instrument lodged in him. Blood flowed over his fingers and he made odd, wet, chortling, gagging sounds. His leg hit his chair, and he lost his balance and went down. He lay writhing on the floor, his body running a race between bleeding to death and suffocating.

He looked up. The evil ice-face was smiling at him.

It was a welcoming smile.

Hiram and Marty helped themselves to four five-gallon gas cans each that they found stored under the tower for its emergency generator. With the help of their special friends, they carried them to Digbee Hall. Throughout the prison similar scenes were being played. On tier one of the Can, Bob Welch had just finished stuffing his face with a meatball sandwich when every cell door on the tier opened. A second later all the lights went out.

His screams went on for some time.

On tier two, Officer Karen Alden, Dave Stirling's replacement, heard Bob Welch scream and started out of the office, heading for the stairs down to tier one. Halfway down the corridor between the cells, the stairway door opened and a grandmotherly woman with gray hair and wearing a flowered housecoat and fuzzy pink bunny slippers came through. She grinned at Karen, showing bloody teeth, and held up an equally gory hammer.

Karen had just enough time to hit her body alarm before the lights went out and she heard all the cell doors open simultaneously. At five foot eleven, 190 pounds of muscle cultivated through hours of work at the local gym, Karen Alden was not the type of woman to scream in this situation. She immediately took her baton out. A hand grabbed her arm and she twisted away, thrust out with the bat and connected with flesh, hearing a loud "Ooomph!" in the darkness. It was the last thing she heard for a while as a pair of huge hands crashed against both sides of her head, boxing her ears and exploding her eardrums. She fell senseless to the floor, unaware of the many hands on her.

On the first floor of I dorm, Boomer Bromley was getting some much-needed sleep while Ray Lever, the second-floor CO, covered. Boomer had spent the day celebrating the holiday with his brothers, exchanging gifts and having a turkey dinner. Christmas Eve had become the family's tradition of late, since they all had families, kids, and in-laws of their own that they now spent Christmas day with.

Boomer was dog tired and still feeling the effects of all the wine he'd drunk that day, and he fell immediately into such a deep sleep that he didn't hear Ray Lever shout, "What the hell are you doing?" or hear the dull, thudding whacks of hard rubber on flesh as one of the cons beat his partner to death with his own baton. Neither did Boomer hear the door open to the small room he was in, or the pack of inmates crowding inside. It wasn't until they grabbed him, lifting him from the cot, that he woke, but by then there were so many hands on him he couldn't move, couldn't fight back or resist much.

One of the cons stepped up. Boomer saw he was holding Ray Lever's bloody baton in his hand and guessed the fate of his partner. It appeared it was going to be his fate, too, as the con raised the baton to strike. Boomer closed his eyes and said a silent Hail Mary.

"Wait. Don't kill him. Remember the doctor said to kill only those who get in the way; all others we have to bring over to Digbee Hall," said an inmate.

A con stuffed a pair of stained boxer shorts in Boomer's

mouth and the others closed around him tightly, dragging him out of the building and down the steps into the soup of wind-whipped snow and fog. The wind staggered the entire group as they pressed against it. Snow hit bare flesh so hard it stung. Boomer tried to look around for help, but the fog was so thick and rushed by with such speed it made him dizzy. If he could have seen clearly, it would not have been a heartening sight. Across the compound, similar groups of cons were transporting overcome guards to the fourth floor of Digbee Hall. For Boomer Bromley, and every other corrections officer on the Hill, their worst nightmare had come true.

The inmates were taking control of the prison.

Jack Roy stumbled out of the tunnel into the basement of C building, back where he and Captain Thompson had started out. He stepped into the light, and if anyone had been there to see him they would have gasped with alarm. He had lost his hat, and his short, crew-cut hair, which had been brown before going into the tunnels, was now snow white. Even his eyebrows and eyelashes were albino white. He appeared to have aged thirty years, and there was something wrong with his face; one side of it sagged, wrinkling against his jawline, as if he'd had a stroke. He had a large bloodstain down the front of his shirt and a river of dried blood running from his nostrils down over his lips, chin, and neck.

Lurching like a drunk, he staggered to the stairs and went up to the first floor.

Jane Mazek sat alone in Outer Control. Between it being flu season and the holidays, the new orders by the supe to have two COs watching the monitors at all times had gone by the boards. She was working alone again. She took off the switchboard headset, placed it on the console, and got up, walking to the window to look out at the storm. She could see nothing but occasional glimpses of the Dead Zone between the fences, the front gate, and beyond in the quagmire of mist and snow. She wondered at the weird weather as much as she had been wondering about Tobi Dowry's suicide. As it had since her death, the question returned again tonight: Why did she do it?

A door closed somewhere below in the building. Jane returned to the switchboard expecting Captain Thompson to come up the stairs at any moment.

"Jane?"

She was in the act of putting her headset on when she heard her name distinctly from downstairs. Only it wasn't John Thompson's voice—it wasn't a *man's* voice. One of the other female guards, she thought immediately, but what were they doing over here? Come to think of it, the only other female guard on eleven-to-seven, Karen Alden in the Can, was new and didn't know her well enough to call her *Jane*.

"Yeah? Who is it?" Jane called, standing again and going to the door. There was no one on the stairs.

"Jane?" Again her name was called, fainter this time, but definitely familiar. Was it Judy, her life partner, come from home for some reason? Jane looked at the storm through the window. It would have to be important for her to come out in this. Why didn't she call?

"Judy?" Jane called. It wasn't unusual for Judy to show up in the middle of the night with a hot lunch to share with Jane, especially on her days off. Though it was a no-no by regulations, Captain Thompson had turned a blind eye to it, but they'd had to give it up when Henderson had become night watch commander. In fact, they hadn't done it since then. Now that John Thompson was back on, maybe Judy had decided to brave the storm and surprise her. It was Christmas, after all, and it would be just like her to do something like this; she was such a romantic. It was the thing Jane loved most about her.

"Judy is that you, you nut?" Jane said louder, laughing,

having convinced herself that it *had* to be Judy below trying to surprise her. She went down to the first floor, pausing before the bottom, then leaping out, arms and legs spread, and shouting: "Merry Christmas!"

There was no one in front of her, but behind her was death.

Jack Roy heard the voice calling Jane Mazek and didn't realize it came from his own mouth. Jane answered and came to the top of the stairs, and he heard the woman's voice call *Jane* again and this time he felt his lips, tongue, and jaw working and sound coming from his voice box. He touched his lips tentatively, moving as though drugged. He worked his jaw open and closed, side to side, as if expecting something else to come out of it.

There were footsteps on the stairs. Jane Mazek was coming down, calling to someone named *Judy*. Jack Roy stepped back into the shadows of the doorway to the left of the stairs. Without a conscious thought, he took out his revolver. With the same thoughtless, routine reflex movement he would use to swat at an annoying insect, he swatted Jane Mazek across the back of the head with the muzzle of his pistol as soon as she jumped out of the stairwell and cried, "Merry Christmas!"

She lurched forward and lay sprawled on the floor, face down. The short brown hair at the back of her head slowly turned dark and wet. Jack Roy stepped up, straddled her legs, and stood over her. He didn't know it, but the entire back of her skull was crushed and she was dying. She breathed her last a second before he wasted a bullet, firing it into the center of her back. He stood there for several minutes, just staring down at the body and the pool of blood spreading around her head and leaking out from under her torso. Abruptly, as though physically grabbed and shaken by some unseen person, Jack Roy shook uncontrollably for several moments, then straightened calmly. Putting his revolver in his holster, he went upstairs to the Outer Control command station and used Jane Mazek's chair to smash the switchboard, radio console, and all the closed-circuit TV monitors.

Returning downstairs, he went out through the pedestrian trap and the front door of C building, leaving it open and blowing in the wind. He did the same with the two front gates, letting them clang open in the wind and get jammed open in the piling snow, unmindful of securing them behind him.

Sans hat and jacket, clad only in his regulation blue long-sleeved cotton shirt and dark blue rayon trousers, Jack Roy faced into the driving snow, rushing mist, and whipping wind, ignored the bitter cold, and trudged through the growing drifts across the road and up the hill to the COs' parking lot. He didn't know why he was there or where he was going, he just went. The howling of the wind was synonymous with the howl of babbling voices in his head that kept him from thinking, but kept him moving, like an automaton, a robot.

He plowed through the deep snow, heading for the last row of snow-covered cars. He turned the corner and walked down to the third car from the end, a small compact sedan. He didn't know it was Tim Saget's Dodge Neon, he just knew it was *the* car. He went to the driver's door, tried it, and found it unlocked. He reached in and popped the levers under the seat that opened the hood and the trunk. He went to the trunk first, where he found a two-foot-long tire iron and a Phillips-head screwdriver. Perfect.

He started with the rear of the vehicle since he was already there. He smashed the taillights with the tire iron, then the rear window. He walked around the car, methodically smashing each window, having to rain down half a dozen blows on the safety-glass windshield before it crumpled into the front seat of the car, destroyed but unshattered. He walked around the car again, stabbing the screwdriver into each of the tires until they were all flat.

He went to the front of the car, grabbed the open hood, and tore it from the car, flinging it behind him, where it was immediately swallowed by the deep ground snow. Within seconds, a light snow cover lay on the black, greasy engine. Jack Roy went to work on it with the tire iron, causing sparks to fly in the night as metal met metal.

Ten minutes later, the engine was ruined and he was exhausted. He dropped the tire iron and screwdriver in the snow, staggered backward a few feet, and lost his footing. He collapsed backward into a snow drift and lay unmoving.

Over at Inner Control, the alarm panel, which kept track of all body and building alarms in the prison, was lighting up as if in celebration of the holiday, but no one was around to hear it. Moments before, Pete Seneca had been overrun by a swarm of inmates who came charging through the front door of Digbee Hall. They quickly subdued him, adding him to the throng of other captive COs whom they were transporting to the fourth floor of Digbee.

In the basement of Digbee Hall, the sound of Pete Seneca's capture reached John Thompson's ears and he stood wondering what that roaring sound was until he began to make out individual voices. Grabbing his gym bag, he ran up the basement stairs. The door opened along the hallway that led to the Can. He crossed though the two locked fire doors before getting to the Inner Control command station, but he was too late. He cursed. Where the hell was Pete Seneca? The sound of footsteps, of an unruly mob, grew louder. He looked at the elevator and saw its dial stop at four before returning to the first floor. He could hear the thunder of many feet going up the stairs at both ends of the building.

John approached the elevator, glancing over at the alarm board, and was torn over what to do—check out the noise from above or answer those damn alarms.

A scream filtered down faintly from above. It sounded like Pete Seneca. John looked out at the fierce storm blowing outside and back at the alarm board. Who was upstairs with Pete Seneca? Was it cons? He tried, calling Outer Control on his radio and got nothing. There was a good chance the radio and the board were acting up because of the storm. He opted to go against what his training told him he should do and headed for the elevator.

As the elevator rose, the noise from above grew louder. There was again the rumbling of many feet making the ceiling shake, followed by a cheer and a scream that was cut off and followed by another cheer. John Thompson unholstered his gun. The elevator reached the fourth floor, settled, and the doors slid open. John drew a sharp breath through clenched teeth at the scene that faced him.

All around the hall in a great arc, most of the cons of New Rome Correctional Institution were arrayed with their former captors, now their prisoners. They were all facing the elevator as if waiting for him. John looked around: Don Juarez, Boomer Bromley, Mike Lecuyer, Bob Welch, Karen Alden, and nearly every other CO on eleven-to-seven were being held captive by cons; some John knew by name, others he did not. There were some guards missing, most notably Jack Roy, Tim Saget, and Chris Frieburg. In fact, there seemed to be no cons from A dorm there either. John wondered what had happened to them.

A singing voice rang out: "If there's somethin' strange in the neighborhood, who you gonna call?"

And all the cons answered, shouting: "John Thompson!"

John raised his gun, took a step onto the floor, and immediately leaped back into the elevator as if he'd been shocked. His chest constricted, and air suddenly seemed scarce. The elevator doors, which had started to close, banged open again with a loud *ding*! A roar of laughter went up from the inmates. The wind rattled the tall windows as though it, too, were laughing.

John put a hand to his eyes and tried to breathe slowly. He tried to stop his lungs from tightening up. He could feel the air barely squeezing in and out. The shock of what he'd just experienced had brought him to the brink of a full-blown asthma attack, and his inhaler was empty. He tried to calm himself by reciting the Lord's Prayer aloud and taking slow, deep breaths between verses. The elevator doors tried to close again, and he kicked out with his right foot, hitting the *open door* button.

The cons hooted and whistled at the sound of his praying and some of them proceeded to torture their captive COs. Ricki Valdez, the six foot, five inch skinner from Venezuela, ripped out Mike Lecuyer's tongue with a pair of pliers he had found in a toolbox left behind by workers. John gathered his strength and as much air in his lungs as he could, then stepped out of the elevator, firing his gun twice as he did. Ricki Valdez, the pliers still in his hand with the bloody tongue in its metal jaw, caught one bullet in the forehead, the other in the nose. His head exploded and his body followed. He crashed backward to the floor, his skull in pieces around him like a smashed melon.

A roar of laughter and cheering went up from the cons, but John barely heard it; he was too busy trying to keep hold of his sense of balance and reality. As soon as he stepped onto the floor, the scene—the *reality*—before him flickered and was replaced with something else. Every con in the room *changed* in front of his eyes and became *someone else*. Some turned into women, some were dressed in medical whites, some were in hospital johnnies. There was that flickering, strobing sensation again, as though God were running a slide show and the projector was jamming, and they turned back into cons, only now the other person they had been remained, wrapped around their physical bodies like a shroud.

It was like existing in a double-exposed photograph. Not only was there double exposure over the cons, there were people in the room who had not been there a moment ago. A topless fat woman ran by him, chased by an old, stooped-over bald man who shuffled along as fast as he could, his arms pumping madly in the air. To the left, three men were having sex with a woman who was on all fours with one man under her, one behind her, and the third standing in front of her, his crotch in her face. To their right, Hiram Pena was raping a woman bent over a large industrial gas can. Against the wall behind them, a thin young man was chained, arms outspread. A tall, blond, muscular woman in leather boots, chaps, thong, and little else was whipping him. Huddled at her feet were a man and a woman, leashed to iron rings in the floor. The woman was licking the dominatrix's boots. The man turned and looked at John.

It was Jim Henderson. Next to him a ghastly Julian James, his face half melted away, sodomized a bloody-faced Jimmy Delilah.

John walked into the hall, gun turning this way and that, trying not to be distracted by the hallucinatory scene around him.

"You men are all in violation of the state penal code and must cease and desist this illegal takeover of this facility!" he wheezed.

The cons hooted, whistled, and laughed. To John's right, Tou Xiong, the Hmong prisoner from the Can, held a screwdriver to a kneeling Pete Seneca's eyeball while several other cons restrained John's second-in-command. Tou Xiong screamed: "Screw the screws!" and shoved the screwdriver into Pete's eye, all the way to the handle. Pete let out the most horrible scream John had ever heard and went into convulsions, flopping to the floor as though electrocuted. Tou Xiong laughed to see such sport and John Thompson shot him and the con that had held Pete's head; both in the chest. Tou Xiong stopped laughing and died. He and his cohort fell on the floor next to Pete Seneca, whose jerky spasms had slowed to an occasional twitch.

The other cons cheered it all.

"Nobody else has to die!" John tried to shout but his lungs wouldn't let him. Instead he got out a hoarse sort of bellow. "You don't realize what you're doing. You don't realize what's going on here. You're all possessed, but you can fight it. Join me in prayer and we can drive this evil out!" He took out his pocket Bible with his left hand and held it up.

This got the biggest laugh of all from the convicts. John

was in the middle of the room now. Directly in front of him, Walter Holstrom raised a CO's baton over the head of Don Juarez, the officer in F dorm at night.

"Don't do it," John whispered, his voice and lungs spent. He leveled the gun at the gray-haired old con.

Walter smiled at him and brought the baton down in a crushing blow to the top of Juarez's skull. John fired at the same moment. The bullet hit Walter Holstrom on the very tip of his chin and took away the bottom half of his face and most of his throat, leaving him aspirating blood into his exposed windpipe as he crumpled to the floor next to Don Juarez.

This time no one cheered. The room grew deadly silent. He had one bullet left. John felt in his pockets for his speed loader but knew it was futile; he had left it in his locker. The cons began to close in on him, forcing him back toward the elevator. He kept his gun up and pulled his father's cross from around his neck, holding it up with the gun.

"In the name of Jesus Christ, Lord and Savior, I command you to stop!"

They grinned at him and kept coming.

John calmly shot Elwin Patoire, a lifer from the Can, who thrust a long shard of glass at him. The cons rushed him, forcing him back against the elevator doors. He looked over his shoulder reflexively, and when he looked back, the few bronchial tubes still open in his lungs completely closed up.

Standing before him was Darlene Hampton.

Behind him, the elevator doors opened on an empty shaft.

John did the human thing and recoiled from the frightening visage. He jerked back, lost his footing, and fell right through the open elevator doors. He went down four floors without uttering a sound, until he landed on the roof of the elevator car. Then he let out a grunting "Oh!" and died.

While Captain Thompson was still in the basement under Digbee Hall, Tim Saget stood at the window watching the weird weather outside. He had never seen a storm like this one; had never seen fog during a blizzard, and what a fog! It swirled along past the windows like gray apparitions chasing the snow. The combination of the two was blinding. He could see nothing, it was so thick. The floodlight over the front door of A dorm illuminated the mist and the snow driving through it but nothing else. A couple of times, when the wind became extra strong and blew the mists clear, he thought he could briefly see the lights from the towers, but he couldn't be sure.

The wind gusted again, chasing the fog away for a few moments, and he saw the walkway in front of the dorm. A mob of huddled figures hurried along, heading for the south gate. With a sense of growing dread, Tim realized they looked like inmates. A moment later, the fog returned and they disappeared from view. He pulled out his radio.

"Inner Control, this is Two-oh-three, over." He waited for a response and tried again after a minute. "Inner Control, come in. This is Two-oh-three, over, I think we have some inmates loose in the yard." He got nothing but airy static. He wondered if the storm could be messing with transmissions, and wondered, too, if he had really seen inmates or if it had been just another ghostly visitation like the farmers he had seen. He paused, listening; was that the roar of many voices as in a cheer, or just the wind?

He shivered and went back to his desk. Not surprisingly, the Chief was up and sitting on the end of his bed, facing Tim's desk. He was still fully dressed in jeans, denim shirt, and sneakers. Tim had noticed that all the inmates seemed restless tonight. He had chalked it up to the storm and the fact that it was Christmas Eve; most of them were probably dealing with some tough emotions. But after seeing what he thought he'd seen outside, he began to wonder if something was up. The Chief's bunk was the closest to the COs' desk, no more than five feet away, but he got off his cot and came closer.

"This isn't good," he said in that strange, whining voice

of his. "I think I miscalculated. I thought we had more time—I should have seen this coming, Christmas Eve and all; the perfect time, you know. Perfect." He looked around. Tim looked with him and saw that half a dozen of the inmates were sitting up, looking at him, including Billy Dee Washington. "We need to get out of here now," the Chief said. He looked scared.

Billy Dee and the others got off their bunks and started coming slowly toward Tim and the Chief. All around the dormitory hall, more cons were waking, getting up, and joining Billy Dee in coming for him. Others just watched with intense interest.

"Follow me!" the Chief cried and ran for the exit.

"Wait!" Tim said, jumping up. "You men go back to bed!" he commanded Billy Dee and the others. Neither the Chief nor the approaching cons listened. Tim hit the body alarm button on his belt and unsnapped his baton. Behind him he could hear the Chief running down the stairs. A moment later, he heard the front door of the building slam.

"Hey! Chris!" Tim yelled to Chris Frieburg, the first floor guard. There was no answer. Tim backed to the stairs and looked down. The stairway was filled with cons from the first floor, some of them with apparent blood on them, slowly coming up the stairs. Tim turned and nearly ran straight into Billy Dee Washington.

"It's time for you to join me, my son," Billy Dee said and reached for him. Tim reacted without thinking. His eight weeks spent at the CO academy came in handy. In a textbook move, he used his baton to deflect Billy Dee's right arm aside, thus creating an opening for him to spear Washington in the Adam's apple with the end of the stick.

Billy Dee's hands went immediately to his throat and he staggered back. "Geck!" he said loudly and began to choke. The other cons froze, watching the biggest and strongest of them flail around, gasping for air.

Tim took advantage of the moment and sprinted for the tunnel door. The Chief was right. It was time to get out of there. Tim had his keys out by the time he reached the door. Thankfully, it was marked with a piece of black electrical tape that made it easy to find. He quickly isolated the key on the ring and unlocked the door before Billy Dee could recover or any of the inmates could react. He slammed the door behind him, hearing it lock automatically. A few moments later the doorknob rattled and fists pounded the other side.

Tim looked around. His heart was racing and he felt on the verge of panic. *The inmates were taking over the prison!* This was a life-or-death situation. He surprised himself; instead of causing panic, that thought calmed him, made him think. He was at the top of a stairwell leading down one flight to a landing where the tunnel door for the first floor was, then down another flight to the actual tunnel. He started down the stairs and the pounding on the door stopped. He looked at the first-floor door and suddenly realized the cons could get in through there. He had to assume that they had Chris Frieburg's keys. He wasn't safe at all, and he didn't have much time. He ran down the stairs, jumping the last three to the first-floor landing. He didn't waste time but kept going, passing the first floor and going around the landing to the stairs that led down to the tunnel.

He reached the bottom and heard a key scratch in the lock of the first-floor door a moment before it burst open. With cries of "Get him!" a swarm of inmates, led by a rough-breathing Billy Dee Washington, streamed through after him. Tim was already running at the first sound of the key in the lock. He held his baton in his left hand and pulled his radio out with his right. "Ten thirty-three!" he shouted into the radio, his voice high-pitched with fear. "Officer in need of assistance! Ten thirty-three!" He got nothing but static.

He reached the locked door that led to the main tunnel. He frantically shoved the radio and baton back on his belt. The key for the door was in a locked box on the wall next to the door. He fumbled through his key ring, dancing in place, with quick glances back the way he'd come. He tried to remember which one was the right key and wished he had used the tunnels at least once before this instead of being a wimp about it. The lock on the box didn't look that large, so he tried the smallest key on the ring and whooped with joy when it fit. The inmates were only twenty feet or so behind him. He opened the box, pulled the key inside it, which was on a chain, out, yanking the chain right out of the box as he did. Trying not to tremble, especially with the growing sound of the mob after him getting closer, Tim slipped the key in the lock and got the door opened. He managed to get through it with just feet to spare, slamming the door behind him as the cons slammed into it. He had the key, so they couldn't follow, but that didn't stop them from trying. He took deep, shrieking breaths and backed away from the thumping door. He hit his head on a low-hanging pipe.

"Fuck!" he said loudly, ducking his head and turning to look at what he'd hit. He felt the back of his head, checking his hand for blood but there was none. The noise from the other side of the door stopped, and he heard the cons moving away, presumably to find another way into the main tunnel. Tim looked at the tunnel ahead. The light was weak and yellow, and the bulbs crackled and dimmed intermittently. Unlike the one he'd just come through, this tunnel was one of the older ones; it was cramped, narrow, and had pipes hanging from the ceiling along its length. He'd have to walk stooped over to get through.

Panic kept trying to erupt in him and he fought to keep it down. He tried to figure out where he was; he'd been in such a hurry just to escape he hadn't paid any attention to which way he was going, or to the signs he'd noticed along the way. He thought for a moment: He had turned right when he entered the tunnel. He didn't know that it was lucky he had; if he had gone the other way, he would have been trapped—the tunnel ended twenty feet beyond.

He again wished he hadn't been such a baby and had used the tunnels before this. He tried to picture the layout of the prison and how the tunnel system should logically follow that layout. If that were true, he figured if he went left, he'd be going toward B dorm, and to the right he'd be going toward the south gate. He went right, walking slowly at first, then quickening his pace the more he thought about how easy it would be for the gang of inmates to gain access to this tunnel through B dorm. He strained to hear a hint of the mob after him, but the only sound in the tunnel was the slap of his feet on the stone floor. He hoped the storm outside had slowed the cons down.

The tunnel became even narrower, the ceiling lower, and he had to slow down. The ceiling lights, which were spaced about every five feet, were dim here. He came to a stretch where the lights were out, and he had to feel his way, stooped over, along the pipes, trying not to burn his fingers. Sweat ran into his eyes. With all the steam pipes running through this part of the tunnel, it was like being in a sauna.

He reached the end of the unlit section, and the passageway connected with another tunnel. He was relieved to see three signs on the walls that confirmed he was going the right way. One pointed back the way he'd come and was labeled *A DORM/B DORM;* the other, to the left, read *KITCHEN;* the third pointed right and read *EAST YARD/D BUILDING.* Tim stood listening, wondering if the cons had gained the tunnel yet. He tried his radio again. Nothing. He took a deep breath; this wasn't good. Where was the captain? Why wasn't anyone answering at Inner Control? There could only be one answer—the inmates had taken over not just A dorm but the entire facility. He had to get out of there. He followed the sign pointing to D building.

"No. This way. They're waiting for you that way."

Tim whirled around. It was the woman in the red headscarf. She was standing about ten feet away, where she hadn't been a moment before.

"It's you!" Tim couldn't believe it. He hadn't thought she was real.

She smiled at him. There was something so familiar about her, but he just couldn't put his finger on it.

"Who are you?" Tim asked. "How did you get here?"

"We don't have time for that. They're coming. We've got to find a place to hide. They won't stop looking for you."

"Why? I mean, the inmates just want to escape, don't they?"

She gave him a look that said: *You know better!*

"Shit!" he swore. "I was hoping this was just a prison break, but it isn't, is it?"

The woman shook her head sadly and touched his arm comfortingly.

"This is about the fire thirty years ago, isn't it?" Tim asked.

"It's that and more," she answered softly. "But we can't talk now. We've got to hurry. Follow me." She led the way, trotting lightly and quickly, her kerchief billowing around her head. Tim ran along behind her, watching the movement of her body as she ran, and found himself thinking of Millie and how much he missed making love to her. In light of his circumstances, all their petty fights and differences didn't seem like much. He wished he had been bigger than that; he wished he had been more of a man.

"This way," the woman said over her shoulder. She took a left turn off the tunnel they were in. Tim kept up with her, noticing a sign saying this was the tunnel to the kitchen. "We've got to hide. They won't give up. He won't let them, and *it* won't let him."

Tim was left to ponder what that meant when the woman suddenly stopped and held up her left hand, halting him. She put her right index finger to her lips to keep him quiet. They stood mid-tunnel, listening. Tim could hear faint voices and footsteps. He tensed. He couldn't tell from which direction they were coming. The woman stood next to him, head tilted, listening.

"Let's go. This way." She took his hand in hers and he was a little startled; it felt firm, warm, real. She pulled him along, running faster than before, passed the stairs to the kitchen, passed the little alcove that had been John Thompson and

Darlene Hampton's trysting spot. Just beyond it, the woman stopped. There was a square opening set into the right wall, close to the floor. It was about four feet high and three feet wide. The woman crouched and looked in, as did Tim. Except for some dust, it appeared dry and big enough for them to crawl through. He could feel warm air coming through. A few feet in, the shaft disappeared into darkness.

Tim swallowed hard. It was bad enough for him to have to be in the tunnels—did she actually expect him to crawl in there? Sensing his anxiety, she reached out and took his hand again. She looked him directly in the eye and smiled.

"It's okay. We'll be safe in here."

At the touch of her hand, Tim felt a curiously deep sense of reassurance, quite unlike anything he'd ever felt before. It was as if her touch was suddenly capable of draining away all his fears and nervousness about crawling into the cramped, claustrophobic, air shaft.

"You can do this," she said.

He nodded. She led the way on her hands and knees and he followed likewise. She didn't go far, just enough so that they were out of the light cast into the shaft from the tunnel. Once they were sitting side by side, facing each other in the dark, Tim was pretty comfortable. It helped that she kept fast hold of his hand.

"Won't you tell me who you are?" Tim whispered. "What's your name?"

"They used to call me Gypsy sometimes . . ." she answered hesitantly, as if unsure.

"I didn't think you were real. I thought you were a ghost, too." He waited, unable to see her in the dark, but she gave no answer. "Are . . . are you a ghost?" Tim whispered tentatively.

"Do you have to be dead to be a ghost?" she asked softly, her words barely audible.

"What?" Tim wasn't sure he'd heard her correctly.

"I don't know what I am . . . sometimes I think I've been here forever, but then sometimes, I go someplace else . . ."

Her voice trailed off, and they remained silent for several moments.

At last Tim had to speak. "What the hell is going on here? You've been in my dreams, warning me about this, haven't you?"

She nodded.

"How have you done that?"

"I don't know. I told you; sometimes I just go someplace else. But you've been in danger since you came here."

"Because of what happened thirty years ago?"

Gypsy nodded.

"Were *you* here thirty years ago?" Tim asked.

She nodded again; she didn't look a day over twenty-five—further evidence that she was not of the living.

"Did you . . . did you know my mother, Lena Saget?"

She nodded a third time.

Oh *shit!* She *has* to be a ghost, he thought. I'm sitting in here with a *ghost!* He felt the kind of terror he hadn't felt in decades—the senseless kind of terror only a kid can experience. He told himself to calm down. She was helping him. He almost giggled with the next thought—she's a *friendly* ghost—but felt that if he did he wouldn't be able to stop laughing. He'd be the proverbial laughing maniac. He tried another question to stifle his shock-induced mirth.

"Were you . . . uh, one of the ones caught in the fire that my mother set?" he asked and immediately thought better of it; he didn't want to remind her that *his* mother had caused her death, especially since she seemed to have forgotten it.

"She didn't set the fire."

"What? Who then?"

"It was *him,* Doctor Stone."

"Why?" Tim asked.

"You read his journal. He was more insane than any of his patients. He uncovered something here, in this hill, a presence that had been here a long time. He thought he had made some great scientific discovery of a new life-form, but he had only discovered the means to his own death and eternal damnation."

"But why did he set the fire?" Tim asked.

"He became convinced that with the help of this thing, he could control and consume the lives of others, making him stronger and adding years to his own life. He started out by gaining control of the patients' minds until they would do whatever he told them, and then he moved on to their flesh." She stopped speaking, and he could sense her discomfort.

"Yeah, the captain said that was in his journal. He ate them?"

"Yes. Four patients, before he got the idea that it was a waste of time to consume lives one at a time when he had thirty-odd lives at his disposal in the hospital. That thing was strong in him by then. It made him believe that he could— 'evolve' was the word he kept using—into a being of pure energy like the thing he was in contact with. It told him it used to be human, too. It convinced him that if he committed mass murder and suicide he could absorb the life forces of his victims and transform himself into something . . . else. It made him believe he couldn't die, could only be made stronger. So he gathered together on the fourth floor of Digbee Hall, which was a men's dorm at the time, all the patients and staff that were under his control. He locked them all in with him, almost all of them went willingly, and set the place on fire."

Tim was confused. "So where does my mother come into this? How did she get blamed for the fire?"

Gypsy looked at him keenly. "She was the only survivor. Just before Doctor Stone lit the fire, your mother managed to escape. In a way, she *was* the cause of the fire, though she didn't actually set it."

"What do you mean?"

"Your mother came here after Dr. Stone was already in communication with the presence here. But when your mother came, that presence got very strong. Your mother had a power of her own—I suspect you have it too. Do you sometimes see things—the future—in your dreams?"

Tim nodded, the chill returning to his spine.

"Your mother's power fed the presence, much as yours has. Your mother fell in love with Doctor Stone shortly after her arrival here and she thought he loved her too. She helped him communicate with the thing out of her love for him, but your mother realized very quickly how evil and bent on destruction it was, and she refused to help anymore. And then it made Doctor Stone turn on her and do terrible things to her. He let the male inmates ravage her even though he knew she carried his baby."

"Me," Tim said softly.

"Yes, he's your father."

It was no big shock; he had figured as much. It made undeniable sense and helped explain a lot. It was why his mother, Lena Saget, had called him "Jason" when he'd visited her. It was why his middle name was Jason. Tim had suspected as much ever since he'd learned from his aunts that Lena Saget, his father's baby sister, was his real mother.

"What did she do?" Tim asked, a lump in his throat thinking about what she must have gone through.

"She did nothing! She refused to help him. Then she found out that he had sunk to cannibalism and threatened to go to Doctor Digbee. That's when the thing that had hold of Doctor Stone planted the idea in his mind that the flesh he had consumed had made him immortal and invulnerable. He became convinced that by killing all the patients and staff, he would become some kind of super being. And by including your mother and you, his unborn son, he thought to consume your powers. But your mother escaped. Because of that, and now, because of your returning here, he—it—has grown strong again and has another chance."

"Another chance for what?"

"Why, for another feast of souls! I thought you understood that. Your soul, and the soul of everyone in here, is wanted very badly; it's what this thing exists for—to gorge itself on human pain, suffering, and death. It wants to devour you and every other soul in this place, just as it tried to do thirty years ago. The orgy of torture and murder has already begun."

"What do you mean?"

"I mean this evil creature now holds sway over the entire prison. All your fellow guards are either dead or soon will be."

"Can't we do anything to stop it?"

She didn't answer.

"We've got to try and get help," Tim said. "We've got to get to an outside phone, call the state police. We're going to have to get over to either D or C building to get an outside line that doesn't need the prison operator to put it through."

She let go of his hand. He reached for her in the dark, but his hand found only the smooth wall of the airshaft. He squirmed around and took out his flashlight, risking clicking it on. The beam revealed that the airshaft was empty. He was alone; she was gone. He shined the light further down the shaft. Empty. The dust on the floor was undisturbed. She hadn't gone that way, and she hadn't gone out the way they'd come in. She'd just vanished.

That cold liquid fear ran down his back again and squirmed in his bowels, but he shook it off. He didn't know what he was going to do, but he had to do something. Gripping his flashlight tightly, he crawled out of the shaft and stood, brushing himself off. He started down the tunnel, turned the first corner, and stopped. From ahead, around the next corner not far away, he heard a soft padding sound; a low drumming, growing louder by the second. It wasn't footsteps, and he could hear no voices, just this smooth, multilayered pitter-patter.

Whatever it was, he didn't like it. He backed up and was about to turn when something small and fast spilled around the other corner, followed by many more. Cats. Hundreds of them, loping around the corner, bounding toward him. Tim remembered the captain telling him about the prison's feral cat problem, but he had no idea—no one did—how many wild, ex-domesticated cats there were in the place.

And right now they were all charging hell-bent toward Tim, their eyes black with the excitement of the hunt, their lips curled back, baring teeth ready to tear into his flesh. He could hear the *clickety-click* of their claws like machine-gun fire on the stone floor as they raced at him.

He turned heel and ran back around the corner and right into the arms of Billy Dee Washington and three other cons from A dorm. Tim looked back; the cats were gone. He felt a strange sense of relief at being caught.

"Jason, my son," Billy Dee said in a weird voice. "It's time for our holiday feast." The other two cons grabbed him, one by each arm, and he didn't resist. They took him through the tunnels, spanning the width of the prison compound underground, and ended up in the basement of Digbee Hall. Billy Dee took out a key ring that Tim recognized as Captain Thompson's. He unlocked the door opposite the basement stairs, and they went into a large room with file cabinets along three walls and elevator doors on the fourth. Again using a key from the captain's ring, Billy Dee inserted it into the elevator call panel and brought the car down to the basement level.

Pulling Tim between them, the two cons entered the elevator car with Billy Dee right behind them. Tim felt something drip on his shoulder. He looked up. There was blood dripping from the emergency exit door set in the ceiling of the elevator car. Billy noticed, too, and looked up, smiling. "Our cousin," he said, nodding toward the bloody ceiling, "the ghostbuster, had a nasty fall." He laughed heartily as the elevator rose.

"I've been waiting a long time for this, son," Billy Dee said. The elevator lurched to a stop. The doors opened and Tim was greeted with a scene from Hell. The vast fourth-floor hall was filled with escaped inmates torturing bound COs. From what Tim could see, it looked like most of the inmates and nearly every guard in the prison was there, but what kept him looking, even as he recoiled in horror, was the way each of the torturers appeared to be two people in one. There was Donny Falcone, the Chief's friend from A dorm, within the shimmering form of a tall, thin black man. Nearer, on the opposite side, a skinny black con was shrouded in the figure of a massive bald-headed white man who leered at Tim through the con's face.

"This can't be real," Tim gasped. He felt faint and nauseous. He felt as though he could suddenly feel the earth spinning madly beneath his feet at thousands of miles per second and felt like he could fly right off into space.

Billy Dee turned to him, laughed and winked. "It's better than real."

The inmates escorted Tim to the center of the hall. All activity in the vast room came to a complete stop. Several of the restrained guards—Tim realized he barely knew any of them—continued to moan, several were weeping, and one kept pleading for mercy, until the inmate who had been torturing him with a lit cigarette kicked him in the face, breaking his teeth and jaw. Tim flinched, recoiling from the scenes of degradation and brutality that were being played out around the room and tried to keep the tears from his eyes.

Billy Dee Washington held out his arms as if to embrace the entire room, and in that one movement, his features shifted, slid sideways, ran, and recomposed themselves rapidly into the image of Doctor Jason Stone. His body followed suit, the color of his skin fading from dark brown to tan, then milky white. His form flowed smoothly into that of Doctor Jason Stone until only he stood there in a white coat that went nearly all the way to his ankles, his long black hair shiny and wavy, cascading over his collar and onto his shoulders, his gaucho mustache framing his smile which showed brilliantly white, though slightly crooked, teeth.

Looking at him up close for the first time, Tim could clearly see a resemblance to himself; they could have passed for brothers.

"As you all know," the doctor said loudly, "I . . . we . . .

have been waiting a long time for my son to come home." He turned slowly as he spoke, so as to address everyone in the room. "Now he's here and we are complete. Now he's here and we can finish the task we began thirty years ago."

The crowd cheered. Sickened, Tim looked around at them. They were all transforming from double-exposed figures into single beings. Standing a few feet away, he noticed a man and a woman dressed like farmers from colonial days. The man wore a wide-brimmed straw hat, a woolen shirt, and canvas coveralls that were so baggy they would have fallen down if not for the shoulder straps holding them up. The woman wore a plain white bonnet that covered her ears and tied under her chin, and a long, green, coarse woolen dress that covered her from her neck to her wrists and ankles. Looking at them, Tim could see a distinct resemblance between the man and Doctor Stone and himself. He could see a lot of John Thompson in the woman. Tim guessed they were Elijah Stone and his wife, Lucy.

They were not cheering.

The insanity of the situation made his head reel.

The lights suddenly dimmed. The wind howled at the windows like a pack of wolves. Shadows in the room grew and began to collect together. A mass of darkness coalesced out of the essence of this shadow and grew until it loomed over Doctor Stone and the rest of the room. The cheering quickly died down. Tim saw that every other person, living and dead, except for Dr. Stone, looked as frightened as he felt.

The dark particles swirled in the air, descending around Dr. Stone like protective, embracing arms. Everyone in the room stood either mesmerized by the shadow particles or cowed by them. Dr. Stone stood stock still, eyes closed, until the darkness wrapped around him and dissolved into him.

He opened his eyes, and Tim immediately knew he was no longer facing his father. What shone in the eyes that gazed upon him now was not human, had never been human—in fact, it loathed humanity. Tim had never seen anything like it, had never seen eyes so alien, so maliciously evil and filled with hatred at all things human.

Looking into those eyes, Tim felt a wave of fear wash over him worse than anything he had felt that night. A horrible emptiness, a black hole of despair, opened inside him. All memory of happiness was sucked into it; any sense of security or self-confidence disappeared into the blackness of despair. He was left with nothing but primal fear and a feeling that life was too overwhelming; there was no point in going on; he would be better off dead, here with his real father and relatives. Tim saw himself for the first time, stripped of all the bullshit; saw the immaturity, selfishness, laziness, and did not like the person he saw. He was weak and cowardly, always had been. He despised himself and saw a lifetime of loneliness stretching before him as punishment for his shortcomings. He saw Millie leaving him, the Sarge disowning him; saw himself become a washed-out barfly, warming a stool, sipping a drink to make it last.

All the while he was having this vision, like a vivid daydream, he was aware of the eyes boring into him, and something else, something oozing out of Doctor Stone—the same black, shadowy streams of dark energy that had entered him. It began to move, flowing into the room in long tendrils of black ooze, like snakes or the tentacles of some giant sea monster. These tendrils curled around the inmates, caressing them, flitting into their nostrils, their open mouths, even their ears, before moving on, leaving each one blank-eyed and grinning.

The thing masquerading as Doctor Stone motioned to one of the inmates, who ran to the side of the hall and brought back one of the five-gallon gas cans that Hiram Pena and Marty Miller had carried over from Ed Isaacs tower. He raised the can of gasoline over his head and turned it upside down. As the pinkish gasoline gushed from the can, dousing the doctor's head and splashing onto his shoulders and over his lab coat, soaking it, his image flickered for a moment and Billy Dee Washington returned, but the eyes remained the same. He let the gas flow over his head until he was drenched in high-test from his head to his knees. All the while, he stared at Tim. Though Tim's eyes were watering and he could barely breathe from the pungent fumes, those eyes did not blink once.

All around the hall, the transformed inmates followed his lead and did the same, passing around gas cans and dousing themselves and their captives with gasoline. Within seconds, the air was thick and wavy with petrol fumes. Doctor Stone stepped toe to toe with Tim, ready to pour the rest of his can on his son. The eyes grew larger and larger until they were all-encompassing. Tim was aware of him raising the can of gas ready to pour it over him, and he stood there, ready to let him. The feeling of utter despair and worthlessness he felt was so crushing he couldn't struggle, couldn't resist. There was a convincing dark voice inside those eyes that never stopped whispering that things would be better this way.

"No, Jason!" The voice came from behind Tim, jerking him out of the spell of those eyes. He turned and there was Gypsy. "Let him go. You can't do this. He's your son!" She was carrying a silver Zippo lighter held up in her right hand, the top flipped back and her thumb on the striking wheel.

Doctor Stone looked shocked and terrified to see her. "Gypsy? How?" he stammered.

"Get out of here," she said to Tim. "Now!" she shouted. She grabbed the back of Tim's collar and pulled while in the same motion striking the lighter to flame and tossing it at Doctor Stone.

Literally yanked from his lethargic despair by her action and the shrill urgency of her voice, Tim pulled his arms free from the grip of the cons holding him and bolted. The lighter sparked into a large blue flame that fluttered as the lighter flew through the air. Before it went more than a foot, the fumes in the air ignited. Doctor Stone looked astonished for a moment, then morphed back into Billy Dee Washington. "Fuck!" Billy Dee commented, a half-second before he was completely engulfed in fire.

There was a sizzling sound, then a loud *whomp*! and the air in the hall instantly combusted. Flames rushed through the hall behind Washington, all the way to the elevators and back again, igniting everything, inmate and guard alike. The smoke, thick and black with human hair and scorched flesh, mingled with the tendrils of shadow, filling the room and blinding most of its inhabitants from seeing any avenue of escape.

Tim was ten feet from the exit door when the air in the hall ignited. He heard the windows explode as he lunged through the exit door, seconds before the flames reached it. He was clambering down the stairs when the door blew off its hinges behind him and crashed against the stairwell wall, just missing his head as he dove the last few stairs to the landing between floors. Flames, funneled by the narrow door opening and the stairs, rushed headlong into the stairwell, rolling down the stairs after him.

He kept running, leaping several steps at a time, aware of the growing heat on the back of his neck. He could smell hair burning—his own. One more short flight of stairs and he'd be at the emergency outside door that would set off an alarm if he used it. The flames caught up with him just as he reached the door and pushed through it, immediately setting off the alarm. Flames licked at his back, setting his jacket aflame. He dove into the fresh deep snow outside the door, feeling the *whoosh*! of hot flame go over his head, and rolled around to put out his flaming jacket before the fire could burn through to his skin. The alarm, a loud intermittent siren, was immediately swallowed up in the fog, snow, and howling wind.

Tim crawled away from the door. His mind was numb. He could only manage one thought: He had to get out of the prison. He had to survive. He was on the north end of Digbee Hall. The snow and fog were so thick and racing by at such a dizzying speed that he couldn't see much more than a few feet. He looked up and back at the front corner of Digbee and could discern only a faint pulse of glowing fire-

light through the thick fog. Pulling his thin jacket tighter
about him, he got to his feet and staggered into the storm,
heading for the rear gate. As far as he knew, it was the closest exit from the prison.

The storm afforded zero visibility. The wind blew so
fiercely he could not face it, but had to walk sideways, tuck-
ing his shoulder into it to try and cut a path. The snow stung
him and the fog soaked him within seconds. Suddenly,
someone jumped on his back, knocking him to the ground.
He rolled away, but the attacker was on him again in an instant. Knees pinned his shoulders to the ground and hands
closed on his throat. Tim could smell burnt flesh. He looked
up and could see flames and smoke rising from the head and
shoulders of his assailant.

Tim struck out wildly with his right hand, grabbing at the
man's face. His fingers sank into the skin, which had the texture of overcooked meat ready to fall off the bone. His left
hand sought out his baton, which was clipped to the left side
of his belt. He pulled a chunk of the guy's greasy face-flesh
off and jammed it into his eyes while bringing up the baton
with his left hand. He cracked it against his attacker's sizzling temple frantically and repeatedly, until the man let go
of his throat and toppled over, his flaming hair hissing out in
the snow.

Tim rolled away from him. The man's blood and melted
skin felt warm on his hands. Shuddering, he plunged them
into the snow to cleanse them. He knelt in the cold snow and
sobbed uncontrollably for several moments before sniffing
back his tears and molding his face into a look of determination. Shifting his baton to his right hand, Tim pushed himself
to his feet, shook off snow and started walking again. After
only a few steps, he realized he had lost his bearings and
didn't know which way to go. His ears and face were numb
with the cold, as were his hands and feet. With the wind
whipping so fiercely, he couldn't keep his eyes open more
than a few seconds at a time when facing into it. Shielding
his eyes with cupped hands, he turned slowly, trying to iden-

tify a building or something to tell him which way to go. The mist flying by revealed little, but in a gap, he found a bearing—several yards away, a group of shadowy figures were coming through the storm toward him. Behind and high above them, Tim could make out the faint outline of Digbee Hall and the glow from the fire raging within before it disappeared again. He figured that if he kept going straight away from his pursuers, he would reach the rear gate station, a large, one-story, square building set into the northern corner of the prison compound not more than thirty yards from Digbee Hall.

He struggled on, the wind doing its best to hold him back. He looked over his shoulder. His pursuers were vague shapes, wraiths in the mist. A blackness darker than the blanketing fog loomed ahead and he went toward it. Before long, he bumped into a brick wall. He leaned against it, hugged it, his breath loud in his ears. Hands tucked under his arms, he followed the wall, keeping his shoulder in contact with it as he went along. He reached a corner and glanced back, but could see no one in the gray wall of air. He went around the corner and continued on. The faint aura of a floodlight became visible through the fog and gave him hope as it grew stronger the closer he got. Under it, he could start to make out the officers' entrance to the rear gate and prisoner trap, where all incoming cons were processed. At the edges of the light, the eddying fog and snow hid anyone, or anything, pursuing. He was almost out. He kept that thought foremost in his mind, excluding all the horrible images and memories that wanted to crush him with fear.

Tim staggered on. He was so frozen he could feel nothing below his thighs. His ears and face were burning severely from the cold. His hands, tucked under his arms, were only slightly less so, and he wasn't sure he could pry the fingers of his right hand off the baton they still clutched. With the doorway in sight, Tim felt a surge of renewed strength. He plowed through the snow, three feet deep in the drifts near the building, and made his way to the door. He leaned against it and fumbled out his keys, moaning with the pain it caused in his fingers. With an extreme effort, he got the key into the lock and had to use both hands to turn it, keeping his baton tucked under his arm as he did.

The door unlocked, he reached for the handle with his hands and fingers that felt like they would shatter if he bumped them against anything. A hand closed on his shoulder. He caught a whiff of burnt hair and skin before being spun around to face a smoldering Billy Dee Washington.

"You can't leave now," Billy Dee said, his voice gurgling in his throat. "The party's just starting." He was horribly burned, his dreadlocks gone, his skin charred and cracked. His flame-split skull showed bone and still smoldered. He glared at Tim through his sole remaining lidless eye. In his burnt, cracked face, Tim could see the other countenance looking through—the leering, hateful eyes of the thing from the shadows. He reached for Tim's throat. Tim screamed and reflexively struck out with one of the first attack moves he had learned with his baton: the solar thrust. He grabbed the stick from under his arm and lunged with the baton gripped in both hands, spearing Billy Dee in the solar plexus, right in the center of his chest at the small cavity between his rib cage. Billy Dee's barbecued flesh yielded easily to the intrusion, and the baton went in and through him, bludgeoning within inches of his heart and coming to rest against his spine.

Billy Dee rose up on his toes, his head bobbing, and said, "*Gah! Gah!*" before falling over backward in the snow. Tim turned and rushed to the door. His frozen hands slipped off the knob repeatedly as he tried to turn it. He looked over his shoulder. Several smoldering figures were coming into the circle of light toward him. He pulled his hands into the cuffs of his jacket, grabbed the knob with both hands, and turned. Agonizingly, slowly, the knob turned. The latch clicked and Tim pushed it open, ducked through, and slammed the door shut behind him. He tried to turn the lock, but he couldn't do it with his numb fingers. Finally, he bent over and, using his teeth, bit the lock and turned it, chipping one of his front teeth in the process. He didn't care. He was out of the storm. It was warm in there. He backed away, shivering and hugging himself as he looked around.

The rear-gate processing building consisted of a large room divided by a long wooden counter that stretched the length of the room. There was a phone on the end near him. He grabbed it, knocking the receiver to the floor with his fumbling hands, but it was dead anyway, no dial tone. The front of the counter was where prisoners were processed; behind the counter were four desks used by the COs. The rear gate handled everything from prisoners to food deliveries and trash pickups. Everything that went in or out of the prison, with the exception of visitors and COs themselves, was searched by the men and women working the rear gate.

The room was empty of COs now—Tim tried not to think of them burning in Digbee Hall—and dark, except for one light on the desk against the wall farthest from Tim. The front wall of the building, which faced the actual rear gate and the access road beyond, was glass from floor to ceiling. With the outside floodlights on, Tim could see glimpses through the fog and snow of the vehicle trap, where delivery trucks and all vehicles going in or out of the prison were checked and searched. To the far right was the concrete base of the tower situated in that corner of the fence. All he had to do was go out the far door and through the rear gate and he could follow the road around to the COs' parking lot, get his car, and get the hell out of there. Looking out at the raging, blinding storm and remembering how hard it had been to get just this far, he realized it was going to be easier said than done.

As if to emphasize that point, there was a huge, window-shaking gust of wind, and all the lights went out. All was quiet but for the sound of the rushing wind. A moment later, that quiet was interrupted by a loud crash as Billy Dee Washington smashed through the door behind Tim, splintering the wood into flying fragments and sending shards of glass everywhere.

"Oh, fucking shit!" Tim screamed and stumbled away from him, bumping into the counter and nearly falling. With a loud hum, the outside floodlights came back on as the prison's emergency generator automatically kicked in. Billy Dee faced him, Tim's baton still sticking out of his chest. He was a horror to behold: burnt so badly his skull showed through the right side of his face. His one lidless eye bulged from its socket, staring balefully at Tim.

"Oh, *fuck!* God, please help me!" Tim whispered. He looked around for a weapon or a way out, but to get to the gate he had to get by Billy Dee. There was the desk against the wall behind him that had its light on and its top drawer half open. Looking around, he noticed a faint glint of metal within. He ran to the desk, yanked open the drawer, and was disappointed to see it was only a metal stapler. As Billy Dee lurched toward him, stumbling into another desk, Tim began pulling drawers. In the bottom one, he found what he was looking for, a correction officer's standard-issue Smith and Wesson .38-caliber revolver. He pulled it out of the drawer and checked the chamber. Full.

Pointing the gun with two hands, keeping Billy Dee in front of him, Tim began circling around the back of the room, trying to get around Billy Dee enough to make a dash for the counter gate. Looking at Billy Dee with his cooked flesh and the baton sticking out of his chest, Tim had to fight the urge to just run or find a place to hide where he could curl up and pray for help. It was obvious that if Billy Dee wasn't dead, he was very close to it, and the only thing keeping him going was whatever possessed him. Since a baton through the chest hadn't stopped him, Tim didn't expect bullets to have much effect, but they might slow him down enough that Tim could make a dash for it. When the lights came back on, a hope of escape appeared to Tim. He noticed the K-9 van parked just outside the door. If he could get to it, and if the keys were in it, he could forget about trying to get his car out of the snow and use the van to go get help.

Tim stopped. "Oh, no! Please, no!" he nearly sobbed. Out

of the corner of his eye, he saw his other pursuers stepping through the wreckage of the door Billy Dee had destroyed. There were three of them; he'd have to move fast before they could surround him. He fired at Billy Dee and sprinted for the counter gate. The shot went wild and shattered one of the large front windows. Snow and wind blasted into the room, sending shards of glass ripping into Billy Dee Washington's toasted hide. He was unfazed. He lunged after Tim, bumping into a chair and knocking it to the ground. He stumbled over it and Tim took the opportunity to scuttle by him.

Marty Miller, the old woman Tim had seen in Digbee Hall on his first day and in Dave Stirling's car, and Donny Falcone, the Chief's friend, now blocked the way. Tim crouched and faced them. All three showed various degrees of burns. Miller was naked, but his body was so badly burned it looked like he was wearing a black suit that was cracking in spots. Chunks of his charred flesh flaked off every time he moved. They fell to the floor where they pulverized into ash on impact. His face was relatively unscathed but for a shiny red burn on the left side that reached from his jaw, up over his ear and to the top of his head, leaving a bald swatch in his hair that still smoldered. The old woman had minimal burns on her arms and hands, which were shiny red. Her face was sooty, and as snow in her hair melted, rivulets of water ran down her face, leaving tracks of clean skin behind. Donny Falcone was the worst off of the three. His flesh had been burned away to reveal raw muscle and tendons. With his right hand he held in his intestines, which were exposed and steaming. His face was still intact, otherwise he would have been unrecognizable. His eyes were lidless, staring from under a crown that was a mush of parboiled skin and hair.

The old woman made her move first. Letting out a banshee scream, she charged Tim. Tim screamed back, thrust the gun at her, and fired. At nearly point-blank range, the bullet went into her left eye and took out the entire back of her head. It proceeded on to hit Marty Miller in the chest, making an ugly puckered crater in the cooked flesh and muscle there. The old woman went down hard, twitched once, and slowly transformed into a crispy Hiram Pena at Tim's feet, his life's blood bubbling from his eye socket and running from his ears and out the back of his charred head.

Before Tim could experience the shock of what had just happened, arms closed around him as Billy Dee Washington grabbed him from behind. Tim could feel the end of his baton poking him in the back. He pushed against it, digging his heels into the floor as hard as possible. There was a muffled *crack!* as the end of the baton snapped Billy Dee's spine and continued on out his back with a squishing, spurting noise. Billy Dee's legs gave out and he let go of Tim. He sank to his knees and slumped sideways against a nearby desk.

Marty Miller, who had been tottering and looking not long for this world, took a stumbling step forward and collapsed in a steaming, twitching heap. Tim looked at Donny Falcone, who also appeared to be fading fast.

"Donny," Tim said hoarsely, his voice shaking and cracking. "Don't do this. Let me get you some help. You're hurt, man. You're a friend of the Chief's; he'd want you to do this. I'll help you. Let's get out of here together."

Donny leaned back against the wall, his head down, and for a moment, Tim thought he had got through to him. But then Donny looked at him and Tim could see his eyes were the same eyes he'd seen in Doctor Stone. Falcone lunged at Tim faster than Tim expected. He awkwardly grabbed for Tim's throat and fell against him. The barrel of the pistol sank into Falcone's gut, and Tim pulled the trigger. Half of the con's midsection sprayed around the room. His charge ended as a slump to the floor, his shoulder bumping Tim's legs as he went down.

Tim stepped over the dead cons, took three steps to the counter gate, and had to stop. He shuddered, and the shudder became a trembling, then a violent palsy. He shook, hunched over, gripping onto himself. He felt lightheaded, nauseous, and his legs did not want to hold him up any more. He slumped against the counter and slid to the floor where his vigorous shivering continued unabated. He looked down. The front of his jacket and pants were stained with blood and human gore. He hugged himself and wished fervently that someone would help him.

"There is no one. No one cares. It's useless to try and go on."

Startled, Tim turned at the voice. It was Billy Dee, still on his knees, slumped against a desk. His face sagged, paled, and became the face of Doctor Stone. Those eyes turned their mind-numbing gaze his way.

Remembering how those eyes had engulfed and dominated him the last time he looked into them, Tim looked away, but didn't count on the power of the doctor's voice that so many inmates had found irresistible.

"You can't get away, son. Stay here with me forever," he said softly. "All you have to do is put that pistol to your head and pull the trigger." His voice was nice, warm. It was an easy voice to listen to and Tim *was* so tired, so cold, so scared, and he was *tired* of *being* tired, cold, and scared. "It doesn't hurt. Come with me. Do it now."

It doesn't hurt? Sure, Tim thought. Why not? If it doesn't hurt. A crushing depression dropped on him. What did he have to live for? A crappy job where he was as much a prisoner as the inmates? A lousy marriage that was like being in prison for the lack of sex in it? The loneliness of the years ahead in that marriage filled him with despair. The shackles of fatherhood and all that crushing responsibility? There was no need to prove anything any longer to the Sarge—he had lied to Tim. He *wasn't* Tim's father. His father was *here*. His family was here. Why *not* stay?

"Yes, stay," his father echoed. He was wheezing now, as Billy Dee Washington breathed his last. "Put the gun to your head, Jason. Do it for me."

Tim did it, putting the cold muzzle to his right temple.

"Pull back the hammer," his father went on.

Tim thumbed the hammer and pulled it back until it cocked with a loud *click*!

"And just pull the trigger."

Don't listen. That is not your father; your father no longer exists. Gypsy's voice rang in his head.

She was right. This was not his father, and if he pulled that trigger he would not be joining his father in eternity, he would become sustenance for that *thing* whose eyes showed through every person it possessed. He didn't know what it was—he knew now that the Chief had tried to tell him about this thing, but he had been too stupid to listen—but there were no ghosts haunting New Rome Correctional Institute and there never had been. The only thing haunting the Hill and anyone who had dared to live or build there was this *thing* of darkness and hatred.

Tim lowered the gun.

"No," his father gasped. "Please, son . . ."

"You're not my father," Tim said and struggled to his feet. Billy Dee fell over onto his face, his last breath hissing from his lungs, Tim's baton sticking up out of his back like a flagless pole. Tim leaned briefly against the counter for support and then went through the gate. He paused and looked back through the smashed-open door to see if anyone else was coming for him, but beyond the reach of the floodlights he could see nothing. Hanging on the wall near him, he noticed, was a state-issue down parka with a fur-lined hood. Tim pulled it down and thankfully put it on, hugging it to himself for several minutes to get warm and subdue his trembling. He reached in the pockets, hoping for gloves, but that would have been too much to ask for.

He went to the other door leading to the vehicle trap and rear gate and unlocked it, venturing outside again. The wind and snow renewed their attack against him. Bent into the wind, Tim staggered to the K-9 unit van, just a few feet away, pulled the driver's door open, and quickly got inside, slamming the door shut behind him. He sat for a moment, breathing on his hands, warming them. Almost out now, he told himself to subdue his shaking. The wind was blowing so hard that just a few seconds of exposure could be brutal. He looked at the ignition and said a tearful, "Thank you, God," seeing the keys dangling there. He sat up and looked beyond the front of the van—the rear gate was *open*! He laughed at himself and batted back the tears. *I'm going to make it,* he told himself.

But where was the dog officer and his dog? Tim didn't remember seeing any of the K-9 unit in Digbee Hall, but the two night dog officers could have been lured into any of the buildings, or attacked anywhere in the compound or not at all. The howling wind let up for a minute, and Tim thought he heard something. The sounds were coming from the back of the van. Tim turned and slid open the panel behind the seat, revealing the heavy mesh screen that separated the cab of the van from the back, where the dogs rode.

As soon as Tim slid the door open, he knew where the dog was; he could hear it eating, hear it tearing at something and wolfing it down. With no windows in the rear of the truck it was too dark to see much more than just the silhouette of the dog's furry haunches as it bent over whatever it was eating. Tim pulled out his flashlight and beamed it into the back of the truck.

He wished he hadn't.

There was a body lying on the floor of the van. Tim could see the legs from the knees down, and knew by the blue pants with the silver stripe down the side and department-issue black combat boots that it was a corrections officer, most likely the night-shift dog officer himself. The dog paused and looked at him, its eyes wild and fierce, its chops bloody. Tim quickly closed the panel. He felt sick. Again the fear and despair—that crushing feeling of being totally alone in the world, totally helpless—grabbed hold of him, shook him, made him want to just get out of the truck and walk off into the storm and the night and keep walking until he collapsed.

He caught himself actually reaching for the door handle but came to his senses.

"No! You're almost home!" he whispered through clenched teeth. He turned the key, started the truck, put on the lights and the heater/defrost. He was glad the van had been sheltered by the rear gate roof; there was hardly any snow on it. He turned on the wipers and eased the automatic gearshift into *Drive*. He pulled out slowly, hugging the wheel, easing the van through the gate while peering between the sweeping wipers for a sign of the road. Finally, he could just make it out beyond a large drift, fifteen feet from the gate. He saw he could follow it as a trough between snowdrifts. He gave the van gas and the back end slid to the left, but he countered, steering the other way, and the van began to pick up a little speed. The van plowed through the drift to gain the access road and Tim held his breath until it had made it. Now he was on the road that would take him along the ridge overlooking the prison, past the kennels, and then past the front gate and down the hill to Route 140. The state police barracks was a couple of miles down the highway.

The road began to rise before him as he climbed the highest ridge on Stone's Hill. The fog was reduced here to fleeting mists scurrying across the white landscape. The back end of the van began to slip and fishtail more. Tim slipped the automatic transmission into second gear and tried not to push too heavily on the gas pedal. He couldn't believe the vehicle didn't have four-wheel drive, but it *was* the older of the two vans Tim had seen the K-9 unit use when he had shadowed there.

Like a parent coaxing a toddler to take his first steps, Tim coaxed the van up the incline, urging it on every time the tires spun, saying a silent, "Thank God!" every time they caught again. Several times the wheels spun, yet the van barely crawled while the speedometer needle jumped to thirty and higher. Something ran across the road in front of the van. Tim couldn't be sure if it was a person or an animal and didn't care to find out. The van was cresting the ridge; a stretch of level ground lay ahead, and he gave the vehicle more gas, causing the tires to spin again, but gaining speed; he didn't want anyone catching up with him on foot.

There was barely any fog on top of the ridge, and ahead he could see the glow of the outside floodlights around the kennels. High above them were the blinking red lights atop the black silhouettes of the old grain silos to warn low-flying aircraft. The two red sparks glowed intermittently in the night, like eyes, searching for him, hungering for him, transfixing Tim for a moment.

He pushed the pedal down, forcing the van faster. There was a thump as he hit a bump in the road—or something hit the van—and suddenly it was out of control, sliding sideways into the five-foot drift piled up along the roadside. In the back he heard the dog slam against the wall of the van and back again, and the body rolling around as the van spun sideways. Tim tried to countersteer, but it was no use. The vehicle came to rest, tilted at an angle, the rear end higher than the front, pointing back the way he'd just come, the rear tires hopelessly buried in the drift.

The engine stalled.

Tim sat stunned for a few moments before trying to restart the van. It would have none of it.

"Fuck me!" he shouted and laughed miserably. The sad chuckles became pathetically close to hysteria, and he bit it back. "You're outside the prison at least," he muttered. Maybe he was safe out there. He hoped so. He wasn't that far from the kennels. He tried to remember if there was an outside line in there. He couldn't remember, but there had to be at least *one* out here that wasn't on the same line as the prison's. At the very least, he could get the other truck, the pickup with four-wheel drive, and use it to get off the Hill. He hoped the other eleven-to-seven dog officer was inside—safely. He prayed it would be so as he trudged through the waist-high snow to the old barn that was the headquarters of the prison K-9 unit.

He reached one of the windows and looked inside. The dog officer was there all right, but not safely. The guy, whose name Tim didn't know, was lying on his back in the aisle between the dog pens, the doors of which were all open. The dogs were all gathered around the downed officer, feasting on him, enraptured with their primal pack feeding instincts. Tim turned away, putting his hand to his mouth to squelch the nausea he felt rising in his throat. He had thought he couldn't get any more grossed out than with the things he'd seen in Digbee Hall and after, but the *dogs were eating the guy's face!*

"Oh, God!" Tim intoned, whispering. "Please, God, get me out of here and I'll never do a bad thing again as long as I live. I'll never drink. I'll love Millie and our kid and I'll raise him to be a good Christian and I promise, promise, *promise,* I'll *never* do another *fucked-up* thing if you'll just let me get the fuck out of here. Don't let me die. Please, don't let me die." He was sobbing, tears running from his eyes, snot running from his nose, and both freezing on his skin from the arctic blasts of wind.

He huddled against the kennel wall and tried to think. The garage was on the other side of the barn. He looked in the window again, focusing on the schedule board hung on the far wall. Next to it was the door to the garage and a couple of pegs to hold the keys to the vehicles. Tim cursed softly, seeing the keys to the other truck hanging there. To get them, he'd have to go in and face the dogs, and he wasn't about to do that.

There was no going that way. He'd have to revert to his original plan: Get to the COs' parking lot, dig out his little Dodge Neon, and hope its front-wheel drive would be enough to get him off the hill. The lot wasn't far, but in the storm and with who-knows-what out there after him, it was not an inviting prospect. But there was nothing for it. Putting his hands in his pockets where he could cradle the pistol for reassurance, he struck off into the storm, heading in the direction he was pretty sure was correct.

It was rough going, even rougher than down in the prison compound. He was on higher ground now, more exposed to the wind and the snow, which did their best to slow him down, turn him around, and generally fuck with him as if they, too, wished him to be captured. The only good thing was that the fog was low and so wind-driven it never had a chance to rise and obscure his vision. He reached the road near where he'd crashed the van and stopped. He stared at the sky beyond the truck. It was glowing red. He walked over and climbed the drift behind the van at the edge of the ridge. He could see the dark outline of Digbee Hall draped in an illuminated fog, the fire licking from its upper-floor windows. It was the scene of his dream.

"Thirty years ago she stood in this exact same spot on this exact same night and watched the exact same scene below."

Tim almost fell over in the snowdrift at the startling sound of Gypsy's voice and her sudden appearance next to him.

"She might have escaped if she hadn't stopped, but she did, and the thing came after her."

Suddenly, there was a deep, bone-resonating thud, and half the roof collapsed. Flames shot into the stormy night. A great black cloud followed the flames, pouring out of the dark chasm in the roof and rising above Digbee Hall.

"It knew her worst fear."

The cloud hovered in the air above the prison for a moment—

Her worst fear—the bats!

—then elongated, stretching toward Tim.

This immediately brought to mind his own worst fear, and before he realized what he had done, they were upon him; not bats, Lena Saget's worst fear, but his own—mosquitoes, only these were monster mosquitoes from hell, as big as his hand and as black as ebony. Ever since he could remember, he had hated the blood-sucking bastards. Just the whine of them in the air was enough to make him cringe like a coward. They swirled around him, jabbing and stabbing at him, trying to alight and plunge their razor sharp proboscises into him. Tim flailed wildly at them, shrieking, his hands striking some, missing most. The ones he did hit disintegrated upon contact and fell on the snow as dark ash.

"Those things aren't *real*," Gypsy said to him. He looked at her, dumbfounded—the insects were flying right through her. Tim saw what she meant: They couldn't hurt him if he didn't believe in them. These demon mosquitoes were just an illusion, just a trick . . . to *distract* him!

He ducked and spun around. The swarm of mosquitoes immediately vanished. The rear door of the van was open, the well-chewed dog officer hanging half out the back. It had not been that way a moment ago. Tim looked around. He was alone; Gypsy, too, was gone. Tim shoved his hands back in his pockets and grabbed the pistol. Trying to look in all directions at once, he trudged on, staying low and bent to the wind, following the slight indent between snowdrifts that indicated where the road lay. He looked back several times at the red glow reaching into the night from the prison below. The entire sky over the prison was aglow and he surmised that other buildings must be on fire too.

Tim surged on, digging deep into himself to find the stamina and courage to go on when fear and shock made him want to give up. The image of those eyes and that voice still lurked in his head, whispering how it was all so futile. He did his best to ignore it and plow on. He was almost there. The wind buffeted him and he staggered to the left. Out of the corner of his eye, he caught something dark and sleek moving fast, parallel to him. He quickly turned in that direction, pistol out and ready, but it was gone. A moment later he saw it again, a fast-moving shape crossing the road about thirty yards in front of him. Then again, off to the right; it was circling him.

Tim held the pistol close to his chest, uneasily trying to keep his hand warm while having the gun out and ready to fire. The road began to slope downward. If his bearings were correct, he should be able to see the lights of the COs' parking lot ahead on the left, but he couldn't. The power must have gone out again. The next thing he knew he was on the ground, face down in the snow. He immediately lunged to his knees, bringing up the snow-covered gun, and caught a glimpse of the tail and hind end of what looked like the dog that had been in the van. He hoped it was only that dog and that the others in the kennel hadn't caught wind of him too.

With quick, awkward, jerky movements, Tim got to his feet and turned in a slow circle, looking for something to shoot at. Within seconds he was on the ground again, his shoulder throbbing from the impact of the dog hitting him and him hitting the ground. He rolled over just as a large silver-and-black German shepherd—the same dog that had been feasting in the back of the van—leaped on him. The dog tore into the thick fabric of his parka hood, trying to get its teeth into his neck. Growling like a wild animal himself, Tim grabbed the dog's neck fur with his left hand, shoved the pistol into the dog's underside with his right, and fired.

The dog yelped and leapt off him, scurrying away into the night, leaving a thick black trail of blood in the snow. Tim leapt to his feet and screamed unintelligible curses at the retreating shadow. A moment later, the sound of many dogs growling and teeth gnashing came to him on the wind. He pictured the other dogs ganging up on the wounded one like sharks drawn to the scent of blood. The sound terrorized him into action. He took advantage of the moment and made a dash to the parking lot. He could just make out the black-and-yellow-striped metal pole that marked the entrance to the lot about ten yards ahead.

The road sloped suddenly and he slipped. His feet went out from under him, and he flopped into the snow butt first and slid for a few feet. He scrambled back to his feet as quickly as possible, grabbing the pole for leverage, when he felt something strong and sharp clamp onto the calf of his right leg. An excruciating pain shot up his leg, making him cry out. He swung at the dog with the pistol, swearing a blue streak, trying to bat it off him, but the animal was too strong, quickly yanking him off his feet. Shaking him as though he were a chew toy, the dog began to drag him back toward the kennel. Tim screamed with pain and rolled to the right, sat up, and got off a shot but it went wide. Though all K-9s were trained not to react to gunfire, the flash from the muzzle and the *pop* of the discharge were so close they were enough to make the dog release him and dash a few yards away.

Tim tried to get to his feet, but another dog struck him from the left, latching onto his arm and driving him to the ground again. "No!" he grunted, landing on his right side, the gun under him. He quickly twisted around, using the dog's momentum, and rolled on top of the animal. Roaring savagely, Tim stuck the pistol under the dog's head and pulled the trigger. The dog jerked once, violently, and stopped moving but for the occasional twitch, its teeth still dug into the thick fabric of his parka, its jaw locked in the biting position. The other dog quickly leaped back into the fray, grabbing Tim's left ankle in its jaws. Tim thanked God for his combat boots, which kept the dog's teeth from piercing, but the biting pressure of the dog, a Doberman he could now see, was crushing. He let out an enraged cry, feeling the ligaments and tendons in his ankle crunching under the force of the dog's jaw. He leaned over and brought the pistol butt down on the dog's head in a rapid series of crushing blows. The dog yelped and tried to get away, but he caught it with a deadly blow to the center of its skull. There was a squishy *crack,* and the dog collapsed immediately and lay twitching, blood running from its mouth into the snow.

Tim fell back against the pole, one dead dog still clamped onto his arm, the other lying at his feet. He waited for the rest of the pack to attack and make a quick finish of him. He didn't know how many bullets were left—he'd lost count—but he was pretty sure the gun was either empty or he had one round left. It didn't matter anymore. He was finished once the dogs came.

He waited for what seemed like a long time; the rest of the pack didn't come. Jamming the barrel of the pistol into the mouth of the dog clamped on his arm, Tim used it as a lever to pry the dog's mouth open and pull his sleeve free. He rolled to his knees and peered uneasily around. The snow had not let up a bit, leaving him visibility of only a few yards. He could just make out the great lumps of drifting snow that had to be the cars parked in the lot, not too far beyond the striped pole.

"Not much further," he said to legs that didn't want to move. "You're almost out of here." His car was less than twenty-five yards away. If he could just make it to the car everything would be okay, he told himself. For a change, the wind gusted behind him, helping him on his way instead of hindering him. Moving as quickly as possible, Tim entered the lot. The rows of cars were white mounds, like sterile, pristine barrows. His car was next to the last in the last row of parked cars. There were supposed to be floodlights on the lot but they were obviously out.

Tim looked back toward the prison. Between the billowing sails of fog the wind blew by, he could see the glow from several fires now; it appeared all of the dorms and D building, in addition to Digbee Hall, were now on fire. Tim pivoted, looking for any sign of the other dogs stalking him, but if they were out there, he couldn't see them. He breached the cylinder of the .38 but in the dark could not tell how many unspent rounds were in it.

"F-fuck it-t!" he muttered through chattering teeth. He didn't know anymore if he was shaking from the cold or shock; his body felt numb except for his bitten leg and ankle, which throbbed constantly and hurt like hell every time he stepped on it. He bit back the pain and trudged on.

Not much further now.

He rounded the corner of the third row of cars.

Wait. There was a break in the white mound that made up the last row of cars. It was his car, only half as covered as the rest of the cars in the row. On closer look he saw why; most of the snow was *inside* his car, having blown in through the smashed windshield and broken windows. It was also piled high on top of the car's exposed engine, the hood being nowhere in sight. As if that wasn't enough, he could tell from the way the car was sitting so low on the lot—and confirmed it with a closer look—that the tires had been slashed.

Tim slumped against the fender. That's it, he thought. Tears welled up in him. *I can't go on.* He slumped to the ground, his back against the flat driver's-side tire, his legs splayed out in the snow. He held the pistol in front of him, tears freezing on his cheeks. The more he looked at the gun, the louder the voice inside became telling him it was the right thing to do; he had nothing to live for. He was better off dead . . .

He put the cold barrel under his chin, pointing up.

He closed his eyes and pulled the trigger.

Again.

He was out of bullets.

He laughed weakly and dropped the gun, drew his legs up, and rolled into a fetal position in the snow. Suddenly he was getting up, through no volition of his own. Someone was helping him; there were hands under his arms and someone was picking him up. He gained his feet and turned. It was Gypsy in the red headscarf.

"You can't give up. You can't listen to that thing. You can't believe anything it tells you or anything it shows you. It will do *anything* to get you to stay here. You've got to get somewhere safe, out of this storm. Come on." She put his left arm over her shoulder and supported him, leading him back through the footsteps he'd made coming in. Curiously, he noticed she left no marks in the snow, though her feet and legs sunk in as deeply as his.

"It's no use," Tim said, dragging his feet, wanting to just collapse, let the snow bury him, and be done with it.

"Don't say that! You've got everything to live for, even if you can't remember what now."

Tim looked down at her. She was easily a foot and a half shorter than he, but she was very strong. She was still dressed in the same clothes he always saw her in, whether in his dreams or otherwise: the signature red kerchief worn over her head and tied under her chin in the Audrey Hepburn style of the 50s and 60s, a gray buttoned sweater, plain white blouse, and a gray, knee-length woolen skirt. He could not see her feet in the snow. She pushed on, dragging him with her, seemingly unaffected by the weather.

"Where are we going?" Tim asked.

"Someplace where you'll be safe," she answered.

Jack Roy heard a voice, far away and faint, calling him. He didn't want to listen, didn't want to respond; it was too warm and cozy here, but the voice got louder, more insistent.

Open your eyes, the voice said. He did. Great clumps of snow fell from his lids and slid down his cheeks. Icicles clung to his eyebrows and eyelashes and hung from his nose and chin. There was someone, a dark figure, not more than fifteen feet away from him in the thinning mists.

Get up, the voice said. Jack struggled to his feet. The dark figure was stumbling away, leaving the parking lot.

Kill him, the voice said.

Covered with snow from head to foot and looking like a displaced Himalayan mythical creature, Jack Roy staggered after Tim Saget.

Tim glanced to the right; several dark shapes were keeping pace with him and Gypsy—the rest of the canines. He looked ahead; they were almost at the road. He looked to the left; more dogs bounded through the snow in an attempt to head them off before they made the gate. As if sensing them, Gypsy stepped up her pace. Tim stumbled, looked down, and saw a kick spray of snow from *behind him.* He turned just as Jack Roy, looking more like Jack Frost with his icicle eyebrows and ice-blue skin, brought his pistol up to shoot. At point-blank range he couldn't miss, and Tim, too tired, cold, and despairing to care, knew it and waited for it. Nothing happened. Jack Roy tried again to fire but his finger wouldn't bend, wouldn't pull the trigger. His hand was frozen, as was the gun.

Realizing something was wrong, Tim turned to run as Jack raised the gun high to strike him. Immediately upon turning, Tim saw a black-and-tan shepherd coming at him, leaping for his throat, teeth snarling. Tim dove to the ground and the dog went right over him, crashing into Jack Roy instead. The dog didn't care. Meat was meat.

Tim crawled away as more dogs came and joined the attack on Jack Roy whose screams were muffled by fur and the storm. Tim scrambled to his feet, shook off the snow and leaned against the last car before the road. His ankle was killing him, throbbing inside his boot. He realized the tight boot was probably keeping him on his feet and the ankle from swelling like a balloon.

"Come on, it's not safe here," Gypsy said, leaning over him. She took his hand and led him out of the lot, across the road and down to the main gate, maneuvering effortlessly through the snow and the increasing windswept fog. Tim was surprised to see that the entry gates, where visitors had to identify themselves, were open, stuck in the drifts of snow. Beyond, he could see the front door to C building flapping in the blizzard gale also. Hurrying through the narrow gauntlet, Tim ran up the steps, ducked inside C building, and pushed the door closed behind him. He took a moment to revel in being out of the storm and in the warmth.

He looked around. The lights were out again. He took out his flashlight with some difficulty, digging under the heavy parka for it on his belt, and flashed it around the reception area and the visitor/pedestrian trap. There was a body on the other side of the trap, lying on the floor. Tim awkwardly jumped over the turnstile of the trap and went to it. He recognized it as Jane Mazek, the eleven-to-seven switchboard operator.

The switchboard.

"Up here!" Tim said, and hobbled to the stairs.

"What are you doing?" Gypsy asked.

"The switchboard is up here. I can call the state police and get help."

The woman looked uncertain.

"Help me," Tim said. With a last fearful look around, the woman took his arm and they went up the stairs. Even before they got there, Tim had an inkling of what they'd find when he stepped on broken glass and plastic on the steps going up to Outer Control. Sure enough, the switchboard had been destroyed.

"Damn it!" he swore. "Now what?"

"You've got to find a safe place to hide."

"No," Tim said, looking toward the darkened stairs uneasily. Anything could be lurking anywhere in this place. "I've got to get out of here. I've got to get off the Hill and get help."

"Do you think you could walk that far?"

Tim saw her point. It was a mile and a half down the Hill to the highway and another two to the state police barracks. The throbbing in his leg and ankle told him she was right.

"Are we going to hide in the tunnels?" Tim asked her as she led him downstairs again.

"They're not safe." She took him to the rear door and opened it.

"Wait!" he cried. "I just remembered something." He limped as quickly as possible down to the basement and the door marked *Armory.* If he was going to go back into the prison, he wanted to be armed. Tim remembered exactly which key opened it—because of one of the few bits of advice the Sarge had given him when he found out that Tim would have only a military baton for protection. "Always know the quickest way to get hold of a firearm in case of emergencies," the Sarge had emphasized. Tim, in case of an emergency just such as this, had made sure to do so.

In the armory he took two .38-caliber pistols, putting one

in his empty holster and carrying the other. He filled his jacket pockets with half a dozen speed loaders. There were other, more powerful and deadly guns in the armory, but he had not been trained on any of them yet. He felt competent and safe with his Smith and Wessons.

He went back up to Gypsy, who stood fretting by the door. "Okay," he said, though he felt *anything* but *okay*. He did not want to go back into the prison grounds, but Gypsy just winked at him, grabbed his arm, and pulled him back into the storm. They were plunged into the tearing wind, swirling fog, and stinging snow.

Right at the bottom of the steps from C building, a half-barbecued convict rushed out of the fog and snow at them. Luckily, the wind was blowing hard, allowing Tim to see him while he was still a good ten feet away. He grabbed his .38 in both hands, aimed steady, and squeezed the trigger. The con fell and was immediately buried under the deep snow.

They went on. Tim hobbled along and clung tightly to the woman next to him while swinging the gun around, trying to keep them covered against attack. Though the fires burning in D building and further on in Digbee Hall made the rushing fog glow eerily, the wind-driven snow flying directly into his eyes made it very difficult to see. He was surprised when they reached the south gate so quickly and safely.

"You need your key," Gypsy said to him. He removed his arm from her shoulders and took his key ring from his jacket pocket and searched for the master that would open the gate. The light from the burning buildings behind him created weird, dancing shadowy effects in the fog around him. He tried two keys that didn't fit. He was searching for another key that looked like it would fit when he noticed a swirl of dark particles—shiny black sparks, like the ones he'd seen around Doctor Stone in Digbee Hall—materializing in the mist on the other side of the gate. Snow and fog seemed to be attracted to the black flecks and collected together, forming a shape that grew to form a person, a little girl.

"Please, Daddy, don't leave," she sobbed.

In a rush of images that felt like long-lost memories, Tim saw and understood that this was his child, the child Millie now carried in her womb. He saw and understood in a flash how miserable her life was going to be with him as her father. Just as quickly, he knew that if he did something about it *now* and stayed on the Hill, her life would improve one hundred fold. The life insurance policy the prison provided would let her and Millie live comfortably, not worrying about money for college. Almost as an afterthought came the fleeting image/memory of Millie meeting someone else, someone who could make her happy.

Because you can't.

"Because you can't," the little girl echoed. "You can never make us happy." And he was nodding, feeling the truth of it in his very bones. It was all so clear now.

"Don't look at it! Don't listen to it!" warned Gypsy behind him, snapping him back to the moment.

He tried to look away, but her eyes were so large, so endearing, so helpless. Suddenly the little girl burst into tears. "Don't go, Daddy! Please! I'm so lonely!" Even though he knew she was not real, he felt pity for her. He couldn't help it. It was as though she had cast an invisible hook into his heart and was now trying to reel him in. He had never felt such compassion and pity for anyone other than himself. Her pain and loneliness touched a deep chord in him, one fine-tuned over a lifetime of neglect and disregard under the upbringing of his placebo father, the Sarge.

"Open the gate!" Gypsy demanded, bringing him back to his task once again.

A sound came out of the fog, carried on the wind and driven snow. It started faintly but was rising quickly in both volume and tone. At first Tim thought it was an engine winding out, then realized it was a human voice. And it was getting louder, which he knew meant *closer*. He spun around from the gate just as a charging mass of flesh and noise barreled into him, knocking him a good five feet backward into the snow. The con, a huge black blob silhouetted against the glowing fog and frozen precipitation, kept coming and kept screaming.

Though the initial hit—reminding Tim of when he had tried out for high school football and had got creamed—knocked him off his feet and hard to the ground, it gave him a few precious seconds to get his hand on the pistol in his jacket before the blob crashed down on top of him. Tim let him come, and when he felt his attacker's weight pressing against the muzzle of the gun in his pocket, he pulled the trigger.

The con barely flinched. He lurched up onto his knees and reached for Tim's throat. Tim pulled the gun from his pocket and emptied the pistol point blank into the con's rib cage, then used the gun to smash him in the side of the head until he slumped into the snow. Tim dropped the gun and rolled away, grabbing the fence to help him stand. Gyspsy ran to his side and began brushing the snow off him. Tim glanced back at his assailant and thought he recognized him as a con named Henrique from A dorm.

"Come on," Gypsy said, pushing toward the gate. "You've got to get it open. There will be more of them. We don't have much time."

He had to fish in the snow for the keys he'd dropped when he was attacked, then his hands were so cold he could barely use them. Randomly, out of fear and frustration, he started shoving keys into the lock, trying not to look at the little girl who had remained and now renewed her crying and lamentions of loneliness. The fifth key he tried worked, unlocking the gate. Pushing it open with some difficulty against the snow that had accumulated around its base, he and Gypsy went through. The weeping child reached out her hand to him as he went by. He tried to ignore her, put her out of his mind and remember that she was an illusion, but looking at her this close he could have sworn she was *real*. And the thought occurred to him, what if she *was* real? What if some poor child had accidentally got into the prison and was now trapped there? The ridiculousness of that notion and everything she'd just said and all the images and false future memories he'd just had concerning her did not occur to him; they were suddenly forgotten, and this new possibility seemed suddenly plausible: *This girl was real and she needed his help.*

He stopped and reached out to her.

"*Don't touch it!*" Gypsy screamed, and grabbed his arm, jerking him away. The child, who had been on her knees, her arms out for him to pick her up, let out an anguished cry and collapsed face down in the snow. The woman had to drag him away from her.

"Quickly," she urged.

Tim looked back. The little girl was gone, but now others were coming out of the darkness, through the gate, some of them still smoking from their burns. There appeared to be seven or eight of them. Tim hiked up his jacket and removed his second pistol from his holster. He quickened his pace, hobbling on with Gypsy's help. To his left he could make out the gym. Ahead, A and B dormitories were engulfed in flames, and the G and E dorm roofs were smoking, flames licking out of their windows. When the wind blew toward him, he could feel the heat from the flames. To his right was the small garden and courtyard where the Chief had been allowed to build his sweat lodge. The fog strung by, and he could see it clearly for several seconds in the light from the burning dorms. The side facing the dorms was bare, the snow having melted from the heat of the flames, while the other side of the lodge was steeped in white stuff.

Tim kept moving, not only forward, but from side to side, trying to keep tabs on the approaching cons. Suddenly one of them charged, kicking up snow, and Tim shot him dead without a second thought.

"Run!" Gypsy cried. "Get in there—it's the only safe place!"

The other cons charged. Tim shot one on his left and another to his right, putting them both down with one shot each. He ran for the lodge. The other cons were gaining on him. Tim turned and fired at the one closest. He fell in the snow but got back up again, only to be crashed into by another charging inmate. Tim ran, and his ankle nearly gave out, causing him immense pain. He gritted his teeth, damning the pain, and went on. He reached the lodge but there was one problem—he couldn't find the door. He couldn't find it on the clear side of the lodge and had to pull piles of the cold white stuff from the other side, feeling for a seam or zipper or something.

He looked back. His crispy and healthy pursuers had stopped chasing and were fanning out around the lodge. One of them tried to rush him but slipped and fell in the snow. The other cons suddenly let out a unified yell and charged. Suddenly his fingers found the edge of a flap. He pulled it back and felt warm air rush out at him. He ducked inside, letting the flap fall back into place, his gun up, ready to take out anyone who followed him.

None did.

"Welcome, Officer Saget."

Tim wheeled around. Sitting on the other side of a roaring fire that burned in a circle of stones in the middle of the circular structure was Chief Tom Laughing Crow.

"I wouldn't worry about them," he said. "I'm not one hundred percent sure, but I don't think they can get in here. They're not supposed to be able to anyway. It's been working since I last saw you."

Tim sank to a pile of pine boughs that were arranged on the ground around the fire and stared at the Chief. His shoulders began to shake. He fought it, but the onslaught of emotion was too much. The shock of the past six hours overwhelmed him, and he could hold it back no longer.

"They killed . . . killed . . . every—" he started, and couldn't finish as the emotion gushed up in him and his voice became a series of squeaks and moans instead of words. He broke down—put his face in his hands and bawled like a child. The Chief sat quietly, waiting for him to finish. He tossed a roll of brown, industrial paper towels to Tim, who ripped off a couple sheets and blew his nose.

The pleasing scents of pine and wood burning reached him when he inhaled. His tears stopped and he looked around, taking in the place. The space inside was much larger than it seemed from the outside. The outer skin of the lodge was canvas, such as is used for sails, but very little of that was visible. An infrastructure of what looked like cut saplings lashed together with rope created a domed skeleton upon which the outer canvas was stretched. The wooden skeleton was hung with long, colorful cloth "God's eyes"—craftworks of different-colored yarns woven on a cross to create a multi-colored diamond—and strings of shells and stones tied in intricate webs. In the middle of the roof, where the lodge was narrowest, the canvas had been cut away to let out smoke from the fire. He noticed there was a hanging flap to close the hole. Around the circular campfire, an array of soft pine boughs, pillows and prison-issue blankets made for pretty comfortable reclining.

A gust of wind buffeted the lodge and Tim looked at the Chief. He tried to keep his voice steady and barely succeeded. "What the fuck is going on here tonight? Do you know?"

The Chief shrugged. "Great-grandfather always used to say everyone has a purpose in life. Do you know how old I am, kid? I'm 82. Not bad, huh?" He held up his hands and regarded himself. "Great-grandfather taught me all he could of the ways of the tribal shaman, but in today's modern world, I never thought any of it would come in handy." He barked out a short laugh of derision. "When Great-grandfather died, he left me all of his things. What I did with those things, I'm not proud of; I used them to hoax white people into believing I was something I wasn't so they'd buy my useless crap. But all the while my life was going one path, I always kept wondering what was my *true* purpose—it seemed that I was never going to find it, until I came here.

"I thought when I got busted, especially at my age, my days were done, but now I see it was all meant to be. I knew it the minute I set foot in this prison. I knew my purpose the *minute* I stepped into the place and sensed the Windigo. I couldn't believe it; it was something right out of Great-grandfather's old stories, but it was *here*! I could actually *feel* it, and when I saw you on your first day my purpose became even clearer: I had to use the knowledge given to me by my great-grandfather to build this sanctuary lodge to protect you. Why? *Fuck!* Damned if I know. I guess somebody up there just likes you, kid." The Chief laughed, and it was the cackling of an old lady.

"Whoa!" Tim said. "I lost you; I missed, like, half of what you just said. First off, what's a Windigo? It sounds like a recreational vehicle."

The chief laughed again. "I like that. No, the Windigo is what is after us, pilgrim. The Windigo is the one spirit of which you find stories in all Native American cultures. Sometimes it is called the *Wendigo* or *Weedeega*. My great-grandfather, who was pure-blooded Mohegan, used to tell me stories at night about the Windigo 'cuz I loved to be scared. What an idiot I was! But listening to him, and seeing that look in his eyes, I always knew he believed they were real. Of course, I never thought I would ever run into one. But now that I think of it, this *is* the perfect place for a demon spirit that feeds on loneliness and despair. What better place than a prison—and at Christmas time no less when all the cons are feeling low. And the cons—like the patients of the insane asylum before this place—are perfect fodder for the Windigo. It loves the weak willed, the perverted and insane. It makes them believe they can be free if they'll just *die,* but their souls become captive of the Windigo in the worst prison of all: having your spirit remain earthbound after death.

"Great-grandfather used to tell me the Windigo is one of the oldest spirits on earth. In the days before civilization ruined everything, when men still respected nature, the Windigo were powerful spirits of the wilderness; spirits of despair, isolation, and loneliness. They preyed on those who ventured alone or in small groups into wild places where few men had ever gone before. In the early days of this country they found easy prey in white men who went into the wild for furs, exploration, and settlement."

"The Windigo starts out slow and works on you seductively, in your dreams, making you miss the things you want most, feeding your loneliness, your isolation. After a while you start to see things you know can't be there, but they are. You start to go crazy. You become careless. If you became careless in the wilderness of colonial America, you didn't live long." The Chief paused and squirmed in place, trying to get something behind him. He pulled out a bag of Hall's cherry cough drops and offered the bag to Tim, who gratefully took one. The chief did likewise before continuing.

"The Windigo are like animals in many ways, Great-grandfather used to say. They have territories and will never stray from them, so if you know where they live, you can avoid them. It's when you don't know where they are that you get caught. And if you were with companions and wandered into a Windigo's territory it would work on each of you, turn you against each other and worse. You ever hear of the Donner Party?"

Tim nodded. "The ones who got caught in the snow in the Rockies and ended up eating each other?"

"Yeah. That didn't happen because they couldn't get through the pass; every Indian of every tribe in this country who knows anything about his heritage knows a Windigo took the Donner Party. It's one of the ways it consumes you—first through the flesh, setting one against the other. When a man becomes possessed by a Windigo he becomes convinced that the flesh of his fellow humans will prolong his life and make him invulnerable to pain and injury. But it's all a ruse."

"In the wild, the Windigo would turn man against man, and murder and cannibalism would be the result, just like what happened to the Donner Party. They also have limited power over certain types of animals—dogs, cats, crows, wolves, bats, and many insects. They'll use them to kill you or drive you mad. As I said, because Indians knew where these spirits resided, they avoided them, but white settlers weren't so lucky. Because of this, whites mostly know the Windigo as some sort of flesh-eating demon, but it's more than that. It doesn't care about the flesh, it wants its victim's life force and soul, adding it to the throng it holds in captive company. It is, after all, the demon of *loneliness*."

Feeling the warmth of the fire, Tim slipped off his parka and sat on it. He checked his injured leg. The dog's teeth had punctured the skin, but the punctures had stopped bleeding. He leaned closer to the fire to dry his clothing and boots. What the Chief was telling him verified what he'd read in the journal and learned from the ghost of Gypsy.

The Chief poked at the fire with a stick and went on. "Over time, though, the wilderness retreated and so did the number of Windigo, or so Great-grandfather always said. Today, they are supposed to haunt only the remotest stretches of wilderness that still exist, high in the mountains, deep in the jungles and retreating rain forests, and in the outer fringes of the world at the north and south poles. But since being here and seeing what's been going on, I've realized maybe the Windigo have not disappeared or are not as remote as Great-grandfather thought. The Windigo that haunts this hill is strong and has been here a very long time. There must be others out there, thriving in little pockets of despair and isolation—like this prison—where they can feed. Maybe a lot of stories we read in the papers—like the Columbine massacre and serial killers—are really the work of Windigos. Maybe every suicide is because of the influence of a Windigo."

The Chief looked at him from across the fire, and Tim thought he winked. "Great-grandfather was a smart man and a gifted healer, and maybe a bit of a seer too. He taught me to build this lodge for worship, and he always said it would protect its inhabitants from *physical* attacks by a Windigo if I ever happened to run into one. I always thought he said that just to scare me, but nothing happens by chance. Now, that doesn't mean the Windigo can't get in your head and try to lure you out, or make you go mad. No matter what you hear or see in the next couple hours or so, between now and dawn—ignore it. The evil is still busy; there are enough weak souls around this place that ain't dead yet to keep it busy for a while. Though it wants you very badly, it will take whatever it can if it can't get you. I figure we're safe for a little while, until everyone outside there"—he pointed his thumb at the lodge wall—"is either dead or is able to escape the prison, though that's unlikely in this storm. Then the Windigo will try and wheedle its way between our ears." The Chief wrapped a prison-issue blanket around his shoulders and curled his knees up to his chest. "Oh, one more thing. Try not to sleep."

Tim tried to digest all he'd been told and all that had happened. A part of him wanted to reject it all; wanted to convince him he was being hypnotized or fooled *somehow* because such things as this *were not supposed to exist!* He badly wanted to deny the truth of his situation, but after all he'd seen and been through, he knew there was no way to do that and survive. After, if he survived this, then he could tell himself anything to be able to keep his sanity, but tonight, if he wanted to live, he had the gut feeling he had better listen to the Chief, just as he had listened to Gypsy. Like the Chief said, for some reason there was a providence looking out for him, and he was thankful for it.

With the warmth of the fire and all he'd been through, Tim was soon dozing. He caught himself nodding a few times. He woke to the Chief chanting and putting more scrap wood, which looked like it had come from the woodshop, onto the fire. He smiled at Tim through the flames and his eyes became the eyes he had seen in his possessed father in Digbee Hall—eyes he now knew must belong to the Windigo.

He woke and sat up. He looked across at the Chief. His eyes were closed and he appeared to be asleep.

"I told you to stay awake," the Chief said, proving him wrong.

Hoping movement would keep him awake, Tim crawled around the fire to the woodpile and fed scraps to the flames. The wind continued to howl outside, throwing itself against the lodge like a child in a tantrum, but the structure held firm. Several times he heard voices outside; once he was certain they were calling his name, but then the wind carried them off.

With the fire roaring again, Tim lay back and stared into the flames. He had the strangest sensation of being drawn into the fire, passing between the flames as though they were solid three-dimensional shapes that moved aside as he glided in toward the center of the conflagration.

Suddenly he was in a hospital room. Millie, her feet in stirrups, was delivering their child. The gynecologist, a woman, crouched between Millie's legs, urging her to push. Millie cried out and grabbed Tim's hand so tightly he thought his bones would fracture. She grunted and screamed.

"Here it is. That's it," the doctor coached. "Just a little mo—oh, my God!" The doctor sprang back from the delivery table. Tim looked just in time to see the baby fall from Millie's womb to the floor with a loud, mushy *splat*. Before he could be outraged, the baby rose up on all eight legs and scuttled away under a table.

Tim screamed and he was back in the sweat lodge. He shook himself and pushed back from the fire, trying not to look into it, but that was impossible. The only way to avoid it was to close his eyes, but he knew he'd soon be asleep if he did that. A few moments later, he was sucked back into the flames and they took him to another reality in his and Millie's apartment. A woman weighing at least 400 pounds sat on the bed, breast-feeding an equally fat baby. Unwillingly, he glided closer. He realized it was Millie, even more obese than her mother. And the baby—he winced and recoiled at a closer look. The baby was deformed; its eyes were too far apart, its nose was like a snout, its mouth was little more than a crooked drooling slash. Its ears were tiny lumps of cauliflower. The baby disengaged its slobbering mouth from Millie's bloated nipple and looked up at Tim.

"Duh-duh!" the baby-thing said, reaching for him.

It was all *so* convincing; it all seemed so *real*. As with the little girl outside, Tim saw it all, his future life extending before him in such detail it felt more like a memory than a premonition. This *was* his future. He knew with a certainty he had never before felt in his life that this was what he had to look forward to—an obese wife who was more hippo than woman, and being shackled with the lifelong responsibility of taking care of a deformed, retarded child. He turned from the baby and was confronted by Millie's dad. He held up a knife. "Look what you did to my daughter! I'm gonna cut your balls off and make you *eat* them!"

A hand shook him back to reality. His face was wet; he'd been crying. The Chief knelt beside him, his hand on Tim's shoulder.

"Remember what I said," he admonished.

Tim nodded. "I'm okay," he said, but his voice was thick with emotion.

"It's nearly dawn," the Chief said. "Listen. I think I hear trucks plowing the road. Tim listened. Beneath the roaring wind he could hear the rumble of a big engine and the sound of a metal plow scraping along. He figured it was the highway department; it was their job to make sure the hill was clear for deliveries and shift changes.

Tim looked at his watch. It was five A.M. He leaned over the dwindling fire, far enough to look out the chimney hole in the top of the lodge, but the sky looked the same as it had all night, white with snow clouds. Crouching, he duck-walked over to the flap to have a peek outside.

"I wouldn't do that yet," the Chief warned. "The plow drivers will see the fires and call for help. We should wait."

Reluctantly, Tim took heed and returned to his spot. He sat straining to hear sounds from outside but could hear nothing but the constantly howling wind. After a while he noticed the sound of the wind had changed, becoming more high-pitched. With the change in the sound came a change in the force of the wind also. It buffeted the lodge severely, causing Tim to look around nervously and remember Alex Torres's prediction that the structure would get blown down in the first big storm.

"Are you sure this thing will hold up?" Tim asked.

The Chief held his hands, palms up, and shrugged.

"You don't know?"

"Either it will or it won't; my saying it will won't make it so. Great-grandfather taught me well. It should hold. It's held all night."

Tim felt a little less than reassured by the Chief's answer and, a moment later, his doubts were verified. A wind gust with a noise like a freight train slammed into the lodge, ripping away a huge top section of canvas that went flapping into the white speckled fog like some strange bird. The lodge teetered—there was the groan of rope against wood and Tim had the sensation that his world was falling over on its side. The lodge collapsed to the left, falling on the fire and into the snowdrifts. The wind immediately caught the canvas and flipped the lodge into the air, and it came crashing down again and began rolling and sliding under the force of the gust. It left behind a debris trail of God's eyes and other of the Chief's trinkets. The edges of the frame went right up and over Tim without touching him, but it caught the Chief, collapsing on top of him. When the wind flipped the lodge over, the Chief was nowhere to be seen. A moment later, something slammed into the back of Tim's head and he lost consciousness.

He opened his eyes. His head hurt like hell and he was moving, but not under his own power. Cons were dragging him by the arms, his feet sliding along behind, across the east yard to the kitchen, which he could just make out ahead. There were other cons there already, waiting for him, some of them burned beyond recognition, smoke rising from their charred flesh. The smell of burnt things was thick in the air.

Tim remembered he still had the pistol in his pocket, though he couldn't get at it with his arms being held. He stayed limp, continued feigning unconsciousness, and waited for his chance. The storm seemed to be abating slightly; the fog, snow, and wind seemed to be thinning. Dawn was approaching, evidenced by a general brightening of everything.

The cons, about twelve in all from the quick count Tim was able to make, dragged him up the steps and into the kitchen. They headed straight for the tunnel door. One of the cons produced a guard's key ring and unlocked the door, holding it open while Tim was dragged through and the others followed. Approaching the top of the stairs leading to the tunnel, Tim realized this was his best chance for escape with the narrow stairway in front of him and most of his captors behind him.

Saying a quick, silent, *Please, God, let me live,* he waited until they were stepping onto the first stair. He kicked his feet out against the top stair's kickboard and lunged to the right, smashing the con there into the railing, forcing him to release Tim's arm. Tim kept pushing with his feet, propelling himself headlong down the stairs and pulling his other captor off balance with him. As he fell, Tim pulled the gun free of his pocket and got it out a fraction of a second before he

424 *R. Patrick Gates*

hit the stairs on his side, bounced, rolled, and crashed to the bottom, with the con falling on top of him.

Tim immediately pushed the con off him and leaped to his feet, despite the raging pain erupting in his shoulder, side, and ankle. He shot the con on the floor in the stomach, then fired twice into the crowd of inmates at the top of the stairs. He knew he hit someone, but he didn't hang around to see who or how many. He jumped over the groaning con on the floor and ran down the second short flight of stairs to the tunnel door at the bottom. Keeping the gun pointed back the way he'd come, he fished out his keys and unlocked the door, breaking his key off in the lock to prevent the cons from following him.

He backed away from the door. There was no sound from the other side. They were probably already going to another tunnel entrance to head him off, but with all the fires, Tim wasn't sure where they would find a clear entrance. He figured he had some time to find a good hiding place; maybe he could get back to the air shaft where Gypsy and he had hid before.

Tim breached the chamber on his pistol and let the shells fall to the floor. He slipped a speed loader in and closed it. He turned to see which way to go and stopped dead in his tracks.

He wasn't in the tunnels.

He was in a cave—a vast cave illuminated by a flickering, dancing light. There was someone there with him, someone familiar, just a few feet away.

"Do you have any concept of *true* loneliness?" the figure said. Tim was startled. If he hadn't known better, he would have sworn the voice was *his*; it sounded just like him. "It's a black hole sucking in the light of hope, happiness, and health. It eats away at your insides until you're hollow and a bottomless void exists in you."

As each word was spoken, the feelings of loneliness and despair that Tim had been battling ever since looking into the eyes of the Windigo returned in force, growing stronger, echoing the force of the voice.

"And as the years head on, that void just widens and consumes you, cell by cell, fiber by fiber."

An image of the Sarge sprang unbidden to his mind. He saw him wandering through his big empty house, not the stern, authoritarian ogre Tim had always known growing up, but just a bitter, sad, lonely old man. Despite his anger at the Sarge, Tim couldn't help but feel empathy and sympathy for him.

"This is what's waiting for you. It's what awaits every man—to grow old, alone, forsaken."

The face of the Sarge suddenly became his own, thirty years from now. He looked sadly at himself and the eyes of the other him slowly turned milky white—the eyes of the Windigo.

"Don't tell me you haven't lain awake at night trembling under the crushing loneliness of being human. Do you remember? As a child, always alone. You're all *so* alone; it is the nature of man to be alone. Your very existence is its own prison—you're all trapped in your minds, completely cut off. And with the years that isolation becomes loneliness and then despair. That old Indian lied to you. I offer eternal companionship, eternal *oneness* with others of your kind. And I can give you any fantasy you desire, for all eternity. It is such bliss, words can't describe it."

His older self came closer. The cloudy eyes held him mesmerized. "It's your choice, Tim. You're strong enough to resist me and just walk out of here; if you weren't I'd have you already. You can do that and go back to your life of isolation and wait until you become old, until you become me, until you become the Sarge or worse. You can join us now of your own volition, just like all the others. They all *wanted* to join me. There is no one here who was forced to be here." His elderly self swept his arm out, and Tim became aware of people around them—the same combination of specters and cons he'd seen on the third floor of Digbee Hall, but now all the cons appeared specterlike also. He looked at them but didn't see Captain Thompson or any of the guards who had been murdered.

As if reading his mind, his older self said: "I can't keep a soul that doesn't want to join me."

Tim felt hot tears on his cheeks. He was so tired of it all. He'd had enough of the gut-wrenching fear and terror he'd been subjected to all night. He'd had enough of the pain and suffering he'd seen and felt. But most of all, he'd had enough of *death*. Everything the Windigo said to him might be true and might come to pass, but *he* was going to *live*. He'd gone through too much not to.

His older self saw the defiance emerge in Tim's face and scowled. His older face changed, running and shifting into a visage of pure hatred and evil. The eyes swelled, the nose grew long and hooked, and the mouth widened, splitting into a razor-toothed maw that opened to roar at him, but the sound of a siren came out instead.

Tim woke to the sound of sirens. He sat up and looked around. He was back in the lodge, or *still* in it, he thought, realizing the cavern had been a dream. He shivered, remembering the true face of the Windigo, and looked at his watch—7:00 A.M. The Chief was gone, the fire was smoldering. Tim put on his parka and went out. It was bright daylight. The storm was over. Tim stepped into the crisp sun-drenched air that still held the stench of burnt things. A and B dorms were nothing more than smoking rubble, while G and E dorms were still burning; little more than their first floors remained intact. Littering the ground around the sweat lodge were at least two dozen bodies. Some of them had obviously died from their burns or as a result of violence, but several appeared to have just frozen to death sitting in the snow around the lodge, waiting for him to come out. He looked toward the perimeter fence and the access road beyond. A line of state police vehicles, ambulances, and paddy wagons were streaming up the road, sirens wailing, lights flashing. Tim looked to the south gate and C building. Smoke was rising from the ruins of D building and Digbee Hall beyond.

Slowly, Tim walked to the south gate and C building.

EPILOGUE

January 10

Tim sat in his car, parked in front of the Sarge's house, as he had so many times in the past. It was the first day he'd had free since the riot. Every previous one had been spent with an array of investigators and a whole slew of people whom Tim had no idea who they were or what their function was. Tim was the only surviving CO of the worst prison riot in U.S. history, as far as the death toll went—fifty COs dead. The body count of inmates was still being figured out. At least twenty were thought to have survived and escaped relatively unharmed. The Chief's name had been on that list, until Tim told investigators he was dead, burned in the fire.

This will be the last time I come here, Tim told himself. The Sarge had something he wanted. Once Tim had it, it would be a long time before he and Joe Saget crossed paths again. Tim sat staring at the house, thinking of the image of the Sarge—old, lonely, and broken—that the Windigo had shown him and felt pity. Maybe he was being too hard on the Sarge. He *was* the only father Tim had ever known.

Lena Saget died the day after New Year's. Tim had wanted to see her again and try to talk to her and tell her about what happened, but he had been tied up with the investigation into the prison riot and hadn't been able to find the time until it was too late. Mostly, he had wanted to ask her about Gypsy—who she was and why she'd helped him. The Sarge had Lena's personal effects and had called Tim to see if he wanted them. Tim hoped there might be answers there.

The Sarge answered the door but wouldn't look Tim in the eye as he let him in. Tim followed him into the kitchen where a cardboard box sat on the table. "I told them to give her clothes away," the Sarge said. "I didn't think you'd want those. These are her personal things—photos, jewelry, you know."

Tim looked into the box, picked up a picture of three little girls—Lena Saget with her sisters—and gasped at the picture beneath. It was a Polaroid snapshot of a pretty woman in a red headscarf sitting on a convertible. Tim couldn't believe it—it was *Gypsy*!

"Who's this?" he asked the Sarge. "Was she a friend of my mother's?"

The Sarge looked at him strangely. "That *is* your mother. Haven't you ever seen pictures of her when she was younger?"

Tim realized he hadn't. He looked again at the photo. How could this be? Her words echoed back to him:

Do you have to be dead to be a ghost?

Feel the Seduction Of
Pinnacle Horror